R ARELY has a storybook family swept into life with such breathtaking reality as the famed White-oaks, who from the moment of their creation enchanted millions of readers all over the world.

"The Jalna saga," says one famous critic, "has an almost phenomenal sustaining interest. It is doubtful if any recent tale of comparable length . . . can match the consistent pace and surging vitality of this long, rich story."

The novels, which span four generations of this fascinating and unique family, rank among the most enduring works of modern fiction. Their appearance in a paperback series is an event hailed by American readers.

Fawcett Crest Books
by Mazo de la Roche:

THE BUILDING OF JALNA   23071-6 $1.50

MORNING AT JALNA   P2411 $1.25

MARY WAKEFIELD   23057-0 $1.50

YOUNG RENNY   Q2842 $1.50

WHITEOAK HERITAGE   P2214 $1.25

THE WHITEOAK BROTHERS   23643-9 $1.75

JALNA   23138-0 $1.50

WHITEOAKS OF JALNA   23510-6 $1.95

FINCH'S FORTUNE   23053-8 $1.50

THE MASTER OF JALNA   Q2797 $1.50

WHITEOAK HARVEST   Q2767 $1.50

WAKEFIELD'S COURSE   23431-2 $1.95

RETURN TO JALNA   23386-3 $1.75

RENNY'S DAUGHTER   Q2550 $1.50

THE
WHITEOAK
BROTHERS:
JALNA—1923

Mazo de la Roche

FAWCETT CREST • NEW YORK

THE WHITEOAK BROTHERS

THIS BOOK CONTAINS THE COMPLETE TEXT OF
THE ORIGINAL HARDCOVER EDITION.

Published by Fawcett Crest Books, a unit of CBS Publications,
the Consumer Publishing Division of CBS Inc., by arrange-
ment with Little, Brown and Company in association with
The Atlantic Monthly Press.

ISBN: 0-449-23643-9

Printed in the United States of America

10   9   8   7   6   5   4   3   2   1

For my children
RENE *and* KIM
with my love

Contents

THE
WHITEOAK
BROTHERS:
JALNA—1923

The Whiteoak Family

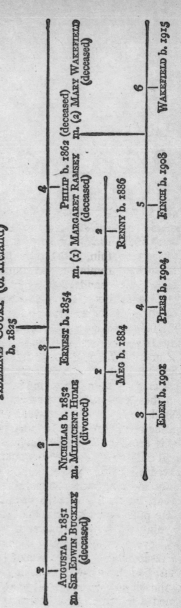

CAPTAIN PHILIP WHITEOAK (of the British Army)
b. 1815 (deceased)

m. 1848

ADELINE COURT (of Ireland)
b. 1825

1 AUGUSTA b. 1851
m. SIR EDWIN BUCKLEY
(deceased)

2 NICHOLAS b. 1852
m. MILLICENT HUME
(divorced)

3 ERNEST b. 1854

4 PHILIP b. 1862 (deceased)
m. (1) MARGARET RAMSEY
(deceased)
m. (2) MARY WAKEFIELD
(deceased)

1 MEG b. 1884

2 RENNY b. 1886

3 EDEN b. 1901

4 PIERS b. 1904

5 FINCH b. 1908

6 WAKEFIELD b. 1915

1.

Jalna — 1923

As FINCH WHITEOAK WAS dressing that morning he noticed the change in his hands. Funny he never had noticed it before. They had, suddenly it seemed, as though overnight, grown long and thin, the fingers finely articulated, the knuckles more prominent, the thumb more individual. They looked like hands that might do something worth while. He grinned at the thought that he should do anything worth while. Then he grew sober and straightened himself. This was the first day of March, his fifteenth birthday. It was natural that he should change. He wondered if possibly he might have the beginning of a beard, but when he ran his hand over his chin it felt smooth as an egg. Certainly he was growing fast, for his jackets were short in the sleeve and his trousers in the leg. When he considered his clothes he scowled. Was he never to have a brand-new suit? Always he was forced to wear those which his brother Piers had outgrown, and by the time Piers had outgrown a suit, who would want it? Not Finch. He wanted a brand-new suit.

Sunday morning was the regular morning for clean underwear, but as this was his birthday he would change today. He pulled off his socks that had holes in the heels, and opening the bottom drawer of the scarred chest of drawers, several of the wooden knobs of which were missing, he discovered clean socks and underclothes as well. These last had shrunk in the washing, so that when he had forced himself into them, he felt scarcely able to move. He performed a few stretching exercises to ease the discomfort, thereby making of himself such a figure of fun that his brother Piers, who had just waked up, gave a derisive chuckle. Piers would be nineteen in the fall.

Finch stiffened and demanded—"What's the matter with you?"

"You."

"Me? What d' you mean?"

"You ought to see yourself."

Finch's voice came out loudly. "It's not my fault if everything's five sizes too small for me."

Piers answered soothingly—"Dear me, no. And it's not your fault you're such a funny shape. But you can't expect me not to laugh."

"You'd laugh," said Finch bitterly," at your grandmother—if you dared."

"I have a cheerful disposition and you help me to keep that way."

"Shut up."

Piers raised himself on his elbow, his pink and white face suddenly serious. "You're not being cheeky, I hope."

There was silence from Finch, as he began to put on his shoes.

"*Are* you?"

"No," muttered Finch. He knew better than to be cheeky to Piers. Anyhow it was his birthday. He ought to be in a good mood. And perhaps Piers had a present for him. He remembered that on his last birthday Piers had given him something. What had it been? Oh, yes, a necktie, a quite decent one. It was still one of his best. He thought he would put it on this morning. It would be a sort of polite thing to do. It would remind Piers that this was his birthday. Strange that Piers had not remarked the day, because he was one who generally gave you a hard smack for every year and a terrific one "to grow on." He glanced at his brother to see if he were noticing the tie but Piers had sunk onto his pillow again and closed his eyes. He was enjoying his Saturday freedom from school. He had that look of blissful carefreeness on his healthy face that Finch both envied and distrusted. He envied it because he knew that never could he achieve such a look and he distrusted it because it sometimes was the forerunner of a teasing mood. He stood staring at Piers for a space, the tie in his hand. Then he saw that Piers had abruptly fallen asleep again, in that way he had, as though he could either sleep or wake at will.

Fifteen seemed, in some way, a landmark to Finch. He felt that he was different. He was no longer a kid. There was a certain dignity attached to the fifteenth birthday. Why, in just six years more he would be of age. What would he be like then, he wondered. A very different sort of fellow from what he was today. He put back his shoulders and held himself very straight. But only for a moment. It really was too much effort the first thing in the morning.

And *what* a morning! An icy rain was beating on the panes, running down in dreary rivulets to form a pool on the sill. The old cedar tree close to the window looked as though it had been dripping from a pool. Surely no rain could make it quite so wet. Beyond it he could see the blurred shape of the stables and the figure of a stableman running toward them. Benny, the English sheep dog, was walking tranquilly toward the house, as though he didn't give a fig for the rain . . . What a day for a birthday. And yet Finch had, deep down in him, that delicious feeling of excitement.

He poured the water in which Piers had washed his hands last night into the slop bowl. He poured fresh water from the ewer into the basin, noticing with distaste the grimy rim round its edge where the wash water had been. Now he splashed the fresh cold water over his face, passed his wet hands across his lank light brown hair and made a pretence of drying himself. Why the hell did Piers have to use *his* towel as well as his own, and drop them both on the floor? He wondered whether or not he would brush his teeth and decided against it.

He wished someone would give him new hairbrushes and a comb. Certainly these were dilapidated. He couldn't even remember whom they had belonged to or how long he had had them, and he could remember a long way back. His hair looked nice and moist and sleek when he had finished with it, but by the time he had finished dressing, that unruly lock was out of place and falling stiffly over his forehead. He cleaned his nails, then with an eager feeling deep inside him, went forth to meet his birthday.

At the top of the stairs he hesitated to look in at Eden, asleep on his back. Always he left his bedroom door wide open. His arms were thrown above his head and his hair, of a bright gold, lay tossed against his pillow. There was something in the sight of Eden lying there that made Finch feel uneasy, almost sad. But then there was something sort of sad about anybody lying fast asleep. Even Eden had a look almost of humility, as though he were sorry for having been suspended from the university last term and would never never do anything wrong again. Yet the moment his eyes were open that look would be gone, and he'd not be pleased to find Finch staring in at him. Finch wondered if Eden had a present for him.

In the passage he met his sister Meg, leading the youngest member of the family by the hand. Why should she lead him as though he were a baby, when he would be eight next June? Why should she dress him and fuss over his hair and spoil him in every possible way? There were others who could do with a little more attention than they got.

"Why, Finch, dear," Meg said reproachfully, "why in the world have you put on your Sunday suit? It's only Saturday. Did you get mixed up in the days, dear?"

He had a mind to shout back— "It's my birthday, isn't it? A fellow has a right to wear his best suit on his birthday, hasn't he?" But he said nothing. He just stared at her with his mouth open.

Little Wakefield tugged at Meg's hand. "I want my brekkus. I want my brekkus," he said, in the whiny voice he kept especially for his sister.

"Listen, Finch," Meg spoke in a reasoning way. "Listen, dear. I want you to go back and take off that suit. It's been all freshly sponged and pressed. I don't want you to gets spots on it. So do, like a good boy . . ."

Finch turned from her and ran up the stairs. "All right," he called back, his voice breaking in anger, "I'll change. I'll come down in my old rags. Don't worry."

Meg raised her blue eyes to him in wonder. "What a

temper to get in, dear. If Renny heard you I don't know what he'd say."

"He'd give him a clip on the ear," put in Wakefield, turning suddenly from a baby into a horrid small boy.

"You shut up," called down Finch.

Now Wakefield was a real little gamin. "Shut up, yourself!" he yelled.

"I will not have such rudeness from either of you," Meg was saying. She grasped the little boy's hand more firmly and began to descend the stairs into the hall below.

Finch fervently hoped he would not have to change his suit with Piers's laughing eyes on him. Thankfully he saw that Eden had been disturbed only enough to make him roll over on his face. Piers was still fast asleep, one hand cradling a pink cheek. Tremblingly Finch jerked off jacket, waistcoat and trousers. As they sank to the floor he gave them a savage kick. He was ashamed and worried by his own temper. From the clothes cupboard he got his most disreputable trousers, the ones with the paint stains on the knees, and an old gray pullover with holes in the elbows. If Meg wanted to see him shabby on his birthday he certainly would give her that pleasure. He couldn't understand Meg. She was always after him for his untidiness, yet when he made himself really tidy, she was after him again.

The rain was coming down harder than ever. That spot in the ceiling was beginning to leak again. He would let it leak. It would serve Meggie right, serve Piers right when he stepped into a puddle. But halfway down the stairs he thought better of it. "Gosh," he thought, "if I was setting out to do a murder, I'd not be able to finish the job. I'd leave the fellow just half killed." He ran back up the stairs, emptied his wash water from the basin and placed it beneath the falling drops. He stood motionless, listening to them as they fell. At first they made almost no sound. Then as a little pool formed, they fell into it with the pleasantest sound. Not just a tinkle but a sweet cadence, like the beginning of a little tune. He stood with head bent, his long light eyes rapt in listening.

Piers opened his eyes, took one look at the basin and rolled over with a groan.

Downstairs in the dining room four of the family were

at breakfast. Meg, who was taking nothing but tea and a sliver of toast, young Wakefield, who was making miniature canals and lakes in his plate of porridge and milk, and the two uncles, Nicholas and Ernest Whiteoak, who were eating heartily of bacon and eggs. All four raised their eyes to Finch as he appeared in the doorway. The uncles said good morning, but no one spoke of his birthday. He sank into his chair and drooped there. Nicholas and Ernest went on with a discussion of the increase in taxation in England since the war. As they had spent the greater part and by far the most enjoyable part of their lives there, even though Nicholas's marriage to an Englishwoman had ended in divorce, their interests and their conversation turned often to London and their past pleasures. There they had spent their patrimony, their prime, returning to Jalna when their bank accounts dwindled and receiving from their younger brother Philip, who had inherited the property, a generous and warmhearted welcome.

Ernest was at this time just under seventy and Nicholas just over it, fine-looking men with an elegance quite unusual in these days, though Nicholas was tending more and more toward allowing his thick black hair that was streaked with gray to grow too long, and to being a bit careless about his cigar ashes. But Ernest was immaculate, looking, as his nephews said, always ready to go anywhere. He thought of himself as intellectual and spent a large part of his time in reading Shakespeare and books about Shakespeare, though he had a tendency to forget what he had read. Nicholas could play the piano quite well and, if he had not been too much preoccupied with other matters in his youth, might have become a very good musician. Now he had an old square piano upstairs in his bedroom and played on it almost every evening. He did not like the tone of the piano in the drawing-room so well, he said. In fact his fingers were getting somewhat stiff from arthritis and a gouty knee caused him to limp a little. But he enjoyed his food. All the Whiteoak family enjoyed their food, with the apparent exception of Meg, though even she could make a clean sweep of a tempting tray when she had it alone in her own room.

Finch helped himself from the bowl of hot porridge and poured milk over it, closely observed by Wakefield.

"What are you staring at?" demanded Finch.

"You're greedy."

Meg interposed— "Eat your porridge, darling."

"I don't want it."

"Aren't you well?" At once her voice had an anxious tone. She scrutinized his pointed, rather sallow face.

"What he needs," said Nicholas, "is a little wholesome neglect."

"Oh, Uncle Nicholas, you know very well that Wake would never have lived if I had not watched over him so carefully."

"Very true indeed," agreed Ernest.

The little boy looked languidly from one face to the other, savoring his delicacy.

A quick step sounded in the hall and the master of Jalna came into the room, followed by three dogs, two clumber spaniels and the English sheep dog.

"The dogs!" cried Meg. "They must be dripping!"

"Not they," returned their master. "They know that this weather isn't fit for a dog. It's a filthy day and no mistake." He laid his fingers against his sister's warm white neck for a moment, then with a good morning to his uncles, went to his place at the head of the table, the dogs majestically ranging themselves on either side of him.

Ernest Whiteoak was of a fastidious nature. He was conscious not only of a pleasant clean smell of Windsor soap from his eldest nephew but also of a slight smell of the stables, and from the coats of the dogs, their characteristic odor. He took out his handkerchief and sniffed the pure scent of Vapex from it.

Renny gave him a quick look. "A cold, Uncle Ernest?"

"No, no. I just use a little Vapex on my handkerchief. As a protection. Nothing more."

"Good." Renny helped himself to porridge and added— "It's a bad time for colds, and, as I said, this is a filthy day." He turned to Finch. "I guess you're glad you don't have to go to school. It's Saturday, isn't it?"

Finch longed to shout— "It's my birthday, that's what

it is! And nobody has the decency to remember it." But he looked glumly at his plate with a muttered assent.

His Uncle Ernest eyed him with mild disapproval.

"It is a good thing," he said, "to form the habit in youth of getting up cheerful in the morning. I formed that habit many years ago and I have found it beneficial to my own health and to the comfort of those about me."

"Yes indeed, Uncle Ernest," agreed Meg, "you are an example to everyone."

"I'm cheerful," piped Wakefield. "But I can't eat this porridge. Would you like to have it, Finch?"

Finch gave him a quelling look and applied himself morosely to his own.

Nicholas wiped his drooping iron-gray mustache on an enormous linen table napkin. "I'm glad," he said, "that we're on the way to spring."

"This rain," said Ernest, "will take away the last of the snow."

"But if it freezes," added Renny, "we shall have the devil of a mess." He turned to Wakefield. "There are twin lambs in the barn this morning."

"Oo—may I go back with you and see them?"

"Yes." He looked fondly at his small brother. "If you eat up your breakfast."

"Renny, do you think I might have a pony for my birthday?"

Now, thought Finch, that will remind them! Now they'll remember that it's *my* birthday.

But it didn't. Everyone began to discuss the question of a pony for Wakefield, as though it were a matter of profound importance. Wragge, the houseman, who had been Renny's batman in the war, had returned with him in 1919, and established himself as a permanent fixture at Jalna by marrying the cook, now brought in another dish of bacon and eggs. He was a small wiry man who imparted an air of jaunty good humor to his domestic activities. He had a pronounced Cockney accent and cherished an unaffected devotion to Renny. He was familiarly called Rags.

Renny Whiteoak was at this time thirty-seven years old, tall and thin, with an elegantly sculptured head covered by dark red wiry hair. His complexion was somewhat weather-beaten and his brown eyes had a wary look, as though thus far in his life he had encountered a fair amount of trouble and was prepared for more. His eyebrows were a salient feature of his face, quickly expressing by their contractions or upraisings, their sudden movements, as though independent of each other, his moods of anger, dismay or jocularity. He raised them now as Eden and Piers came into the room, and glanced at his wrist watch.

"Sorry," said Eden, bending to kiss his sister.

"But you're not really late, dear, only your porridge will be cold."

"Preserve me from it hot or cold. Morning, everybody." He smiled at the faces about the table and seated himself at the left of his eldest brother who said, while helping him to bacon and eggs—

"What I was remarking is his clothes."

It was obvious that Eden wore jacket and trousers over his pyjamas.

"If I had appeared at table in such undress when I was a young fella," observed Nicholas, "my father would have ordered me to leave." He glanced with reminiscent pride at the portrait of the handsome officer in Hussar's uniform which hung above the sideboard beside that of his wife. The dominating presence of this portrait, painted in London seventy years ago, had influenced even the second generation of Whiteoaks to be born in Canada. In their earliest years the splendor of the uniform had attracted them, and as they grew their grandfather was often pointed out to them as the model of what a British officer should be, firm in discipline, quick in decision, inexorable in justice. His gallantry had been equaled only by his strength of character. No one told them of his weaknesses, which were charming.

Eden shrugged his shoulders in a new and irritating way he had and said—"Well, he was a martinet, wasn't he? He'd not have done for these days."

"It is a good thing for you," said his Uncle Ernest, "that my mother did not hear that remark."

"I didn't mean to be rude, Uncle Ernest, but things have changed, you know. Especially since the war."

"For the worse," put in Nicholas. "Where the young are concerned."

Eden laid down his knife and fork and laughed. His blue eyes regarded his uncle across the table with ironic amusement. "Come now, Uncle Nick, were you always well behaved?"

"I was human."

"And so am I—very."

"That has nothing to do with coming to breakfast in pyjamas and uncombed hair."

"You have just remarked how things have changed."

"Not that much."

Renny now spoke. "Say the word, Uncle Nicholas, and I'll see to it that he goes upstairs and dresses."

"No, no. Let Meg decide. If she doesn't mind . . ."

Eden leaned back in his chair smiling from one face to the other.

"It doesn't matter in the least to me," cried Meg. "Eden looks so nice no matter what he has on."

"Thank you, Meggie, darling. I should have hated to be sent upstairs to tidy myself like a little boy." He attacked his bacon and eggs with appetite.

Finch was thinking—"How does Eden get that way? Doesn't he mind what's said? Or is he just so darned proud?" Yet Finch had seen Eden look blacker than he had ever seen one of his other brothers. But when Eden looked black you didn't know what it was about. Last year, he had remained cool in the storm which had raged about him, yet Finch had heard him walking about his room in the middle of the night. Perhaps he felt things more than he showed.

Nicholas must have been thinking about that time too, for he remarked to Eden—"Of course, you've heard that I was sent down from Oxford."

"Oh, yes, and you have no idea how that endears you to me."

"Grandfather," said Renny, his eyes full on Eden's face, "had more money to waste than I have."

The upbringing and education of his young half brothers was his responsibility and a father he was to them. The smile faded on Eden's lips. His smile always had the shadow of pain in it and now that shadow deepened before it faded. Ernest gave him a sympathetic look and began to talk of the weather, which had greatly worsened. The rain now slashed furiously on the window panes, making a wall between those in the room and the desolate world beyond. No one who was not forced to would venture out on this day.

More thickly buttered toast with marmalade was eaten, the huge silver teapot was replenished and emptied, while the windows trembled in their frames and down the roof poured the rain, washing away the last of the snow that lay in little ridges on the northward side. Wragge, with an air of ceremony, as though he were performing a juggling trick and showing the family something they had never before seen, opened the folding doors that led to the sitting room, grandly called the library though there were no more than a hundred books on its shelves. Nicholas, Ernest and Eden kept their own books in their rooms. One of the shelves in this room was filled with books on the breeding of show horses, care of the horse in health and disease, a history of the Grand National, books on the judging of show horses and their training. These were only a portion of the books and magazines on the same subject which were perused by the master of the house, and many of which were in his office in the stable or littered the shelves of his clothes cupboard.

"It is cold in here," remarked Ernest with a glance at the fireplace. "There is an east wind."

"If there's an east wind," said his brother, "the chimney would smoke."

"The wind is from the south," Meg declared, "right off the lake."

"I'm positive it's from the east," persisted Ernest.

"If it's from the east the chimney will smoke like the devil," said Renny.

"It's from the south," said Meg. "Finch, just go out to the porch and see if it isn't from the south."

Everybody looked at Finch, as though quite suddenly he had become interesting. He stared back truculently.

Why should he be chosen to go out into the wet and cold to discover which way the wind blew? And on his birthday. "It's from the east," he muttered. He did not want a fire lighted for he would probably be sent to fetch wood for it. Always it was he who was sent to do unpleasant things.

"Get a move on," ordered Renny, raising an eyebrow at him. Glumly he went to the hall and opened the front door against the blast. He stepped out into the porch and shut the door with a bang behind him . . . Here was an icy-cold dripping world, filled with the thunder of rain and wind. The heavy branches of the evergreen trees swayed senselessly, the bare branches of maple and birch, but dimly visible against the rain, were without meaning, as though never would life run through them again. Their sap was sunk into their roots, and their roots clung to the wet clay in fear of being torn up. Where had the birds hidden themselves? Were there perhaps, deep down in the sodden ground, flat-faced worms which knew that spring was coming? The first day of March—and his birthday and no one had thought it worth noticing! He did not care which way the wind blew. Let it blow. Let it blow the chimney down.

The door opened, and closed. Renny was standing beside him. "What's the matter with you, Finch?" he demanded. "How long does it take you to discover which way the wind blows?"

"It's blowing every way," growled Finch, standing where the rain beat full on him.

"This is a pretty way to behave—and on your birthday too."

At last the words were out. At last the day had been mentioned. But how? In what a way? Flung at him, in rebuke. Renny too drew back, as though he wished he had not mentioned it. Doubtless he was sorry he had mentioned it, as he had no present for him. Now Renny was saying—"The wind is blowing the rain into the porch, so it's from the south. We can have a fire. Come in."

He took Finch by the arm in a jocular way and propelled him back to the library.

"The wind," he announced, "is straight from the south. Get some logs, Finch." He himself knelt in front of the fireplace, crumpled a newspaper and took a handful of kindling from a small battered oak chest.

Finch brought logs from the basement, laboring up the stairs with them, as though they were made of lead. Outside his grandmother's bedroom, which was opposite the dining room, he hesitated, wondering whether or not she would remember his birthday. Well, she made a great fuss over her own. Surely she might give a thought to other people's. As his eyes rested speculatively on the door, the rappings of her stick sounded on the bedroom floor, and she called out—"Come in!"

He could not very well go to her with his arms full of logs, yet there was that peremptory note in her voice which took for granted that you would run at her bidding. He stood still, wondering what to do.

Again she called out, and this time more sharply—"Come in!"

Holding the six logs to his breast with his left arm, the sweetness of the pine filling his nostrils, he gingerly opened the door and put his face in the opening. In the room was a different world, the world of the very old. The heavy maroon curtains were drawn across the windows, and the still air was laden with the scent of sandalwood, camphor, and hair oil. In the dimness the pale shape of the bed was visible and a nightcapped head on the pillow.

"Which of you is it?" demanded the voice, old but vibrant.

"It's Finch, Granny."

"Well, come in and let in the light."

"I . . . I can't. I'll come back and do it."

"Do it now."

"But Gran, I've got an armful of wood."

"Put it down and come in."

Finch's voice broke on a note of anguish. "Gran, it will make a mess on your carpet and I'm supposed to take these logs to Renny for the fire."

That was enough for her. If there was to be a tug of war over who was to be waited on first she was ready for it.

"Put down the wood," she ordered, and he could perceive her struggling to sit up.

He laid the logs carefully in the doorway and went to her. She was propped on one elbow. She gave a chuckle, as of pleasure in her little triumph. "Kiss me," she said.

He put his arms about her old body in its heavy cotton nightdress that was trimmed with much embroidery, and hugged her. That was what she liked from her sons and grandsons, a good hug and a hearty kiss. It seemed to put fresh life into her. She was almost ninety-eight years old. Her arms, surprisingly strong, held him close.

"Now open the curtains."

"It's an awful day, Gran. The worst sort of day you could think of for the time of year."

"What time of year is it—I mean what date?"

"The first day of March." Now he had drawn the curtains wide and the window, streaming in freezing rain, was disclosed. The bare branches of an old lilac tree bent before the gale.

"The first of March, eh? And coming in like a raging lion. Well, well, what a day for . . ."

Now she was going to say it! What a day for your birthday. But she said only—"Put my pillows behind me. Prop me up." She gave a sniff, as though she had a cold in the head.

He placed the huge feather pillows at her back, his eager eyes on her face beseeching her. My birthday, his heart pleaded, don't forget my birthday, Gran . . . But how could he expect an old woman, almost a hundred years old, to remember his birthday?

When he had her propped up he looked down into her face. He could remember it since he was little more than a baby and it had always fascinated him. The dark eyes were so alive, the nose so finely arched, there was a look of courage, of boldness, in the very structure of the face, so that, toothless as she was, dominance was enthroned there. There was craft in the face too. It might have belonged to an old empress, seasoned in the intrigues of a court. Yet her realm had been Jalna. She was little known beyond the surrounding countryside. In Ireland, where she had spent her youth and in India, where, in a British military station, she had spent the first three years of a happy marriage, she was forgotten.

"My teeth," she now demanded, "give me my teeth."

The two sets were in a tumbler of water on a bedside table. Finch held it in front of her while she, with a look of pleasurable anticipation, retrieved them and, with a clicking sound, put one denture, then the other, in place.

"Good," she said, "now . . ."

But her eldest grandson's voice interrupted her. "Finch! What the devil are you doing?" he shouted.

"Oh, gosh," groaned Finch, "the logs!"

Renny was striding down the hall. Before Finch could intercept him he was at the door of the bedroom and had stumbled over the logs and almost plunged onto the bed. Old Adeline Whiteoak held out her arms to him.

"Bless me, what an entrance!" she exclaimed. "What a clumsy fellow you are. Can't you see where you are going?" She knew she was to blame and so smothered his explosion of anger in an embrace. She held him close while Finch gathered up the logs. She drew strength from Renny.

Finch found the fire merrily burning up the kindling and the family group at ease. Meg was knitting something for Wakefield.

"Let me put on the logs," begged the little boy.

Finch gruffly pushed him away and built up the fire, laying the logs carefully, almost caressingly in place. The sweet scent of these pleased him. Wakefield crouched close beside him, the flames reflected in his large brown eyes. He held up his little hands to the fire. Finch had a sudden desire to hold him close. He picked him up and pressed his small body against his own, rejoicing in its weakness, finding sensuous comfort in it.

Meg beamed up at them.

Wakefield whispered—"It's your birthday, isn't it, Finch? I know." He looked mischievous.

Finch quickly set him on his feet. "Forget it," he said.

Renny appeared in the doorway. He said, in his decisive voice—"Gran's awake, Meg. I've rung for her breakfast, can you go to her?"

Meg rose at once. She would be thirty-nine in a few months but already had a matronly figure and a strand of gray in her light brown hair at the temples. She had a particularly sweet smile but a stubborn nature. She was devoted to her brother and her young half brothers and was held up by all the neighborhood as the model of what a sister, a niece and a granddaughter should be.

The spaniels were stretched in front of the fire and now two other pets entered the room, passing Meg in the doorway with a supercilious air. These were Nip, a Yorkshire terrier belonging to Nicholas, and Sasha, a yellow tortoise shell cat, which was Ernest's. Each made straight for its owner, Nip scratching Nicholas's leg in a peremptory way till he was lifted to his knee; Sasha, in a graceful bound, reached Ernest's chest and then his shoulder, rubbing her cheek on his.

"Lucky little brute," observed Eden, stretching his supple body to its indolent length.

"This is a perfect morning for study," said Ernest. "You should bring your books down here by the fire, boys."

"Good idea," agreed Piers. "I'll race you upstairs, Eden." As though shot from a bow both darted into the hall and up the two flights of stairs. Eden flew up so lightly, with such eager grace, it was hard to believe that only a moment ago he had been as relaxed as the cat Sasha.

Nicholas was filling his pipe, Ernest was reading aloud something from the morning paper. Renny was putting on his mackintosh. Wragge was about to carry a tray into the grandmother's room, from where her voice and Meg's came, amiably discussing the weather. Grandmother was saying—"It was just a day as this when he was born. I will remember it and his mother in labor six hours."

Meg interrupted—"Sh-h. He's just outside in the hall. He'll hear you."

At the same moment Grandmother's parrot broke in with vigorous imprecations in Hindustani, directed, the old lady liked to think, against the weather. She exclaimed —"Poor Boney, poor Boney. How he does hate this climate—and so do I."

Wragge's voice came. "Your breakfast, madam."

She said, with gusto—"Good—good—I'm ready for it too."

Finch, whose heart had halted at mention of his birthday, now slowly mounted the stairs.

What was the matter with everybody? Why did they treat him with such indifference? On his fourteenth birthday they'd been very decent to him. What had happened? He had not been in disgrace or complained about by his schoolmasters. Yet not one present, not even one good wish, had come his way. Three times had it been spoken of and then hushed up as though it were a disgrace. Of course he knew he was not as attractive as the other boys but what was the sense of rubbing it in? There was no sense—no sense in anything. The world was a senseless bewildering place. He wondered how he could endure it for fifty or sixty or—if he lived as long as Gran—eighty years more. But then he'd probably die young. Yes, he was pretty sure he'd die young.

He looked into the bedroom he shared with Piers. Bessie, the maid, was making the bed. Her round pink wrists and capable hands were moving above the sheets. He wanted her to say a kind word to him but she was smiling to herself—busy with her own thoughts. There was no place for him in the house or in anyone's thoughts. He was alone—as perhaps few in the world were alone . . .

There was a long narrow box room at the end of the attic, where trunks, old clothes, old magazines, old picnic hampers, bird cages, fishing tackle and a thousand odds and ends were kept. There was the old brass-bound leather trunk where was kept the splendid uniform which his grandfather had worn. Every spring there was a ceremony when the contents of this trunk were carried to the grassy lawn at the back of the house, hung on a clothesline, brushed and aired. The grandmother always presided over this ceremony, supported on the arm of one of her sons and ejaculating in her harsh old voice that had once been one of the sweetest in Ireland—"Oh, but he was a fine-looking man! You don't see his like nowadays. Nor even in his time. How the women stared at him. But I kept him for my own . . . Is that a moth hole, Nicholas? Let me see . . . Thank God, no . . . Let me feel the cloth in my fingers . . . Ah . . ." And tears would roll down her cheeks.

Finch laid his hand on that trunk wherein was locked his mother's wedding dress and veil. Who kept the key of that, he wondered. Meg, he supposed. And why had he never been shown these things? He had as much right to mourn over relics as anyone. His mother had died soon after Wakefield's birth and she'd had a hard time at his own birth. Six hours in labor, his grandmother had said . . . on such a day as this . . . He shuddered . . . Why might he not see the things in the trunk? Why was he treated so? Downstairs this miserable day was being tolerably passed by the group about the fire, by Gran snugly eating her breakfast in bed, by Renny in the stables. Only he was the outsider. Alone . . . alone on his birthday . . . Not a present—not a good wish—not even the customary whacks on the back from Piers!

A little moth miller zigzagged past him and he had all but put out his hand to crush it, then changed his mind. Let it lay its eggs where it would. Let the worms they produced devour what they would. They had as great a hunger as Grandmother at her tray and perhaps, in the sight of God, as much right to eat.

The rain thundered on the slope of the room, made gurgling noises in the eaves. The roof leaked in one corner. There was the spot adjoining his own bedroom . . . Let it leak. It was none of his business. Let the moth and the flood share the house between them . . . In weary melancholy he lay down on the bare floor, resting his head on a canvas dunnage bag. Tears filled his eyes, and somehow he felt the better for them. He was alone. He was at the end of things. He did not care. He heard someone give a hoarse sob and wondered if it might be he . . .

When he woke he felt cold and stiff. The rain had somewhat lessened but the sky had darkened with its load of rain to come. The clear treble voice of his youngest brother came to him. "Finch," he called, as he mounted the stairs. "Finch, where are you?" Timidly, as though he remembered stories of ghosts and witches, he opened the door and put his small pointed face and curly dark head inside.

"Why are you lying on the floor?" he asked, in surprise.

"Because I'm not standing up and poking my nose into other people's business."

"Oh." Wakefield now assumed the manner of his Uncle Ernest. "Well, you're wanted, my boy."

"Who wants me?"

"Everybody. It's dinnertime." The family at Jalna still held to the country custom of dinner in the middle of the day and still drank tea at that meal. "Tea" itself was eaten at five o'clock and a substantial supper at eight.

"Why—why, it's impossible." Finch got up and stretched. "I've only been here a little while. I was studying and I . . ." No, he would not say he fell asleep.

"What were you studying? I don't see any books."

"Did you never hear of doing problems in your head? Well, that's what I was doing."

"It's dinnertime. You're to hurry."

The sound of the rain was broken by the crescendo resonance of the brass gong, sounded by Wragge.

"There! Didn't I tell you?" Wakefield jumped up and down in excitement. He ran to Finch and tugged at his hand. "Do hurry."

"I ought to tidy myself."

"There's no time."

Finch suddenly felt gentle toward the little brother. He let himself be led down the two flights of stairs to the door of the dining room. Strangely it was shut. With a flourish Wakefield opened it and shouted.

"Here he is! Here he is!"

Finch was dazed by what met his eyes. The family were assembled, standing about the table—Meg and Renny at either end—Grandmother and the two uncles on one side —Eden and Piers on the other, with his place awaiting him between Piers and Wakefield. Wakefield had run to his own chair beside Meg, on which was a thick volume of the *British Poets* to raise him to a comfortable level. But why were they standing up waiting for him? And as for the table—surely it had not been made to look like this for him.

The yellow velour curtains had been drawn to shut out the weather. The heavy silver candelabrum had been set on the shining damask on the table. The candlelight glimmered in the eyes of the smiling family, made their smiles beautiful. Grandmother stood bent, her knuckles on the table, eager to sit down, the purple ribbons in her best cap trembling. She grinned up at Finch. "Happy birthday, you young rascal," she called out. "Come and kiss me."

"Happy birthday! Many happy returns of the day!" sang out his brothers, sister, and uncles.

It was almost too much. Indeed it was altogether too much—the transition from melancholy and neglect to this warmth of kinship, this beaming acknowledgment of the day, this glory of candlelight, fruit, and little dishes of nuts and raisins, as though it were Christmas . . . He stumbled over Renny's spaniel, Merlin, because his eyes were strangely blurred, and almost fell into his grandmother's arms. The spaniel yelped and scuttled beneath the table.

"Steady, steady, old lady," said Nicholas, supporting her. "What a clumsy fellow you are, Finch."

The grandmother gave him a resounding kiss. His uncles slapped him on the back. Meg held out her plump arms and enfolded him.

"We thought we'd give you a nice surprise, Finch, dear, by pretending we'd forgotten all about your birthday. Wasn't it fun? It was all my idea."

"Wonderful fun," mumbled Finch, against her cheek.

"Now sit down and eat a good meal. You are so dreadfully thin. Then we shall have the presents."

Wragge had placed a platter on which was a joint of beef surrounded by Yorkshire pudding in front of Renny, who, after testing the edge of the knife with his thumb, at once set about carving it.

"I know what you're getting," said Wakefield. "I wish my birthday would hurry up. June is a better time to be born in than March."

"Attend to your food," said Nicholas.

"I haven't any. No fat, Renny, please."

"Dish gravy," put in Grandmother. "I do like dish gravy. *And* Yorkshire pudding."

"There you are, Gran. You know what's good for you."

When it was Finch's turn to be served, such an enormous helping was put on his plate that even he, with his growing boy's appetite, was a little abashed. "Oh, look here, Renny, what do you think I am? A rhinoceros?"

"More like an ostrich," Piers said.

"He'll be better looking as he gets older. He has the Court nose. He cannot look quite undistinguished with that," said Ernest kindly.

"What's that about the Court nose?" demanded Grandmother, having herself been a Court.

"Finch has it," cried Wakefield.

She peered across the table at Finch, a bit of Yorkshire pudding clinging to her underlip. "I don't see it," she said.

"He's just wiped it off," laughed Piers. "He's been crying."

Grandmother retrieved the bit of pudding with her tongue. "I won't have the nose made fun of," she declared.

A spirited discussion on the personal appearance of both Courts and Whiteoaks ensued. Finch was forgotten. He had, for a wonder, little appetite. Even when the birthday cake, with fifteen candles, arrived, he felt no hunger for it. When he tried to blow out the candles with one great puff, he had to make three attempts before he managed it.

"I could do better myself," said Grandmother.

Later he was presented with a number of quite expensive gifts. The year before he had been given a bicycle. He was a lucky boy and he knew it, yet somehow the spiritual clouds of the morning were not quite shifted by the sunshine of this hour. He had been the subject of good wishes, yet could not feel as he knew he ought to feel. He stood staring out of the library window at the rain that had become only a gray drizzle. From the hall he heard the sound of the grandfather's clock preparing to strike— a kind of rattling wheeze. But before it reached the point, the black marble clock with the gilt face, which stood on the mantelshelf in this room, gave out its musical, effortless notes. *One-two-three.* Instantly, as though in resentment at this forestalling, the grandfather's clock struck harsh and strong. The Dresden clock in the drawing room made its sweet response. All three eager to push forward into the mystery ahead.

His sister came up behind him and clasped him about the middle, she so plump, he so thin.

She said—"I do think it was fun, don't you, Finch, our pretending we'd forgotten all about your birthday? You really were taken in, weren't you?"

"Sure. It was lots of fun."

"It was all my idea."

"It certainly was fun."

"And do you like the fountain pen I gave you? And all the presents from the others?"

"It's a beauty. Everything's fine."

"Last birthday you were given a bicycle."

"Yes."

"I think you're a lucky boy."

"I certainly am."

"You'll remember this birthday."

"You bet I shall."

2.

Indigo Lake

EDEN DID NOT OFTEN MAKE a confidant of Piers, so that when he beckoned Piers to follow him into his room, shut the door after them, and asked—"Can you keep a secret?" Piers felt a glow of pleasure.

"Of course I can," he answered.

Eden perched himself on his desk and lighted a cigarette. "I'm an idiot for telling this but I simply can't help it. It's so interesting."

"What is it?"

"Well . . . I know a way of making quite a lot of money . . . if I can get others interested."

Piers liked money. All the young Whiteoaks liked it, but, though they lived well, there was seldom much cash available to them. Their grandmother had a fair-sized fortune, comfortably invested, but she hated to part with money. Indeed she liked to pose as rather badly off and never dropped a hint as to whom her will would benefit. But it was usually taken for granted that Renny would be her heir. He had inherited the estate from his father, her youngest son Philip, and it was natural that she should make her home with him, as she had with his father. Indeed it had been stipulated in her husband's will that Jalna should always provide a home for her. Nicholas and Ernest, so long as they had plenty of money to spend, had spent it in London, only returning to Jalna during the war. They were welcome doubly, for their family held them in great affection. Their brother Philip and his second wife had died within a few months of each other, while Renny was with his regiment in France.

Piers now said—"I'm interested in making money. How's it to be done?"

A smile flickered across Eden's lips. He said—"I hadn't thought of you. But, of course, if you'd like to invest in this thing—if you have any capital—you're welcome to."

Piers was disappointed. "Oh, I thought you meant me."

"I do mean you—if you have the wherewithal."

Piers had, during the past two years, helped with the work of the farm in his holidays, ploughing the land, learning the methods of spraying the apple orchard, grading and packing apples for shipment, as well as helping to school polo ponies. At the end of the coming term he would matriculate, quit school, and settle down to the work he loved. He strained toward the day.

He now said—"I have two hundred dollars saved." He could not keep the pride out of his voice.

Eden looked at him in wonder. "However do you do it?" he exclaimed.

"I've worked pretty hard, haven't I? All you do in your spare time is to write poetry."

"I'm no good at physical labor."

"Well, of course, you're going to be a lawyer. What a life! Gosh, I'd hate it."

Again Eden smiled. "I believe I am going to hate it too," he said. Then his voice became confidential. "Listen, Piers. The other day I met a man named Kronk in the city. He's a mining man and he's one of a company who are developing a new gold mine in the north. It's called the Indigo Lake Mine. They've found rich deposits there. As they are just in the early stages of this project they are interested in quite—well, what you might call insignificant shareholders—like you and me."

Piers was astonished. "Have you money too?"

"No, not exactly. But I should get a commission on the shares I sell. Why, look here, Piers, this Kronk told me the stock is rising so fast that he knows a man who is making ten per cent on his investment and if he chose to sell out today he could double his money. But naturally he wouldn't dream of selling."

Piers's prominent blue eyes were bright with the lust for gain. He asked—"How much are the shares?"

"Fifty cents each."

"Fine! I'll take four hundred."

Eden gave Piers an approving smile. "Good man! I thought you would."

Then Piers's face fell. "What will Renny say? He'll never let me."

"He mustn't know; he has nothing of the speculator in him, except in horseflesh. We must keep it dark. Then—when you have made a good fat profit, you may like to tell him." He gave Piers a cigarette, adding—"I'm going to tackle the uncles now and see if they'd like to join in the fun."

Piers laughed skeptically. He was feeling immensely exhilarated and mature. He said, blowing a smoke ring—"They'll never speculate again. Uncle Ernest lost a lot of money once, didn't he?"

"This is different. It's absolutely safe. You should hear Mr. Kronk talk of it. He's put everything he owns into it. And his wife too. She's put everything she owns into it."

Piers was now even more impressed. He asked—"How did you meet him?"

"Met him on the train. I must introduce you. He's quite an amazing fellow. Come up from scratch. Look at this prospectus he gave me."

The two pored over the bright-colored prospectus, Piers's muscular hands now and again touching Eden's slender, loosely-put-together ones. When Piers had gone Eden sat down by the desk, as though weary. Why, he thought, resting his head on his hands, was he forced to go through all this in order to secure enough money for his heart's desire? His uncles, when they were young, had taken the pleasures of travel as a matter of course. Renny had been about a good deal—to Ireland, to England, to France during the war, to New York to ride in horse shows. But he—he who wanted with all his soul to go to France and Italy—must be stuck in this backwater where the chief ambition of his family was to preserve the traditions of the past. There was more in life than mere good living, well-bred horses, healthy fruit trees, going to morning service on Sunday in the little church his grandfather had built. It was all very well for Renny. It suited him down to the ground. And Piers—it would suit him down to the ground—the earth to which he would willingly be tied. It was all very well for a woman nearing one hundred, but she had had a colorful past in Ireland and in India—not that she lived in the past, as did most very old people. She lived greedily in the present and quite often spoke of the future—bless her heart. But before long she must die . . . she was worth at least a hundred thousand dollars . . . supposing she left fifty thousand to Renny and divided the remainder equally among her other grandchildren. Ten thousand to each. What could he not do with ten thousand dollars! He would slough off the study of law like the abominably stifling skin of a snake, and go forth and see the world. But he could do it on so much less than ten thousand. Just a little money! He was not greedy.

He found Nicholas comfortably disposed after a nap—gouty leg resting on a large ottoman, massive head with its untidy graying hair lolling against the back of his padded leather chair. His large brown eyes were but half open and in one handsome hand with its seal ring he held a meerschaum pipe, the mouthpiece of which disappeared beneath his shaggy moustache. He had responded to Eden's knock with a lazy—"Come in," but when he saw who entered his eyes opened wide and he said—"Hello, Eden. Finished your work for the day? And what a day! What a hopeless looking day. The time of year one should spend on the Riviera."

"And you used to, didn't you—in the old times?"

"I did indeed. Sit down."

"Shall I make you uncomfortable if I sit on this thing? No? I want to talk." He sat down on the ottoman careful not to incommode Nicholas. It was only then that he noticed Nip, the tiny Yorkshire terrier, luxuriating on his master's relaxed middle—the gray of his long silky hair so blended with the gray tweed. Nip gave Eden a defensive look and wriggled a little closer to the massive comfort of Nicholas, who answered:

"He hates this weather too."

"Lucky dog, to be able to forget it."

"Well, he was put out this morning as usual but stayed not a minute longer than was necessary. What's that you've got?"

"A prospectus, Uncle Nick, of a gold mine called Indigo Lake Mine. Wonderful new veins have been discovered there."

Nicholas laid down the law with his meerschaum. "Keep away from speculation. Nothing in it but worry—and loss. God—what your Uncle Ernest has lost!"

"I know. But this is different."

"They're all different till you get involved. Then they're all the same. Loss and anxiety and—more loss."

Eden said—"I have nothing to invest and don't expect I ever shall have. But—if I had—this is what I'd go into. Look here." He put the prospectus almost caressingly into Nicholas's hands. It crackled across the little dog's body and he twitched in annoyance. Eden, in his freshness and strength, pressed close to Nicholas's leg. With the professional air of a mining promoter he poured out the benefits of this investment.

"But what is there in it for you?" asked Nicholas, "if I let you persuade me? Which I shan't."

"I'd get a commission from Mr. Kronk."

"Depending on how foolish I am. Better let me give you something and have done with it."

Eden drew back stung. He folded up the prospectus. "It isn't in the least like that, Uncle Nick. This is purely a business deal. One chance in a lifetime. I wish you could meet this man Kronk. Will you let me bring him out?"

"God, no. It would never do at all."

"Well. I shan't try to persuade you. Though it is a wonderful opportunity. The gold's just lying there waiting to be dug out. What will happen is that American speculators will jump in, the way they do, and buy up all the shares." Eden put the prospectus in his pocket, leant forward and laid his cheek against Nip, who, opening his eyes, gave Eden a swift lick with his pointed tongue, then resolutely went to sleep again.

Nicholas looked down at Eden with a sudden pity—inexplicable, for the boy was young and—what was he, besides being young? How little one knew of those who were nearest one. And Eden was near, very near, though more comfortably so when he brought in a new poem to read to him.

"Look at this day," Eden was exclaiming. "Look at it —and you might be in Rapallo or Venice or Taormina if . . ." He smiled into his uncle's eyes.

Nicholas looked out at the day, then down at his gouty knee. "I'm not fit for travel now," he said.

"But you could get rid of that knee. Look how much better it is in the summer. Why, Uncle Nick, you're not going to spend the rest of your days stuck here at Jalna, are you?"

Nicholas took the prospectus from Eden's pocket. He put on his glasses and studied it.

"It's nicely got up," he said. "If I had any spare cash to play with I shouldn't mind."

"This is what they call getting in on the ground floor, Uncle Nick. You'd be there before the big speculators send the stock soaring."

"How you talk," laughed Nicholas. "How much are the shares?"

"Only fifty cents each. Tempting, eh?"

The window was blinded by rain. But now Nicholas saw a sapphire sea, a wall overhung by wisteria, and mimosa. He saw too the face of his wife from whom he had been divorced for many years. But her face faded. In truth he could not clearly remember what she looked like. The sea and the garden remained. He shifted in his chair . . . He repeated—"Fifty cents each . . . two thousand shares for a thousand dollars."

Eden's face came closer. "Uncle Nick," he breathed, "you ought to come into this."

"Now I won't be stampeded," growled Nicholas.

"Of course not. Not for the world. But these shares are going like hot cakes. By the end of next week they'll be oversubscribed, Mr. Kronk says.

Nicholas blew through his moustache. "I'll take two thousand shares. Not going to let a chance like this get away. I'll take four thousand."

They laughed in triumph, as though over an enemy defeated. "Not a word of this investment to the family," cautioned Nicholas. "If your Uncle Ernest knew he'd want to be into it himself and he has already lost too much in stocks."

"I'll not tell him you've invested in this, but believe me you won't lose. This is safe, Uncle Nick. It's gold—right there in the rocks. You'll be spending next winter in Italy."

Nicholas heaved himself out of his chair, deposited Nip carefully on the bed and limped to the piano, on which stood a siphon of soda water and a tantalus with a bottle of Scotch, one of brandy, and one of gin.

"Must have a drink to celebrate," he said, and poured a fair amount of whiskey into a tumbler, adding a splash of soda water. "Have one?" he asked.

"No, thanks." And he thought—"Better not smell of spirits when I interview Uncle Ernest."

Outside in the passage he hesitated. What if this stock were not as sound as it seemed? What if—but then he remembered Mr. Kronk and that air of security exuded by him and his well-furnished flat. The broker had taken him there, instead of to his office, because, as he said, he had such a special feeling for him.

In the passage, dim because of early falling darkness, Eden overtook Finch. He caught the boy's wrist in his hand. "You couldn't look sadder. You *are* a funny kid. I believe you were so upset by the joke we played on you that you haven't recovered. You know it was one of Meg's subtle ideas. Fun on a rainy day sort of thing."

"It *was* fun," Finch said heavily.

Eden was so happy in his success with Nicholas that a feeling of affection for the awkward boy warmed his heart. He threw an arm about his shoulders and gave him a hug. Finch's eager response startled him. It was almost as though Finch would embrace him in return. Why—he was like a lonely dog you had patted.

Now he gave Finch a little push and said—"I must go in to see Uncle Ernest—" and he could not resist adding—"on business."

"Business?" Finch echoed vaguely.

"Yes. But don't mention it to Piers or to anyone."

"I never talk to Piers—about anything." Finch was

pleased that Eden should have confided even so little in him.

Left to himself Nicholas refilled his pipe, refilled his glass. He seldom allowed himself to take so much whiskey at a time because he knew it was bad for his gout. What was that newfangled word they had for it? Arthritis. Yes—that was it. A miserable sounding word. He'd rather call it gout. But now he was exhilarated by the speculation in which he had indulged. There was no doubt about it, these gold mines did exist and there was no reason why he should not make a little money when the chance came his way. That prospectus had been very attractive indeed. It showed photographs of the actual operations. Indigo Lake. That was a name you couldn't forget. He felt restless and yet happy. The winter had been very long. Lately, he thought, he'd had a touch of claustrophobia—another newfangled word. There was nothing like a little fling with one's money, and, if this Indigo Lake business prospered, he'd invest more. He might even advise old Ernie to buy a few shares. But for the present the transaction should be secret between Eden and himself.

But Eden was already displaying the prospectus to Ernest, repeating all he had told Nicholas of the unique nature of this investment. Ernest had a strain of the gambler in him. It was a long while since he had been offered anything so enticing as these shares in the Indigo Lake Mine. His color rose and he walked eagerly about his bedroom. Nicholas had been persuaded to buy four thousand shares. Ernest jumped at eight thousand. He too would like to spend the following winter in Europe. He too felt restive. Life which had once been an exciting affair—a very pleasant affair, especially as he had never put his neck under the yoke of marriage, as Nicholas had done—but now it had become a little tame. A good deal of time spent in attendance on his irascible old mother, who, though he loved her dearly, could be very trying. He was very fond of his nephews but there were so many of them and they were often noisy and difficult. A change would be delightful. Why, he and Nicholas had been nowhere since they had returned from England during the war.

He agreed with Eden that it would be well to keep the Indigo Lake transaction between themselves for the present. Nicholas would be against it and he had a very unpleasant way of recalling one's past unfortunate speculations. Such things were better forgotten. He enjoyed the intimacy of conspiring, as it were, with Eden. He had an especial feeling for this nephew who undeniably had poetic talent and a face that matched it, who appreciated Ernest's own literary interests. They two were different from all others of the family. They two spoke a language in common. The other nephews were dear boys, but Eden . . .

As for Eden, any doubts that assailed him were dispersed by his next meeting with Mr. Kronk. Nicholas and Ernest had bought their shares in the nick of time. By the end of that week there would not be another share available. Mrs. Kronk too had taken a great fancy to the frank young man. The Kronks, man and wife, were eager for the family at Jalna to have as many shares of the Indigo Lake Gold Mine as possible. Mrs. Kronk, a tall large-boned woman, with straight fair hair brushed severely back from her intelligent face, was especially interested in Eden. He wondered what she had found to attract her in the little bilious looking man whom she appeared alternately to bully and to mother. He could not help noticing how her attitude toward himself changed when they found themselves alone together. Then she would stretch out her arms along the back of the sofa and speak to him in a low, matter-of-fact tone, as though they had years of familiar conversation behind them.

3.

Awakening of Spring

SPRING, AS FAR TOO OFTEN, seemed reluctant to come into the open. Like a chick in a hard-shelled egg, it pecked faintly at the hard shell of winter till its moist infant presence could just barely be perceived. Then apparently disheartened it lay curled up dormant for a time, as though never to be hatched. Finally, after a night of wind and rain at the end of April it burst forth in an agony of threshing and writhing and in the morning perched on the earth, its pale gold plumage drying in the sun, its eyes little bright pools. And, like bits of the shell it had cast off, soiled patches of snow and ice lay in the hollows.

As the sun mounted it showed once more what warmth could be, how every twig that had life in it, every root that had health in it, responded. Soon the countryside belonged to spring. At Jalna none of the family was more conscious of its power than Piers. It appeared to his elders that they could see him growing, and he grew, not in a lanky awkward fashion but with all his parts in serene accord. His neck and shoulders became more muscular, his legs fine pillars to support him. The fair skin of his cheeks and chin produced an authentic yellow beard. His shaving was now worth Finch's attention.

Piers was a favorite of his grandmother's.

"Ha," she would exclaim, in admiration, "here's a stalwart fellow coming on! A back like his grandfather's. And he's the only one of the whelps that has. I do like a well-set-up man."

42

And her son Ernest would reply—"To my mind, all the boys are well proportioned."

"Well proportioned! Ha—I grant you that none of 'em has legs that are too short or a neck that's too long, with a great Adam's apple. That I do hate."

Nicholas would put in—"Take Renny. He's a lithe wiry fellow."

"Aye. Take him. You may have him. He's the very likeness of my father—old Renny Court—and you know what he was."

"We've heard such different accounts of him, Mamma."

"And different he could be—to suit the occasion—smooth as silk—or rough and tough."

To draw her on Nicholas would add—"You can't deny that Eden has looks."

"Looks! Of course he has looks. The looks of his poor mother . . . No—not one of 'em will ever match your grandfather." And she would raise her eyes from beneath their shaggy brows to the portrait of her long dead husband Captain Whiteoak. Her eyes would glow with a love the years could not dim and one of her sons would take her handkerchief and gently wipe away the drop that hung on the tip of her arched nose, and she would put out her shapely old hand and grip his hand, as though to gain strength from him.

Piers, very conscious of this approval, held his back straighter, tried to put into his eyes that very expression of having been born with a silver spoon in his mouth and a sword in his hand which distinguished the eyes in the portrait of his grandfather. Once in the seclusion of the attic Piers had got into that dashing uniform and stared at his reflection in an old mirror. Piers had been disappointed in the reflection. The uniform had hung loosely on him. It would take several years of growth before he could fill it out. Still, he had made a fine figure of a hussar and he wished he might have presented himself as such to the family.

But on this lovely morning two months after Finch's birthday and the first Saturday in May he was happy to be as he was—free as air for the day—filled with an incomparable zest for life. He whistled to the dogs but none answered. As usual they were at Renny's heels. He crossed the lawn where the yellow heads of dandelions were rosetted against the green velvet of the new grass like brass buttons. He passed through the wicket gate in the hedge, followed the meandering path that led down into the ravine. The stream had overflowed its banks that spring, torn at them, tried to tear down the rustic bridge, but now, its early ardor spent, had subsided to a cheerful gurgling among the stalks of cattails and clumps of watercress.

Piers stood leaning on the handrail of the bridge, considering what he would do with the day. A succession of pleasant possibilities crossed his mind. There were so many things to do, but at the moment he was content to do nothing but lounge against the bridge, his strong hands stroking the handrail, from which the bark had long disappeared, pulled off by the destructive fingers of boys. Initials had been carved on it. His own—his brothers'—his uncles'— why had young Finch carved his name Finch, instead of just his initials? He was a conceited young duffer. There was *NW* for Nicholas and the date 1865. Pretty dim it was. And there were his sister's initials, entwined with the letters *MV*. Piers had to think for a moment before he could remember. Ah, yes—*MV* stood for Maurice Vaughan, their neighbor, and once years ago he and Meg had been engaged to marry. The engagement had been broken off because of a scrape Maurice had got himself into with a village girl. There had been a baby deposited on the Vaughan's doorstep in truly Victorian melodrama —a tremendous row and the engagement broken off. Piers remembered, with a grin, how shocked he had felt when Eden had told him the story of it when he was fourteen . . . Somehow Piers seldom connected Pheasant Vaughan with that story—Pheasant, a funny little kid—rather nice —he'd known her all her life. It was months since he'd seen her. It had been on a bitter cold day in January and they'd met on the road. She'd had her head bent against the wind and worn a skirt too long for her that was caked with snow nearly to her knees. She'd looked a funny figure —rather like a little old woman. When they'd said hello and parted and he had looked back at her, she'd been looking back too—her eyes large, as though she were half afraid of him. She must have a dull time of it, being in a house with only Maurice Vaughan and his grim-faced housekeeper, Mrs. Clinch. Casually he contrasted it with Jalna, teeming with activity, and gave a moment's pity to the child.

But she had passed from his mind when he saw her, or just glimpsed her, crouching among the reeds at the stream's edge. She must have been there all the while peering into the water. Had she seen him, he wondered. Whether or not she had she plainly saw him now, for she raised her eyes to look straight into his and beckoned.

That was all he needed, that and a warning finger she held up, to bring him to her side in a dozen stealthy strides. He crouched beside her, feeling a sudden inexplicable excitement.

"What is it?" he whispered.

"Look—a water snake."

It moved lazily, beautifully, near them, in dappled sunlit folds. Piers wondered at her not screaming, as most girls would. But she turned now to him, her lips parted, a rim of white teeth revealed, in a smile that seemed to him an invitation to a moment's comradeship. But she was only a kid. If she had been older she probably would have screamed, as a girl naturally would.

"Isn't it happy?" she whispered.

Well—that was a silly thing to say about a snake. As though it could be happy!

"Like to see me kill it?" he asked.

"Oh, no. I—love it."

He broke into laughter. He had a musical laugh, and, as though she could not help herself, she laughed too. The snake, its secretive golden eyes wary of them, moved without haste into the shadowed recesses of the reeds. It had dominated the pool, now it was gone, and the little white faces of the thronging bloodroot stared out from the bank.

A tremulous silence enveloped the boy and girl. The moist sweet scent of the ravine, the chatter of the stream, closed in about them. They gazed into the pool where the snake had been, and saw there the reflection of their own faces. Her dark hair and eyes turned amber in its shallow.

The pink of Pier's cheek, the blueness of his eyes, the fairness of his hair were merged into the semblance of a golden youth about to discover the meaning of spring. They gazed in silence for a space. Then his arm found her waist—his hand, her side where the heart fluttered like a hovering swallow. They turned their heads and looked into each other's eyes.

Piers had never before felt tenderness toward any human being. He had felt it toward young lambs. But now tenderness toward Pheasant welled up through all his sturdy body. Tenderness and an urge to protect her, and an urge to love her. But he only said laconically—"You're funny."

"So are you," she breathed. "Not a bit like I thought you were."

"I guess we're both funny. Will you kiss me?"

She nodded without speaking. But the kiss was not a success. Their faces merely bumped gently together. But in some inexplicable way it drew them very close. They felt less shy, more familiar, and strangely happy.

"How old are you?" he demanded.

"Seventeen in a few weeks."

"I'm eighteen. Soon be nineteen."

They could find nothing more to say. They squatted side by side in silence, as though the sum of their years had left them speechless in wonder. Only the stream spoke. A small bird flew by carrying a piece of white string in its beak, its wing beats ardent in its urge for nest building.

At last Piers said—"Well, I must be getting along."

She did not say stay.

"Shall you be coming this way tomorrow about this time?" he asked.

She nodded, pulling up a blade of grass and examining it.

"I'll be here," he said. He left her, running across the bridge and up the steep toward the lawn, as though to show his power.

4.

A Rise in Stocks

"POETRY AND MAKING MONEY," said Eden, "go extremely well together. I wonder that poets in the past have never tried it."

His Uncle Ernest was the only member of the family to whom he openly spoke of himself as a poet. Of course they all knew he wrote poetry and, according to their various temperaments, looked on it as a pleasant pastime, a weakness inherited from his mother, or a waste of the valuable hours which he should be devoting to the study of law. All but Ernest. He appreciated the promise shown by the young poet and, when Eden came to his room and read him his latest verses, he was gratified. Their literary gifts were a link between them. He himself had been engaged, for some years, in the preparation of a book on Shakespeare, though he had never yet produced a manuscript to show his family and Nicholas openly doubted the possibility of his ever producing one.

Uncle and nephew had had many an agreeable talk in the comfortable privacy of Ernest's room where the walls were decorated by water color drawings of English scenery he had done in his earlier days. In fact there was at least one of these in every room in the house. But never before had they enjoyed a talk of this nature. In the past their talk of money had concerned the lack of it, on Eden's part, and how quickly it went, on Ernest's. But since the speculation in the Indigo Lake Mine, the subject of money had taken on a new and delightful aspect. Today they were hilarious.

From the very week of Ernest's investment the price of Indigo Lake stocks had been rising. Not in a spectacular fashion, but steadily, firmly, in a way to give the investor confidence. Mr. Kronk kept Eden informed on the matter each day. Another bright-colored brochure arrived confirming these reports. Almost every day after his lectures he went to Mr. Kronk's apartment, and, if he were not there, Mrs. Kronk was and always with good news for him. She would give him not tea but a cocktail. Never before had he enjoyed himself in this way. A commission of twenty-five per cent on the investments of his uncles and Piers was paid to him by Mr. Kronk—paid with a smile, just as though he'd earned it. Nicholas, picturing a winter on the Riviera, doubled the amount he had invested. After a month of watching the rise of Indigo Lake, Ernest had also doubled his investment. Now he saw a gain so splendid that his fingers fairly itched to write still larger cheques.

He was an agile man, an affectionate one. In the hilarity of the moment he threw an arm about Eden, clasped him in a dancing position, and they waltzed the length of the room. Sasha, his cat, rose from her sleep on the bed to watch them, arching her back, making her legs long and her face a mask of disdain.

"I couldn't have believed it," Ernest exclaimed, panting a little, at the end of the waltz. "I had become very nervous about speculation since my last misfortunes. But this —my dear boy, it's wonderful. To think that a chance meeting on the train . . ."

"And if you could meet him! He doesn't look capable of big business enterprises. Just a confiding little man, with a cozy manner. But there's nothing he doesn't know about mining. Knows all that north country like the palm of his hand. Apparently taken a real shine to me."

Ernest squared his shoulders. "I shall invest more. Do you think we ought to bring your Uncle Nicholas into this? It does seem a shame that he should not share in it."

Eden considered. He felt himself to be getting into a corner. He said—"I think we'd better not. You know he doesn't like speculation." Eden now rather wished that there had been no secrecy in the affair. But how was he to know that it would be such a stupendous success?

Nicholas, though waltzing was beyond him, was enormously pleased. He beat the arm of his chair with his clenched fist and exclaimed—"By God, this is the best thing that's happened to me in many a day!" He did not suggest letting his brother in on the affair but rather took a rise out of how surprised old Ernie would be when he discovered what an astute speculator he was.

Piers, on his part, had never shown such eagerness to help with the work of farm, stables or orchard. No work was too hard or too tedious. Good farm laborers were scarce and he hired himself to Renny with a zeal for work that amazed his elder. At the same time he showed rather a disconcerting greed as to wages. Whatever he earned he handed over to Eden to invest for him, with childlike trust. Eden had opened a savings account in a city bank and in it he almost religiously deposited all that he earned in commission. Half a dozen times a day he would take the little deposit book from his pocket and examine it, relishing the way the amount increased. He kept a map in his desk, and when he had saved enough to pay his passage to Europe, he drew a red line from Montreal to Le Havre and from there to Paris. He calculated what it would cost him to spend a month there and the day came when he dared print, still in red ink, A MONTH HERE. He borrowed books about Paris from his uncles. Ernest brought out an old album of photographs and picture post cards of Paris, the French and Italian Rivieras, Florence, Rome and Sicily, and, he pored over them with Eden, read him bits from a journal he had kept on his travels. It required the greatest self-restraint on the part of Ernest and Nicholas to conceal their exhilaration from each other and from the family. They made no attempt to conceal their feeling of well-being and good humor. Things that in ordinary times irritated them now brought only a tolerant smile to their lips. Wakefield's noise and naughtiness, their old mother's irascibility, did not ruffle them. Piers consistently worked and all he earned he handed over to Eden to invest for him.

Before the summer had well begun Eden had persuaded his sister to invest in the Indigo Lake Mine. Meg had little of the speculator in her nature and was averse to acknowledging to the family that she had anything more than enough for her barest needs. Yet she was tempted and at last succumbed. When Eden was able to tell her of the rise in the stock of Indigo Lake she was so elated that, if he had not restrained her, she would have hurled all she had into the speculation.

But his young brother, his sister, and his uncles were small catches for Eden. He longed for an investor possessed of substantial means and more and more often his thoughts turned to his grandmother. The great obstacle was her age. Could he make her understand what the proposition was? Would it be possible to accomplish a transaction without the knowledge of her lawyer, Mr. Patton? All the family were aware that her fortune was invested in the most conservative way and her sons held it regrettable that this was so and that consequently her income was not so large as it might have been. Not that they ever saw more of it than sufficed for her few needs and the occasional presents she gave.

Several times Eden went to the door of her bedroom before she was up with the determination to sound her on the subject but each time his courage failed him. She might give the whole affair away to the family and bring down blame on himself for having suggested such a speculation to her. Of late he'd had quite enough censure about his failure in his exams to last him the rest of his life. Yet—he could not keep his mind off the delightful prospect of landing such a glittering fish as she. And it would be all for her own good! She might indeed be so grateful to him that she would increase the legacy he was sure she had already left him in her will.

This indecision could not continue and it ended one morning when, in passing her room, he saw that the door stood open and she herself was seated in a low chair beside a stool on which stood a basin of water. She was washing the rings which she wore every day—her wedding ring, her engagement ring, and five others, too many to be in good taste for any woman, to say nothing of a woman of her great age. But somehow they suited her and her family could not picture her shapely old hands without them.

She saw Eden's reflection in the mirror and called out—

"Come in, Eden, come in, and tell me what mischief you're up to."

Their eyes met in the mirror. They smiled and he came into the room, closing the door behind him.

Once he was inside that room and the door shut, its atmosphere enfolded him. She had been reared in a less sanitary period than this. She distrusted night air and did not mind having her parrot free in her room or his seeds or feathers scattered about.

Now, however, it was almost noon, the window stood wide open, and the heavy white plumes of the lilac tree beyond it added their scent to the air.

Eden bent over her and kissed her between the eyes. The hairs of her eyebrows were strong and he was conscious of the fine white ruching on her cap.

"What mischief now?" she demanded.

"No mischief, Gran. Business."

She appeared not to take this in but applied herself, breathing audibly, to the washing of her rings.

"I like that ruby ring," he said.

"Aye. It's a fine stone. A rajah gave it me."

"I wish I knew all your past, Granny."

That caught her humor and she chuckled.

"Some day I'll tell you and you may make a poem about it."

"An epic, Gran."

"You'll not get it out of me by flattery."

"You've tremendous suds in the basin. Would you like me to wash the rings for you?"

"No, no. I like something to busy myself with. When you get to my age it doesn't take much to amuse you . . . A little soap and water. A few rings to wash."

Eden dropped to his knees and his bright glance sought her. Seeing his face thus close she had a good look at it. She said—"You're too handsome. You'll have trouble with women."

"Renny's the one they're after."

"Him! I hope he'll make a better husband than did my father that he's the spit of."

"I love you when you're common, Granny."

She grinned. "Who was it—Longfellow?—who said that about not losing the common touch?"

Hilarious, Eden answered—"Longfellow. The best thing he ever wrote."

She dried the rings and restored them to her fingers, then spread out her hands to admire.

"Not bad-looking hands for a woman of my age, eh? I've had them for near a hundred years."

"I've always admired your hands, Gran."

She clasped them on her stomach and flung at him suddenly—"This business. What's it about?"

He'd half made up his mind not to tell her of his scheme. It was too dangerous. She perceived the hesitation on his face. "Come now," she said, "tell me. I like to hear about business affairs—if they're sensible."

"I don't think this would interest you, Gran."

"Then why did you shut the door?"

The moment had come. He could not resist it. He took her hand, with the rings still moist and warm on it, in his. He said low—"It's a gold mine, Granny. Up in the North. A wonderful chance for anyone who has money to invest. It's just being developed. A wonderful rich vein. Fortunes are being made out of it. I know a man—"

"Gold!" she interrupted with avidity. "Gold, eh?" Had it been silver or any other metal she would not have been interested. But the word "gold" fired her imagination. Gold she could understand.

Her parrot, which had been tossing seeds from his cup in search for his favorites, now cocked his head and rapped out—"Gold! Gold! Gold! Pieces of eight! Pieces of eight!"

Adeline Whiteoak clapped her hands together. "Hark to him! He knows every word we say."

"It's a good omen," laughed Eden, taking her two hands in his. "Listen, Gran."

"Yes, yes. Tell me all." She was not only interested but complacent to hear the whole story of the Indigo Lake Mine. Eden, now becoming a glib promoter, poured it out, embroidering the material recital with colorful and poetic words. She leant closer, drinking it in, her mouth open a little, the strong curling hairs on her chin quivering. The parrot sprang from his perch and alighted on her shoulder screaming—"Gold! Gold! Pieces of eight! Pieces of eight!" in passionate repetition.

Eden showed her the colored folder, the machinery of the mine pictured against a turquoise blue sky with Indigo Lake beyond. She made him fetch her magnifying glass from the bureau and she pored over the pictures. She had investments, sound ones, good ones, but nothing in gold. Her imagination, with little to feed it nowadays, was fired. A smoldering resentment she was feeling for her lawyer, Mr. Patton, because of his, as she considered, overbearing ways, made her relish the thought of deceiving him.

"I'll do it!" she cried, giving a thump to Eden's knee. "I'll do it today."

Eden's heart quickened its beat. "How much, Gran?"

She frowned, then exclaimed—"Fifty thousand. I'll invest fifty thousand dollars."

He drew back in horror. "You can't do that, Granny. It's too much."

She grinned. "I never do things by halves."

Eden felt panic. He wished he had not spoken. He folded the prospectus. "This is very tiring for you, Granny," he said. "Better put it out of your mind."

"Now you talk like your Uncle Ernest. This doesn't tire me. Does me good."

"But you mustn't invest so much."

"Who says must and mustn't to me?"

She was taking things out of his hands—and she going on for a hundred!

He said—"Supposing you should lose the money? What then?"

She arched her neck and her voice came harsh and strong. "I never lose. If the gold is there—it's there. *Is* it there?"

At the mention of gold Boney reiterated—"Pieces of eight! Pieces of eight!" Then he added in Hindustani —"Kutni! Kutni! Paji! Shaitam ka katla!"

Eden said—"Yes. The gold is there all right. It's a wonderful investment but I do advise you to go slowly at the first. My broker would advise that."

"A hundred dollars then."

This was a terrible decline. Eden hesitated, not knowing what to say.

She perceived this and said, with sudden sweetness— "You tell me then."

He could not stop himself. He heard himself saying— "What about ten thousand?"

"Just the right amount," she agreed and he felt that she could no longer differentiate between one sum of money and another, though she loved all gain. What troubled him still more was, now that she had agreed to invest in the mine, how to put through the transaction. He knew nothing of business, and dare not inquire of his uncles or Renny.

Over and over he made her promise to divulge nothing of the scheme to the family. She was becoming very tired and docilely nodded her head, on which the lace of her cap trembled, in agreement. He himself felt tired and wiped his moist brow with his hand when he had closed the door behind him. He was torn between exhilaration and anxiety. Then the image of Mr. Kronk rose before him. There was the man who would know just what to do. He would go to see him that very day.

He did go to the city, taking the opportunity of driving in with Renny. As he sat beside his elder, bumping over the rough bits in the old car, his eyes slid every now and again toward that hard profile he knew so well. Certainly it was an arresting profile—the nose handsome, with its proud nostrils, so like his grandmother's. Now the mouth and eyes expressed contemptuous concentration, for he disliked motoring and distrusted the car, having rather the attitude toward it of one of his own horses.

In the city he asked—"Where shall I drop you?"

Eden hesitated, then said—"Oh, anywhere."

"Anywhere? But where do you *want* to go?"

"Which way are you going? Anywhere will suit me."

Renny gave him a quick look. "What did you come in for then? Just to have a look around?"

"Well, actually I came in to see another student about some books."

"Do you mean he's going to lend you books? I hope he is, for your books cost like the devil."

"He might, if he has what I want. He lives in the Norfolk Apartments."

"Good. I can easily drop you there. You'd better go home by train."

It was in the Norfolk Apartments that the Kronks lived. Eden found the husband away and the wife at home. Eden was conscious of how glad she was to see him. She used more lipstick than was usual in those days and he saw a touch of eye shadow beneath her clear light eyes. She was as tall as he, so that their eyes met on a level. She wore one of the long-waisted short-skirted dresses of the time, and when they sat down and she crossed her legs Eden noticed how shapely they were. Her silk stockings were more sheer and lighter in color than any he had seen. She saw the glance he gave them and exclaimed:

"Since you were last here I've been down to New York. I did some shopping. I hope you don't think these too sheer." She stretched out her legs side by side, close together, the high-heeled shoes looking ridiculously small for her height.

"I think they're very pretty," Eden said rather nervously, for she was a type new to him. Then he added—"I suppose New York is wonderful. I've never been."

"Ah, *wonderful!* I did something else besides shop. Haven't you noticed?"

He looked her over but could discover nothing different about her. He murmured—"You always look so well dressed."

"It's not clothes. Look!" She bent her head and he saw that her hair was cut short.

"You've had your hair bobbed!" he exclaimed.

"Not *bobbed,* it's shingled. Do tell me you like it. My husband hates it. He liked my hair but it was such a nuisance."

"I think this looks very nice."

She straightened herself and gave him that confidential smile of hers. "I am so glad," she said. "I couldn't have borne your not liking it."

"But I do. I like it awfully well." His color rose. He did not quite know what she expected of him and he had but one desire and that was to talk business.

With sudden matter-of-factness she said—"I'm going to get you a drink." She went into the dining room, which was separated by only an archway from the living room, and began to busy herself at the sideboard. He stood, rather shyly, watching her from this distance. But while they were drinking their Scotch he began:

"I suppose Mr. Kronk was in New York on business."

She gave a little chuckle. "He certainly was. Nothing but. My, how those New Yorkers gobble up the Indigo Lake shares." She finished her drink with an audible smack of the lips.

Compared to this his news seemed insignificant. He said —"My grandmother has money she'd like to invest but . . ."

Instantly Mrs. Kronk gave him the full attention of her clear light eyes. "Your grandmother? Aren't you lucky to have so many affluent relations!"

He did not quite like this. He said, a little stiffly—"The difficulty is that she doesn't know, nor do I, how to go about selling government bonds and reinvesting. You see, she can't go to her bank. She's rather old."

"About eighty or more?"

"More. Considerably."

"Couldn't those uncles of yours arrange it for her?"

"She'd rather they didn't know. They'd be all for caution where she's concerned."

"Well, then, all you need is a power of attorney. I have the forms right here. Just get her to sign them."

It was all so simple. When Eden left the apartment house with the forms in his pocket, his exhilaration was such that he had walked some distance before he noticed rain coming down. By the time he had boarded a street-car big glittering drops were bouncing on the pavement and the bottoms of his trousers were soaked. On the way to the railway station the street lights came on and by their light he saw at the corner the ten-year-old family car and at the wheel his brother. There was no time in which to buy tickets. Eden thrust his fare to the conductor and pushed his way through the closing door just in time. Through the downpour he reached the running board of the car, rapped on the pane, and was inside just before the jolt with which the master of Jalna invariably started the car threw him on to the seat.

Renny said—"Well, that was neatly done."

"I was mighty glad to see you!"

"Did you get the books?"

"The books?"

"Your friend was going to lend you."

"Oh, those! Unfortunately no. The ones he has aren't of any use to me."

His brother threw him the glance of suspicion that seemed always ready beneath his mobile brows, and asked —"Who is this fellow?"

Eden thought—"Once you've been in trouble everyone's so ready to suspect you—especially old Redhead." His brain was so excited by the interview with Mrs. Kronk, by the thought of the power of attorney in his pocket, that he was less agile in self-defence than usual. He stammered —"Oh, he's a fellow by the name of—" before he could stop himself he said—"Kronk."

"Kronk," repeated Renny and put the most sinister implications into that syllable. "Who is he?"

"Oh, you wouldn't know. He comes from Saskatchewan."

"Studying law?"

"Yes."

"What's he doing here in the holidays?"

"He's got a job."

"How can he afford to live in such an expensive apartment house?"

"Well—you see—his father's a very rich man."

"Rancher?"

"Yes—that's it."

"Then why doesn't this fellow go home to the ranch where he might be of some use instead of taking a job in the city?"

"Well, you see he's had words with his father and doesn't want to go home."

"Hm." Renny apparently thought none the better of young Kronk for that. His expression was grim as he took out an old cloth and wiped the steam from the streaming windshield.

Eden asked pleasantly—"When do you think of buying a new car?" Instantly he realized that this was about the last question he should have asked. There was a taciturn silence before his brother returned—"I never think of it."

"*Never!* Good Lord."

"There are other things I need much more."

The traffic was dense at this point, or so it seemed to them, who could not realize what later it would become.

"In 1903," said Renny, "there were one hundred and seventy-eight motor vehicles on the road in Ontario. Now, twenty years later, there are two hundred and seventy-eight thousand, seven hundred and fifty-two."

Eden stared in wonder. "How on earth do you remember those figures?"

"Because I'm interested. I dislike 'em so." He gave a savage grin at the driver of a large new car who had tried to cut in on them.

Eden said, letting out his breath—"Whew, that was a close call."

"He needed a lesson."

There was silence till they had left the city behind and the road was almost deserted. On one hand lay wet summer fields, the heavy heads of the grain drooping under the rain, woodlands where coming night was already welcomed, and on the other the gray expanse of the lake. Renny stopped the car, lighted a cigarette, and offered one to Eden, who asked—"Did you buy the filly you've been speaking of?"

"No. Worse luck. A man from Pittsburgh got in ahead of me. Bought her yesterday."

Eden made a sound of sympathy.

Renny continued—"I should have made a lot of money out of that filly. She's a beauty. But that is what comes of being short of cash." He sighed, wiped the windshield and started the car.

"That was quite a bump," Eden said, recovering himself.

"She always starts like that," returned his elder laconically.

"Like me to drive?"

"No, thanks."

Eden had a sudden feeling of pity for him. Here he was

in need of money, and there was money to be made and so easily made, in the Indigo Lake enterprise. He had a mind to tell Renny, then and there. Indeed it would be unfair, even heartless not to tell him. He need not let him know that any others of the family had invested in the stock. He said:

"A chap I was talking to this afternoon has been making quite a lot of money out of stocks."

"Oh, what stocks?"

"Mining. A gold mine."

"He can have them. Eventually he'll lose. I'd not put a dollar into mining stocks. There are enough suckers without me. Now I'll tell you what does interest me. There's a sale of livestock near Stead next week. Like to come with me?"

Well, thought Eden, there is no use in trying to do anything for Renny. He simply won't be helped. But how he'll regret it when he finds what he's missed. A thrill ran through his nerves when he thought of the power of attorney in his pocket. The rain continued steady and the wind from the lake was cool. When they passed through the tiny village into the road which led to Jalna only the lights from windows twinkled through the darkness, and they passed or met no one. The massive pines, two hundred years old, that still lined this road were embracing their final decade, and beneath their arch it was black night. In their own driveway they splashed through puddles between hemlock and spruce and passed the brightly lighted house. Eden would have liked to get out here but they were chatting amiably and he would not interrupt their good fellowship.

A dim light came from the stable. Wright, the cheerful head stableman, opened the door to them.

"Heard you coming, sir. What a night it's turning out to be."

"How's everything, Wright?"

"Fine, sir. May I ask if you got the filly?"

"No. She was sold yesterday."

"Too bad. She was a promising one."

"Yes."

There were fifteen horses in the stable—show horses,

polo ponies that were bred and schooled here, and the farm horses. They had been fed, watered and bedded down for the night. Some had lain down to rest but others stood watching out of lustrous eyes the approach of the three men. Renny moved past stalls and loose boxes speaking to each, putting out a hand to caress a pet. The mare Cora, his favorite saddle horse, got up with a clatter of hooves when she heard the loved voice and uttered a deep-throated whinny. Renny went into the loose box to put an arm about her and she swung her carven head to nuzzle him.

Eden, with the smell of clean straw, the smell of well-cared-for beasts in his nostrils, studied the picture made by man and horse in the loose box. He found in them a curious resemblance. It was in the bold naked lines of the head, in the look of wariness; of sensitivity to the physical world. As Renny talked with Wright, Eden saw how the two recovered from their disappointment. Renny was cheerful when he said good-night to Wright and went out into the rain with Eden.

The air was full of heady scents from the earth. The house, all lighted, looked larger than it really was. As they passed into the porch the wet leaves of the Virginia creeper, shaken by a gust, sent down a small deluge on their heads.

"Oh, boys, I'm so glad you're back," their sister exclaimed as they appeared at the door of the drawing room. "What a night it's turning out to be!"

"And cool for the time of year," added Ernest.

"Quite a relief after the heat," said Nicholas. He was seated at the piano and had been playing one of Mendelssohn's "Songs without Words." Young Finch sat on the window seat, his head bent, listening. Piers came to meet Renny asking—"Did you get the filly?"

"No. She was gone."

"Oh, hell."

His grandmother peered at him round the wing of her chair. "Hell?" she repeated, with relish as it were. "*Hell.* Is that what I heard you say?"

Piers grunted assent.

"Well, I won't have it. I won't have you bring your

swearing and cursing into the house. Too much of it here. I heard someone else use bad language not five minutes ago. Who was it?"

"Boney," grinned Piers.

"He swears in Hindustani. That's different."

Renny bent and kissed her. "Have you had a good day?" he asked, playing with the ribbon rosette on her cap.

"Yes. Very good, thank you. But I'm hungry. Why doesn't Wragge sound the gong?"

"Because it's not quite time for it."

She stretched out a hand to Eden, who brought the beaded ottoman and sat himself by her knee. She stroked his hair, exclaiming that it was moist.

"I was out in the rain, Gran."

"What wouldn't many a girl give for your hair that keeps its wave in the wet!"

Renny asked—"Where is Wake?"

Meg came quickly to his side. She took his sleeve in her fingers and said in a low ominous tone.

"I must speak to you about him. I told him I should."

"The little rascal bit her!" the grandmother exclaimed, suddenly full of energy. "He must be flogged."

Ernest remarked that this sort of viciousness should be nipped in the bud, and Nicholas, either at the thought of the deed or the prospect of its punishment, gave a sardonic chuckle and put down the loud pedal.

Meg led Renny into the hall where the two spaniels and the sheep dog had come up from the basement to seek him, and now crowded each other for his attention. Patting them he demanded—"Why did he bite you? Where did he bite you?"

She closed the door behind them and with a nod toward the closed door of the library, said—"Speak low—he's in there. He's been terrible all day—just as naughty and disobedient as could be. I was trying to put him someplace —I forget where—and he kept saying—I won't—I won't —I won't—and then he bit me."

"Why didn't you punish him on the spot?"

"It was too serious. I said I would tell you." A frown of exasperation dented his brow.

"Show me the place."

"Oh . . . I scarcely can."

He grinned. "Nonsense."

She drew up her skirt, her petticoat, her knickers, and scanned her plump white thigh.

"It's faded a good deal," she said. "It looked terrible at first."

"Hmph." He bent to look at the almost invisible marks. "Did he draw blood?"

"Well—not exactly. But that is not the point. The point is that he *bit* me." She let down her skirt.

Renny opened the door of the library and looked in.

It was dark in there except for the line of brightness which showed where were the folding doors that led into the dining room. But now the light from the hall discovered a small figure sitting on his hands in an armchair beside the clean-swept fireplace in which flourished a large fern which it was Meg's habit to keep there in the summer.

"Wake," ordered Renny sternly. "Come here."

Wakefield at once slid from the chair and came into the hall. His long-lashed brown eyes blinked in the light.

"I hear that you've bitten your sister."

Wakefield hung his head. "Yes."

"Very well. Come with me." He held out his hand and the small supple one was meekly put into it.

The two mounted the stairs while Meg looked after them, already half regretting what she had done.

"This is a bad business," observed Renny, when the two were inside his bedroom and the door shut against the dogs.

"Yes."

How small and weak he looked!

"You know what we think of a horse that bites."

"Yes."

"And a dog."

"Yes."

"You know what happens to a dog that bites?"

"He's allowed two bites before they kill him. I've only had one."

"But you know you must be punished."

"Yes." His lower lip began to tremble and tears filled his eyes.

Renny had unbuttoned his own jacket and was taking off his belt.

"Ever hear of a whipping boy?" he asked cheerfully.

"No." Apprehension of this strange new procedure transfixed the culprit.

Renny gave a flick of the leather belt toward the nearest bedpost. "Well, that's one. That's your whipping boy."

"No! Renny, *please!*"

"Yes. It's going to take your whipping for you. Like this." He struck the bedpost a sharp blow. "It takes the licking for you and you do the yelling for it—see?" He grinned down at Wakefield. "You understand?"

"You mean you hit the *bedpost* and *I* scream?"

"Just that."

"Really loud?"

"Certainly. So they'll hear it downstairs."

"What fun! Wait till I get my breath."

"Four whacks. Four yells."

"Go!" Wake jumped up and down in his relief.

Six times Renny struck the bedpost and six times Wakefield rent the air with a shrill scream. At the sixth they heard Meg thumping up the stairs. The dogs were barking loudly. Wakefield tottered toward his sister as she flung open the door. "Meggie!" he bleated.

With a glance of terrible reproach at Renny she gathered her small brother into her arms, clasped him to her breast and lugged him along the passage to her own room, followed by the dogs.

Half an hour later she sought out Renny with a bewildered air.

"After all that, he hadn't one little mark on him."

"They've faded," he said mildly. "Like the marks on your leg."

5.

The Power of Attorney

IT SEEMED AN UNCONSCIONABLE time to Eden before he
was able to have his grandmother to himself long enough
for the signing of the power of attorney. He kept it con-
venient in his pocket along with his fountain pen, but
certainly as they two were alone, some other member of
the family would as certainly come into the room or knock
on the door. Adeline herself appeared to have forgotten
about the scheme and Eden had moments when he
wondered if it would not be better that he also forget it. He
fancied that Boney, the parrot, had a jeering regard for
him. Hanging head downward from his perch he would
stare at Eden as though from that angle he had a better
view of his machinations.

His perturbed thoughts kept him uneasy. A poem he had
half written lay unfinished in his desk. Instead of rejoicing in his lonely walks in the day or in the quiet of his
room at night, with the necessity of study no longer dog-
ging him, he was brooding on Indigo Lake, poring over
Mr. Kronk's latest report. "I'm turning into a beastly
financier," he said to himself. "It's got to stop." He took
the power of attorney from his pocket and would have
torn it on the spot, but his sister appeared, wearing a hat
and carrying a basket. He returned the paper to his pocket.

Meg said—"Oh, Eden, will you like a dear boy sit with
Granny while I take these raspberries to Miss Pink? She's
having such a time with carpenters working in her house
that I thought some nice ripe raspberries would do her
good."

"Where are the uncles?" asked Eden, as though unwilling.

"Uncle Nicholas is having a tooth out and Uncle Ernest has gone with him. Of course he said he didn't need anyone but you know how it is with a tooth."

"Where's young Finch? Why couldn't he sit with her?"

Meg was reproachful. "I do hope you're not getting selfish, Eden. You used to be so fond of Gran."

"I still am. I just wanted to know. Where is she?"

"Darling, she's just where she always is at this time of morning. Sitting up in her room."

"Good. I'll go straight to her. Where did you say Renny and Finch are?"

"Oh, where they usually are, you know. They'll not be about. Don't give her anything to eat. She'd a hearty breakfast."

He found his grandmother making a show of tidying her top drawer. She was seated in front of the marble-topped dressing table with its crocheted wool mats, fumbling among the mass of ribbons, yellowed lace, gloves, fans, smelling-salts bottles and odds and ends which filled the drawer. Boney, perched on her shoulder, was admiring himself in the glass, occasionally turning to peck at the ribbons on her cap or to rub his beak against the fine arch of her nose.

"Good-morning, my grandson." She greeted him in a strong cheerful voice that showed her to be enjoying one of her good days. "Come and kiss me, do."

Wary of the parrot he put his smooth lips to her ancient cheek. "Morning, Gran."

"Sit you down. I'm busy, as you see. But you can talk to me. Repeat some of your verses to me. I like poetry. Used to be able to rattle off pieces by Tom Moore. But I've forgotten 'em."

"I remember, I remember, Gran."

"Say a verse then—if you can."

He repeated:

"I saw from the beach, when the morning was shining,
A bark o'er the waters move gloriously on;

I came when the sun o'er that beach was declining,
    The bark was still there but the waters were gone!"

She said, the tears springing to her eyes—"Good.
Good boy. Ah, how I wish I could do it now. But me
memory's left me. I'm getting on, you know, I'm ninety-
eight on this coming birthday. D' ye think I may live to
see a hundred?"

"I'm sure you will, Gran." A sudden pity for her made
him put out his hand to take hers. What did it feel like to
be old, he wondered, and what would he do in the long
years that lay ahead of him?

Because of a feeling of sadness that had risen between
them, he said to lighten it—"I know another."

Swinging her hand gently in his he half chanted:

"I have a fawn from Aden's land,
    On leafy buds and berries nurst;
And you shall feed him from your hand,
    Though he may start with fear at first,
And I will lead you where he lies
    For shelter from the noon-tide heat;
And you may touch his sleeping eyes
    And feel his little silvery feet."

He asked—"Remember that, Granny?"

"I do. I do. And did you learn it from me?"

"Yes. I've a good memory, you know."

"It's a grand thing to have."

He could not stop himself. He asked—"Do you remember what we talked of the other day? About making
money in investments?"

"I do not."

"Of course you do. The gold mine, you know. Huge
profits, just for the taking. Indigo Lake Mine. Magnificent
vein of gold. You said you'd like to invest."

At the word "gold" Boney shook himself so that his
plumage vibrated with a rustling sound, and shouted:

"Gold! Gold! Pieces of eight! Pieces of eight!"

Though Eden's words brought no recollection of the
interview to her, the voice of the parrot did. She struck
her hands together, her eyes brightened.

"I do—I do remember. I was going to invest in gold. That's what it was. Gold."

The parrot fairly shook himself off her shoulder.

"Gold!" he screamed. "Ruddy gold! Shaitan! Shaitan ka bata! Piakur! Jab kutr!"

Eden drew the power of attorney from his pocket. "You can't sell your government bonds without signing this. Not unless you have your lawyer out."

"He'd never let me. He's an old slow coach. Never risked anything. His wife never risked even one child. My mother had eleven."

He spread out the paper in front of her, his hands trembling a little. "This is what you must sign, Gran. If you want to invest in the gold stocks."

"Gold! Gold!" shrieked Boney. "Ruddy gold!"

She peered at the paper. She seemed not to like the look of it and drew back. "I'd not be signing anything away, should I?"

"No, no, just giving me the power to sell government bonds for you."

"I don't want to sign anything away. I like to hang onto the bit I have."

Eden folded up the paper. "All right, Gran. I'll let someone else have the stock."

"Gold!" cried Boney, pulling out a feather and letting it fall to her lap. "Gold—you old devil!"

Adeline took up the feather—itself of a bright gold—and flourished it. "It's a sign!" she exclaimed. "A good omen. Give me my pen. I'll put down my name."

Eagerly Eden sought the pen and at last discovered it behind Boney's seed box. He spread the power of attorney on her worn leather writing folio, then discovered there was no ink.

"Will you use my fountain pen, Gran?"

"No, no. I don't like these newfangled notions. My father always used a quill pen. And when he went to sharpen it—"

"Gran," Eden interrupted, "I'll fetch the ink. Just a jiffy and I'll be back." He darted from the room.

When he returned two minutes later with the ink bottle in his hand, he found Wakefield leaning against his grandmother's shoulder and holding up his thin brown knee for sympathy.

"He's given his knee a rasp," she explained, "and he's come to be comforted, bless his heart."

Eden, longing to take the child by the scruff and put him out, bent to look. He said, patting Wakefield's back—"That's a very small scratch. Do you feel able to walk as far as Mrs. Brawn's for some pop and a chocolate bar?" He found some small coins in his pocket and put the necessary into Wake's hand. "Better hurry or you'll be late for lunch."

"Thanks," murmured Wakefield. "But I think I'll go to Mrs. Brawn's this afternoon. I want to be with my grandmother just now."

"He's the apple of my eye," cried Adeline.

The power of attorney fell to the floor. The little boy picked it up and read—" 'Know all ye men by these presents . . .' "

Eden snatched it from him.

Wakefield asked—"What is that paper, my grandmother?"

She answered blandly—" 'Tis rubbish. Throw it in the wastepaper basket."

Boney fluttered his wings and cried—"Iflatoon! Haramzada!"

"Now look here," said Eden sternly, leading his small brother to the door. "You're to get out and stay out. Do you hear? I'm reading aloud to Gran."

"But—"

"One word more and I take that money back." Eden thrust him into the hall and shut the door on him.

"Now, Gran," he said, cheerfully but masterfully, "let's get this little job done."

"What job? I'm tidying my drawer."

He put the paper before her and pen into her hand.

"Just sign here—like a dear."

"Where? I don't want to sign away anything."

Exasperated he cried—"My God—you're not signing away anything! You're only—"

"Don't swear at me, young man. I won't have it."

"Forgive me, Granny. But you do remember, don't you,

about the stocks you want to buy? The shares in the gold mine?"

"Gold! Gold!" screamed Boney. "Pieces of eight!"

"Of course I remember." She spoke brusquely, firmly. "Give me my pen."

He dipped it in ink for her, showed her just where to sign. She gripped the pen handle, made one or two false starts, then signed her name, Adeline Whiteoak, quite clearly.

It was done.

"Don't breathe a word of this to anyone," Eden warned. "All the family will be up on their hind legs, if they hear of it. Please remember, Gran. It's *our* secret, isn't it?"

"And I shall make a pot of money, eh?"

"You'll double your investment."

"Ha, that's what I like to hear."

Meg found them tidying the drawer together, Adeline's best cap perched on Eden's fair head, Boney busying himself with a crust of toast.

"And how did you get on?" cried Meg. "You do look happy."

"Haven't had such a good time in months," said Adeline.

Boney cocked an eye from his toast. "Pieces of eight!" he screamed. "Gold! Ruddy gold—you old devil!"

6.

Room for Scope

OH, TO BREATHE FREELY—away from that room—away from everyone! Eden fairly flung himself along the winding path across the fields. The sandy loam was hard and dry and warm beneath his feet. Among the shining spears of stubble, glossy black crickets darted. A daddy longlegs, having lost one of them, steered a wobbling course. The wind, cool in the shadow, hot in the sun, blew against Eden's body, and an answering movement stirred his spirit.

But even while he reached out toward freedom, he thought—"All these experiences I pass through are making me into the being that will be the ultimate me. They are necessary to me. They are a part of me." Remote pictures, almost of babyhood, flashed into his mind—himself, tossed up and caught in his father's hands—himself, carried on Renny's shoulder, supporting himself by a clutched handful of Renny's red hair—then a sudden vision of that middle-aged woman who had captivated him four years ago, not from his love of her but from hers for him. He laughed when he thought of that affair, which now seemed almost as far away as childhood. The glory of the sun, the brightness and expanse of the fields ran through him like a poem, and he longed to write something far, far better than he had yet done. For the hundredth time he thought of the verses he had sent to an American magazine more than a month ago, and no word of them yet. Time was as nothing to the magazine's editors, yet his impatience was almost unbearable for he knew, yes he was certain he had never written anything better than those verses. What he would write tonight was already stirring his imagination.

The path led him into the pine wood, ancient trees of the primeval forest, with massive trunks and boughs heavy with pointed foliage. Here and there a fallen branch lay, and in one spot a whole tree had sunk down, not blown by a gale, but, from a rotting within, had just sunk quietly to join the earth. About it there were a few bright red mushrooms and a pallid plant called Indian pipe. He sat down on the trunk of the fallen tree, lighted a cigarette, and gave himself up to dreaming. All thoughts of the Indigo Lake Mine left him and the first lines of a poem sprang into his mind. Birds did not like this dark wood, but now an unseen small bird, having found himself here, began a pensive song. Never did he get past his first lines but sang them over and over, while Eden sitting on the tree trunk got no further with his.

He heard steps approaching and turned a defensive face toward them. Finch appeared scuffling the carpet of pine needles as he slowly advanced. Eden looked into Finch's face, his own expression of defensiveness melting into interest. What an odd face the youngster had! Long and rather melancholy. But his eyes were a good shape and his nose too. Eden felt rather sorry for young Finch, sharing as he did a room with Piers and often rather roughly treated by him.

Finch raised his eyes and saw Eden. With a deprecating grin he quickened his steps, as though to get himself as quickly out of the way as possible.

"Hullo," Eden called out, suddenly hospitable, as though the pine wood were his private room and the log his easy chair. "Come and sit down."

Finch dropped to the big log beside him, miscalculated its width and all but toppled over backward.

"Well," remarked Eden affably, "holidays are nearly over. I suppose you're counting the days till school opens. Nice thought, isn't it?"

"Uh-huh," groaned Finch. And he added, like an elderly man—"It's terrible how time flies."

"What do you want to be, Finch?"

"I dunno. I've never thought."

"Horse breeder, like Renny?"

"Gosh, no."

"Go into farming, like Piers?"

"Gosh, no."

"Lawyer—like me?"

"Gosh, no."

"Look here, brother Finch, can't you say something but gosh, no?"

"Gosh—I mean—I didn't know I was. What I mean is I haven't the least idea."

"But you know what you don't want to be."

"That's pretty well everything, I guess. I don't seem to have an inclination to be anything I've ever heard of."

"I remember when you wanted to be a railway engineer."

"Gosh, I'd hate it now . . . Eden, do you like the idea of being a lawyer?"

"Not in the least."

"Then, why—"

"Well, it seems an easy life, and I thought that as I shall probably have no clients it will give me plenty of time for other things."

"Like writing poetry?"

"Doubtless. I shall likely come home to eat."

"I guess you'll be a famous poet sometime."

"Me! Never. But I like to hear you say it."

After a slightly embarrassed pause Finch said—"There's something sort of mysterious about words."

"Yes?" Eden gave him an amused but penetrating look.

"They can turn things you know into something different. I mean more beautiful and better."

"You feel a power working within you, eh, Finch?"

Scarlet from embarrassment Finch burst out—"I'm not like you. I'm not talented. I'll never be anything." He got to his feet. "Well, I must be going. I'm on an errand for Meg."

"Who isn't? I've never known anyone who keeps so many others busy. What's your errand?"

"I'm to find Noah Binns and tell him Meg wants him. He's cutting down trees for Mr. Warden."

"Trees? What trees?"

"Those two silver birches."

Eden sprang up. "No! He can't do that. Why should he want to cut them down?"

"I don't know."

"I'll go with you."

The brothers, now as active as a moment ago they had been languid, strode along the bridle path together. They left the wood, crossed a field and passed through a gate on to a country road. On its either side were scattered houses with well-kept gardens owned by retired farmers or businessmen retired from city life. In front of the most pretentious of these lay two birch trees, not quite full grown, their pure white stumps, now no more than two ridiculous white posts, standing beside them. Resting on his axe was the middle-aged laborer, Noah Binns, triumphant but panting a little, his parted lips showing his black teeth.

Not waiting to open the gate in the neat white picket fence Eden vaulted it and demanded:

"Why the dickens have you done this?"

Noah Binns grinned. "Hired to. That's why. Hired by the owner."

"He must be mad. There weren't two lovlier trees in the countryside."

"Well, they'll be firewood now and serves 'em right. They ate the good out of the ground."

Eden gazed down at the two fair forms bright in their summer leafage. "It's a crime," he mourned.

Finch came and stood beside him. "They don't know yet what's happened to them," he said.

Noah chuckled in derision. "But they will when the hot sun blasts 'em. They'll wilt then, dang 'em."

The door of the white house opened and Mr. Warden, its owner, came out. He was a large gentle-looking man with a grayish cast on the skin, as though from suffering. He had a speaking acquaintance with the brothers and now gave them a polite good-morning. He was a widower.

He said—"I'm afraid you are not pleased by what Noah's been doing but those trees had become a nuisance. I can't persuade the grass to grow under them. Time and again I've sown the seed. The grass comes up and it dies. If there's one thing above another I've set my heart on it's a nice green lawn."

"But anyone," cried Eden, "can have a lawn. Those birch trees—look at them, Mr. Warden—why, I'd give a year of my life to see them standing again!"

"Ah, no, you wouldn't. That's just talk, young man. As for life—it's given me a new lease of life to see them taken down." Raising his head as though he breathed more freely and putting his shoulders back, he left them with dignity and went back into his house.

Looking after him Noah Binns remarked—"What he needs is more room for scope."

Finch gave a snort of laughter which caused Noah to repeat with great firmness—"Room for scope. That's what he needs." He began with ferocity to lop off the delicate branches of the nearest tree.

The brothers turned away. Suddenly Eden began to laugh.

"I suppose that's what we all crave," he said. "Room for scope."

They walked in silence for a space, enjoying the free movement of long legs in unison over the quiet country road, Finch happily aware that Eden was pleased by his company. He moved closer to Eden as though he would touch him. At last Eden spoke.

"You know that Aunt Augusta is coming and bringing a forty-second cousin with her—Dilly Warkworth?"

"Yes, I know," Finch groaned. "I wish she weren't."

"My God, so do I . . . I don't mean Aunty. Just the horrible girl. She's been jilted or something."

Finch gave a giggle of delight. "Lovesick damsel in the house, eh? Hell—what a thought!" Then, seriously—"Did you ever see one?"

Eden said—"I don't remember seeing one. I ran away when I perceived the sickness developing." He spoke in a pompous tone, putting on an act for Finch.

"All love is rather sickening, isn't it?" Finch gave his brother a sidelong glance.

"My advice is—keep away from it." Now Eden spoke as the experienced lover of a dozen affairs.

"Never shall I fall in love."

Eden gave him a smile of pity. "My poor Finch, why should I waste advice on you? You'll be helpless. Victim of the first female who goes for you—tooth and claw. As for this Dilly, she'll forget the lad she left behind her when once she sets eyes on our red-headed brother. Mark my words."

7.

A Secret Among Them

WITH THE POWER OF ATTORNEY signed it was all so easy for Eden, with Mr. Kronk's accomplished help. Adeline's government bonds, to the amount of ten thousand dollars, were sold and the money invested in the Indigo Lake Mine. Eden's intention had been to deposit all that he acquired on commission into a saving account and watch it increase, bit by bit, till he had enough saved for the trip abroad. Once abroad who knew what might happen? But with this investment of his grandmother's, his saving account reached such proportions that boyishly he one day boasted of it to Mr. Kronk, who showed, by the way he spoke rather than by what he said, how shortsighted he considered this. What he said was that it reminded him of peasants who hoarded their gold in a stocking. Eden, who had taken a serene pleasure in watching his little pile increase and had examined his deposit book at least five times a day, now swept all from the bank and handed it over to Mr. Kronk to invest in Indigo Lake. Mr. Kronk could not resist pointing out to him what he had lost by not investing it earlier. By the time the first leaves were beginning to fall the stocks of the Indigo Lake Gold Mine had soared to a still more spectacular height. Typewritten reports arrived at intervals giving exhilarating "market information." Eden, Piers, their uncles, and their grandmother were walking on air—if a woman of almost one hundred years could be said to walk on air. So eager was Piers to make more money to invest that he was ready to do the work of two on the farm. Renny was actually worried about the boy and his passion for work combined with parsimony.

One day he demanded abruptly—"Piers, what are you doing with all this money?"

Piers, never communicative, drew back, with a defensive stare in his prominent blue eyes.

"*Doing* with it? Why saving it, of course."

"How much have you saved?"

Piers's defensive stare became a scowl. He muttered— "Nearly all of it."

"What are you saving for? Any special object?"

"No. Just saving."

"Well, school opens next week. You'll be working with your brain for a change."

Piers said eagerly—"Oh, I shall find time to work. I was just going to speak about that. I can work for an hour before I go in the morning, and another hour at night. And most of Saturday. Is that O.K.?"

As for Eden, there were times when he almost wished he never had drawn his grandmother into the secret speculation. Far from investing her ten thousand dollars and then letting the affair slip from her mind, as he had expected, she never seemed to forget it. At the most inopportune times she would fix him with her still dominant gaze and give him such a grin of complicity as made him grow hot all over.

She would even ejaculate—"We know a thing or two, don't we, my beauty?" or "We weren't born yesterday, were we, you rascal?"

Her two sons were considerably disturbed by these signs of a secret bond between her and Eden. They wanted no interloper of his generation to come between them and their mother's fortune. They loved her dearly. No one could deny that they had been devoted sons. Yet with her end so nearly approaching, it was only natural that they should guard her against the designs of younger members of the family. No one, with the exception of her lawyer, Mr. Patton, knew the contents of her will. She had let it be known, however, that her money was to be left to one heir alone. "I will not have the bit I leave cut up into pieces like a cake."

After one of her indiscretions Eden snatched the first opportunity of speaking to her alone. He leant over her chair and whispered fiercely—"Look here, Gran, you must *not* talk about our secret in front of the others. You'll let the cat out of the bag and where shall we be then?"

Peering up into his face, wheezing a little, she said— "You're like your poor mother—afraid of people. I'm not afraid."

"It's not a question of courage, Gran. It's whether or not you want Uncle Nicholas and Uncle Ernest to know about your investing in Indigo Lake."

"It's none of their business."

"But they'll make it their business."

"Yes, yes, we must keep it secret. Ha, I do enjoy getting the best of them. How much am I worth now?"

"*Worth,* Gran! You mean how much have the stocks risen?"

"Yes, what am I worth?"

"The price of the stock has doubled."

"Then I've doubled me money." She gave a hilarious chuckle. "I invested ten thousand dollars, didn't I? Now it's doubled. It's twenty thousand."

"Good God, Granny, don't talk so loud."

She looked suddenly keen. "And you're sure it's all safe and sound?"

"I never was more sure of anything."

"Are you making a little yourself?"

"A little."

"And what will you do with it?"

"Go abroad. To France—Italy—Greece."

"Ireland, too. Don't forget Ireland."

"Yes. Ireland, too."

She put up two long arms and clasped him to her. "Ah. what fun it is! I feel ten years younger. What age would that make me?"

He hesitated, struck by pity. "Why—just over eighty, Gran."

"That's not young enough. I feel twenty years younger."

"And you promise not to be indiscreet?"

"I promise."

But she could not keep her promise. It was too much

for her. Over a cup of tea, over a game of backgammon, this feeling of well-being, of adventure, would overtake her and she would utter such enigmatic remarks, make what almost amounted to strange prophecies, that her sons grew quite anxious about her. They would have been much more anxious had she not been so well. She walked less bent and her appetite, always good, became so much better that Ernest sometimes feared for her.

"Mamma," he said, when she demanded more gravy on her second baked potato, "do you think it is wise?"

"If I haven't learned wisdom at my age I never shall. More gravy, Renny." Then, across the table she caught Eden's eyes. Warningly he returned the look.

She said—"We can keep our mouths shut—when we choose—can't we? And open 'em when we choose."

She did then open hers and introduced a fork mounted with potatoes. This rendered her, for the moment, speechless and in that moment Eden was able to introduce a new topic of conversation. It was one of many escapes for him. Yet the temptation to allow Adeline to increase her investment in the Indigo Lake Mine became more insistent as the price of the stock rose. What a benefit to her and to her heir (whichever he might be) after her death! And what a benefit to himself at this moment! In truth, the fire of speculation was burning brightly in him, as it was in Nicholas, Ernest, and Adeline. The two uncles had already increased their original purchase. Ernest, who was a born speculator, did not rest till Eden had arranged a meeting between him and Mr. Kronk. Eden was not eager to do this. He preferred to act as go-between and doubted if such a meeting would be successful. But he had no need to doubt. Mrs. Kronk was present at the meeting, her manner more suitably dignified for the occasion. Mr. Kronk's manner was even cozier and more confidential than usual. Ernest Whiteoak, who flattered himself that he was a judge of character, told Eden afterward how greatly his feeling of security had increased with this meeting. And seeing the three together in earnest and sincere talk had added to Eden's own confidence in Indigo Lake. He pocketed his commission and allowed his grandmother to sign another power of attorney for the further sale of government bonds.

The tangled web of his machinations so complicated his life that he looked forward, almost with relief, to returning to the study of law in the fall. Now the family at Jalna were divided into two parts for him—those who were investors in Indigo Lake and those who were not. On the one hand, himself, Piers, Meg, his uncles, and grandmother. On the other, Renny and the two young boys. Knowing Renny's constant shortage of money he ingenuously longed to draw him into the golden net. But any reference to speculation, except in horseflesh, brought no response from him but rather a nervous drawing back, as though in fear of having his pocket picked.

Eden was constantly having conferences, as Mr. Kronk called them, with his fellow investors, behind closed doors with the older ones, in the open with Piers. With Piers it was largely a matter of showing off in front of his junior. They would stride along the bridle through the woods, now and again stopping to eat the wild blackberries and smoking cigarettes, always supplied by Eden, who was as openhanded as Piers was the reverse. Eden would boast of the money he was making on commission, taking care not to implicate any others of the family, but referring to nebulous "clients" who were literally falling over each other in their eagerness to invest in Indigo Lake. He talked of France and Italy and Greece and knew almost to a week the date of his sailing and the steamship of his choice. But he did not intend to spend the rest of his life in Europe. He would always want to visit those at Jalna.

Driven partly by his grandmother's insistence, partly by his own desire to increase his own holdings, Eden at last gave in and allowed her to invest another two thousand dollars. After this transaction he thought to restrain her speculative ardor by making no reference to a rise in stocks, but the only effect of this was to cause her to demand, at every opportunity:

"Have they gone up or down?"

There were times when Eden wished she had never been introduced to Indigo Lake. Twice he answered— "They're stationary"—but that only excited her interest

the more. Then, in a moment of irritation, he said curtly
—"They've gone down a little."

At that she struck the closed fist of one hand into the
palm of the other and exclaimed—"I'll sell out! I'll sell
out at once."

Eden thought it might be well for her to sell at the
profit she had made and have done with the nervous strain
of keeping the affair secret. He went to see Mr. Kronk
and to place the selling of her stock in his hands. Mr.
Kronk at once said that he had customers who would
be delighted to buy any shares that came into the market.
However, it just happened that a sharp rise in the price
had taken place that very day and he foretold a really
spectacular rise in the near future.

"Tell the dear lady," he said, smiling, "to hold onto her
shares a little longer. To buy more shares, if she's so
inclined. She's due to make a lot more money in a very
short while."

It was irresistible. With Mr. Kronk's expert aid Adeline,
Nicholas, and Ernest all invested more of their capital in
the gold mine. Eden invested the greater part of his commission from these transactions. Piers almost wept to
think he had nothing further to invest. Mr. Kronk said
how wise they were because the Americans were sweeping
the shares off the market. He showed Eden letters from
the United States, the writers of which were investing to an
extent that made the investments of the Whiteoaks paltry.

Now Eden had a few serious words with Adeline.

"Look here, Gran, you *must* stop these mysterious remarks about our business affairs. Today at dinner you said
'Indigo' was your favorite color and then you looked at
me and asked me what was *my* favorite color. Please,
please, don't give the whole thing away."

"And I shall make a deal of gold, eh?"

"You will."

Boney puffed himself up, closed one eye, and remarked
in a hoarse whisper—"Pieces of eight. Pots of gold, you
old devil."

"*Do* promise, Gran." Eden took both her hands in his
and held them close. "Promise."

"I promise."

And for a few days she kept her word. But the strain of self-control was too much for her and she became testy and inclined to moods. This did not at all trouble Eden, so long as their secret was guarded. He was living in a dream in which materialistic calculations of gain were merged into romantic visions of the future. Sunk in his seat in the train which carried him, Piers, and Finch to their several seats of learning, he felt himself being transported through the fields of southern France toward Italy. His spirit was not in the lecture room, but wandering in the Greek theatre in Taormina. In his fancy the rich harvest fields of Jalna were transformed into the steep slopes of Sicily and the sweating harvest hands into laughing dark-eyed girls carrying sheaves on their heads. With a Midas touch Mr. Kronk had transformed his world for him. And on top of all this glitter, he had a letter of acceptance from the editor to whom he had sent his latest poem.

So greatly was he elated, he could not stay in his bed that night but wandered about his room in the moonlight listening to the last faint pipings of the locusts, so soon to be chilled into silence. That night he wrote a new poem, longer and more ambitious than any he had yet composed, and the following day he had a feverish cold.

8.

Learning

DURING THAT SUMMER PIERS was too much engaged—physically in farm work, mentally in the exciting development of the Indigo Lake Gold Mine—to have much time for Pheasant Vaughan. But he did not forget that meeting with her by the stream and every now and again he would go down into the ravine and stand on the rustic bridge gazing at the spot where he had knelt beside her, with a kind of shame-faced longing. She was only a kid, he thought, and he would not have acknowledged, even to himself, that he had gone down there in search of her. He could not know how she haunted the little stream in the hope of seeing him again, how she did see him again on more than one occasion, but contented herself with peering at him through the bushes, her heart beating wildly at the sight of him, almost afraid to breathe for fear he should discover her. Yet all the while she looked forward to the day when they should meet again. She would lie flat on her back in her bed, staring through her open window at the stars, picturing that meeting, imagining how they would exchange a kiss, born of loneliness and longing on her part and a great tenderness on his. And there would be something alive in that kiss—something she could not understand, did not try to understand. Yet it was as real as the starshine in the window, and the reaching out of her being toward it sent a tremor through her nerves that made her turn in the bed and hide her face in the pillow. A kindling excitement ran through her and she would whisper his name—*Piers—Piers*—into the night.

She had never seen a woman's magazine. She knew nothing of the technique of being a modern adolescent. She was as awkward, as graceful, as innocent, as wild, as a colt. The life she lived with her father and the elderly housekeeper, Mrs. Clinch, in that quiet house was the only life she knew. She had had lessons from Miss Pink, the organist of the village church—reading, writing, arithmetic, geography and history and learning Goldsmith's "Deserted Village" and Wordsworth's "Yarrow Revisited," by heart, with other poems, none of which interested her greatly and all of which she found difficult. In truth, she found all these subjects difficult. Perhaps it was that Miss Pink was not a good teacher or it may have been that she was a dull pupil. She was inclined to the latter view because neither her father nor Mrs. Clinch had ever intimated that they had a high opinion of her intelligence. She had spent a large part of her life in mooning about the house or wandering through woods and fields. Her only playmate had been the old pony which her father had ridden as a boy. She had ridden him along the country roads, even as far as the lake, where he would bend his shaggy head to drink. He had jogged along cheerfully but with a will of his own, taking her, when so he chose, through a ditch to where he espied fallen apples, and then stood munching one, with the apple juice running down his lip. Pheasant had never thought of his dying and leaving her but he had done just that. He had died suddenly one morning. He had been thirty years old, rather gray in the face, but still active. That was a year ago but she still could not think of him without such a contraction of the heart as made her quite giddy. It was only since the meeting with Piers that the pain of this loss had eased a little.

She had always been fascinated by the family at Jalna. There were so many of them and they were so diverse. Mrs. Clinch had not a high opinion of their behavior and had gossip with which to back her opinion. In the kitchen with Mrs. Clinch, cozy by the big coal range, these stories about the doings of the Whiteoaks had helped to pass many a blustery winter afternoon. The housekeeper had so far nothing to say against Piers, and Pheasant hoped she never would for she knew she would have to spring to

Piers's defence and then there might be words between them. But it was summer now and Pheasant spent little time indoors. Who knew what might happen before winter came?

Of all the Whiteoaks it was Renny she knew best. He came quite often to Vaughanlands to talk about horses with Maurice. Sometimes he stayed for a meal and then what a different atmosphere he brought to the table! Maurice became animated, lively. There was noise and laughter. If Renny remained for the evening Maurice brought out a bottle of Scotch and when those glasses were to be washed next morning Mrs. Clinch would look grim and mutter—"Poor young man," in the way she always did when she considered temptation thrown in Maurice's way and its evil results in the past. This exclamation always made Pheasant uncomfortable as she knew that she was the most evil result of all.

On this day in the first week of September Renny had come to lunch. If only she had known in time she would have changed into a fresh dress but it was not till she hurried to the table, anxious at being late, that she was aware of him.

"I'm sorry," she began, then stopped as she saw his tall figure, his back drooping a little from much riding, his lean face tanned the color of mahogany, his hair bleached by sun to a lighter shade.

"Hullo, Pheasant." He came to her and took her hand. "Where do you keep yourself? Now that your pony's gone I never see you on the road."

Pheasant put up her other hand to hide the safety pin that held together the rip in her pullover. There was something in his touch which gave her confidence. She forgot the safety pin and smiled up into his face.

"Poor old Jock," put in Maurice, "he went quite suddenly, but he was past thirty." When they were seated he added pensively—"I shall never forget my joy when he was given to me. Remember, Renny? Of course you already had one, and a little beauty he was. But I don't believe that any kid ever loved a pony as I loved Jock. We weren't horsy people like you Whiteoaks, and he came as a complete surprise."

Pheasant was pressing her eyelids together to keep back the stinging tears. To herself she was saying—"You loved him so? Yet, since I can remember, you've never bothered your head about him. And when he died . . ." The tears pressed between her lids and ran down her cheeks.

Neither man noticed. Both were with gusto attacking the steaming stew set before them.

Renny was saying—"Now my young Wakefield begs for a pony, and on his birthday I think I'll get him one."

Maurice said—"Well, if Wake enjoys it half as much as I enjoyed Jock . . . Lord, how I loved that pony!"

With the back of her hand Pheasant contrived to wipe away the tears. She put a bit of dumpling in her mouth and sat up straight. Now Renny Whiteoak's penetrating gaze was on her.

"I have an idea," he said.

"I've never known you at a loss for them," returned his friend.

"I believe this is a good one. You may remember, Maurice, that promising little mare I bought two months back. Well, I intend to enter her in the horse show for the ladies' saddle horse class. I need someone to ride her. Of course, Piers could, but I'd like someone who would give zip to the show. Look like a sylph on her. I believe you're just the ticket, Pheasant."

"Me? Why, I should be terrified."

"She's as gentle as a lamb. Perfect manners."

"I don't mean her. I mean the crowds."

"Why, they'd love you. Come now. Say you'll try." Maurice put in—"Pheasant can't ride."

"I've been riding all my life," she exclaimed hotly.

"On old Jock!"

Renny said—"I'll teach her. I'll soon find out if she's got it in her."

"Want to do it, Pheasant?" asked Maurice.

"I'm still afraid but—I'd like to try."

"Good," said Renny. "Come back with me after lunch and I'll find out if you've got it in you to ride in the show."

Maurice said—"She's nervous."

"Oh, that's nothing. So are horses often. The very best."

Her appetite was gone, and as soon as she could she stole away and up to her room. The two men, drinking their coffee, did not notice her going till she was on the stairway. Then Renny called out:

"Will you change into your riding things as soon as possible, Pheasant? I must be getting along."

"Yes, I will." She darted up the stairs wishing she had a new pair of riding breeches. Hers were shabby and had a tear on one knee. Would Piers be there, she wondered, and rather hoped he would not. It would be enough for her to face the mounting of a show horse under the eye of Renny Whiteoak, to be told by him, as she probably would be, that she was only fit to ride the little old pony.

As they drove to Jalna in his old mud-splashed car he talked reassuringly to her of the new mare, her gentleness, and of the schooling and riding of show horses. Scarcely ever had she been inside his gates. She knew only too well that her birth had broken off the engagement between her father and Meg Whiteoak. She felt a sad responsibility and at the same time a romantic pride in the thought of the shadow her coming had cast upon two lives. Jalna, to her, had an air of mystery, of elegance, and of abounding life.

The clumber spaniel Floss stood with hind legs on the back seat, forelegs resting between Renny's and Pheasant's shoulders, and every now and again she would raise her head to lick him on the ear. Each time he would exclaim—"Down, Floss!" She would lift her lip in a sheepish grin, but never was she really rebuffed and soon would rise up for another kiss.

The car stopped in front of the open door of the stables and Scotchmere, the old weather-beaten, bowlegged groom came out to meet them. He had a bottle of liniment in his hand which he occasionally shook in an absent-minded way, then raised to his nostrils and sniffed.

"This is Miss Vaughan," Renny said, assisting Pheasant from the car. "I'm going to give her some lessons in riding."

It was the first time in her life that she had been called Miss and she strove to appear dignified. But Scotchmere only grinned. "Oh, her and me's acquainted. I once took a stone out of her pony's shoe, didn't I?"

Anyone who had done anything for Jock seemed a friend to Pheasant. She said—"Oh, yes, you were so kind."

They went into the stable, clean and cool, almost empty, for the horses, with the exception of three, were out in paddock and field. One of these was a big bay gelding whose legs Scotchmere had been rubbing. The second was a mare which was that day expected to foal. She was in a loose box carpeted in clean straw but she was restless, walking nervously about, her large expectant eyes seeming to protrude from her stark head. When she saw Renny she uttered an anxious whicker. He called out:

"All right, old girl, I'll be with you very soon."

It was to another loose box that he led Pheasant and opened the door.

"Here she is—Silken Lady," he said, "and I expect you to fall in love with her."

The mare stood eying them, not askance but with a kind of elegant interest.

"Dare I come in?" asked Pheasant.

"Of course. She's an angel for kindness. Will you dress her up, please, Scotchmere?"

Pheasant stroked the shining shoulder of the mare, who lowered her head as though in humility, while the lines of her neck remained proud. Scotchmere brought bridle and saddle, equipped her and led her out, his thin bow-legs, ending in heavy boots, somehow not incongruous beside her beauty.

Pheasant forgot about Piers. All her being was concentrated upon the will to remain in that saddle. Now they were out of the stable into the bright late summer air, their feet on the sandy soil. The sound of thudding hooves came to them from the paddock.

Renny said—"We'll just see what the boys are up to. Then I'll take you for a nice quiet ride." He led the way to the paddock.

A lively scene was presented to them there.

For the first time Pheasant saw the brothers gathered together—Renny at her side, Eden lounging against the railing of the paddock talking with the groom, Wright. She never would forget a walk she had had in the woods with Eden when she was a little girl. He had been so different from anyone she had ever known and for months she had hoarded in her mind those things he had said to her that had kindled her imagination. Oh, to know him better, now that she was older! To walk with him, as she had that day, holding his hand and trying to talk as he did. But now he gave her an absent-minded nod and his eyes returned to the horses which were being schooled in the paddock.

Renny said—"A couple of good ones. I expect great things of them at the horse show."

How beautifully, she thought, they flew along the track and skimmed the barrier. The mare, Silken Lady, appeared to observe them with an appraising eye, as though she, if she had the chance, would do better. Pheasant saw that one of the horses was ridden by a stableboy and the other by Piers.

Now he saw her and his face tightened, as though to deny the little amorous passage between them, but the next time he trotted past he looked her full in the eyes and she saw that he remembered. She glanced up at Renny to discover if he had seen the look Piers had given her but he saw only the horse as it took the next jump, saw the power in his hind legs, how his tucked-in forelegs cleared the bar. He saw Piers shift his weight over the horse's neck, how lightly he rose in the stirrup.

Renny grinned down at Pheasant. "A good pair. A good jump, eh?"

"Oh, yes. They're wonderful."

She hoped Piers would ride over to where they stood but instead he dismounted, did something to his horse's girth, his back turned to her. Renny's roan was now led out to him and Eden joined them, with little Wakefield clinging to his arm in an effort to draw him into a romp. Finch, lolling against the railing, gave Pheasant a shy smile. He looked no better than a stableboy, she thought, with his torn shirt and a straw between his teeth. There they were, so many of them and she with not one brother.

"Now," said Renny, "I'll put you up."

"Let me." Eden came and helped her into the saddle. She was nervous and mounted clumsily.

"Don't be anxious," Eden said. "She's a gentle creature. What's all this about, anyhow?"

Renny's bright glance swept over mare and girl. "They're being schooled for the show. Don't you see how well they become each other?" He sprang into the saddle. The roan moved forward and the mare, with delicate condescension, followed.

Pheasant's fear vanished. She had not known that a horse could move as did this, with such ease and grace. They moved sedately along the path. Were those left behind looking after them, she wondered, and held her body well to make up for her clumsy mounting. They followed the bridle path through the woods, where the blackberries shone among the bushes and red squirrels were sampling the green acorns, and Michaelmas daisies showed when the sun found his way through the branches.

At last Renny judged that she was ready for a canter. Then her happiness made her want to sing. This soft thud of hooves made the sweetest music in her ears. She felt that Renny understood her and the mare understood her as she had never before been understood. But she wished Piers might have seen her.

"Now that you and Lady are acquainted," said Renny, "we'll call this the first lesson. Can you come tomorrow?"

"Oh, yes. I never have any engagements."

"It won't go on being easy, you know. There'll be lots of hard work."

"I don't mind."

"You'll be a good rider—with training." He gave her a swift appraising look, then went on:

"You must come every day that weather permits. If I'm not here Wright will look after you."

When they returned past the paddock it was empty. An afternoon quiet had descended. Wright met them and took their horses. He said in an undertone to Renny—"The mare's foaling."

Renny halted. "Good-bye, Pheasant." He patted her shoulder. "Tomorrow, come in the morning. Run along now. You've been a good girl."

The two men disappeared into the stable.

"Whew," Pheasant whispered to herself. "This is the life." Something was happening here every minute, she was sure.

Wakefield ran along the path to meet her. "Like pears?" he asked. "Here's one. A bird's pecked it but it's still good."

"Thanks." She took the pear he offered and then asked —"Where are Piers and Finch?"

"Here's Finch! Right here!" he cried.

Finch came from behind the pear tree. A derisive grin lighted his face that had a little while before worn a shy smile. He said—"Piers will be here in a jiffy. He's gone up to put on a clean shirt and wash the smell of the stable off him. He wants you to wait."

These remarks for some reason sent little Wakefield into shouts of laughter. He danced along the path laughing. Pheasant, greatly embarrassed, asked—"Did Piers say that?"

"Sure," laughed Finch. "He wants to look his prettiest for you."

She stood on the path hesitating, not knowing what to believe, what to do. In front of her loomed the house, that house she never expected to enter, where lived Meg Whiteoak, whom her father might have married but for her. To her right was a path into the ravine. That way she could return home without the risk of meeting any of the Whiteoaks on the drive.

But now Piers came out of the house, wearing white trousers and a soft white shirt.

"Look at him," Finch giggled. "Isn't he sweet?"

Wakefield was suffocating with laughter. "Isn't he sweet? Isn't he sweet?"

Both fell silent as Piers strode near.

He gave a little start, as of surprise, to see Pheasant still there. He asked, with an indifferent air—"How did you get on?"

Indifferently she returned—"Oh, all right."

"Going on with the lessons?"

"I think so."

He saw the pear in her hand. "Where did you get

that?" he demanded, and took it from her. "It's not fit to eat. It's been pecked by the birds." He threw it away. He turned to Finch. "Get some decent ones."

Pheasant exclaimed—"Oh, that one was lovely. We haven't any half so large."

"These are the best in the countryside," he returned frowning. He continued to frown while Finch, with ridiculous alacrity, rushed to the tree and began to gather pears as though his life depended on it.

"Not so many, you lunatic!" shouted Piers.

Wakefield swarmed up the tree and hung there like a monkey. "Ripe pears!" he cried. "A kick apiece!"

Piers selected half a dozen from those Finch proffered. "I'll carry them for you," he said, and turned with dignity toward the ravine at Pheasant's side.

"How are your uncles?" she asked, in a proper conversational tone.

"They're fine, thanks."

"And your grandmother?"

"Splendid, considering her age."

"It must be wonderful to have uncles and a grandmother."

"I suppose it is."

"And a sister and four brothers!"

"I could do without those two youngest."

"Oh, don't say that. What if anything happened to them?"

"Are you superstitious?"

Now she spoke like Mrs. Clinch. "Doom is always near us."

Piers began to wonder if he really liked her very much. He felt annoyed at himself for having changed into those white trousers. He felt a sudden fury at Finch for the laughter in his eyes. He felt ridiculous carrying the pears. He wanted to give them to her and have done with it.

They passed through the little wicket gate at the bottom of the lawn and descended the path that led to the bridge. Whether to precede or follow he could not for a moment decide, so they wavered at the top of the path before she took the first steps downward. The stream was so low as to be almost hidden by the eager growth that hungered for its moisture. One of the cattails had burst and its soft down glistened in the deep shade of the ravine.

Pheasant pointed. "That's where I saw the snake."

"Ever been here since?"

"Yes."

"See any more?"

"No. But once I saw you."

He gave a little laugh, unaccountably pleased.

"Saw me?"

"Mm-hm."

"What was I doing?"

"Just standing there on the bridge."

"Looking like a fool, eh?"

"No. Looking—thoughtful."

"Thoughtful, eh? Thoughts too deep for words, I guess."

Now they were on the bridge. She asked—"Do you like poetry?"

"Gosh, no. You don't, do you?"

She felt that she ought to say she didn't but she was naturally truthful. "I don't like many poems," she said. "Only a few."

"Well, of course, there are a few," he conceded. "Like 'The Revenge' and 'Horatio.' "

Her face lighted. "Oh, yes, I love them. They make me feel strong and brave."

Now he liked her very much. "Let's sit down for a bit," he said. "It's nice here and you could eat a pear."

They sat on the bridge, their legs dangling. He laid the pears near her hand. He said—"Now you can begin." They smiled into each other's eyes.

"You have one too."

"No, no, they're for you."

"Oh, *please.* I won't, if you don't. People look so disgusting eating fruit—juicy fruit."

"Do they? I hadn't thought of that." He picked up the smallest pear and began to eat it with exaggerated daintiness, his little finger crooked.

"Do I look disgusting?" he asked.

She reddened. "I wish I hadn't said that."

"*Do* I look disgusting?" he insisted.

Driven, she answered—"You look—nice."

Now they both were embarrassed and sat eating pears in silence till he said—"Let's finish them. I'll give you more tomorrow."

Pheasant said—"I'm ravenous. I didn't eat much lunch and—I've been so happy. It makes you hungry to enjoy yourself. Don't you think so?"

"I haven't thought about it."

"I have often."

"You think a lot, don't you?"

She answered sedately—"Well, I have a good deal of time for thought. I'm not like you."

Like a man of action he returned—"I've very little time for thought." Then his sunburnt hand moved to hers and he added—"But I've thought a lot about you—since— you know when."

They sat silent, holding hands.

After a time he wanted to free his hand but did not quite know how. If he drew his hand away, it might appear that he wanted to go. If he left it where it was . . . She settled it for him by gently withdrawing hers.

She asked—"Does your brother Eden ever read his poetry to you?"

"Gosh, no. He and I have other things to talk of."

"Oh." She looked surprised and interested.

He had an almost irresistible desire to tell her all about the Indigo Lake Mine but he conquered it and said only— "Eden has some quite good ideas. He and I are going to make a lot of money some day."

"How wonderful."

"Oh, I don't know. It's natural for a fellow to try to better himself while he's young."

"I suppose so. Mrs. Clinch says it's wise to take time by the forelock."

"You're quite a one for proverbs, aren't you?"

"Mrs. Clinch says there'd be a lot less misery in the world if people gave heed to them."

Piers gave her a look of mingled amusement and severity. "Look here, you're too young to be always quoting Mrs. Clinch."

Suddenly coquettish, she demanded—"Whom should I quote? You?"

"That's the idea. Quote me."

A warm intimacy of atmosphere rose, as though from the stream, and enveloped them.

He said, rather breathlessly—"Shall we move on?"

She nodded and they rose and climbed the steep path that led up from the ravine into a little grove. The path then crossed a field beyond which was Maurice Vaughan's house. Once they were in the grove he put his arm about her waist. A feeling of power enriched all his being.

Pretending not to notice his arm, she asked—"What will Eden do with the money?"

"Travel. Go to Italy."

"And you?"

She turned her eyes full on him and he became aware of their beauty.

He gave a little laugh. "Oh, I have other plans. I'd be satisfied right here, if . . ."

"Yes?"

"If I knew there was someone who cared a lot about me."

She could not speak. His arm tightened about her. Once again they kissed, but briefly, shyly. Then he asked:

"You'll come to Jalna tomorrow?"

"Yes."

They stood, reflected in each other's eyes, eyes that expressed no desire, but rather a beaming surprise as though each discovered in the other a new person. He put out his hand and touched her.

"Well, good-bye," he said.

"Good-bye."

"We'll come back this way tomorrow."

"Yes."

"You didn't mind, did you?"

"Oh, no."

"Good-bye—" He had heard Eden talking on the telephone, call some girl "little one." So after a moment's hesitation, he added—"little one."

He turned and almost ran from her. He did run down the path into the ravine, and exulting in his power, he would not cross the bridge but leapt over the stream, a flying white figure, and panting a little, mounted the steep.

9.

Aunt Augusta and Dilly

PIERS HAD A DESIRE TO protect Pheasant, even a desire to
fight for her, if there were anyone to fight. This new
sensation of love made him feel aggressive, rather like the
young turkey cock on the lawn which spread his handsome tail with a rustling sound, shook his fiery wattles,
and turned round and round in front of his favorite hen.
But there was none to challenge the young turkey. He
stood on the green lawn before the house, his inward eye
picturing who knew what combat? The glossy hen turkey
trilled softly to herself.

Piers stood watching them for a little, not quite knowing what to do with himself. By dressing in white he had
precluded any further work that day. Well, he'd worked
hard that summer, he deserved a rest. He saw Finch loaf-
ing in the porch and remembered the ridiculous way he'd
behaved over gathering the pears, and what he'd heard
him say. There'd been a jeering look on his face, a very
irritating look. Piers felt he ought to do something about
that.

He strolled across the lawn, the turkey cock with great
dignity making way for him. Finch gave rather a sheepish
smile because of something he saw in Piers's eyes.

Neither spoke till Piers said quietly when he stood
beside Finch—"I supposed you thought you were being
funny."

"*Funny?* When?"

"You know when. I have pretty good hearing and I
heard you say wasn't I sweet."

Finch giggled—"Well—*aren't* you?"

"Not a bit."

"But l-look here," stammered Finch, "I didn't mean any harm—not—anything at all."

"Did you expect me to like being called sweet by you?"

"Why—I didn't think you'd mind."

"Then why did you stop when I came near?"

"I—I dunno. Honestly, Piers."

Piers moved closer to him. He moved right against him and crowded him against the wall. Finch scowled in discomfort as Piers's muscular body inexorably pressed on him. Now Piers's eyes were laughing into his. Finch would not speak, he would not groan. He thought—"No matter what Piers does to me I won't give him the satisfaction of hearing me—" but in spite of himself he gave a gasp, as though air were being pressed out of him.

The door opened onto the porch and their eldest brother stood beside them. His eyebrows shot up when he saw the look on Finch's face.

"What's this?" he demanded.

"Nothing," answered Piers, moving away from Finch, who still remained as though plastered against the wall.

Renny gave a glance into Finch's flushed face. He could see that he had been hurt. He said—"You two are not very well matched. And Piers—if you feel like pushing anyone about, try me."

The boys remained mute, looking at him. Authority and the atmosphere of the soldier emanated from him. He said —"Remember that Aunt Augusta and Miss Warkworth are here and don't let's have any roughhouse. You know Aunt Augusta doesn't like it."

"Gran does," said Finch in a belligerent voice. He straightened himself, nursing his aching shoulder.

Renny laughed. "It amuses Gran but it does not amuse Aunty."

"Why did she bring that girl with her?" asked Finch.

Now Renny's eyebrows came down in a puzzled frown. "Damned if I know."

"I know," said Piers.

"Why, then?"

"You won't like it if I say."

"I shan't mind."

"Well, then, to marry you. She has money."

Renny gave a short laugh and wheeled to re-enter the house.

Finch asked—"What are they doing in there now?"

"Having tea. You're late. Tidy yourself, Finch. You look elegant, Piers."

"Well, I thought it only decent to please Aunty."

In spite of the ache in his shoulder Finch gave a hoot of derisive laughter. Renny said to him—"Let me see you raise that arm."

Finch raised it and grimaced with pain. A small smile dimpled Piers's sunburnt cheek.

Renny said to him—"Don't do that again." He gave Finch a gentle push. "Go upstairs and make yourself presentable." He followed Finch into the hall.

Finch muttered—"I don't feel like going in for tea."

Renny asked sharply—"Did he hurt you badly?"

"No. But . . . there's that girl."

"Get upstairs with you and brush your hair. The girl won't notice you."

"How long will she stay?"

"A month or more. She's a sort of connection you know. Her mother was a Whiteoak."

"Hmph. Meg says she's been ill."

"Nothing worse than a disappointment in love."

"Good Lord—she's had time to get over that. How old is she, Renny?"

"Twenty-five."

"Old enough to know better."

They were having tea in the drawing room where a table was spread with thin bread and butter, strawberry jam, scones and raisin bread, brittle ginger cookies, and an iced cake. The group appeared much more feminine than was usual, with the addition of the two visitors. The elder was Adeline Whiteoak's only daughter Lady Buckley, a widow whose husband had inherited a baronetcy. Her title had always been a source of irritation rather than pride to her mother, who, being the granddaughter of an impoverished Irish marquis, looked on an English baronetcy of only two generations as insignificant, and, as she sometimes remarked, did not approve of titles. Yet it might have been noticed that she was never in the company of a new acquaintance for long before she would mention the name of her grandfather; being very old, she had forgotten many things but never did she forget that.

Lady Buckley was in her early seventies, an imposing figure, as tall and stately in her bearing as her mother was bent with the weight of years and in bearing waggish, rather than stately. Lady Buckley still wore her hair in a Queen Alexandra fringe, and her dresses were in keeping with this style. Her hair was very thick and of a purplish brown. Her complexion was rather sallow and her prominent dark eyes gave the impression that what she saw was not pleasing to her. Yet her nature was amiable and her kindness to her family never failed. All her married life she had spent in Devonshire but with frequent visits to Jalna. During these visits old Adeline was inclined to be irascible or what Meg called "showy-off." This she was being at the present moment, eating more cake than was good for her and audibly drinking her tea.

The young woman whom Lady Buckley had brought with her was Dilly Warkworth, a distant cousin whose home was in Yorkshire. She had had an illness, though her round face showed no sign of it, and the doctor had recommended a sea voyage. She had been visiting Lady Buckley and so it had been arranged that she should come with her to Jalna. She had dark brown fuzzy hair, large light eyes of an uncertain color, and a complexion so exquisite that her features seemed unimportant.

Now as Finch entered the room, his aunt exclaimed—"This boy has grown inches since I saw him two years ago. And I do think he's better looking."

Meg said—"Well, I'm glad you think so, Aunt Augusta. The poor fellow is at the awkward age and it is good for him to feel that he has improved." Meg raised her voice as though Finch were deaf. "Aunt Augusta thinks you are much better looking, Finch."

Wakefield put it—"She didn't say *much* better. She only said *better*."

Augusta put out a long hand and stroked the little boy's

hair. "There is no lack of looks here," she said, "but such delicacy."

"Yes indeed," Meg spoke sadly, "his health gives us a good deal of anxiety. His heart, you know—"

Renny frowned. "Please don't discuss it in front of him."

Miss Warkworth drew Wakefield on to the chair beside her. "Never mind, I'm delicate too."

Wakefield looked up into her face. "I think you're nice," he said, "and pretty."

She laughed and hugged him to her.

"What's she laughing at?" demanded the grandmother of Ernest. "I want to hear the joke."

"Sh, Mamma," he whispered. "There is no joke."

"Hmph. I want some cake. That dark sticky cake."

Ernest brought it to her. She said—"Tell Eden I must speak with him."

Eden, hearing his name, came and sat beside her. He said, in a low voice—"Remember, Granny, not an indiscreet word."

She chuckled. "Not a word. But listen. That girl has brass . . ."

"For God's sake, hush, Gran!"

But she persisted. "Get her to invest. Why not?"

"Yes, yes, but we can't talk of it now. Have some more tea."

"Thanks. I will." Then she turned her aquiline face, surmounted by a beribboned lace cap, toward the girl. "This is a wonderful country, isn't it? A rich country. We have gold mines here."

"Yes," answered Dilly. "So I've heard."

"Did you hear of any mine by name?"

"No. Just that it is a great country for investors."

Nicholas and Ernest were amused by their mother's sudden interest in mines. Neither had an inkling that the other or she had put money into Indigo Lake. Eden felt something approaching panic.

Now she said—"What you should do, my girl, is to marry out here. You've a choice right in this house. Invest in a husband and a gold mine."

Eden for the hundredth time wished he had never

drawn her into his net. Sometimes he almost believed she took pleasure in teasing him. Yet she had the good sense to refrain from pursuing the subject. He felt sure the day would come when the temptation to speak outright of Indigo Lake would be too much for her. By the time that day came he hoped to have enough put by to pay for a year or even two years in Europe. The mounting of his savings account ran through his thoughts like a golden thread. And now his thoughts turned to his aunt and the visitor. Why not give them the opportunity to increase their income? On her last visit he had heard Lady Buckley remark that, since the war, certain of her investments did not yield what they formerly had. Indeed it seemed a shame that the entire family should not put all they possessed into the gold mine. Especially Eden wished this for Renny, who was often pressed for money. Yet it would be useless to try to interest him.

Lady Buckley asked of Wakefield—"Do you still have lessons with Miss Pink?"

"No, Aunt Augusta. My sister Meg has been teaching me."

"And do you enjoy your studies?"

"Very much, thank you."

How mannerly he is, thought Meg, and was proud of him. But Finch regarded his junior with a pessimistic eye. Smug little hypocrite who always slacked on his homework and played up his delicacy!

"And do you still recite poetry?" Lady Buckley inquired, leaning toward her youngest nephew so that a tinkling sound came from the several strings of jet and amber that overhung her firmly corseted bosom.

"Yes, Aunt. I know several new pieces."

"Do you indeed? Well, supposing you recite one for us now, so that Miss Warkworth can hear you."

Wakefield at once slid from his chair, took out a crumpled ball of a handkerchief and wiped his lips.

"Make it short," growled Finch to him in an undertone, and was rewarded by an unobtrusive but well-aimed kick on the anklebone.

Wakefield stood up straight, a thin pretty child with

curling dark hair and large dark eyes, and declaimed without hesitation in his clear treble:

> " *The Eagle*
> " He clasps the crag with crooked hands;
> Close to the sun in lonely lands,
> Ring'd with the azure world, he stands.
>
> The wrinkled sea beneath him crawls;
> He watches from his mountain walls,
> And like a thunderbolt he falls."

"Thank you. Very, very nicely spoken," said Lady Buckley.

"Oh, what fun!" exclaimed Dilly Warkworth. This was the latest catchword in London and she introduced it whenever possible.

Meg did not think this expression at all appropriate praise of her small brother's performance and her fair face expressed her disappointment.

The grandmother said—"Now I don't call that poetry at all. 'Like a plum cake he falls'! Whoever heard of such a thing? Why don't Meggie teach him something sensible?"

"Not plum cake, Gran, thunderbolt," several voices corrected but she liked her own version and repeated the word several times, adding—"I haven't had a piece of plum cake in a long while. Have some made, Meggie. I like it very much."

Eden said to Dilly Warkworth—"I hope you won't find your visit here too dull, after London."

She gave her gay laugh. "Oh, it's great fun."

"Isn't my grandmother amazing for her age?"

"Oh, she's wonderful fun!"

Eden looked into her eyes and wondered what went on inside that head. If she had been disappointed in love, as they said, she was certainly taking it well. She gazed admiringly at Wakefield, who now was perched on Renny's knee. She asked—"Is he delicate? He doesn't look very strong."

"He's not strong. Renny took him to a specialist a few months ago who says he has a weak heart. I think Renny's afraid he will never raise him but Wake will probably outgrow the trouble."

"What fine eyes he has. But then your family run to fine eyes. Yet none of you resemble one another."

"Not Meg and Piers?"

"Oh, yes—they do. What fun!"

The windows stood open, the window curtains gently fluttered. The sunshine, broken into darkling splashes of gold by the moving branches of the old trees, shone on the silver tea tray, the massive blue and gold teapot, the polished mahogany of the cabinet that held curios from India, the rings on the grandmother's hands, planted firmly on either knee now that her tea was finished. It also showed up the worn spots on the carpet, the scratches on the side of Ernest's chair made by the claws of his cat, Sasha, how certainly Ernest's hair was receding at the temples, Renny's scraped knuckle, the two spots on Finch's chin, the peculiar purplish shade of Lady Buckley's hair.

Dilly Warkworth leaned close to Eden to whisper— "Tell me all about your eldest brother. I'm so glad I've come."

10.

More Investors

A FEELING OF AFFLUENCE SUCH as had not existed at Jalna for some years now emanated from those who were the lucky holders of shares in the Indigo Lake Mine. Adeline Whiteoak, who was not given to reckless spending, now changed her habits in a way that was quite alarming to her sons and her daughter. Augusta expected nothing more than a memento on her mother's death, but she hoped greatly that her favorite brother Ernest would be the principal legatee and she saw no sense in the frivolous spending of good dollars in which the old lady now began to indulge. After decades of spending almost nothing, for she had a supply of clothes to last the brief while remaining to her, she suddenly decided that she wanted a new fur coat.

"But, Mamma," her daughter expostulated, "your seal coat is still in good condition, Meg tells me. Don't you think you can make it do?"

"It's out of date. I want something with style to it."

Here Nicholas had a word to say. "But you haven't had your seal coat on your back for at least five years. You never go outdoors in the winter, you know."

"I shall this winter."

"What if you caught a bad cold?"

"I shan't catch cold if I have a new warm coat on me." Suddenly she remembered something. "Where's my little old mink jacket and muff. I want to see them."

Ernest said—"Don't you recall, Mamma, how you gave

105

them to the boys' mother? She was delicate, you remember, and felt the cold of our winters."

"Aye, I remember. But she died. Where's the coat?"

Meg spoke up. "I wore it for a while but it was old-fashioned and the moths got into it."

Her grandmother returned, with sudden shrewdness—"Mink is well thought of in these days. Perhaps I'd better have a new mink coat."

Meg cried—"But your seal coat is not Hudson seal, Granny, it's real seal. Do try to be satisfied with it."

"Why?" rapped out Adeline.

"Furs are so expensive."

"I have plenty of money. And I'm making more, I may tell you."

Still no one suspected what she was up to. Yet no one could help noticing how alert, how lucid was her mind, compared to what it ordinarily was. Not only did she insist that the new coats should be inspected and several sent to her on approval but she began to talk of other expenditures—a new carpet for her room, fresh silver plating for certain old Sheffield pieces (What if the copper *does* show through, Mamma, it only proves that they are Sheffield!), new upholstery for the dining-room chairs, new cushions for the pews in the church. To be sure, much of this was only talk but some of it was earnest and rather frightening.

Eden, from being thrown into panic by her every reference to money making, now became reckless of consequences. In fact, he could scarcely restrain his mirth to see her spreading of her ancient wings, and the family's fears. When he and she were alone he would throw his arms about her, hug her, and exclaim:

"We were not born yesterday, were we, Granny?"

And she, rejoicing in his youth and freshness, would stroke his bright hair and plant a kiss on his smooth cheek.

Nicholas and Ernest were tempted to disclose to each other their activities on the stock market, but both had at various times declared their determination never again to speculate and held back from the disclosure till a more substantial sum should have accumulated. But Ernest could not resist confiding the secret to his sister Lady Buckley. She had been complaining of the cruel increase in income tax when he said, with that affectionate note in his voice which always drew her to him:

"Gussie, dear, it does seem a shame that you should be troubled by this when the means to overcome it is right at hand."

She raised her arched black brows inquiringly.

"Mining stock," he brought out. "Indigo Lake, gold."

"But, Ernest—"

"Oh, I wouldn't urge you. But only let me tell you my little story. And remember it's in confidence. I heard of this mine through Eden. He met a mining broker, by sheer lucky chance, who has these shares for sale. Through Eden I have invested just under five thousand dollars and—let me tell you—I've practically doubled my money!" His blue eyes sparkled with pleasure.

"Does Nicholas know of this?"

"No one knows but Eden and myself. The Americans are buying up the shares so fast that I doubt if there are any to be had, but—if there are—you couldn't do a better thing than . . ."

She said judicially—"The thing for you to do, Ernest, is to sell out while the price is high and conserve your gains."

He could not help smiling at the idea of her giving him advice. He said—"Not I. Not till I've made a nice thing out of it."

"But you already have."

"Oh, I mean a *really* nice thing. Gussie, it's a wonderful opportunity. Do let me have Eden tell you all about it." She agreed to that. Eden, who had acquired the almost professional tone of a seasoned broker, was delighted to show his aunt the brightly colored brochure depicting the Indigo Lake Mine in action. The persuasion of Ernest, Eden, and the brochure was more than Augusta could resist. She owned some stock in a Canadian railway and these she arranged with Eden's help to sell.

She demanded to be taken to interview Mr. Kronk, that she might see for herself what sort of man he was and hear the details from his own lips. Eden had no hesitation in arranging the meeting, for he was sure Mr. Kronk would be able to instill perfect confidence in the mind of any speculator. And he was not wrong.

Ostensibly going to visit a dentist she asked Eden to accompany her. They borrowed the family car and set out, an oddly assorted pair, for the city. She was far too honest to have said she was going where she had no intention to go, but her visit to the dentist was brief, being no more than to have a denture which caused some irritation eased a little. She had a pleasant sense of adventure.

Mr. Kronk had lately acquired an office in the rear of a rather shabby building. You approached it by way of a long narrow passage that smelt a little of drains. His name was not on the door, which was kept locked. After a knock, a fat pale office boy opened the door, inquired your business, and if Mr. Kronk were free to receive you, you were admitted. Certainly he was not only free but eager to meet Augusta and Eden. When the introduction took place he looked up into Augusta's face with an expression so kind, honest, and intelligent that she was drawn to him at once. He held her hand a little longer than was usual in his hand that was rather remarkably large for his size. He had black hair, a sallow complexion, and dark eyes in which there were greenish flecks. The office, though so small, was luxuriously furnished.

11.

Dilly

"TELL ME ABOUT YOUR ELDEST brother," Dilly had said to Eden. "He has such an interesting face."

On a day of extraordinary heat for October they were sitting on a garden seat under the old mulberry tree whose fallen berries lay wasting in the sun, and she repeated the question.

"Why," Eden returned, "there's not much to tell. He's a distinct character, either good or bad, according to your conception of good and bad."

"What fun!" she cried.

"Yes, he can be great fun. On the other hand, he can be quite—intimidating."

"Should I think him good or bad?"

"I think you'd call him good. He's a kind brother—if you behave yourself—a devoted grandson and nephew —a lover of this land and his horses and dogs."

"Then how could he be bad?"

Eden made a small movement of irritation. "Bad is an old-fashioned word. Let's discard it."

"But it was you who brought it in."

"I suppose I meant that a certain type of person might use the word bad about him."

"Could I be that type?"

"Never."

"Am I a type?"

"Do you want to be?"

"No indeed."

"Then you're not."

With such youthful sparring they became better acquainted. But she did not interest Eden except that he envied her the things she had done which he had longed to do. London was familiar to her. She had been to France and Italy. What she had acquired from her travels, other than a pat knowingness about sight-seeing and foreign hotels, he could not discover. Yet the glamour of her experience hung like an aura about her. When he told her confidentially that he expected to go abroad next year she was ready with the advice of a seasoned traveler though her journeys had been brief and with a group of girls under the care of a teacher and guide.

She irritated Eden with her curiosity about Renny. He himself was not without experience, he thought, and he had a mind to punish her. He would like to give her something to say besides—"What fun!" To invest. That would put a different face on affairs. Eden had an almost tender feeling toward any possible investor in the Indigo Lake Mine. If Dilly could talk largely he could do a bit of boasting himself.

He said—"I suppose you're not interested in gold mines."

She stared. "I've never thought about them. But I have a friend in South Africa whose husband is in mining. I may be going there to visit her next year."

"I wasn't thinking of South Africa. We have gold mines right here, you know."

"Not really!" Her tone implied disbelief.

"Well, look here." He took the folder from his pocket. He had got a fresh uncrumpled one from Mr. Kronk. He showed her the pictures, read from it what she could understand and ended—"Please don't mention it. My family know nothing of it."

She stared. "But I thought you were studying law."

"So I am. This is just on the side." He could not keep from adding—"Large fortunes are being made out of this mine. Not by me, of course. But—well—I haven't done too badly."

It came, just as he had expected.

"What fun!"

The midday sunlight discovered no flaw in Dilly's complexion. The whites of her eyes were exquisitely clear. Eden put an arm along the back of the seat in a new intimacy.

"Remember, this is a secret—between you and me," he said. "Renny'd be in my hair if he found out."

"Oh, I'm such a one for secrets! Everybody tells me their secrets. I wonder why."

Eden also wondered why, but he said—"I suppose you have the gift of inspiring confidences. But this is scarcely worthy of you. It's just hardheaded business."

She exclaimed—"But I come from a business family. Cotton mills. I know a great deal about business. I wish I were into this gold mine affair—if it were ever so little. It would give me something new to think about." A shadow crossed her face and Eden remembered she had had a disappointment in love.

He said gravely—"These shares cost little, considering the potentialities. But they're being bought up very fast."

"What do they cost?" She broke with almost abrupt shrewdness.

Eden explained the present position of Indigo Lake shares with a skill equal almost to Mr. Kronk's. He smiled as he heard himself use the broker's very phrases. He had little hope that she would buy shares, yet the mine loomed so large in his thoughts that he could not resist talking of it. But Dilly was surprisingly receptive and showed herself eager to learn all he had to tell her of Indigo Lake. Suddenly she said:

"I have a thousand dollars which my trust company has deposited in a bank here—for traveling expenses or in case of emergency. But I don't want to travel. I want to stay here in this delightful house—that is, if you think your family can tolerate me."

"Oh, they all—we all, love having you."

She said happily—"Then I'll do it!"

"What if an emergency crops up?"

"Then I could sell my shares, couldn't I?"

"Of course. And at a profit."

It was too easy, he thought. The girl had more money than brains. Almost he wished he had been more reticent. Now there would be six investors at Jalna. Eden smiled to himself, considering all he had accomplished in so short a while, and to the benefit of all six. Looking up into the mulberry tree, he forgot Dilly, and saw himself strolling along a street in Paris, past shrubs in green painted tubs, in front of pavement *cafés* where those seated at the little tables had a gaiety he longed for. Their glances seemed to beckon him. Then he was on the Corso in Taormina watching the goatherd driving his little flock to be milked in the purple twilight.

"Dreams," said Dilly, and he felt her hand on his hair. He started, bringing himself up with a jerk.

"Now I've shocked you," she cried.

"Lord, no."

"But I had to touch it. It's so beautiful."

"Thanks." He stroked down the rumpled lock.

"I know you think I'm forward," she said, "but I never was what you'd call shy and this coming to a new country has excited me. I feel ready for anything. Have you ever felt like that?"

An odd smile bent Eden's lips. "A few times."

"Oh, tell me."

He was relieved by the appearance of Pheasant Vaughan, who could be seen through the trees that rose above the ravine, making her way toward the stables.

"Who is she?" demanded Dilly. "Is she in riding clothes?"

"Yes. She's the daughter of a neighbor. She's going to ride one of our horses at the show."

"What fun!" But Dilly, for some reason did not look amused. "How old is she?"

"Sixteen."

"How ridiculous—she'll never do it properly."

"She couldn't make a fault on that horse. Beside she's very good, though my brother has been training her for only two months. Should you like to come over to the paddock and watch them?"

Dilly sprang up with an elastic strength and buoyancy. "I'd love to." She led the way, as though restive. "Do you think your brother would lend me a horse to ride? I adore riding."

"I'm sure he would," Eden promised, not being at all sure.

At the white-painted palings they found Renny and the two grooms, Scotchmere and Wright. Piers and Pheasant were trotting round the paddock mounted on two beautifully groomed show horses. To see them was to feel the happiness that emanated from them. Two stableboys set up a bar and the two riders leaped it with graceful ease.

Scotchmere, chewing a straw, remarked—"She's coming on—the young lady I mean. But she ain't got the judgment she needs for the show—when the band is playing and the crowd cheering. You'll find that out, sir. I told you at the first you'd made a mistake and I stick to it."

Wright said—"All that little mare asks is someone to set on her and hold the reins. She'll go over the jumps herself."

Scotchmere spat out the straw. "Of all the silly remarks I ever heard that's the silliest," he said bitterly. "Any horse needs to be rid properly."

"Well, now, just look at her," exclaimed Wright and his ruddy young face glowed in admiration as the mare skimmed lightly over the bar now somewhat raised. Piers followed, feeling in this moment of splendid exhilaration a desire to follow Pheasant to the ends of the earth.

Renny turned to Dilly. "Pretty sight, isn't it?" he asked.

"Isn't it fun!" she laughed, showing more of her white teeth than he had heretofore seen any woman show. He looked speculatively into her mouth, as though she were a horse whose age he was about to assess.

Pheasant, proud of her increasing skill, filled with love for Piers and the mare, was careless. Down rattled the bar to the ground. Piers's horse shied. The mare danced skittishly, and Renny sang out:

"That won't do!"

Round the corner of the stable Meg appeared. It was seldom she came in this direction, for not one member of the family was so little interested in the activities of the horses as she. And of all the family she was the one whom Renny least wanted to see there. He knew how bitterly Meg would resent Pheasant's riding one of his horses at the show. He had hoped, in a primitive masculine way, to hide what he knew could not be hidden, or in any event to conceal it to the last possible moment, even to the moment when Meg, in their box at the show, would see Pheasant ride onto the tanbark. His brothers had taken care not to mention Pheasant's daily presence in the paddock to Meg. Eden indeed thought little about it, for his mind was intent on other matters, and Piers, of his own desire, was even more eager than Renny to keep the secret.

But now she was upon them and saw the girl mounted and flying, with happy thud of hooves, toward the next jump. In the first moment Meg could not be sure who was the rider, for it was seldom that she saw Pheasant. Then, as the mare passed close to the palings, she was made certain indeed and her heart caught up the thud of hooves and joined its own wrathful beating.

With her hand pressed to it, she went to Renny, who watched her approach with a grimace of chagrin.

"What does this mean?" she demanded.

"Keep your voice down," he said.

"What does it mean—that girl *here* on one of your horses?"

He returned, frowning sulkily—"I had to find someone to ride for me."

"What utter nonsense!" she cried.

"Keep your voice down."

She raised it. "She did not ride for you last year or any other year!"

"I was not then entering a horse in this event. Now I can."

"But Renny—" now tears came bright into her eyes— "think of me."

"That's right," he said, "tell your whole history to the world . . . Anyhow that's more than sixteen years ago. Everyone has forgotten it."

She spoke more quietly. "I have not forgotten it."

He too spoke quietly and laid a sympathetic hand on her arm. "Meggie, you know how badly I felt over that. But I see no reason for remembering it in this instance. It is a matter of business that I should have someone to ride this mare for me as she should be ridden."

"I will refuse to go to the show."

This to him was not only unreasonable but was to deny herself one of the great pleasures of the year. Now she not only looked at him with tears in her eyes but a sob shook her plump body. At the same time things were going badly in the paddock, for Pheasant—with a shock—had seen Meg. The mare, conscious of her nervousness, twice refused, then when at last she jumped did so in helter-skelter fashion. Piers's mount, temperamental and excitable, danced about like a skittish colt though he was eight years old.

Scotchmere approached Renny and Meg, a scowl darkening his wizened face.

"What do you think of that?" he asked.

Young Wright, looking as though the end of the earth had come, ran into the paddock to tighten the mare's girth. Finch, hanging over the palings, gave vent to hysterical giggles.

"I've said all along," continued Scotchmere, "that the little lady is too young. She hasn't experience and it ain't possible to give it to her in a couple of months."

Though Pheasant was astride the mare her spirit was gathered tremblingly into the little group now discussing her. She could not see, she could not hear, but in a chaos of bewilderment and apprehension, felt that she knew all.

As Wright straightened himself and drew away Pheasant said in an undertone to Piers:

"Your sister . . . she doesn't want me."

"Nonsense. Come—forget them all. We'll show them." He patted the mare.

His own horse was still misbehaving and he brought the whip down on its flank. The pair trotted back to the starting point. No one quite knew how it happened but at the first jump Pheasant was thrown. She was tossed off and was on her feet by the time Renny had vaulted the palings and reached her side.

"Are you hurt?" he asked.

"No—oh, no. I don't know why I was thrown. . . Just stupid, I guess." She was panting and she gripped her elbow.

Renny pushed up the sleeve to discover a skinned spot. Patting her arm, he said:

"I'm glad it's no worse. But you had better go home and take it easy for the rest of the day."

He hesitated, then added—"Come into my office first and let me put some ointment on it. I have the very best kind."

Wright was holding the mare by the bridle. She looked gently at Pheasant out of her great liquid eyes. Her head, in naked beauty, was motionless, as though carven from bronze. Only her nostrils moved with her breathing.

Pheasant laid her hand for a moment on the mare's neck. "Good-bye," she said, and followed Renny into the stable.

Piers had dismounted and now walked beside them. He said—"Everybody has a bad day now and then."

She turned her face away.

Renny said—"You had better take Pheasant home, Piers. She's a bit shaken. But leave her to me now."

In the little room that he called his office there were a shiny desk and a revolving chair, a file containing the records of all the horses he and his father had owned, and lithographs of famous horses decorated the walls. After closing the door he said—"It's just as Piers says—" Then he stopped because he saw that in comforting her he was going to break her composure. Opening a cupboard on the wall he took out a small pot of ointment. But after another look at her elbow he frowned. "I must put iodine on it, I'm afraid. It will hurt."

"Go ahead. I don't mind."

"Good girl." He made a swab with cotton wool and applied the iodine, asking—"Does it hurt very much?"

But she was glad of the pain, hugging it to her as a relief from the sharper pain.

When the elbow was neatly bound he looked down into her face. "You know, Pheasant, it's not that I haven't a good opinion of you, as a rider; you've come on wonderfully. You have fine stuff in you. You have good hands on the reins—" He broke off, thinking how terribly young she looked.

"I know," she said, in a small shaky voice. "But I'm not good enough for the show."

"I was wrong to think I could train you in so short a while."

The sound of the mare's hooves on the cement of the passage came to them. She was being led in, and either in protest or in pleasure she raised her voice and whinnied. It was too much for Pheasant.

"I'm going," she said breathlessly, and ran toward the door.

But he caught her by the back of her jacket and held her. "No, no," he said, "not like that. Come now, be a brave girl. You'll ride for me some other time—"

She interrupted—"You know I shan't. Please let me go."

She struggled and he released her. Almost ceremoniously he held open the door for her, then watched her run along the passage through the wide door of the stable and vanish. Scotchmere appeared, carrying a saddle in his hands. He looked after Pheasant with a speculative grin.

"Too high-strung," he said. "But she'll get over it. I guess we've done with her."

With a taciturn look Renny turned back into his office, reflecting on how difficult it was to do anything without interference. Yet he was not altogether sorry that things had turned out as they had, for in these last days his doubts of Pheasant's ability to face such an important event had disturbed him.

Scarcely had the door closed when it was again opened and Meg stood there.

"Come in," he said genially, but the look on his face was forbidding.

She spoke gently. "Scotchmere tells me that you have decided not to allow that girl to ride for you. I'm so thankful."

"I've said nothing of the sort to him."

"Oh, but he knows you so well. And—after what I saw—"

"Your appearing on the scene had a lot to do with it."

"Good heavens, Renny—am I such an ogress?"

"You have never shown Pheasant any friendliness."

"And no one in his right mind could expect me to."
Now her blue eyes were swimming in tears, their pupils
enlarged.

He flung himself into his chair with an exasperated
"Ha," and picking up a nail file, concentrated on a broken
thumbnail.

She exclaimed—"It sets my teeth on edge to see you do
that so roughly. Look—let me." She took the file from
him and also taking possession of his hand proceeded
tenderly with the operation. "Such nice hands," she said
in a cooing voice, "and you use them so badly."

Ignoring this he said—"If the mare won at the show I
could sell her for a good price, and I may remark that I
need the money. You know this has been an expensive
year both for repairs to the house and the stables. You
know that one of our best horses died."

She clasped the hand she held against the delicious
softness of her bosom. "I know, I know, and don't imagine
I'm not sympathetic but I couldn't bear—" her voice
trembled and she broke off, actually not knowing, for
once in her life, what to say next.

He said—"Then you put your own personal prejudices
above my welfare."

She found her tongue. "Never! But—oh, you see how
it is. I could not go . . . she must not ride . . . even
Wright says she won't do . . . why not ask Dilly to ride
for you? She's dying to."

"Dilly!" He was astonished.

"Well—she's been hinting, hasn't she?"

"She's always hinting about something. Why Aunt
Augusta brought her here I can't imagine."

"She is a charming girl!"

"Our ideas differ. What experience of riding has she?"

"She was practically brought up in the saddle. You
know what life in Leicestershire is. Do let her ride the
mare. In any case give her a trial."

"Gladly. Where is she?"

Meg's smile was ineffably sweet. "Oh, she has gone to
the house to try on my riding things. You know, I can't
get into them now. I'm sure they'll fit her."

12.

Pheasant

SHE RAN ALONG THE PATH homeward faster than she had ever run before. Her feet scuffed through the fallen leaves, making that sound she ordinarily delighted in, but now she heard nothing. Oh, to be home—in her own room—with the door locked! In that safety she longed to be hidden.

A projecting root caught her foot and she fell. So confused was she that for an instant she thought she had again been thrown from the mare. She felt disgraced to be thrown a second time and gave a little whimper of protest. Then her mind cleared and she lay still, looking up into the blue depths of the sky through the russet oak leaves.

She heard footsteps padding on the path and scrambled to her feet. For a wild instant she thought it might be Renny come to take her back to say all was well. But now she saw Piers running toward her.

"Oh, Pheasant," he called out, "here you are," and hesitated, a little embarrassed to see her tragic expression.

Now he moved toward her slowly, his healthy fair face clouded by concern.

"It's a damned shame," he began, but she put out her hand as though to ward him off.

He stood motionless, reflecting on the peculiar change going on within himself. He felt at one and the same time a confusion of spirit and a sense of power, a desire to be alone, and a longing to take Pheasant into his arms and comfort her. Yet the sense of power was so demanding that the longing to comfort became a wish to dominate.

"I'll tell you what," he began, but she interrupted:
"I won't talk about it."

"You needn't talk. Just listen to me." He drew nearer.
"Pheasant—"

She let him put an arm about her and for an instant laid her head on his shoulder. Then she pushed him from her and turned and fled along the path. He did not follow but stood looking after her, considering how easily he might overtake her if he chose.

She, as though she heard footsteps in pursuit, ran her swiftest, her heart beating fast in her throat. She did not stop till she was within sight of her own home. Then she slowed to a trot and entered the cold dim hall on tiptoe. This house, in spite of Mrs. Clinch's efforts, always had a faint smell of dust and mustiness. To Pheasant this smell was always associated with the thought of home, and with the loud ticking of the clock which stood at the foot of the stairs and sent its metallic ticktock and—what always seemed to her—its angry strike, both below and above.

Surprisingly she met her father on the stairs.

"Hullo," he said, "and how did the riding go?"

She forced her voice to be steady. "Not very well. They don't think I'll do after all."

He gave a short laugh. "I could have told them that."

"You've never seen me try," she exclaimed hotly.

"No, but I can imagine. Jogging about on an old pony is a very different thing from riding a show horse. I think Renny Whiteoak showed very poor judgment in allowing you to try."

"Well, it is all over now." She spoke in Mrs. Clinch's very tone, as though rather glad to have done with frivolity.

This meeting braced her to self-control. When she was in her room, with the door shut behind her, she went to the window and laid her forehead against the cool pane. She pressed her fingernails into the palms of her hands. The hurt she had given her elbow began to throb and she welcomed the pain. She repeated again and again, as though she were at the end of all hope in life—"It is all over now."

The trees that crowded too close to the house, which

was in a hollow, were conifers and made a dark background for a picture of herself victorious at the show, the leaping mare, glistening like a horse in bronze, clearing every barrier, the band filling the air with the flourish of her triumph. How often she had imagined this scene. Yet now she lay as in the dust defeated, and the mare whom she loved would not give her another thought.

Her breath made a film on the pane and on this she drew with her fingers an outline of the mare's head and wrote beneath it the one word *Farewell*.

Somehow she felt more self-controlled after that, and before long, hunger gnawed at her stomach, for she had scarcely in her excitement eaten properly before going to Jalna. Now she descended the steep backstairs into the kitchen. Mrs. Clinch was making a pie. The parings she took from the apples were so thick that the apples, after the operation, looked very small and naked.

Pheasant took a lump of brown sugar from the bowl and put it into her mouth.

"How did you get on?" asked Mrs. Clinch.

"Fine," she answered.

She opened the tin cake box with the picture of Balmoral Castle on it and took out a currant bun. She held it up for Mrs. Clinch to see.

"All right?" she asked.

The housekeeper nodded. "You'll spoil your appetite," she added with severity.

"Oh, no, I shan't."

The sun was deliciously warm in the kitchen garden. There had been frost but a few flowers had survived. Strangely these were the most fragile—the little pink petunias and the sky-blue morning glories. These last were climbing along a picket fence, holding up their blue cups as though in a gift to heaven. Two of them, coming from the same stem, were so close that they touched each other, the taller casting its shadow on the other and so turning it to a deeper, tenderer blue. Pheasant, munching her bun, stood watching as a last lonely bee tumbled the twin flowers for honey. "He's hungry," she thought, "and he's like me—he wants to live."

13.

The Vegetarian

HE WAS FULL OF RAGE, through and through, yet scarcely knew at what he was raging. He felt a moment's surprise at his own powers of feeling in these days, and a kind of panic because of the sudden sweep of his emotions. What had come over him, he wondered. Yet he would not have had it otherwise. Though often he felt bewildered by the change in him, he felt at the same time a voluptuous relish of his own strangeness. Everything he saw was in stronger colors. He felt himself more and more of an outsider, looking on at this strange highly colored world about him.

But now he was in a rage and banged things about in his bedroom, as though to prove it to himself, for there was no one else to see. Yet it was Saturday. His homework was done—all but those blasted French verbs and he would wrestle with them tomorrow. Something had gone wrong right after breakfast. Now he remembered. His sister Meg had told him to go out and gather vegetables for the harvest festival at the church and he had asked why couldn't somebody else do it and she had told him not to be so lazy and he had answered there was a fat chance of his being lazy with everyone in the house ordering him to do things. Meg had said no more nonsense please, and at that moment Eden had appeared and told him to hop on his bicycle like a good kid and take this pair of shoes to the shoemaker's to be half-soled. Eden had put the shoes into his hand and smiled at him, and Finch, in spite of himself, had given a half-grudging smile in return. He had taken the shoes to the shoemaker's. He had gathered the vegetables, and, surveying the great overgrown pumpkins in their golden ripeness, the rosetted cauliflowers in their crisp leaves, the long pale vegetable marrows, his anger had melted from him and he had felt wildly, boisterously happy. He had sung as he collected the vegetables, glad of the noise of the wind that drowned his voice.

But now it all returned to him. That was the way with him in these days. He would be swept by some sudden gust of feeling, then it would pass, only to return again like a recurring wave, weaker perhaps but still powerful enough to shake him.

He flung down his books. He stumbled against a chair and his arm struck his clothesbrush that lay on the chest of drawers, knocking it off. He kicked it beneath the bed. He set his jaw and glared after it. He made up his mind he would leave it there till next he needed it but a moment later found himself on his hands and knees fishing it out. Shamefaced he brushed the knees of his trousers with it, as if to convince some onlooker that all his movements were intentional and sober.

He went down the two flights of stairs in a loose jog trot, his hands in his pockets. Late summer warmth was claiming this day and more to follow. The front door stood open. All that showed beyond it appeared of a more serene yet deeper temper than on the days before. The leaves, still thick on the trees, had in what a short while turned to a rich mahogany, a pale gold like the first dandelion, a blazing red, or a tender pinkish gold. The last to Finch were the most beautiful. The tips of these pinkish gold leaves of the maples were as though dipped in a deeper essence, so that the variegated splendor of the tree far surpassed the freshness of its spring.

Finch stood staring in wonder, the clement air moving gently across his face, pungent scents of the fall rising from the ravine. He had a vague desire to be absorbed into the scene, to forget himself and be a part of it forever. Now anger was gone out of him and when Eden called from an upstairs window—"Hullo there, did you take the shoes?" he answered docilely—"Yes. He said he'd have them ready by Tuesday."

"Good," Eden returned and added—"Thanks."

Finch sauntered round the house to where he had left the vegetables mounded in a wheelbarrow. He felt proud of them—so clean, fresh and well grown. He had disposed some glossy red peppers among them and some bunches of parsley that had become dark green, strong, and curly in the autumn cold. At the last moment he had not been able to resist adding a few onions, stripped of their outer skin and as pretty as could be, he thought.

Wright drove across from the stables in a light wagon drawn by an old horse, thirty-two years old but still handsome, with her thick arched neck and blond mane. And from the flower border came Meg, her arms fulls of chrysanthemums and the intensely red blooms of salvia that seemed to be dripping blood.

Wright, jumping down from the wagon, asked:

"Is that the lot, miss?"

"Yes. Have you the pears?"

He held up a basket of late pears. "I picked out the best-shaped ones, miss, and put in a few big pippins. I thought they might come in useful."

"Very, very nice," she said, examinging them with an experienced eye; then remarked the onions.

"Oh, not onions, Finch, not onions."

Wakefield came running out of the house.

"They smell," he shouted, and bent over them. "Ugh, they *stink!*"

Finch took him by the scruff and pressed his face against the onions. "Have a good smell," he urged.

Meg interfered. "Now, boys. *And* Wakefield, don't let me ever hear you use that horrid word again."

Wakefield assumed an elegant air, his finger tips shielding his nose. "*Quelle odeur,*" he said mincingly.

Meg smiled at Wright and Finch, her eyes saying— "How clever he is!"

The little boy, suddenly clinging, caught her hand and begged—"May I go with you, Meggie, to decorate the church?"

"Indeed you may. And here comes Piers with the car."

Piers drove up in the family car, which still showed signs of its last muddy journey. He sat smiling serenely while Wright arranged the vegetables and fruit in the back of the car.

Finch wondered, why does he always look so pleased with himself?

On the seat beside Piers was a basket of purple grapes and a bunch of Michaelmas daisies. The grapes, with their bloom as though of a breath blown on them, had so closely grown in the bunch that not one more could have forced its way in.

Piers smiled, as if he had invented them.

"I thought they were pretty," he said.

Meg leaned over the door of the car to look. "Oh, how nice! Where did you get them, Piers?"

"I picked the Michaelmas daisies at the edge of the woods. The grapes I bought in Mistwell."

"You must let me pay you back."

"No, no. That's my contribution."

Wakefield cried—"I picked the salvia and with nice long stems. Finch brought onions! What do you think of onions in a church, Piers?"

"Good Lord!" exclaimed Piers.

"Well, the good Lord made them too, didn't he?" Finch's voice broke out in that uncontrolled way it had.

He stood, shaken again by anger, looking after the car as with Meg and Wakefield and the flowers established in it, it moved off. The wagon, driven by Wright, followed, the blond mane of the horse and the blond hairs on the back of Wright's neck glistening in the red sunlight.

No one had asked him, Finch thought bitterly, to help to decorate the church. No one had thanked him for what he had taken so many pains to do properly. Why, he must have examined twenty pumpkins before making his choice. And there lay the onions discarded on the grass, their tender tubular stems bruised.

Suddenly he burst out laughing at himself. Sentimentalizing over a bunch of onions—what a fool he was! No wonder his brothers made fun of him. Hands in pockets he jigged up and down on agile feet. He was feeling very much alive, almost jocular at the thought of his own peculiarities.

The spaniel Floss appeared from beneath the hedge and, seeing him so lively, rose and stood up against him, grinning into his face. Finch romped with her, thrusting her from him while she returned each time with all her weight against him. At last the two came down together on the grass and clasping her to him he rolled shouting with laughter . . . Then, as though galvanized, he leapt up and ran toward the stables, calling to her to race him there. She ran a little way, her long ears flopping, but seeing Renny in the distance turned abruptly in his direction.

This defection sobered Finch and he felt unaccountably hurt, for after all Renny was her master and she adored him. Still, why should she run after him at the very first glimpse? "It's true," thought Finch, "that I can't hold any-one—not even Floss. And I've been so good to her." He remembered the times he had taken burrs out of her long ears and plumed tail, brought her in out of the rain and dried her underpart on a towel.

He thought he would not go out of the sunshine into the stables, though he wanted to inspect the new colt. But instead he would go to the small enclosure beyond and play with the six lambs that lived there. But before that he would smoke the cigarette he had pinched from the battered box on Eden's desk. He looked at it rather dubiously, for it had got a crack in it from lying in his pocket. He went to a secluded spot where the silo jutted out from the barn and lighted the cigarette carefully, holding the crack together between finger and thumb. He inhaled and the sweet scent of the tobacco—Eden refused to smoke cheap cigarettes—mingled with the sweet scent of a brushwood fire which a farm hand was tending.

A little black hen with a single half-grown late chick was scratching about in the bits of straw and the weeds near by. At the most insignificant find she clucked ex-citedly to her chick, who ran to examine and, if possible, devour, though its crop was already bulging. When the cigarette was finished and the stub thrown down the little hen hastened to offer it to her chick, who several times picked it up and dropped it, with inquiring bright glances at its parent.

"Why, look here," Finch said, "haven't you got any sense? Now, I'll tell you what, I'll get you something you'll really like." He thought he would go into the barn and fetch a handful of chopped corn.

He went in at the door and stood motionless a moment in the cool sweet-smelling dimness. From below came the contented moo of a cow and the sound of water running from a tap. Then, from the yard there was the sound of a lamb bleating. Were they moving the lambs to a new place? He ran down the steep stairs. He saw a farm hand filling a bucket at the tap and asked:

"Are they moving the lambs?"

The man was a Scot. He answered with a grin—"Well, they're moving one o' them. They're butchering it."

Finch ran along the cement floor and looked over the half door. The lamb was lying on its side, held down by one man, while another with a knife . . .

"Stop!" shouted Finch. "Don't!"

The man with the knife turned his head.

"Why?" he asked.

"Because you *can't*—not on a morning like this!"

"I have orders. You'll soon be getting nice roast lamb for dinner."

The lamb raised its head and looked at Finch.

"I tell you to stop!" he shouted. He vaulted over the half door and ran across the cobbled yard.

Before he reached the lamb it had uttered its cry of pain. Its white woolly breast was reddened by the blood that ran from its throat. Its disproportionate woolly legs moved, as though to run, then were still.

"Ah, now," said the Scot, "don't you worry. It didn't hurt the wee thing at all."

Finch turned and fled, as though from a massacre.

Over the paths, across the stubble fields he ran till he hid himself in the darkness of the pine wood. This pine wood was not large. Like everything at Jalna it was not on a grand scale, though the trees themselves had grandeur because of their great age and massive boughs. They seemed to create silence. Even the migrating birds, when resting here, ceased their twittering. The carpet of pine needles muffled the thud of horses' hooves on the bridle path. At its edge a few mushrooms, smooth as pearls, thrust upward toward the light. Finch could hear the silence of the wood broken by hoarse sobs as he ran. Yet he did not know he was crying.

In the deepest part he threw himself down on the ground and hid his face in the crook of his arm. The lamb lay beside him, its trusting eyes close to him. "You will save me, I know." Then its bleat of pain—its death that penetrated his very marrow . . . It had trusted him. It had trusted the man who butchered it. It had lived the few months of its life trusting and gamboling in joy of its life. And they had killed it to eat it! To devour it! Again he saw its gashed throat with the blood gushing onto the snow-white wool. His stomach revolted. He raised himself and was sick. Then he lay back, relieved a little, and was quiet.

He got up and covered the place where he had been sick with pine needles. He was shivering and moved to the edge of the wood where the warm sunshine touched him. He discovered a small mushroom and picked it. Its earthy scent came to him and it was damp and earth-cold against his palm.

He could see the lamb resting against the breast of the Good Shepherd, its woolly legs dangling. "O Lamb of God that taketh away the sins of the world, grant us Thy peace," he kept repeating, "grant us Thy peace." The words, as though loosing a river of grief, brought blinding tears to his eyes. He neither saw nor heard Eden's approach and was aware of him only when he dropped to the ground beside him.

"Oh, hullo," said Eden. "What's the matter?"

"Nothing."

"Do you want to be left alone?"

"I don't care." Finch flung an arm across his face to hide it.

Eden lighted a cigarette and clasped his hands across his knees. He said—"I see plenty of trouble ahead of you. You take things too hard."

Finch's eyes were hidden by his arm but his mouth was drawn into a grimace. He tried to speak but made only incoherent sounds.

Eden went on—"You should be like me. I don't let things worry me—either at home or abroad."

There was silence except for a sudden breeze that whispered among the pines. Then, without uncovering his eyes, Finch asked—"Eden, have you ever seen a lamb killed?"

"So that's what's the matter! Why did you see it?"

"I just happened to."

"Well, you know they are killed, don't you? What about lamb and mint sauce?"

"I'll never touch it again."

"What about the poor steers and pigs?"

Finch sat up. "I'll never eat meat again! Why should I? People get on without it. Why—Eden, the look in the lamb's eyes . . ." Again his mouth was contorted.

"They do indeed. Whole nations have given up eating flesh and survived." And Eden began to quote:

" Life which all creatures love and strive to keep,
    Wonderful, dear, and pleasant unto each,
    Even to the meanest: yea, a boon to all
    Where pity is, for pity makes the world
    Soft to the weak and noble for the strong.
    Unto the dumb lips of his flock he lent
    Sad pleading words . . . tum-te-te-tum . . .

"I forget the rest." Eden frowned crossly.

Finch asked—"Who wrote that?"

"I forget. But I don't think much of it as poetry, do you?"

"I dunno." But Finch was flattered by having his opinion asked.

"Orpheus taught men to abstain from slaughter, yet he himself was torn to bits. But you know all about that."

What would it be like, Finch wondered, to have Eden for a friend? But Eden would soon tire of him, he knew. Even now he fell silent, looking straight ahead with an odd, unseeing look. Finch examined his profile. He was like his mother, Finch had heard said, heard his grand-mother say, in her harsh, sardonic voice—"Like his poor flibbertigibbety mother." It must feel strange to be beauti-ful like Eden. Not that he would have wanted to. It would have been embarrassing to him. But he could have done with a few good looks, he thought.

Eden took a notebook from his pocket, found a stub of a pencil in another pocket and looked inquiringly at Finch.

"Must you stay here?" he asked politely.

"Why—why—I don't know," stammered Finch.

"Because the first lines of a poem have just come into my head and I should like to be alone to write them down. If I wander off I shall probably forget them, but a walk will do you good. There's lots of room."

Finch scrambled to his feet. "Oh—all right. I'll go." He looked vaguely about, then turned to Eden. "You won't tell, will you?" he asked, reddening.

"Tell what?"

"Wh—what I said about—the lamb?"

"Not a word. I'm good at keeping secrets. But are you really going to reject it when it comes to the table?"

"You wait and see."

"Knowing your appetite, I'll believe it when I see it—not before."

Finch spoke loudly. "You'll see it! I'll never eat meat again."

He felt a constriction in his throat. Tears scalded his eyes. He stumbled over a fallen branch as he hurried away and all but fell.

Eden called out—"Don't hurry. I wasn't *driving* you off."

Finch turned back. "Eden—you won't tell that I—" he could not go on.

Eden finished for him—"That you were crying? God, no! What a little duffer you are! Get out! You've made me forget that first line."

Finch had his midday meal at the school to which he went each day by train. During the following week he refused meat, and if he left it on his plate at supper no one noticed. But when Saturday came it was a different story. It was a day still warm, and doors and windows stood open.

When the family collected for the one o'clock dinner they were met by an excellent smell of roast lamb and mint sauce. The grandmother, supported by a son on either side, sniffed the rich odor and made a gallant attempt to walk faster. "Don't be so slow," she said to Ernest. "I'm not a centurion yet."

"Centenarian, Mamma."

"Ha—well, what was a centurion then?"

"He was commander of a hundred men in the Roman army."

She gave a roguish grin. "Well, I never commanded a hundred men—not *quite* a hundred, no!"

Her son Nicholas patted her back that once had been supple and straight but was now stiff and bent. He looked down at her with admiration. "You certainly commanded 'em in your day, Mamma—in three countries."

The rest of the family, with the exception of Finch, were standing about, waiting. The visitor, Dilly Warkworth, was as usual trying to captivate Renny. In these days when she was engaged in schooling the mare Silken Lady, this was easier to do. He was drawn to any woman who could ride well. He had thought her to be a bit of a fool, but now he admired her, in an impersonal way.

Ernest and Nicholas steered their mother around the end of the table to her own place between them. There they could attend to her wants and try to restrain her appetite, which was all too zestful. They lowered her into the chair where she arrived with a "Ha" of satisfaction, put up her two hands to straighten her beribboned cap, and fixed her eyes, surprisingly bright and clear for her age, on the platter Rags was about to place on the table in front of Renny. This he did with an air of especial deference and solicitude, as though the wiry and weather-beaten master of the house were a particularly aristocratic invalid. Nicholas and Ernest found this irritating and it always took them a moment or two to get over it.

"Roast lamb!" exclaimed the grandmother. "Nothing I like better. Plenty of brown gravy and mint sauce, please."

Renny tested the edge of the carving knife with his thumb. He began to carve.

Finch came in and slid into his chair with a glance of apology at his sister.

Meg said—"I must ask you to be on time, Finch. You know perfectly well how long it takes you to tidy yourself."

Finch did not hear her. He was staring at the juicy brown roast on the platter. When it was his turn to be served, he said loudly—"None for me, please."

Renny threw him a piercing look—almost of consternation. "What's the matter?" he demanded.

"I'll have just vegetables, please."

"Vegetables! Why—this is roast *lamb!* One of our own."

Unable to control himself Finch broke out hoarsely—"That's just it! I was there. I saw it *killed.*"

"Now don't let's have any nonsense." Renny spoke with some severity. He cut a thick slice from the roast and laid it on a plate.

"I won't eat it, I tell you," shouted Finch.

"Come, come," soothed Piers, "be a little man."

Nicholas, who was becoming somewhat hard of hearing, demanded—"What is all this about?"

The grandmother, with the first luscious mouthful on her fork, put in—"If the boy wants more, give him more. He is growing fast—needs feeding."

The plate was set in front of Finch. He looked down at it with loathing. He repeated—"I won't eat it, I tell you."

Replying to Nicholas, Eden said—"He saw the butchering and he's turned vegetarian. Who can blame him?"

"If the boy wants more, give him more," put in the grandmother, her mouth full of roast lamb.

"That's not the trouble," Renny said, testily. "He won't eat what I have given him because—"

Ernest interrupted—"My mother should not be told unpleasant things when she is eating."

Him she now interrupted fiercely—"I won't be kept out of things."

Piers declaimed—" 'He never loved a dear Gazelle but it was sure to die.' "

"Baa-a," bleated Wakefield.

Meg helped him to mint sauce. "This lamb," she said, "is very nice indeed and very good for you."

Finch, with flushed face and trembling lips, sat staring at his plate.

Renny said—"Let's have no more of this sentimental nonsense. Behave yourself and eat what you're given."

"I tell you, I won't—I can't," Finch got out hoarsely.

"Baa-a," bleated Wakefield.

In sudden fury Finch caught his arm and twisted it. The little boy uttered sounds of anguish disproportionate to his hurt.

Old Mrs. Whiteoak rapped the table with her fork. "Take them out and flog them, Renny," she ordered. "Boys fighting at table! I won't have it."

"Such fun!" cried Dilly, who had been listening open-mouthed.

"I am ashamed for you, Finch," said Lady Buckley on a deep contralto note.

Renny rose from the table, took Finch by the arm and led him into the hall. Closing the door behind them he said—"I am going to be forced to give you such a walloping as you have never had, one of these days."

With his mouth contorted, Finch began—"But don't you see . . ." He could get no further. How could he make Renny see what he saw—the gaping wound, the pleading eyes, the blood on the snowy wool? And, if he could make him see . . .

Renny was saying—"Now you go up to your room and stay there till you get over this. Then go down to the kitchen and get something to eat. Whatever you want. If you won't eat lamb—"

"I'll never eat any meat again."

"Very well. Be a vegetarian if you like but for goodness' sake, don't make a fool of yourself as you did just now."

A vegetarian Finch remained, as the days marched on. What amazed him was that no one made any further remark on his abstinence from meat. He could not know that it had been agreed to ignore him in this matter. Wakefield did indeed call out "Baa-a" to him from the shelter of Piers, but got such a savage look after the first occasion that he desisted. Finch's relief was almost physical, so greatly had he shrunk from the chaffing, the derision he had dreaded. Now he could face a future untainted by the shame of devouring his fellow creatures. If they could but know! Indeed, many a time he pictured them, as by some miracle, discovering he had not shared in the cruelty they suffered. Surely when he died word would pass among them and they would mourn him. It seemed hard to him that the cows, sheep, and pigs of the farm appeared to trust Piers more than him—Piers who was so zestfully a meat eater.

That zest—that appetite—unfortunately remained with Finch. He was growing fast—bones and muscles were hardening in him, he came to his meals ravenous. The smell of the breakfast bacon or sausages was torture. No amount of toast and marmalade filled the yearning cavity of his inside. Scarcely an hour would pass before he would be hungry again. And when there were pork chops or veal stew or roast beef! Renny would inquire solicitously if he would take a little of the Yorkshire pudding with a little gravy on it. A bit of the pudding— yes. The gravy—no. Almost he resented the masklike faces about the table. They were making it too easy for him. It was unnatural. They didn't care! That was it— they didn't care!

He tried to fill up upon chocolate bars and nuts. He ate large numbers of apples and bananas but his stomach cried out for meat. Meg had fish cooked especially for him but he had never liked fish. He did like macaroni and cheese, but that same night he was teased by the delicious scent of baked ham. Wakefield would lean forward to watch him eat as though he were an animal in a zoo. Otherwise his abstinence was unnoticed.

One night when all the household were out with the exception of himself, studying in the library, and Grandmother and Wakefield tucked up in bed, his resolve broke. There had been cold roast pork for supper, fine and tender, with a crisp rind. He dropped his books and stole down the stairs to the basement. He turned on the light in the kitchen where there was a pleasant warmth from the fire in the coal range. Some copper utensils, brought from England by his grandparents, but now unused, hung on the walls. They caught the light eagerly, as though meaning had been given back to them. He could see his reflection moving in them from one to another.

He opened the door of the larder. There were leftovers in bowls on the shelves. There was a side of bacon hanging from the ceiling. There was a platter of uncooked sausages and half a meat pie. But beneath a large dish cover he found what he wanted—the remainder of the roast pork. It had been cooked with stuffing and some of this lay crumbled on the platter. He collected a little mound of it with his fingers and put it into his mouth. Oh, the delicious flavor! He tore a crisp rind from the joint and crunched it almost savagely. How long was it since he had tasted meat? He could not remember. It seemed half a lifetime. He found a sharp knife and cut himself a large slice of the fine white meat. He felt like the discoverer of roast pork. He ate a second slice. Then he turned his attention to the cold meat pie. His hunger surprised even himself but at last it was satisfied.

He turned out the lights and stole softly up the stairs. He heard his grandmother snoring as he passed her door.

No more study for him that night. He lay back in Nicholas's leather armchair replete. He did not think but merely felt a deep animal content—like a tiger that has devoured his prey.

But the next day the problem was there. How to make the complete about-face. All day long at school it kept nagging at him. Could he go to Meg and persuade her to say the doctor had ordered meat for him, that if he did not eat meat he would die? But everyone knew he was not ill. There was nothing to do but face the music. Meat he must have.

At supper there was a very substantial dish of beef stew with dumplings, for Renny and Piers had been at a fall fair at some distance. Their cheeks were ruddy from the strong northwest wind they had faced. And there, sitting opposite him, was his grandmother, who had had no exercise whatever, waiting eagerly for her share.

"Granny, dear," Meg was saying, "don't you think you had better have a poached egg?"

Ernest added—"I agree that she had better have a poached egg."

His mother peered up at him truculently from under the lace frill of her cap. "I want a dumpling," she said.

"But, Mamma, they are so hard to digest."

"Speak for yourself," she retorted. "I can digest 'em."

Ernest said, out of the side of his mouth nearest Renny —"A small one then."

"What's that he says?" she demanded. "A small one? Nothing of the sort. A big one! I say a big one, Renny. You would not starve your poor ould grandma, would you?" She spoke these last words in the rich Irish brogue she had heard in her girlhood days.

Nicholas chuckled—"Give her a dumpling, Renny, and let her put up with the consequences."

"What fun!" exclaimed Dilly.

Finch looked glumly down at the fried potatoes, fried eggs and rather watery stewed tomatoes which Wragge had set before him.

Meg inquired—"What is the matter, dear? Aren't you hungry? Would you rather have just some blancmange?"

"Yes," Finch answered loudly. "I am hungry. No I don't want blancmange."

Renny leant toward him, with a cajoling air. "Have a little of the stew," he said.

Every eye was on Finch. But he did not care.

"Yes," he said firmly, "I'll have some of the stew— quite a lot."

Everyone watched fascinated while Renny mounded a plate with the juicy meat, the rotund dumplings, the rich gravy, in which small mushrooms were smothered.

With an unrestrained giggle Wragge removed the fried eggs from in front of Finch and set the stew in its place.

"If he's been rude," said the grandmother, "he shouldn't have his supper. Take him out and cuff him, Renny. That's the way my father kept them polite."

"He's all right," grinned Renny. "Go to it, Finch."

Amid an outburst of laughter Finch applied himself to the steaming stew. All about him he heard—"Ha-ha-ha! Ho-ho-ho! He-he-he!" and from Wakefield—"Ba-ba-ba!" One would think, he said to himself, that nothing quite so funny had ever happened before, but he was impervious to derision or chaffing. He continued doggedly to enjoy the stew. Fortunately at this moment Grandmother mislaid her dumpling.

"Where is it?" she demanded, peering all about her.

All eyes were now on her. She could not have lost it. But certainly it was not on her plate. At last Wragge discovered it on her lap. He gathered it up in her table napkin and she was given a fresh one. This effectively took the attention of the family from Finch. She herself was vastly amused.

"A dumpling," she chuckled, "a dumpling in my lap—of all things!"

The talk then turned to the fall fair and the meal ended on a high cheerful note.

It was so mild this evening that the front door stood open. The dog saw a rabbit cross the lawn and rushed out to chase it. Then Wakefield scampered after them. And after him—all the others—even the grandmother.

"Give me your arms, boys," she said to her elderly sons. "I want to see the moon."

The harvest moon was indeed a sight of great splendor. The sun had sunk, a resplendent red ball, in the luminous west. Now it was as though it rose again, in the dark blue east, so like it was to the red harvest moon. The Virginia creeper that covered the front of the house had, in the frosty night, turned to a rich tapestry of bronze and gold and scarlet. Adeline Whiteoak, as a young woman, had planted it there, had guided its puny tendrils in its first year, had held a watering can high above it to refresh it in the drought. Now she stood bent, nearly a hundred years old, gazing up at it as it embraced and beautified the house, clung to it, fastened its hold in every crevice, draped its tendrils over the porch, and soon would cast down its leaves and rest till its next budding time.

Already many of the leaves of birch and maple had fallen and had that day been raked into a heap on the lawn. Wakefield ran into its midst and began kicking the leaves about, throwing an armful in Finch's face. Now Finch was after him, showering leaves on him. And Piers was after Finch, and Eden after Piers, and Renny after Eden, in a storm of flying leaves. Now Eden was down and his brothers were burying him in leaves. He lay acquiescent while they made a great mound on him.

"Here lies a dead poet!" chanted Piers, and Eden was up again and the leaves flying about him.

"Ha," said old Adeline Whiteoak, "I like to see the whelps rioting. I like to see the harvest moon. Now I shall go to bed . . . A dumpling in me lap. Who would have thought of it! Tck-tck."

14.

The Falling Leaves

NOW ALMOST ALL OF THE LEAVES had fallen, though the strong brown oak leaves were slow to loose their hold, and when they did sailed majestically to the ground with an air of intention rather than defeat. There seemed no end to the leaves that fall. Their density on the trees seemed scarcely to account for their great numbers when they had fallen. They were raked into heaps and burned, blazing brilliantly for a little, then declining to a quietly glowing mass, the sweet-smelling incense from which rose to the blue sky. But no matter how many were burned or how many lay in hollows or in the ravine, many were left to be blown about by the untiring wind. It was not a playful wind but a strong chill wind that spoke of icy gales to come. The leaves were blown across the paths and roads, first in one direction then another. Scarcely were they settled in one spot than they were hurled back where they had come from. And so, like refugees without a country, they could find nowhere to rest.

The time of the horse show was one of the high spots of the year at Jalna. This year it was especially so because of the pleasurable excitement of speculation that ran through the house. Even Renny, who knew nothing of this, who never had heard of Indigo Lake, was conscious of the undercurrent of exhilaration and was pleased by it.

Meg remarked to him—"How gay the uncles are! I haven't seen them so animated in a long while."

"It's having Aunt Augusta here," he said.

"It's more than that," she insisted.

139

"It's Dilly then."

"Nonsense. They're not at all that sort of elderly man. And Aunt Augusta too. How lively she is."

"It must be Dilly."

"No. Aunt Augusta said only yesterday that she rather wished she had not brought her."

"Why?"

"Well—she laughs too much."

He stared. "Laughs too much?"

"Yes. She's not the sort of girl Aunty thought she was."

"You mean suitable for me?"

"Well, possibly."

He put his arm about her plump middle. "I shall never marry, Meg. Nor you, I guess. We have our hands full with these young brothers."

She sighed. "Yes indeed."

The youngest now came running up. He had been in the apple house, as they called the squat little building which was half underground, where a quantity of apples were stored till the prices should rise. From its open door the scent of the apples came to Renny and Meg. Wakefield carried a large Northern Spy in one hand and in the other a small Tolman Sweet and a russet.

"Look," he said, "aren't they nice?"

"You must not stay long in the apple house," said his sister. "You will catch cold."

"Look," he repeated. "Try one."

His elders looked, not at the apples but at him, with the solicitude of parents. The small boy was a posthumous child whose mother had died not long after his birth. But he was stronger than he appeared.

Renny took the apples from him and, one after the other, held them to his nose and sniffed the fragrance.

"How distinct they are and how good," he said. "I'm glad our orchard is still untampered with, but in twenty years, Meggie, when these damned experts at the agricultural college have had their way, no one in the towns will be able to buy apples with the flavor of these. All varieties will look fine but they'll all smell alike and taste alike."

"Hm," his sister agreed absently. She was still brooding on Wakefield. He had now run to meet Piers, who, standing on a light wagon laden with barrels of apples and drawn by a dappled gray gelding which he greatly prized, was on his way to the railway station.

"Hullo," he called out. "Anything you want me to do in the village?"

"May I go?" shouted Wake. As the wagon drew up he was already clambering into it.

"Oh, I don't think he should," said Meg.

"Don't coddle him. The more he is outdoors the better for him."

"I wish he were able to go to school."

"Why, Meg, I thought you liked teaching him."

"I do. But he's become so difficult. He needs a *man*."

"Well, I certainly haven't the time. I wonder if the uncles would undertake it."

"It would be no better."

The pleasant sound of the gelding's hoofbeats was dying away. A fresh storm of leaves was blown from the elm by the apple house and scurried down its moss-grown roof. Renny went and shut its low broad door. When he came back Meg said—"I wonder if he might go to the Rector for lessons. Mr. Fennell is so kind but quite firm. Firmness is what Wake needs."

"He needs his behind warmed," said Renny.

"He'll talk of anything but his lessons," complained Meg. "And he won't sit down. He stands leaning on my shoulder, playing with my hair or my earrings. How can I teach him when he won't listen?"

"I'll see Mr. Fennell about him." Then he added, reflectively—"Piers is a fine healthy boy. No trouble with him. I wish Eden were more like him."

"Oh, I wouldn't have Eden different. I'm sure he has a brilliant future ahead of him. Uncle Ernest is convinced he will."

"I wish I were."

"Think of the poems he's had accepted by magazines—and he not yet twenty-three."

"Poetry and law—what a combination!"

"Has he read you any of his poems lately?"

"No. But Uncle Ernest showed me one about a door

in a wall. To tell the truth I thought it rather silly and very obscure."

"Oh, I love that one and the one about trees. Here he comes—and Finch too. They have walked from the station. How the day flies!"

"Yes, and I still have things to do."

The two youths were carrying their books and their hair was blown by the wind. Against it Finch held his head down but Eden was looking up into the treetops. Neither saw Meg and Renny till they were near by. She called out:

"Hello, boys! What a lovely day it's been. Did you have a good day?"

"A hell of a day," returned Eden. "They had the heat on and I was roasted—boiled—suffocated."

"We had no heat at school," said Finch, "and I was frozen."

"What a shame," said Meg to both of them. "Do go to Mrs. Wragge and she will give you a nice cup of tea. It cools and it warms, you know."

"Thanks, no," they murmured sulkily.

"What a pair," laughed Renny. "Come over to the stables with me and I will give you some exercise."

But they did not intend to be drawn into this. They turned with one accord and a muttered something about study to be done and went toward the house. Inside Finch clattered straight to the basement kitchen to get something to eat. Eden went through the hall and out of the side door. He stood concealed, till he saw Meg return indoors and Renny go to the stables. Then he followed the path past the orchard, across a stubble field, and entered the wood.

Here the wind had lost its power. Scarcely could it stir the pine needles that lay on the ground, but it whistled through the highest branches like a wind at sea. The golden evening sky bent above them and now and then a pine cone fell. Eden's mind was weighted with the accumulation of the day—the voices of the lecturers, the faces of the other students, the smell of the overheated air, the sound of shuffling feet and coughing, the return home by train with young Finch sitting opposite and obviously taking a cold. The air beneath the pines was delicious. He drank it to the depths of his lungs and held it. "For all my dreams of the south," he thought, "I am a northerner." A flurry of snow fell from a sudden cloud and he raised his face to it. It was the first of the season and lasted only a few minutes, then there was the clear gold again, and a flock of blue jays moving southward above the treetops.

The two first lines of a poem he had conceived in the night before came into his mind, but the third line eluded him. It had been clear enough while he had been dressing that morning but now it was mingled with the prosaic happenings of the day. He stood for a little, motionless, trying to recall it. He tried passionately to draw it back to him, as though his future happiness depended on it, and at last he did. Yet after his first relief he was disappointed in it. He had felt that it was one of the best things he had written. Now, declaiming it aloud, it sounded less impressive. Still it was good—all but one word. He tried other words as he strode along but none quite satisfied him. He found it difficult to concentrate. Then, abruptly, before his mind's eye, he saw the little form of his bank deposit book. It obliterated all else. Worse still, he found himself willing. Willing to be dragged—no, not *dragged* but *drugged*—by the entrancing figures written therein. He experienced a feeling of shame that this should be so, then thought—"It is not the wonder of possession that holds me, but the thought of what it can do for me—free me from this study of law which I hate."

He had not realized that he had come out of the pine wood and was already on the path that led across a pasture field to the country road. Then he remembered that not since the spring had he walked on this road. That was the day when he and Finch had discovered the felling of the two silver birches by Noah Binns. He was in a mood to look morbidly on the place where they had stood and to picture them in their autumn beauty fluttering their thousand delicate golden leaves.

Now he stood before the white picket fence staring somberly at the dry lawn, from which even their stumps had been removed. The blinds of the house were drawn and Noah Binns was raking the dead leaves into a tremulous dry mound. When he saw Eden he clumped across the grass plot to his side with a peculiar bending at the knees, as though he were trying to avoid a creaking board on a floor.

Eden gave a dramatic gesture toward the place where the young trees had stood.

"I'm glad you've taken the stumps out," he said. "They were a sickening sight. I hope Mr. Warden is satisfied."

Noah grinned, showing his black teeth. "He's satisfied, all right."

"Did the grass do well? I hope not."

"Do well? No. He would have a load of manure dug in, though I warned him what would happen. And happen it did. That manure was full of weed seeds and up they sprung and choked the grass." Noah leant against the fence in silent laughter.

"Serve him right."

Suddenly sober Noah said—"There's two ways of lookin' at that. He wanted room for scope and them trees hindered him."

"I say it serves him right and you may tell him I said so."

"It ain't possible."

"Why, Noah, have you suddenly turned polite?"

"It ain't possible—because he's dead."

Eden drew back *"Dead?"* The thought of death was horrible to him.

"Yeh." There was triumph in Noah Binn's grin, for he had a relish for the thought of death. "The weeds killed him."

"When?"

"We buried him today."

"Poor man."

Noah gripped the pointed pickets of the fence in both hands and bowed, as though to destiny. He said:

"That man wanted room for scope. The two trees hindered him. He took their lives and the weeds took his."

"You mean to say he felt so badly?"

"See here, young feller, how old are you?"

"Twenty-two."

"You ain't found out yet what it is to be hindered. You don't understand."

"Oh, don't I?"

"You wait till you're that man's age and longing for scope. Every morning he'd take one sorrowful look at them weeds, then shut hisself up for the rest of the day."

"Did he ever say he wished he hadn't cut down the trees?"

"Not he. He sort of blamed them for all his misery."

"Well, Noah, let's hope he'll find room for scope now."

"There's one thing he'll have," said Noah, "and that's plenty good grass in the graveyard." He watched with contemplative gaze Eden's figure recross the field and disappear among the pines. Then he returned to his raking of the leaves with a muttered—"Dang him."

15.

The Falling Stocks

EDEN HAD FOR SOME TIME led a double life. He was the law student who could, when occasion demanded, talk quite earnestly of his studies and make pretence of being ambitious to become Mr. Justice Whiteoak. Yet he never seriously believed that that life, so foreign to his nature, could really claim him. There would appear some way of escape—a door in the wall, beyond which would lie the garden of his desire. Once let his poems be collected between covers and he would open the door and be gone from the study of law for ever. But now he had entered on a third life—the life of the mining promoter. If things went on as they were with him . . . but when he tried to picture what was opening up before him, he could not think clearly. His imagination became a kaleidoscope of fantastic shapes and bright colors. He would lie on his back in a delicious languor, relaxed in the supreme indolence that only youth can know.

Yet there were times when he was troubled not a little by the manner in which the Indigo Lake Mine had pressed in upon his imagination. Poems were begun in fervent fancy but left unfinished because thought of rising stocks took possession of him. Worse still the other investors under that roof were continually desirous of discussing the condition of the market with him. With an air of almost overpowering secrecy Lady Buckley would draw him into her room and, in a contralto whisper, inquire if the stock were still rising.

"A little," he would say. "You were lucky to buy when

you did. Still, the price is not prohibitive, and if you would care to buy—"

"No more—no more. I am quite satisfied. I just want to be sure I am safe."

"Nothing could be safer, Aunt Augusta."

Then she would say—"I do feel rather selfish in keeping this so *secret*."

"Don't worry. The others would probably object. I'm sure Renny would."

"Foolish young man that he is, when he so often finds it difficult to make ends meet."

"I shall soon be off his hands."

"I do hope you are applying yourself *strenuously* to your studies."

"Oh, I am."

"I saw your light burning late last night when I went to investigate a rattling window."

Eden tried to look the dedicated student.

Lady Buckley said—"But you must have plenty of rest, dear, for your health's sake."

"I'm strong enough, Aunty."

Then his sister would corner him with—"Let's calculate just how much I've made, Eden. Tell me just what my stocks are worth today." Her smile would be extraordinarily sweet, as she contemplated the rise in her fortunes. "There's no reason," she asked, "is there, why I should not make a great deal more?"

"None whatever."

"What fun—you and I having this secret!"

"Great fun." All these secrets were beginning to weigh on him. But what need he care when he had sloughed off the irritating skin of law and was loitering free in Rome?

As though she read his thoughts, she asked—"How much have you made out of this?"

He gave her the amount he had received as commission on her investment.

Meg opened her very blue eyes wide. "You must take care of it, Eden. A very nice little nest egg. And *so* easily earned."

He returned her look crossly, she could not think why.

Dilly seemed to have forgotten her investment. She was absorbed by two things, her preparation for the horse show and her pursuit of Renny. Between the two, the rest of the family saw very little of her, excepting when he was present. She was almost always in riding clothes and could talk of nothing but the behavior of her horse. She still laughed rather more than Lady Buckley thought suitable, her complexion became more dazzling than ever and there was an added gleam in her eyes when they rested on the master of the house. Her pursuit of him hung about her like a too heavy perfume. Even Finch noticed it and felt both fascinated and repelled. He was not aware of the pursuit but her concentration on the horse show did not account for the intensifying of her personal attributes. He would stare at Dilly, with his mouth open, till his aunt would catch his eye, shut her own mouth firmly and nod to him to do the same.

For some reason Piers was rather touching to Eden, in his complete trust in Eden's perspicacity. He handed over almost all he earned and did not even ask for a receipt. "Why, he's a child," thought Eden, "no more than a trusting child. That's what's the matter with us all, I believe. We're too trusting. We've been too sheltered. We're all of us, even the uncles, clinging to our innocence—clinging to our childish idea of a family."

With Nicholas and Ernest he was most at ease in these days, for, secure in the privacy of their rooms he could indulge in happy forecasts of the future. He had given up all study. When he retired to his room to work it was only a pretence. He idled, he wrote a little poetry and read much.

One evening he carried a book to Nicholas's room and rapped.

"Come in," Nicholas sang out.

"Here's a book I think you'd enjoy." Eden put *South Wind* into his uncle's hand. "Are you busy? May I come in?"

"Thanks for the book. Alluring title—on a night of north wind. Upon my word, I can't remember a windier fall. Sit down, Eden. I have been waiting to see you alone. Have a drink?"

"Thanks." Eden bent to pat Nip, curled up on the bed, who rose, arched his back like a cat, and uttered a complaining yawn.

"Hates this weather," said Nicholas, pouring the drinks. "Catch a spider, Nip!"

The little dog hurled himself from the bed, raced round and round the room, snuffling in the corners and barking hysterically.

"Gives him exercise," said Nicholas. "Good for him."

They sat down with their drinks and Nicholas then asked—"I suppose you have lots of work to do?"

"Well, not much tonight."

His uncle looked at him keenly. "Working very hard?"

"Not particularly." There was a defensive note in Eden's voice. He knew well how he was wasting his time but he could, in these days of high hope, endure no probings from his elders.

"Well, well," said Nicholas, settling himself in his chair and gathering Nip onto his knees, "I idled too, when I was your age. Regretted it afterward—though not greatly. But now it's different. A young man needs to be keen, doesn't he? How are the stocks?"

"Fine."

"Do you know what I've decided to do?"

"No idea."

"Sell out. I shall make a good profit and not run the risk of a drop in prices. By Jove, I don't want to lose anything."

"No danger, Uncle Nick. But if you want to take your profit now, I'll see Kronk tomorrow and he'll fix it for you."

Nicholas smiled up at Eden. "This affair of the Indigo Lake Mine has given us a deal of excitement," he said. "It's years since I have done any speculating, and then not very successfully. But this—well, as I say, I think I shall take the profit and be satisfied. Now, if I were Ernest, I'd go on and on, till I should probably end by losing."

"Not in this, Uncle Nick. But you are right, I dare say, to sell out. You've made a tidy sum and you're satisfied."

The following day Eden went to Kronk's office to arrange for the sale of his uncle's shares. The broker had a stenographer with him but he asked her to leave, and when Eden and he were left alone, turned to him with his cozy smile. Mr. Kronk, although well turned out and well groomed as to hair and fingernails, always had a slightly soiled look, as though no number of baths could get him quite clean.

He said—"I sort of hope you are not here to talk business but just to have a nice quiet drink. I've been fairly swamped by business the last few days. Americans ring me up and buy Indigo Lake by phone. What wouldn't I give for a rest." And he sighed, as though for the unattainable.

But when Eden told him he had come to arrange for the sale of Nicholas's shares, his eyes narrowed and he looked almost disapproving. He said:

"Your uncle can sell if he wants to. Certainly. Certainly he can. But I really don't advise it. He'd make a fine profit but not as good as if he held on a little longer. Have a drink, won't you?"

"No thanks. Why would it be better for him to hold on?"

Mr. Kronk had all the physical habits of self-confidence. He smiled into Eden's eyes. "Because," he said, "the price has dropped a little, owing to fluctuations all through the market. Wall Street is really at the bottom of it." And his smile became faintly reproving, as though if he had Wall Street on the spot he would be quite firm with it.

Eden was quick to take alarm. He asked—"Do you think there is danger of a further drop?"

"Possibly a very slight decline. But don't worry. Tell your uncles and your aunts and your cousins—that's Gilbert and Sullivan, isn't it?—not to worry. Indigo Lake will take care of us all. Are you yourself thinking of investing something more?" He looked at Eden in a way that made him feel rather like a specimen under a magnifying glass.

Eden had still in his possession one thousand, six hundred and fifty dollars which he had got on commission. He had intended this very day to invest this, as he had already invested his earlier earnings.

"Now is the time," Mr. Kronk said, "when the price has fallen a bit."

"It's still high."

"And will go much higher. I think I'm safe in saying that inside the next three months it will reach the peak— and remain there. You can put in your money and forget about it."

"Well, I'll think about it," said Eden. "I haven't very much, you know."

"Every little helps," beamed Mr. Kronk. "But do just as you like. It doesn't matter to me."

The telephone on his desk rang. He took up the receiver and a very brief but somewhat cryptic conversation took place, during which Eden decided that he did not like the look of Mr. Kronk, that indeed he had one of the most objectionable faces he had ever seen and that he should like to take hold of it, as one might a face of putty, and mould it into a different shape.

"Long distance from Detroit," said the broker. "A client wanting to invest another five thousand. He chose a good time."

"Just the same, I think I shall wait for a bit."

"Please yourself," Mr. Kronk said curtly, and his expression was rather like that of an animal trainer who senses a rebellious spirit in one of his troupe.

At the first opportunity that evening, Nicholas drew Eden into the empty library. He asked—"Well, did you get the thing settled?"

"No, Uncle Nick. I went to see Kronk and he says you should wait for a bit. You see the stock has dropped a few points and you will make a bigger profit if you wait till it goes up again."

"I'm quite satisfied with the profit I've made. I want to sell. So please go to him to-morrow and say so."

"Very well."

"No matter what objections this man Kronk makes, tell him that I want to sell. Mind you, I'm very pleased by what he has done for me. But—I'm running no risks. I'm going to sell."

Eden found Mr. Kronk in his office on the following day and gave him the message from Nicholas. Eden half expected the broker to try again to persuade him to use his influence with Nicholas against the sale. But no— Mr. Kronk smilingly agreed. There was nothing he liked better, he said, than giving people their own way, guiding them when he could but always, above all things, anxious to see them mentally at ease. As for himself, he never worried. He had his own philosophy of life and that kept him steady through all vicissitudes. His greenish eyes had a soothing, almost hypnotic power. He asked—"What about that little nest egg of yours? Don't you think you would be sensible to invest it now, while the price is down? Remember, it will rise sharply in a few days."

Eden disliked the term "nest egg." It made him think of hens and he did not much like hens. Then something in him rose against being guided, though ever so gently, by Mr. Kronk. He said rather stiffly:

"I think I'll not invest anything more at present."

Mr. Kronk gave a little shrug. He said—"About your uncle's shares, I'll sell them tomorrow and send him a cheque."

16.

Wakefield's Day

WAKEFIELD HAD FELT VERY important when first he had gone to the Rectory for lessons from Mr. Fennell. On the whole, he had thought, it was rather nice being too delicate to go to school. He had seen Finch rushing off to catch the train on bitter winter mornings. He had seen him hugging the stove in the hall when he had returned home on bitter winter evenings. You could tell by that stove when winter had really come. In the spring it disappeared into the basement. The stovepipes were taken down and there was a great cleaning of walls and rugs. The hall seemed larger and the front door stood open, letting the outdoors into the house.

Now it was November and the stove once more dominated the hall. The dogs had welcomed it. But now, without warning, Indian summer had poured its blessing upon the countryside. The last of the bird migrants forgot that they were migrating and settled down to enjoy this respite from flight. They perched on the mountain ash trees and gorged themselves on those scarlet berries.

This delay in the onslaught of winter, this coy backward glance of summer, had a pleasant but relaxing effect on Wakefield. His legs seemed to weigh more and his head less. He meandered across the field, through which was the short cut to the Rectory, at a snail's pace, while his brain felt as light as a bit of thistledown. But there were pictures in it—of his grandmother giving him a kiss when he went to say good-bye while she was eating her porridge, a kiss that was a little milky. Then she had wiped his cheek on her table napkin. A picture of Mrs. Wragge, seen through the window of the basement kitchen, kneading bread. Pictures of horses—jumping, cantering, galloping—for in these last days before the show little else was talked of. Renny, Piers, and Dilly Warkworth were seldom seen out of their riding clothes. Nicholas and Ernest spent hours by the palings of the paddock where the horses were being schooled.

The satchel of books on Wakefield's shoulder seemed to grow heavier with each step. He wriggled out of it and dragged it along the ground after him for a change. By the time he had reached the fence at the edge of the field he noticed that the satchel had come open and he examined the contents to discover if anything were missing. Yes—the arithmetic was gone! He looked back across the field and thought he saw it but was not sure. Well, the ground was nice and dry. It would do the book no harm to lie there till his return.

He flattened himself on the ground and crawled under the fence and attained the road. The church on its knoll rose opposite him, the graveyard peaceful about it. He made up his mind that he would visit the graveyard on his way home. His parents, in Heaven, would be pleased to know that he visited their graves. Surely they would be pleased to see him going off to lessons every day—so studious, in spite of having a weak heart.

The door of the Rectory stood open and Wakefield entered without knocking, as he thought best, considering that he was late. He sat down at his desk in the library and swung his legs. It was some little time before the Rector appeared. He was wearing his surplice.

He apologized—"Sorry to keep you waiting, Wakefield, but I had a Communion service this morning. I wore my surplice across the yard because it must be laundered for Sunday."

"That's nice," said Wakefield, "because my grandmother is going to wear her new fur coat on Sunday."

"Fur coat," exclaimed Mr. Fennell, emerging from the surplice. "In weather like this? I'm afraid she'll be much too warm."

Wakefield emphatically shook his head. "Not my grandmother. If she wants to do a thing she'll be comfortable doing it."

"I think you are rather like your grandmother," said Mr. Fennell.

Wakefield was pleased. "Yes," he agreed, "except for the difference in our ages. There's ninety years between us."

The Rector looked at him speculatively. He said—"If you live to her age, I wonder what sort of world this will be. The year 2013—hm."

"I hear my uncles say there's less fun in it even now."

"There are more important things than fun, Wake. There are your lessons. Where is your arithmetic book?"

Wakefield diligently searched his satchel. "I can't find it," he sighed. "I'm afraid my brother Finch has borrowed it. He's very backward in arithmetic and it helps him to do problems out of my little book. Shall I go home and see if I can find it?"

"No, no, no. We'll do geography. Where is the map of Ontario I asked you to draw?"

Wakefield instantly produced it.

Mr. Fennell examined it, while stroking his untidy brown beard. "Why, this is beautiful," he said. "But why is it signed Ernest Whiteoak?"

Wakefield ran his hand through his hair. He said—"I asked my uncle to help me a little with it and he got so interested that he finished it, and he's used to signing everything he draws and I didn't like to stop him."

"I see. How much of the map is your own work, Wakefield?"

"The lake, sir. I did all of the lake. I drew that little sailboat on it, the way they did in old maps. My uncle liked that."

"Well, I hope that next time he will leave you to do your own work. Now let us settle down to learn some history."

The rest of the morning was passed quite agreeably but Wakefield was glad when it was over and he was free. Mr. Fennell gave him a large greenish-gold pippin to take with him, but as he did not very much like pippins he fed it to the cow that was in the little field next the church. She seemed to have great difficulty in swallowing it and made such crude choking noises that Wakefield hurried on.

He thought he would go into the churchyard for a little and possibly even into the church. He never had been inside it alone and he thought this might be a good morning for inspecting it. The gate that led into the churchyard closed with rather an ominous click, and there seemed to be a good many steps to mount before he reached the level of the churchyard. He gave no more than a glance at the family plot where lay buried Captain Whiteoak, his son Philip and Philip's two wives, also several infant Whiteoaks who had preceded Eden in Philip's second marriage. Wakefield knew the inscription on the granite plinth. He knew the names on each of the several headstones. There was nothing there to delay his intention of entering the church. A spiral of smoke was ascending like incense from a mound of leaves near the church and a rake lying on the ground beside showed that someone had been at work. Wakefield wondered if that someone had gone into the church and he moved very quietly on tiptoe and gently pushed open the door. He closed the door as gently behind him and hesitated a moment in the porch.

Certainly there was someone in the church. Wakefield could make out soft shuffling noises and then an odd metallic sound. Fear quickened his heartbeat. He was ready to turn and fly. Then curiosity overcame fear and he opened the inner door, just a little way, and peeped in. The church looked brighter than usual and strangely smaller, though there was no congregation.

But who was moving about? Yes, there was someone, at the very back of the church, so near that door that Wakefield could almost have touched him. It was disappointing to discover that it was Noah Binns, and Wakefield was about to steal away when he became fascinated by what Noah was doing. He had taken the poor box off the wall and was cautiously shaking it above one curved earthy palm. Then, out of the slot, a coin dropped—then another—and another. Noah peered at them, rather disappointed looking, but after a firmer shaking a fifty cent piece plopped out, and then two quarters. There was not much money in the poor box, but it looked a good deal to Wakefield and he envied Noah Binns for having come by such wealth with so little effort. He opened the door wider to have a good look at him.

Noah must have felt that he was being watched, for he gave a start. Two of the coins fell from his palm and rolled under the nearest pews. His eyes and Wakefield's met in a concentrated stare. Then Noah pocketed the coins and, still holding the box in one hand, shuffled forward and caught the little boy by the shoulder. He dragged him inside the church and shook him right off his feet. Wakefield would have fallen but that he was held up in that angry grasp.

"Let me go," he said and would have screamed but Noah now spoke soothingly and held him quietly.

"Come, come," he said, "don't you be scared. I won't hurt you. Sure I won't."

Wakefield saw that Noah was even more frightened than he. His teeth were knocking together with fright. The poor box was rattling in his hand.

"Let me go," Wakefield repeated, in a quite different tone, this time one of authority and accusation. "I'll tell what you did—see if I don't!"

Noah's face looked all mouth. He said—"It ain't the way you think. I'll tell you how it was. I come into the church to fix a window that was loose and I noticed a coin stuck in the slot of this here box. It was a fifty-cent piece. Well, that ain't right, I thought, and I tried to push it in. It wouldn't go in. Then I thought I'd shake it out but a few little ones come first. See? That's the way it was."

Wakefield said nothing. He just stood speechless, his large eyes fixed on Noah's scared face. A tiny brown field mouse moved across the matting of the aisle. Bright splashes of color fell from the stained-glass window, memorial to Captain Whiteoak.

Noah said—"You just come in time to see me put all the money back in the box. P'raps you'd like to put it back for me, eh?"

"All right."

Noah dived into his pocket, brought out some of the coins—coppers, five and ten cent pieces. He held the box, more steadily now, while Wakefield dropped them one by one through the slot.

Now Noah was grinning. "There y'are," he said. "Now we'll put the box back on the wall, eh?"

"Where's the fifty cents and the two quarters?" asked Wakefield.

Now Noah was laughing. "Well, I am a forgetful feller," he said. "Did you ever see the like? To forget them quarters!" He took them from the depths of his pocket and gave them to Wakefield. "Here y'are! Put them in."

Wakefield dropped them through the slot. "Where's the fifty-cent piece?" he asked.

Noah was shaking with laughter. "Darned if I won't forget my own head next!" he said. He recovered the large silver coin and Wakefield restored it to the box.

"There are some on the floor," he said.

They went down on their hands and knees but Wakefield could not find the money. He was by this time more interested in finding the little mouse.

Noah, first on his feet once more, said—"I found them coppers and put them back. Coppers—that's what they was."

"Oh," said Wakefield, from under a pew, "just coppers."

"I'm going to make you a present," said Noah, sucking the air through a broken tooth, "out of my own money, see?" He took two quarters from his pocket and put them into Wakefield's palm. "That's for being a good boy and helping me with my work."

Wakefield stared astonished at the money for a moment, then his fingers closed on it. "Thanks," he murmured, "and when you want any more help let me know."

Noah's attitude became suddenly firm, almost menacing. He said—"Don't you go talkin' about what happened here."

"No," agreed Wakefield, not liking the look on Noah's face.

"I don't want no enigmas to get around about me."

"No." he backed away a few steps.

Noah raised his voice. "This place is an awful place for talk," he said, "and I don't want no enigmas about me. If I hear of any, I'll know who done it. I'll get even with them. Nothing could be fairer than that."

Wakefield turned and ran out of the church. "Goodbye," he called out and never stopped running till he was in the road. He then slowed down to a trot, adjusting his school satchel more comfortably on his shoulders, then examined the two bright coins in his hand. One of these had the King's head on it. The other the head of Queen Victoria. Both were good to spend.

He stood to look in at the window of the one little shop in the road. It was on beyond the blacksmith shop and its window was simply the window of the cottage. In the window stood a table and on it were displayed bottles of ginger ale, orange squash and lemon soda, as well as a pan of homemade buns and two pies. Inside, on the counter, were chocolate bars and candies and fancy biscuits.

The bell gave its small but peremptory clang when he opened the door. He thought it was rather a mistake to have placed the bell there, as otherwise the customer might have examined what was offered for sale at leisure and even sampled the goods. But now Mrs. Brawn, redfaced from her oven, bustled in and inquired what he would have. He chose lemon soda, with marshmallow biscuits, which came to ten cents, and ten cents worth of mixed candies. These last were put into a paper bag to carry home, but he stood by the counter, nibbling the biscuits and taking the drink through a straw. Mrs. Brawn knew him well and liked a little chat with him. When he had paid she inquired:

"How's the lessons going?"

"I'm doing Latin," he answered with dignity.

"Latin! Well, I never! At your age!"

"Mr. Fennell thinks they don't begin it soon enough in the schools. My brother Finch didn't begin it till he was twelve. By the time I'm that age I shall be able to converse in it. Do you know what converse means?"

"Well, I should hope so. I've had some education. It means have a conversation. Let's hear you say some Latin."

He drew up the last of the lemon soda with a sputtering sound before he said—"*Amo, amas, amat, amamus, amatus, amant.*"

"Well, I never," declared Mrs. Brawn. "Whatever does it mean?"

"It's different ways of saying I love you."

She gaped, then frowned. "I call that shameful," she said. "Putting such ideas into the head of a little boy. The Rector ought to be ashamed of himself. Time enough for you to talk about different ways of loving when you're twenty."

"I guess that Mr. Fennell thinks as I'm not likely to live till I'm twenty, I may as well begin early."

Pity filled Mrs. Brawn's eyes with tears. "My, it's too bad you're so delicate."

"Yes, isn't it?" he agreed, then added—"I think I'll have a bottle of ginger ale now. And will you please charge it?"

As she set it in front of him she reminded him—"You owe me ten cents already. Don't forget that."

He applied himself to the ginger ale for a moment before answering—"I won't forget. And there'll be plenty of money in our house after the horse show. My brother Renny will take a lot of prizes, you know."

"Ah, he's a fine figure on horseback. I see him pass most every day and that lady visitor too. I guess there's lots of talk about horses in your house just now."

"There's nothing else. Everybody's going to the show every night excepting me and I'm going twice. And even my grandmother talks of going because of her new fur coat."

"Land's sake—would she go?"

"We're trying to make her understand that church is better for her—but it's not easy."

With such amiable conversation his visit to the little shop ended and he found himself again crossing the field on his way home. With mild surprise he came upon his arithmetic textbook, little the worse for lying there all the morning. He replaced it in his schoolbag and trotted on and at last into the house. There he encountered Wragge, who said:

"You'll be eating in the kitchen, young shaver. The

three gentlemen 'as all gone into town. Also Miss Wark-worth. Your grandmother 'as gone to lunch with the Miss Laceys, and your aunt and Miss Whiteoak gone with 'er. And a solid two hours it took to get her dressed and into the carriage. Wot 'as come over 'er I don't know but she gets livelier every day. She says to me yesterday, 'Rags, I'm making money, I am.' Fancy that, at her age."

Down in the kitchen Mrs. Wragge asked Wakefield what he would like for lunch.

"A sandwich, with plenty of mustard, and a piece of pumpkin pie."

"That ain't much of a dinner."

"I'm not very hungry."

"It's all the studying," cried Mrs. Wragge. "That clergy-man works him too hard."

"What did you learn today?" asked Rags.

Wakefield perched himself on a corner of the kitchen table. He said—"Mr. Fennell wore his surplice today."

"When did he wear it?"

"All the while he taught me."

The Wragges gave each other a look. "Never 'eard of such a thing," said he. "And why did Mr. Fennell do that, I'd like to know?"

"Just to look holy," replied Wake.

The cook screamed with laughter. "He must be crazy. No wonder you ain't hungry."

"Was he teaching you out of the Bible something spe-cial?" asked Rags.

The sandwich was ready and Wakefield bit into it with interest. He then said—"The first question Mr. Fennell asked me was, what is the difference between a hackney and a hunter."

"The man's out of his mind," said the cook.

"And did you know?" asked Rags.

"Of course I knew."

"And what was his next question?"

"He asked me, what are the points of a harness horse."

"He's demented," said the cook.

"I'll bet you didn't know," said Rags.

Wakefield said, through a mouthful of sandwich—"He

must lift his feet high enough to kick flies off his belly. He mustn't plait or dish or go wide behind."

Mrs. Wragge said—"This whole thing is made up. I don't believe a word of it. Come now, eat your pie and move on. I want to clean up my kitchen."

Wakefield ate half his piece of pie as he walked slowly through the hall. In the library he presented the other half to Boney, the parrot. He then sat down to consider the fact that he had the house to himself. He could not remember this having happened before. He savored the largeness and silence of the house for a short while, then with the slow majestic walk of complete possession, he set out to explore.

Boney, his beak plastered with pumpkin pie, looked after him quizzically, tried to speak but could utter no sound.

Wakefield thought he would begin at the very top, in Eden's room. The door of this room was usually kept shut, excepting when Eden was in bed, for he liked to sleep in a draft. Wakefield went in and closed the door behind him. The window was wide open and it was pleasant up there among the treetops. He opened the drawer of the desk and saw Eden's latest verses, written in pencil on pages from a notebook. There were poems in typescript too and several printed slips beginning with the words—"The Editors have read your manuscript with interest but regret . . ." It was very dull, with the exception of the poems which had been printed in magazines. These Eden had cut out and pasted in an ordinary school scribbler. Wakefield liked achievement and these printed poems made him feel proud of Eden, as he knew Meg and the uncles were.

He sprinkled his hair with a nice-smelling toilet water that was on the wash stand. He then strolled into the bedroom where Piers and Finch slept. He found nothing of interest there but half a chocolate bar which he nibbled, then liked so well he finished it.

He slid down the banister to the floor below. He had suddenly remembered his savings bank which Meg kept in her room and the twenty-five-cent piece he had been given by Noah Binns. He found the bank in Meg's clothes cupboard. It was in the shape of a little house and you dropped the coin down the chimney. But first he turned the bank upside down and gave it a good shaking to see if it would render up its contents, as had the poor box. The bank, however, was obdurate. Nothing came through the chimney. He frowned and said aloud—"No enigmas, please."

Suddenly, inexplicably, he decided against putting the money in the bank. He returned it to his pocket and the bank to the clothes cupboard. It was wonderful having the house to himself. He ran along the passage, waving his arms and chanting—"No enigmas, please." He threw his leg over the banister and slid to the hall below. As he arrived on the newel post he was startled to hear the piano being softly strummed. He scrambled down and glided to the door of the drawing room and put his eye to the keyhole. He could make out the figure of Finch seated at the piano. Finch—of all people—who couldn't play a note! But the strumming was soft and rather pretty till it became a torrent of strange and noisy chords.

Wakefield opened the door and went in. He stood just behind Finch till his hands rested on the keyboards, then he said, in a highfalutin tone:

"*Very* nice, my boy. *Very* nice indeed."

Finch wheeled on the seat and faced him.

Wakefield produced the silver coin. "Here's a quarter for you," he said grandly, "for playing such a pretty tune."

"I like your cheek," said Finch. "Who do you think you are?"

"Your Uncle Wakefield, dear boy."

"Where did you get the quarter?"

"Out of the church poor box."

"You little liar."

"No enigmas, please. Do you want the quarter?"

Finch took it from him, caught him by the arm, and put the coin down inside his collar. He said—"That's how much I want it. And look here, don't mention to anyone that I was at the piano, will you? I know I can't play but—well, don't mention it."

Wakefield could feel the coin slide down his spine. He

wriggled and it appeared from beneath his shorts. He pocketed it and said, eager to be on a confidential footing with Finch—"All right. I won't say, Finch. Let's have a secret together. Let's do something together. You know the sort of thing."

"Like what?"

"Let's see what Gran keeps in the small drawer in the wardrobe."

"I've never noticed it."

"I have, and yesterday she shut it quickly when I peeped in. Let's go and see—*together!*"

Finch leaped past him, then halted. "Where is she?"

"At the Laceys' with Meg and Aunt Augusta."

Finch opened the door of the bedroom. Wakefield pressed close beside. He said—"I believe it's a skull."

"We shouldn't be doing this," said Finch. But he could not stop himself. He would have this secret with Wake, so that Wake would not tell of his piano strumming. Of late he was ridiculously sensitive to teasing.

He drew open the drawer.

"That's what I thought was a skull," Wake whispered. "It's just a big new sponge. And there's the sachet Miss Pink gave her, and there's the little box with the Chinamen on the lid."

"We've no business to look in here," said Finch ashamed. Then something caught his eyes. On the very bottom of the drawer lay the certificate of the shares in the Indigo Lake Mine. It was the word "Indigo" which held him. He remembered his grandmother's cryptic uttering of that word and how Eden, more than once, had appeared embarrassed by it. But it was none of his affair and he was about to shut the drawer when a particularly hard head was thrust between those of the two boys.

"What are you up to?" Renny demanded.

"Oh, nothing—nothing at all," stammered Finch.

Wakefield added—"We're were just having a little look at my grandmother's treasures."

"You ought to be ashamed of yourselves, and I have a mind to take a stick to your backs." Then he saw the certificate. He bent lower for a moment to look at it, then sharply shut the drawer.

"Don't come in here again," he said, "when Gran's not here. I'm ashamed of you."

"You looked at it too," said Wakefield. "What does it mean?"

From the library came Boney's voice screaming: "Gold—you old devil! Pieces of eight!"

17.

After the Show

NICHOLAS WAITED, NOT WITH anxiety, but with some impatience, for his cheque from the sale of his Indigo Lake shares. But like all those at Jalna his mind was filled by the excitement of the horse show. Renny's horses were doing well. He himself was awarded the prize for the best performance in high jumping in the hunter class. Dilly Warkworth achieved a third prize. Piers, riding polo ponies, carried off several. One of their Jersey cows won a prize and a team of their Percherons received honorable mention. By the time the show was over and the animals restored safely to their stalls everyone was satisfied and almost sated. The weather had turned wet and the old car with its buttoned-down sides did not keep out the wind and scarcely kept out the wet. The rag with which Renny wiped the misted windshield was often in his hand. Those who had been to the show alighted from the car rather stiff and dazed. The trees, blacker than the darkness, were sucking up the moisture into their roots. The dogs came barking into the porch to welcome them. Rags could hardly wait to hear the news of the day's success or failure. He himself went twice to the show, once taking his wife with him. On the night when he went by himself he got tight and did not show up at Jalna till the next day.

After the return, those of the family who had been to the show had a late supper. They sat long about the table, relishing the cold roast beef, the cheese, the homemade bread, the crisp sticks of celery. A decanter of wine and one of whiskey stood on the damask tablecloth, catching and holding the light. Even through two closed doors, the talk and laughter would rouse the grandmother and she would thump on the floor with her stick, and to the one who went to her, would exclaim:

"Tell me who won. I don't want to be left out of things."

She liked best to have Renny answer her call, because from him she had the show in greatest detail. He would sit on the side of her bed relating the prowess of each of his horses in turn. He would excite her till her old eyes would shine and she would say—"I can smell the tanbark. I can hear the band but—Lord, you should see the shows in Ireland!"

"I have seen them, Gran, and they're no better."

"Ah, that's the country for horses and the hunt. You should have seen me when I was a girl, and my horse scrambling over the walls and me clinging to him for dear life. It was at the hunt in Ireland that I met my dear Philip."

"Why, no, Gran, you met him first in India."

"So I did. So I did. What a bad memory I'm getting. To think I would forget that—of all things. But now I remember how I'd tell him of it and he'd say he wished he'd been there. And now I imagine he was there, dear one! But you must tell me more about the show. How did that girl Dilly ride the mare?"

"She should—the mare, I mean—have had a first but the way Dilly handled her it was a third. Now I'll show you what I mean." And he took a small chair and perched himself on it and bobbed up and down, beating it with an imaginary whip, so that his grandmother pulled her nightcap over one eye and laughed so loud that they heard her in the dining room. Ernest came to the door and put his head in and said—"All this excitement is bad for you, Mamma. You'll not sleep."

"Mind your own business, Ernest," she retorted. "I want to see this show out."

Boney took his head from under his wing and stared at them sleepily with one eye shut.

Adeline Whiteoak did indeed lie awake for a long while

but her thoughts were pleasant. Indeed she had no actual thoughts, but a succession of pictures moved through her mind—she counted the leaping horses as one might count sheep to put one's self to sleep. She saw the scarlet coats of the Mounted Police. She heard the band and saw the applauding crowd. In the dim night light she saw her eldest grandson bouncing on the chair, his head the color of the autumn leaves that were blown against her window that day. She heard laughter from the other room. The flying leaves, the leaping horses were mingled in her dreams.

The last upstairs were Dilly Warkworth and Renny. At the foot of the stairs she said:

"I know you are not pleased with me."

"What makes you think that?"

"I've never ridden so badly. I could kill myself."

"Nonsense. You won a ribbon."

"A third! It should have been a first."

"Yes, it should," he agreed.

"And I tried so hard—for your sake. Do you hate me?"

"It's time you went to bed. You're tired out."

She put her face against the newel post and began to cry. He just touched the nape of her neck, which was extremely pretty. That was enough. She twined both arms about his neck and drew his face down to hers. He kissed her without feeling, but he thought he never had seen her so attractive. She looked tired and pale, yet somehow younger and rather touching. He noticed that she had long eyelashes and charming little ears.

He said—"You're not to worry about tonight. You're to go to bed. You're tired."

"We are made for each other," she said breathlessly. "You know that. We can't help coming together, can we?"

He stroked his left eyebrow with his forefinger. "I don't see why," he said.

"We are so much alike. We love the same things."

"We don't love each other."

"I do. I adore the ground you walk on."

"I'm not the marrying sort," he said. "If that's what you have in mind."

"I have never thought of anything else."

"You surprise me," he said, "and that's putting it mildly."

"What did you think I was?"

"Oh, rather lighthearted. You're always saying what fun things are."

She made her large eyes larger. "I have had tragedy in my life."

"Girls are disappointed in love every day."

"Not girls with the deep feelings I have."

"Come, come, get to your bed."

"Bed—bed—why do you keep talking of bed?"

He gave her a shrewd look. "You have a funny mind, Dilly."

"I feel faint," she said. "Will you get me something to drink?"

"You've had enough to drink."

"What a brute you are! I ought to hate you. But I don't—I don't—I don't—"

The repetition became smothered in sobs. Her head moved about, feeling for his shoulder.

"My God!" he exclaimed in exasperation, "I wish you'd go to bed."

"I'm faint. I simply couldn't—couldn't walk up those stairs."

She did look pale.

He moved behind her, took her by the arms, and half carried, half pushed her up the stairs. He opened the door of her room, which was across the passage from his own, and put her inside. Still she clung to him. She had ceased her crying and now, half laughing, she said, on a deep cajoling note—"Let's get engaged. It would be such fun."

"Dilly," he said mildly, "I will go to bed with you if you want me to, but I'm damned if I'll marry you."

Her answer was a sharp slap on the face.

"You devil," she said.

He returned—"Some men enjoy being slapped by a woman. I don't happen to be one of them."

As though she were the one who had been hurt, Dilly again broke into unrestrained weeping. The door of Lady Buckley's room opened and she, in a massive purple velvet dressing gown and her Queen Alexandra fringe done up in curling pins, bore down on them.

"Whatever is going on?" she demanded. "What has he done to you, Dilly?"

"Nothing."

"That's the trouble," said Renny.

Lady Buckley looked from one to the other with concentrated disapproval. She said—"I'm shocked to think that such a scene would be made over nothing." After a pause, she added—"I heard the slap. Who gave it and where?"

"She did," said Renny, "here." And he touched his cheek.

"This is disgraceful," said his aunt. "I shall remain here till I hear both your doors locked on the inside."

She stood planted, her curling pins detracting nothing from her dignity.

"Good-night, Aunty." Renny kissed her long sallow cheek and, with a swift glance at Dilly, disappeared into his room and locked the door behind him.

18.

The Bubble Burst

BEFORE EDEN LEFT FOR THE TRAIN Rags brought him a message from Nicholas. He said—"Your uncle would like to see you in his room just for a minute, sir."

Eden looked at his watch. "Good Lord—I have no time to spare. I shall miss my train." He darted up the stairs two steps at a time and appeared at Nicholas's bedside. His uncle was sitting up with a breakfast tray in front of him. His crest of iron-gray hair, his handsome profile, gave him dignity but he was not mindful of the toast crumbs on his chin.

Eden asked—"Is it about Indigo Lake, Uncle Nick?"

"Yes. I want you to find out why I haven't had my cheque."

"I will."

"Even if the stock has fallen I want to sell out. Make that Kronk fellow understand."

"I'm sure he has sold your shares. Probably you'll get your cheque today."

But the cheque did not come and Nicholas was hovering near the door when Eden and Finch appeared that evening. The horse show was over. Darkness settled in early. The two young brothers stamped off the snow in the porch, but still they brought a certain amount into the hall.

Eden said,—"It's a hell of a night. Why couldn't we have been met, I wonder."

"Wright had to take the car in for repairs."

"What we need is a new car."

"No chance of that. Finch, run upstairs like a good fellow and bring me my glasses. They're in my room. Bring Nip down too."

How good was the feel of home, thought Finch, to be in the warmth, to hear the sounds of home—his aunt's voice, reading aloud to Wakefield—his grandmother's laugh as she defeated Ernest at backgammon—Meg and Rags having a heated discussion as to the relative merits of two brands of silver polish. Their voices came from the dining room. Finch found the spectacles and discovered Nip curled up on his master's bed. The little dog rolled over, turning up his pink belly and making small grunts of protest. But Finch picked him up, kissed the top of his head, and rattled down the stairs with him. Nicholas and Eden were still in the hall.

Nicholas had asked—"Well, did you see him?"

"No, Uncle Nick. I telephoned both the office and the apartment but there was no answer. That was at noon. In the afternoon I went to the office. He wasn't there. Then I went to the apartment and found Mrs. Kronk. She told me he'd been called out of town. She was surprised by my being a bit urgent but I told her you were surprised by the delay in sending your cheque. She said she was sure it was in the post."

Nicholas ran his hand through his hair. "Well," he said, "if it doesn't arrive in the morning, I will go and see him myself."

"I wish you would."

"Here are your glasses, Uncle Nick, and here's Nip." Finch set the terrier on his feet and he, for some fancied insult, flew at the great woolly sheep dog, barking in rage. Good-humoredly the big dog moved away from the stove, but that was not enough. Nip gave him no peace till he went to the very end of the hall and sat himself there in complete isolation.

"Naughty fellow," said Nicholas. "Poor old Ben."

There was a fresh stamping in the porch and Renny and Piers entered.

"What a night," exclaimed Piers. "Winter."

"We had to walk from the station," Eden said in an aggrieved tone, "facing the wind."

"Oh, I walked farther than that."

"Facing the north wind?"

"Well, no."

Renny, from the shelter of his three brothers and his uncle, threw a wary glance into the drawing room. He saw Dilly perched on the arm of his grandmother's chair, watching the game. It was his first glimpse of her that day, for he had spent it with Maurice Vaughan. Dilly's face, in the light of the lamp and the heat of the open fire, was blazing pink. She wore a self-conscious smile, as of an actress acknowledging applause after a scene of tragedy.

His aunt, reading to Wakefield in the library, saw Renny through the door which stood ajar. She closed the book and said—"Wakefield, go to your brother Renny and tell him I wish to speak to him here. We can finish the story later."

The little boy, already becoming restive because Augusta's choice of books and his did not agree, ran gladly into the hall and tugged at Renny's sleeve. "Aunt Augusta wants you. Where have you been all day?"

"I've been with Maurice." He bent and kissed the child. "Have you been well? Did you go to the Rectory?"

"Yes and yes. Aunt Augusta wants you. Is it private? May I hear?"

Renny sighed. "It's private." He went into the library and shut the door. He stood with his back to it, like a man at bay.

"Well, Aunty?"

She said reproachfully—"You are making the last days of my visit very difficult for me."

He returned her fire at once. "You have made it difficult for me by bringing Dilly Warkworth here."

"She is a fine-looking girl and healthy. I thought something to the benefit of you might come out of the visit."

"Oh, Aunt Augusta, how could you? She's not at all my style."

She regarded him sternly. "That scene last night . . . why . . . I blush for you when I think of it."

He returned her look wryly, as though trying to discover the blush. He said—"I like to do the pursuing myself."

"Then why did Dilly slap your face?"

Augusta's contralto tones, her expression of exaggerated censure, were too much for him. He grinned but did not speak.

She said—"Remember that you are the eldest brother and have an example to set."

He came and plumped down on the old leather sofa beside her. "Aunty," he said, "if you knew what a time I've had preserving my virtue."

"From Dilly?" she boomed.

"I should have put it the other way," he answered. "I should have said Dilly's virtue."

"I have believed her to be a young woman of high principle."

"Well—it's marriage she wants, if that's what you mean."

"My dear, she has a very tidy fortune."

"And a very untidy seat on a horse."

"You two have been inseparable of late."

"I hope to see less of her, now that the show is over."

Augusta looked at him with some reproach. "Never mind, I shall soon be leaving and she with me."

He put an arm about her. "Aunt Augusta, you know I should like to have you here always."

At that moment. Wragge drew open the folding doors that led to the dining room. The table set for eleven people was revealed, its centrepiece a tall silver dish of polished red apples and purple and green grapes. On the platter, on which the Wragges had inflicted several chips, lay four cold roast ducks surrounded by parsley, and in small dishes were pickled red cabbage, red currant jelly and applesauce. Beside each plate was a chunky piece of homemade bread, and the butter, also homemade, lay in a slab inside the silver butter cooler the high lid of which was shaped rather like a bishop's mitre. There was cider on the table in a yellow glass jug, and a huge pot of tea. Wragge now added the last dish to this course—a casserole of scalloped sweet potatoes. These Wakefield disliked and he made a face at them as he passed. Once in his place he slyly got rid of his portion of bread, for he disliked it too, by handing it to Ben, the sheep dog, who carried it into the library and hid it beneath the sofa.

Ernest remarked—"I am rather glad that the show is over. Now some other topic of conversation is possible. For weeks it has been nothing but horse—horse—horse."

Dilly said—"Well, on my part, I'm thankful. I've disgraced myself."

There was a chorus of oh, noes, except from Renny, who with calculated concentration was carving the first duck.

She reiterated that she was disgraced and that it would have been better to have let that funny little girl of their neighbor's ride the mare. This remark was so unfortunate that Nicholas and Ernest at once began to talk with great animation about the weather.

Nodding her cap with satisfaction their mother agreed that winter had come. "I'm glad of it too. I shall wear my new fur coat to church tomorrow."

Ernest cried—"Do you think you should venture out in such cold, Mamma?"

"I must wear my new coat. Just once. Then I'll put it away for the winter."

A groan went around the table at the thought of such extravagance.

She went on—"And I want to sit on the new cushions I'm giving for the pews. Have they come yet?"

Meg said—"They are due next week, Granny."

"Good. Everything will be spruce for Christmas. Shall you buy yourself a new coat, Eden?"

"Me, Gran? Out of that ten dollars I got for my last poem?"

A mischievous gleam brightened her eyes. "I'll buy you a new top coat, boy. Any color you like. What about blue? Indigo blue?"

"Good idea, Gran," said Renny. Then the word "Indigo" struck him. He recalled the certificate, which, during the stress of the show, he had forgotten. He leant toward her, with a penetrating look. He asked—"What's this about Indigo? I seem to have heard that word before. Is it some secret password?"

Now she looked sly. "I don't know what you mean," she mumbled, but she was enjoying herself.

He jabbed the carving knife in her direction. "Gran, the truth! What about Indigo?"

He unaware of the intricate web of deception woven about that table, and she unaware that any but herself was involved, they faced each other with a mixture of playfulness and antagonism. A tremor of amazement tightened the nerves of the other investors. Was she also into it? At her age! Her sons and daughter looked from her to Eden, from Eden to one another, and back again to her.

Eden thought—"Now it's coming out. The whole damned thing is coming out." Somehow he did not mind. Everybody had made a lot of money. Everything was bound to come out. He caught Dilly's eye and his lips formed the words—What fun! But, after one intimate glance and the flash of a smile, her eyes turned toward Renny, with a look of—what was it, Eden wondered. It seemed almost like hate.

Nicholas thought—"That rascal Eden. Now I understand Mamma's behavior of late. I wonder if old Ernie is into it too. I shall advise her to sell."

Ernest thought—"No wonder Mamma has acted mysteriously. The fur coat . . . the cushions for the pews . . . I wonder how much she has made."

Piers squeezed Eden's knee under the table. Piers was shaking with suppressed laughter. Eden caught his wrist. The two dared not look at each other. Piers said out of the side of his mouth—"Gold, you old devil."

Renny, having with considerable expedition served the company, now persisted—"Out with it, Gran. What about Indigo Lake?"

She answered tartly—"Mind your own business. Indigo Lake is a mine and a very lucrative business it is." She put up her hand and set her cap at a jaunty angle. From under its lace edge she gave him a daring look. She repeated—"A lucrative business. Don't you wish you had a share in it?"

Her eyes sought Eden's and he laughed. "Now the fat's

in the fire," he thought. On the whole he did not mind. He laid down his knife and fork and prepared for battle.

Renny turned to Nicholas. "What's all this about?"

Nicholas answered—"My mother has told me nothing."

"Is this a secret, Gran?" asked Renny.

"It's a secret," she returned stoutly, "between Eden and me."

With the eyes of his uncles and his aunt on him Eden flushed. His heart quickened its beat, but he did not speak.

Augusta demanded, in rather an accusing tone—"Are you telling us, Mamma, that you have been speculating?"

"There's naught to hinder me, is there, if I take a notion to?"

"Of course not."

Dilly said—"Mrs. Whiteoak and I are a reckless pair. We've a bit of the gambler in us. Haven't we, dear Mrs. Whiteoak?"

"This is no gamble. This is solid gold, eh, Eden?"

Renny turned to him sharply. "What have you to do with it, Eden?"

Before Eden had framed an answer Ernest broke in with—"I don't like this secrecy. I don't like it at all. If Eden—if Eden—if Mamma—"

He became tangled in words and could not go on for a space, then he got out—"I like openness—frankness."

"Then," asked Nicholas, "why weren't you open and frank yourself?"

Ernest reddened. "I had made mistakes before. I acknowledge it. I didn't want to be accused of—of folly."

Meg said—"Folly is scarcely the word, Uncle Ernest. Not in an investment as safe as this."

Renny stared at her astounded. *"You too,* Meg?"

"And why not? I like to make a bit of money as well as anybody."

"Well, I'll be damned." Renny scrutinized faces about the table. "I seem to be the only one who isn't into this!"

Eden said—"I gave you an opportunity."

"I don't remember."

"You weren't interested."

"What do you think you are? A broker?"

"Well—I've had some experience."

Meg put in—"I call it very clever of Eden."

Renny said to him—"I'll see you later."

Wakefield's child's treble broke in. "Has somebody been stealing? Is there an enigma?"

"There's a pot of gold," said his grandmother. "Indigo Lake gold."

Rags had been changing the plates. He now placed a sizzling hot dish of pancakes and a large jug of maple syrup on the table.

Meg said to Wakefield—"Sit up straight and don't make a noise eating your celery. You should have finished it by now."

"Finch makes a noise. So does Gran."

"Finch has not yet learned table manners," said his grandmother. "I've forgotten 'em. When you reach my age you haven't time for 'em." She bit off a morsel of celery with gusto.

Augusta remarked with some severity—"The child is too much inclined to making personal remarks."

"He is so observant," said Meg. "He notices everything."

"And what eyes he has," exclaimed Dilly.

"Aye," agreed the grandmother. "We run to fine eyes in this family." And she opened hers wide and rolled them at her eldest grandson. "Blue or brown, they're well shaped and bright. Now, that rascal there—" and she pointed her stick of celery at Piers—"he has the eyes of his grandfather, him in the portrait—blue as the sky on a May morning, ha!" She gazed for a rapt moment at the pictured face. "You'd look into those eyes and your heart would melt."

Dilly also gazed rapt. She said—"I always admire a blue-eyed man."

Old Adeline craned her neck to look at her. "You do? I thought you admired yon dark-eyed devil at the end of the table."

Dilly stared. "Are his eyes dark? I hadn't noticed."

"Dark they are and his hair is red and you hadn't noticed! What a girl. Not like most of them, eh, Renny?"

He replied—"When Dilly and I are together we have no time for frivolities."

Rags was whispering to Renny, an annoying habit he had. "I heard you mention Indigo Lake, sir and I thought this item in the evening paper might interest you." He laid a neatly folded page of a newspaper by Renny's plate.

"Thanks." Renny bent his head to read the marked article.

Wakefield said—"No enigmas, please."

Grandmother was talking of the approach of Christmas. "Well do I remember when I was a girl in Ireland how we had a roast peacock for dinner and his tail feathers spread like a fan above him. No turkey ever tasted so good."

"What fun!" cried Dilly.

The pancakes were golden brown, delicious. Butter lay in little shining globules along their edge. The maple syrup filled every crevice and formed a pool on the plate. It was amazing how many of them Piers could tuck away. But the master of Jalna seemed to have lost his appetite. He gazed abstractedly at his plate, then his eyes searched the faces of those about the table, as though he were making some sort of calculation.

Ernest was saying, with almost a simper—"I think we should have a sort of general confession in the drawing room, when the young boys have retired. I feel that the time for subterfuge is at an end. We all have, apparently, done so well—so extremely well, that I think . . ."

Nicholas took the words from his mouth. "It's time we had a celebration, in short. I don't mind telling what I've made."

"Nor I," laughed Eden. "It's going to change things a lot for me."

Piers said, raising an imaginary glass—" 'Then let us the cannikin clink!' "

"Good idea." Nicholas beamed at him. "I shall go to the cellar and bring up something special I have stored there. Some really good port."

Finch said—"What's all this about? I wish I could ever make any money."

Wakefield cast a reproving look on him. "Once I gave you a quarter," he said, "and you wouldn't have it."

Meg asked—"What's the matter, Renny? You're not eating."

"He is brooding," said Dilly, "on my bad horsemanship."

Wakefield asked—"Shouldn't you say horsewomanship?"

Ernest gave the little boy an approving smile. "I have never known a child," he said, "with such a feeling for words."

"I've never known one," said Finch, "so conceited."

Ernest returned benignly—"The point about conceited people is that usually they have something to be conceited about. They value themselves."

Dilly exclaimed—"How I wish I did! I think nothing of myself."

Piers put in—"Why don't we talk about Indigo Lake? I'm dying to know what everybody has made."

Now came Augusta's contralto voice. "I think Eden is the only one who can tell you that."

Nicholas wiped his drooping gray moustache. He said—"I think we all are shy. No one wants the rest to know how much he has made."

"I don't mind," said Dilly. "I invested a thousand dollars and I've doubled it."

"Dilly!" Augusta said, on a deep accusing note. "You should not have done that without consulting me."

Wakefield, spurred on by Ernest's approval, quoted, in a high-pitched chant:

"You should not go down to the end of the town
Without consulting me!"

"What a memory he has," said Ernest.

Dilly apologized—"Sorry, Lady Buckley."

Nicholas helped himself to a bunch of grapes. "When I get the sweet taste of the syrup out of my mouth," he said, "I'll go to the cellar and fetch that port."

"I'll go with you," said Renny.

"Let me come too," cried Dilly. "I must see that cellar before I leave!"

"You'll get all cobwebby," objected Nicholas.

"I don't mind."

Renny gave her a sulky look, nevertheless she sprang up. It required a formidably repressive one from Augusta to put her back in her seat. The two men retired, followed by the sheep dog, descended the stirs to the basement kitchen, where Nicholas paused to compliment Mrs. Wragge on her pancakes, went along a passage, out of which opened the Wragges' bedroom and a storeroom, and reached the locked door of the wine cellar.

"It's scarcely worth locking up nowadays," said Renny.

Nicholas groaned. "What a cellar my father kept!"

The light of the candle Renny carried fell on starkly bare bins and shelves and those which still boasted a fair store of spirits and wines. It illuminated the strongly marked features of the two men, at the same time heightening the contrast between them—Nicholas, the man of the world, his mind enriched by experience and travel, detached, not given to extremes of joy or sorrow—Renny, his life cencentrated on the activities of Jalna, circumscribed by his own tastes, high-mettled as one of his own hunters, with a kind of virgin elegance about him.

With the bottle of port in his hand, Nicholas said—"I expect you had quite a surprise tonight."

"Yes. I had."

"A pity you aren't in this too."

"I'd as lief not."

"You are an odd chap. Aren't you interested in making some easy money?"

"I don't like losing it."

Nicholas chuckled. "That trait must have come from your Scotch grandfather. I mean caution. Not that I think you are generally cautious. As for me, I've sold my shares of Indigo Lake. Thought it well to get out while the going was good."

Renny looked relieved. "I'm glad of that. Did you get your money?"

"A cheque is on the way."

"Are you positive?"

"Why are you looking like that?" Nicholas asked this question with an abruptly startled air.

"Read this." Renny took the folded newspaper from his pocket and held it in the candlelight.

Nicholas said testily—"I can't, without my glasses. What is it?"

Renny read—" 'Disappearance of Lemuel Y. Kronk, Mining Broker. Promoter of Nonexistent Mining Stock.' That is the heading, Uncle Nick. The article just goes on to say that he has fleeced a lot of people and skipped out."

"I can't believe it! Let me see the paper." He frowned at it and was able to make out the gist of the article.

"What sort of man was he? How did you meet him?"

"I didn't meet him. Eden did the investing for me. I guess for all of us."

Renny drew back from him in consternation. "My God, Uncle Nick, are you telling me you handed over your good money to that boy and an unknown and unlicenced broker?"

"Was he unlicenced?"

"This article says so. He's been swindling people not only here but in the United States. Lots of them."

Nicholas raised the bottle of port as though he would like to break it over Mr. Kronk's head.

"The scoundrel," he said. Then he remembered the other investors, waiting upstairs to celebrate, and a sardonic smile bent his lips. "What will my brother say? And my mother! Good God—my poor old mother!"

Steps approached along the passage and Finch looked in at the door. He said—"Meg sent me down to find out if anything is wrong. They're all in the drawing room waiting. They've brought out the best wine glasses and there's a fresh fire. I wish I had something to celebrate."

Nicholas ruefully asked of Renny—"Shall I bring the port?"

"Brandy might be better."

"Right. We'll drink brandy."

"Why? asked Finch. "Why change?" In the candlelight his pink-cheeked boy's face shone bright with curiosity.

They did not trouble to answer him. The port was

replaced and Renny produced a bottle of French brandy in its stead. The candle was on a slant so that the wax melted and fell in hot globules on his hand. Abstractedly he rubbed them off. The little procession forced and marched back to the drawing room. The fresh fire in the fireplace had a quantity of dry kindling in it. The flames leaped and crackled, as in joy at being set free. The light of the lamp paled beside them. Those present appeared to have arranged themselves as for a ceremony. Her chair in the full light of the fire, old Adeline Whiteoak was a figure strangely resembling that of the parrot, Boney, whose tall perch stood behind her. Both held their heads forward a little. In her extreme age her profile tended to a predatory outline, as did his. He was clothed in bright plumage, while she wore a tea gown of dark green velvet, its wide sleeves lined with red and with a red collar. With his claws he firmly gripped the perch, while she as firmly held to the arms of her chair, for she was stirred to a pleasurable excitement not often experienced of late. The rubies, diamonds and emeralds of her rings caught and held the firelight. "Come, come," she was saying, "what's all this delay? Let's get together and celebrate. Let's hear what money everyone has made, eh, Boney?" And she raised her face to the parrot.

Uttering throaty caressing sounds he shook his plumage, then said a few words in Hindustani.

"Hear that?" she cried. "Pearl of the harem he calls me . . . Ah, the darling!" And she stretched up a hand to him which he fondled with his beak.

Wakefield had thrown himself on the fur rug at her feet. It was his bedtime but no one gave him the command to go. He lay sprawled at ease, his dark eyes roving with indolent assurance from one point of interest to another.

Eden and Piers sat side by side on the window seat, fresh-colored, eager for the coming disclosure. Piers felt himself a man among men. He had made money. He had speculated on the stock market and made more money. He laughed to himself when he remembered how he had that morning overtaken Pheasant on the road and given her a lift as far as the post office. She had been on her way to post a letter for Mrs. Clinch. She had looked prettier than he had ever seen her. He could not get the thought of her out of his head. Yet strangely he could not see her face with clarity. It had been so changeful during that drive. It had gone from shyness to composure and then to mirth, when something he said had made her laugh. It was her laughter, high and pure, that remained with him so clearly, and now hearing it in imagination, he laughed within himself.

Ernest and Dilly were seated side by side on the sofa, their expectant faces turned toward the door. They had exchanged brief but exhilarating confidences on the subject of speculation. Each had declared that the act was the exciting thing about it. The profit was of only secondary consideration. Dilly was smoking a cigarette, a spectacle which Meg looked on with disapproval. She and Ernest shared an ash tray. He looked like a man about to propose a health.

Lady Buckley and Meg had pieces of embroidery in their laps but their hands were idle and their eyes fixed on the three who now entered. Nicholas came first, with the air of a French aristocrat on his way to the guillotine. After him came Renny bearing the bottle of brandy, and lastly young Finch wearing, for reasons known only to himself, a hangdog air.

Renny set the bottle on the small table beside the glasses.

"Well," he asked, "who's for it?"

His grandmother peered at the bottle.

"I thought 'twas to be port wine," she said.

Meg added—"Yes. I have the port glasses ready."

Ernest exclaimed, disappointed—"Why the change? Cognac does not agree with me, nor, I think, will the ladies wish for it."

"They'll need it," said Renny.

"I like a drop of cognac," his grandmother declared. "Let me have the glass in the curve of my hand to warm it." She eagerly watched the ceremony of filling her glass.

Lady Buckley asked—"May I inquire why this air of mystery?"

"Yes," said Meg, "we're curious to know what was going on down in the wine cellar."

Renny said—"There is no mystery, Aunty. The plain fact is that this man Kronk has skipped out with the spondulics." He stood, with the tray of glasses in his hands, like a man dispensing poison. Yet a flicker of mordant amusement crossed his lips as he scanned their faces, observing the effect of his words.

"Incredible," said Ernest. "I don't believe a word of it."

Nicholas heaved a noisy sigh. "It's true enough."

"Who told you?"

"It's in the evening paper. Read it to them, Renny."

Renny set down the tray, took the paper from his pocket and began to read aloud. " 'Disappearance of promoter of Indigo Lake Mine. Swindled many thousands of dollars from credulous investors both here and in the United States.' " He hesitated, letting the words sink in, then finished the brief article, inconspicuous on a back page of the paper.

A palpable movement ran through the room, as though each were conscious of sudden physical discomfort. Then Ernest rose, with an unfolding of his long person, and crossed to his mother.

"Mamma," he said, "don't you think you had better go to bed?"

"Why?" she demanded. "It's still early."

"You've had a tiring day . . ."

"All my days are tiring now . . . What did Renny read from the newspaper?"

"Oh, that was nothing," he lied. "Nothing of interest. Do please let me help you to your room, Mamma." He patted her back, encouraging her.

Eden had sprung up, come to Renny, and was devouring the article over his shoulder. "It's impossible," he said but even while he denied its possibility, a chill gripped his heart.

Nicholas rumbled, in an undertone—"We've been fleeced. Among us we seem to have lost a tidy sum."

Old Adeline caught the word "lost." "What's lost?" she demanded. "Let me be, Ernest." She struck at his hand that patted her. "I want to know what's lost. Is it a dog? A horse? A reputation? Come now—out with it!" She took a sip of brandy and sat up straight in her chair. She looked alert, eager.

Renny said in an undertone to Nicholas—"She'll have to know it eventually. I think I'd better tell her now."

"My money!" cried Meg. "Don't tell me that man has run off with *my* money!"

"I'm afraid he has, my dear," said Nicholas.

Meg's face flamed to scarlet. "Eden, *you* led me into this! I trusted you."

Piers, equally flushed, glared at Eden. "I trusted him too. I put everything I had earned into Indigo Lake."

Renny said—"Without my leave. You young rascal! Well, now you've lost it." He turned to Eden. "You've made a pretty mess of things."

Eden's face had gone white. "I've lost too."

"What had you to invest?"

"What I made on commission. Quite a lot."

"Good Lord!"

Lady Buckley said—"I went with Eden to that wicked man's office. He talked most convincingly. I trusted them both."

"You would have done well, Aunty," said Renny, "to have consulted me. I'd have warned you."

She gave a groan. "Oh, how I wish I had!"

The grandmother's eyes had moved from one speaker to the other, her face expressing both frustration and an arrogant will to delve to the bottom of all this. She thumped on the floor with her stick. Her voice came out harsh and strong.

"I will be told," she said, and turning to the most vulnerable—"Meg, explain. Has somebody lost money?"

Through tears Meg answered—"Yes, Granny."

"Who?" she demanded.

The answer came, with a grin, from Renny.

"You, Gran."

"Me? I couldn't."

"Oh, yes you could. It's quite easy—with a young fool like Eden and a swindler like Kronk to help you."

Ernest said—"That is not the way to break the news to my mother."

His mother said—"Hold your tongue, Ernest. I want the plain truth." And sitting upright and resolute there she looked well able to bear it.

"After all," growled Nicholas, "she's not ruined." But thought ruefully—"She'll have that much less to leave behind her."

She said—"It was a gold mine. What happened to the gold?"

"There was a mistake, Mamma," said Ernest. He took out his handkerchief and mopped his high white forehead.

"I made no mistake," she said, emphatically. "I invested my money, safe and sound, in a gold mine."

Ernest asked, almost tremblingly, for he expected to be her heir—"How much money did you invest, Mamma?"

She snapped out—"Twenty thousand dollars."

This was a shock indeed. Eden hastened to say—"She forgets. It was far less."

She heard him and demanded—"How much have I made?"

"Nothing," said Renny. "You've lost. Look here." He took the newspaper to her and held it under her nose.

"Is it in print there?" she asked.

Nicholas said, under his breath—"She may as well know the truth."

"But what a shock for her," said Ernest.

Augusta put in—"Mamma is able to bear it, and the loss. It means less to her than to any of us."

Renny tapped the newspaper with his forefinger. "See, Gran? Can you read it? The broker has skedaddled, taking everybody's money with him." He threw a glance over his shoulder at Dilly. "Fun, isn't it?"

Dilly gave an hysterical laugh.

Adeline demanded—"You others—have you lost money too?"

"Everybody," answered Renny for them. "All but me."

She shook her head dolefully and a momentary heavy silence enveloped them.

Finch had been too embarrassed to remain in the room.

He had left but had lingered in the hall, listening, not so much to the words that were said, as to the tones of the voices which went tingling through his nerves. He now heard his grandmother say loud and clear—"Come here, sir." He saw Eden cross the room with an almost lounging step and stand in front of her.

"You rascal," she then said raspingly. "You scallywag. You led me into this."

"I'm sorry, Gran," he said, "terribly sorry." He knelt with his body very straight, in front of her, as though deliberately making the picture of a penitent. But he went on composedly—"I was as much deceived as you. I thought the mine—everything—was authentic. Even now there may be a mistake."

"You brought these pictures to me. You persuaded me with all your talk. You can't get out of that. How much have I lost?"

Nicholas, a little too eagerly, added—"Yes. How much has she lost?"

That was enough to make her recoil from what she thought of as prying into her affairs. She said tartly—"I will not tell what I have lost—not till every one of you comes out with his folly. Now, Nicholas, what about you?"

Nicholas blew into his moustache, then tugged it into place. "Enough," he said. "A tidy sum. I don't want to talk about it."

"I see . . . Now, you, Ernest—what did the rascal get out of you?"

He answered with dignity, though his voice shook—"I think I agree with Nicholas that we should refrain from giving figures."

She retorted—"Aye, but Nicholas asked how much I had lost. That was different, eh?" She turned to her daughter, speaking with mock formality. "Lady Buckley, pray how much lighter is your purse?"

Augusta said—"I cannot remember clearly at the moment. I shall tell you tomorrow."

Old Adeline gave an ironic smile. "She'll tell me tomorrow." And she imitated Augusta's manner of speaking. Then, fixing Meg with a compelling look—"You, Meg— what are the damages?"

Meg sprang up, as though suddenly conscious of Wakefield's presence. "The child," she cried, "up till this hour! I must take him to bed." She heaved him from the rug and led him to the door.

There he halted, turning back into the room.

"I must say good-night to everybody."

"Very well, but do be quick about it."

He felt himself small and good, aloof from all the mysterious and troubled talk going on about him. He made the round of the room, giving a hug to those he liked best, offering a cool cheek to those not so favored. Meg waited by the door on tenterhooks till the good-nights were accomplished, then bore him off. Finch had already disappeared.

The grandmother still held the centre of the stage, determined that no loss experienced by the others should equal the dramatic quality of her own. She said—

"This means little to the rest of you but think what it is to be impoverished at my time of life."

Nicholas said—"You will never notice the loss, Mamma."

"How do you know," she retorted, "when I haven't told you what I invested?"

He could not say to her that her needs now were few but she guessed what was in his mind.

"I have my ambitions," she said. "There's things I want to do." The remembrance of her new fur coat smote her. "And there's my Persian lamb coat to be paid for! Dear, oh, dear, I wonder if I can return it to the shop."

Ernest answered—"I'm afraid not. You sent a cheque for it yesterday, Mamma."

She threw up her hands in despair. Then she turned to Eden, who had risen to his feet and was standing apart, with folded arms and hanging head. "Oh, Eden, you deceitful rogue! You came to me secretly with the bright pictures to entice me into a thimblerig. If only your uncles had been with me, you'd never have trapped me but you came in the time when I was alone." A tear of pity for herself glistened in her eye.

Renny said—"Have another sip of brandy, Gran?"

Trembling she took another sip and was refreshed.

"This means little to you others," she repeated. "Little to any but me."

Piers was saying under his breath, through clenched teeth—"It means little to me, eh?"

Eden did not hear what was being said. While kneeling in front of his grandmother, in his nostrils the scent of the Eastern perfume she used, the aquiline contour of her face, the bright colors of her gown, filling his eyes, the thought of a new poem had come to him. It was no more clear than a pale star in early twilight, but it was there, challenging the futile flow of words about him. If only he dared to take it up to his room, to capture it on paper, to forget all the turmoil of disappointment and chagrin that seethed within him. But he dared not leave.

His grandmother was saying—"Then there are the new cushions I bought for the pews. Do you think we might stop the making of them?"

"They are to be in the church tomorrow," said Augusta sombrely.

"Still, if I sent word quickly that no one is to sit on them, mightn't they be returned?"

"It is too late," said Augusta.

"Too late—too late—too late." She repeated the fateful words, between each repetition taking another sip of brandy till the small glass was empty. She then asked abruptly—"What was I grieving about?"

"The money you have lost in Indigo Lake, Mamma," said Ernest.

Nicholas growled—"Better let her forget it."

"I have no intention of forgetting it," she said. "And how could I? Now I'm dependent on charity." The final sip of brandy had been a little too much for her. She stretched out a trembling hand to her eldest grandson.

He clasped it. "Nothing will be different at Jalna, Gran. Your living here has cost you nothing, nor will it ever."

She did not like this reference to her freedom from responsibility in that house for so many years. She turned to Ernest. "I wonder," she said, "if I ought to see the doctor. I feel strangely weak."

"It is the cognac," said Nicholas. "What you need is bed."

Ernest said to Eden—"This is a terrible thing you've done to my mother."

"I know, I know," he said absently, and wondered if he might decently escape. His artist's imagination had perversely chosen this moment for activity. The poem was taking shape.

"Help me up," he heard his grandmother say. She was raised to her feet and, brushing aside those who had aided her, walked a little unsteadily to the window.

"No moon," she said. "A dark night. And a black night for me. A black night indeed."

Meg now returned to the room, with an inquiring glance about her, to discover what had happened during her absence. Avoiding her grandmother she went to Piers and dropped to the window seat beside him.

"What have they been saying?" she whispered.

He gave her his angry boy's stare. "Nobody has a chance to say anything. Nobody but Gran. Talk of egotism!"

"It is ridiculous," she agreed.

Old Adeline turned from the window. She asked—"Was Eden's name in the paper too?"

"Thank God, no," answered Ernest.

"Well, it should be. He swindled me too."

Eden said loudly—"Everything I did, I did in good faith. I thought it was a sound investment. So did a lot of people."

Nicholas said—"You did very wrong to approach my mother."

Ernest demanded—"Why did you keep everything secret?"

Eden answered—"Because you all wanted it kept secret."

"The truth," said Augusta, "was bound to come out."

Eden fairly exploded—"It did come out—tonight, and look how happy we were till Rags brought in the newspaper."

Now the talk broke out in full volume. Accusation, self-defense, reproach, tears from Meg, an outburst of swearing in Hindustani from the disturbed Boney. In the midst old Adeline stood leaning on her stick, a rock about which the storm of words beat. She was not without a certain pleasure in this letting loose of emotion, for hers was an emotional nature that was irked by self-restraint. She liked to watch her descendants at it, hammer and tongs. But by now she could not add more than her presence to the scene, for her brain was more than a little confused and her body very weary. Lower she bent over her stick and finally suffered herself to be assisted to her room. In the doorway she halted, gathered her wits together and said:

"My husband, he that built this house, would turn over in his grave if he knew the swindling that has gone on inside it."

Dilly had taken no part in the scene but had sat leaning forward, a fascinated spectator, unnoticed by the Whiteoaks.

19.

Scenes at Night

EDEN WENT TO THE TABLE where the cognac stood and poured himself another drink.

Meg said, her voice ringing clear—"You may well need something to support you, considering what you have done. Oh, Eden, what responsibility to take—the investing of the fortunes of your own family! I don't see how you had the temerity."

His hand shook a little. He said—"Oh, I have plenty of that."

"It's the secrecy all round that staggers me," said Renny.

Ernest gnawed his lip in chagrin. He said—"I blame myself for speculating. I should have restrained Eden if possible."

"You should have told me," said Renny, "what he was up to."

Nicholas blew through his moustache. "Good-bye," he said, "to all our airy castles. I think we each should tell what they were and then try to forget about 'em. What had you in mind, Ernest?"

"Travel, Nick. London and Paris."

"And you were going off without me, you dirty dog?"

"Well, I knew what you would say if I spoke of speculating. You'd call it gambling and remind me of former losses. I little thought you were into it too."

"Lord, I wish I hadn't been."

"What was your particular castle?"

"The Riviera. Egad, I could smell the mimosa."

Meg said—"I had no such dreams. I just wanted to

193

add to my poor little pile of savings. And now, instead of that, I've lost."

Renny asked—"How much did you invest, Meg?"

"I forget the exact amount," she hedged. "But it was much more than I could afford to lose."

Renny smiled across the room at Dilly Warkworth. "There is one investor," he said, "who has not squealed, and I admire her for it."

Her face was as though the sun had shone on it. She said—"I don't mind. It was fun."

Piers said—"Perhaps you can afford to lose. I can't. I put every dollar I had into it. Five hundred and fifty dollars."

"You got what you deserve," said Renny. "You led me to believe that you'd put it all in the bank."

"I believed Indigo Lake was as safe as any bank."

"Why didn't you ask my advice?"

"Because Eden wanted everything kept quiet."

Meg cried—"It's the same with me. Eden said he wanted everything kept quiet."

Lady Buckley, after settling her mother for the night, now returned.

Renny said—"I suppose, Aunty, that you're another victim whom Eden told to keep mum."

"I don't like your way of putting it," she said, "but that is how it was." She swept to her chair by the fire, with the effect of wearing a train. "Eden gave me to understand that secrecy was advisable."

Piers said—"And all the while he was lining his own pockets."

The villain of the piece stood sipping his cognac. An odd half-smile lighted his face. He stood—"I know it's pleasant to have someone to blame for your mistakes. But I must remind you—every single one of you was ready and eager to keep his part in it a secret."

"I admit that," said Nicholas. "Nevertheless I think you had acquired a plausible way from this Kronk fellow and you exercised it on us."

Ernest said—"I cannot help thinking that there has been a very deliberate manipulation on Eden's part."

Piers added, his tone in almost brutal contrast—"Eden deserves to be kicked and I'd like to do it."

Eden turned to smile at him. "My poor little man," he said. "And only a short while ago you were so pleased to be in my company."

"I'd be pleased to see you outside and give you what I said."

"Boys, boys," put in Meg. "Everyone is so tired. It's been such an evening. And Christmas coming on!"

"Nobody need expect a Christmas present from me," said Piers.

"Let's see," mused Eden, "what did you give us last year?"

"Oh, I know I didn't give much. I hadn't the money to spend—but this year I had."

"Poor Pheasant," said Eden. "She won't get her present."

Meg drew back startled. "Pheasant!"

"Why, Meg, didn't you know he's sweet on Pheasant Vaughan?"

Now every eye was on Piers.

"I'm nothing of the sort," he denied. "I hardly ever see the girl."

Meg said—"I'm very sure she is the last person Piers would take up with, knowing what he must know."

Piers gave his sister a bold rustic stare. "What about her?" he asked.

Her face flamed. "Don't tell me you haven't heard!"

"I haven't heard anything against Pheasant."

"Can't you understand that who she is is against her?"

"No." He looked still bolder.

Ernest put in mildly—"We must remember that we have a visitor."

"Rather late for remembering that, eh, Dilly?" laughed Renny.

Dilly exclaimed passionately—"I wish that girl had ridden for you at the show instead of me."

"You did very well," he returned, with more kindness in his eyes than he usually gave her.

"A *third!* She'd have got a first, I'm convinced."

Meg said darkly—"The horse show is neither here nor there."

The fire crackled loudly for a moment, then abruptly died. The dogs, sleeping on the mat, gave it a suspicious look, then moved farther off, the spaniel Floss laying her head on the sheep dog's furry side; he, with a grunt of satisfaction, again subsiding. The ormolu clock on the mantelshelf struck eleven.

Ernest yawned and his eyes watered. He said—"Let us hope that Piers will cultivate wisdom. It is something we all need to cultivate—no matter what our years. We can always learn. For my part I am going to bed. What a different evening from what we expected."

"Good-night, everybody," said Nicholas. "I'm going too."

Piers crossed to the table where stood the brandy.

Renny gave him a sharp shake of the head and framed the word "no" with his lips.

Piers exploded. "Why mayn't I? I need it if anyone does."

"Go to your bed."

"I've lost everything. And look at the way I worked!"

"I know."

"Everyone is howling about his own loss. Not a word about mine."

"No cheek, Piers. And no drink."

Nicholas said—"I did no howling, my boy. What I say is—we've all had confounded bad luck. Let's to bed and forget it." He put his arm about his sister. "Come along, Gussie. Be thankful Edwin isn't alive to see you making ducks and drakes of his fortune."

Augusta did not like this and showed it.

He added to mollify her—"You're a brave woman. No woman could have made less fuss over a heavy loss. What did you say the amount was?"

"I did not say."

She suffered herself to be drawn to her feet and the two moved to the door with an air of almost jocularity on the part of Nicholas and sad dignity on Augusta's. She said a good-night to each in turn, her voice taking on a deeper note when she uttered Eden's name.

"Good-night, Aunty," he said. "Better luck next time."

Ernest said, pouring himself another drink—"I consider that remark in very bad taste."

"Sorry," said Eden.

Augusta said from the doorway—"There will not be another time." She and Nicholas disappeared.

Meg, with an audible yawn, also rose. She said—"I shall not sleep a wink tonight. Oh, how lucky you are, Renny! How I envy you. When I think of my tiny bit of money that I had hoarded through the years . . ."

"Hoarded is good," observed Piers, watching Ernest sip his cognac.

She was not taking that sort of remark in silence. She said—"I notice a tendency to insolence in you, Piers. You must curb it."

"Huh," he grunted.

"There is nothing nicer in a young boy," she went on, "than good manners toward his sister." She gave him a reproving kind of kiss, winked hard, then brought herself to kiss Eden, then came to Renny. To him she whispered —"You must be severe with Piers—about that girl."

"Eden was only teasing him." He kissed her cheek. "Sleep well, Meggie. Don't worry."

She gave a groan, then asked—"Coming, Dilly?"

"I think I shall find a book to read and relax by the fire. I'm a nighthawk, you know."

"I'll build it up," said Renny. He knelt by it, blowing its embers into little green tongues of flame with the bellows upon which Augusta had, in her youth, painted a spray of maidenhair fern and three trilliums.

When he rose and looked about him he found the room empty but for Dilly. He stood, bellows in hand, regarding her warily. The bellows might have been a weapon and he at bay. The room looked as though some physical encounter might have taken place in it. No chair was in its proper position, every cushion was shapeless, empty glasses stood about, one of them snapped off at the stem by Ernest's tense fingers and concealed by him behind a begonia in a pot. Renny's eyes came to rest on it and Dilly exclaimed:

"Poor dear, he was so wrought up. First by the bad news—then by breaking the glass."

"No wonder," said Renny. "It's one of our best. Old Irish glass."

She gave a little laugh. "Doubtless you have plenty more."

If that was her mood he wasn't afraid of her. He came and sat down on the sofa beside her. He said: "I can't tell you how much I admire the way you're taking this, Dilly. You've been a trump."

She fixed her eyes on his breast. She said low—"What is the loss of a thousand dollars—compared to what I feel here?" She struck her own breast.

"Now, Dilly," he said, almost as though he were reasoning with one of his young brothers. "You can't make me believe that you're suffering from frustrated love. I know the signs too well."

"That," she said, "is one of the vainest remarks I've ever heard."

Imperturbably he lighted a cigarette. "I haven't lived thirty-seven years for nothing."

"I wish I knew," she sneered, "how many hearts you've broken in that time."

"One thing is certain," he said. "Yours is not among them."

"I suppose you're accustomed to seeing women in storms of tears."

"I have seen you cry and you were very touching."

"I haven't a tear in me tonight. If you were to beat me black and blue, I wouldn't cry."

"You are a very primitive girl, Dilly."

"Me?" She was astonished.

"Yes. When you are angry at me you strike me. When your mood changes you talk of my beating you."

She said desperately—"Whatever way I approach you, it's sure to be wrong."

"I think you were splendid tonight. When every single thought of the others was concentrated on their own loss, you made light of yours."

She cried—"What I said was that it is nothing compared . . ."

"I know, I know," he interrupted. "What I say is that you shall not suffer any loss through Eden's bright ideas. I'll see to that."

"I don't want anything," she said doggedly, "but that you should care for me."

"I admire you enormously."

"Admiration—pooh!"

"I'm very fond of you."

"Fond of me—bah!"

The fire brightened, striking answering brightness from the amber of the cognac, the crystal glasses, the eyes of the two on the sofa. Dilly turned her supple neck to look him in the face. She said, as though musing:

"That hair . . . those eyes . . . and a heart like ice."

"Dilly," he said, "you make me laugh." And he did laugh, so infectiously that she laughed too.

Then she caught herself up in anger, frowning, and he noticed that her eyebrows were a little too heavy. She repeated—"A heart like ice," then added, to make it worse, "like an ice-cold stone!"

His spaniel Floss had come to him and he fondled her ears. Dilly thought she saw annoyance in the bend of his lips and she was impelled to anger him still further.

"Your position is rather unique," she said. "Do you realize that?"

He raised his head to return her look.

"Unique?"

"Decidedly. How many young men are there who are in the patriarchal position you are? You own the estate. Everyone here is more or less dependent on you."

"My grandmother and my uncles aren't."

"They prefer to be. Everybody kowtows to you."

"*Kowtows!* Good Lord. I wish Gran could hear you say that."

"When she discovered that she'd lost some money she turned at once to you and you said everything would be as it had always been. You are the patriarch and it's very bad for you. If you don't watch out you'll never marry and you'll become eccentric."

He regarded her with some curiosity. He said—"This is something new, Dilly, this role of a preacher."

She answered, in an offhand way—"It simply means that I am concerned about you."

"That's very sweet of you but I like you best as you were."

"Nothing I could do would make you like me."

He said, with decision—"I have told you how much I admire the way you've taken this loss."

She exclaimed—"You've despised me ever since I rode so badly at the show."

"Now," he said deliberately, "you are taking a hectoring tone. I wonder why." He had ceased to fondle Floss's ears and, demanding his attention, she had raised herself, with paws on his chest, and bumped his face with her muzzle. He kissed her between the eyes.

Dilly said bitterly—"You think more of that spaniel than you do of me."

His eyebrows shot up. "Who could doubt that? She and Merlin have been my companions for years . . ." He did not finish. Merlin, on hearing his name, rose from his place by the fire and came to Renny.

Dilly sprang up. She exclaimed—"You and your dogs! You'd drive me mad. I'm glad I am going home."

"I'm sorry you leave us with such feelings," he said tranquilly.

"I love every member of this family," she said with violence, "but you."

"Even Eden?"

"Even Eden."

A voice asked from the doorway—"Did I hear my name?"

"Yes," returned Renny. "Dilly has just said that she loves you."

"And I love her for that," said Eden, coming into the room.

Renny gave them a benign look. "Bless you, my children," he said.

Dilly sprang up and went to the fireplace, and Merlin at once took her place on the sofa. She picked up the hearth brush, made by a disabled soldier, and began to sweep the hearth. She did it vigorously, with the concentration of an immaculate housewife, as though unconscious of the presence of the two men. Yet in her every fibre she was conscious of them.

Renny, dispassionately observing her figure from the rear, wondered how he ever could have expected her to have a good seat on a horse. Eden's quick glance moved from one to the other and he felt he had perhaps better leave them alone. Renny settled it by saying—"So you're still about."

Eden came in and leant over him. "I've been telephoning the Kronks' apartment."

"Good idea. Any news?"

"Mrs. Kronk was there alone. She has no idea where he is. She feels her position very badly."

"I'll wager she's as guilty as he."

"No, no. She knew the mine was there. She'd been up north to see it. But there was no capital to develop it with. That she didn't know."

"What about the pictures?"

"Oh, they were faked—pictures of another mine. She didn't know that, of course. She was crying."

"Poor little soul," said Renny sarcastically. Then he added, in a different tone—"I'm coming up to your room before I go to bed."

Eden thought—"Oh, Lord, will this night never end!" But he nodded his acquiescence, with his faint half-smile, and, for some reason he could not have explained, tiptoed out of the room.

Still Dilly persisted in her tidying of the hearth. She took the poker and poked and scratched at the fire.

"It's all right," said Renny. "A very nice performance. But please stop."

Without looking round she asked—"Why?"

"Because it's getting on my nerves."

"I wasn't aware that you had any."

"You are aware of nothing," he said, "but your own headstrong emotions."

She wheeled and faced him, holding the poker upright like a lance.

"What a picture," he laughed.

"I can tell you," she said, "I feel dangerous."

He could not resist saying—"Yet you would like me to believe you'd be an amiable companion."

"I should not be a tame one, at any rate."

"I like a placid woman."

"Oh, I know," she sneered. "A woman like a cow. Chewing the cud of her adoration of you all day long."

He gave her a hilarious grin. *"Dilly!* Don't tell me you're becoming literary."

She looked pleased with herself. "That was pretty good, wasn't it?" Then she added, in a tragic tone—"Of course, you don't credit me with brains."

"I haven't weighed you in that balance but I have never liked you as well as I like you tonight."

"Patronizing brute! Your vocabulary isn't great but it has more power of infuriating a woman than any I have ever heard."

He said tranquilly—"I think you enjoy getting in a temper."

She returned hotly—"You've never seen me in one before tonight."

"I've never seen you enjoy yourself so much."

She brandished the poker. She said—"I enjoy a bit of sparring."

"I can see that."

Her arm fell to her side. She spoke in a low, almost trembling voice. She said—"You see only the surface—never the aching heart beneath."

Gently he pushed Merlin from the sofa to make room for her. "Come and sit down," he said, "and tell me about this aching heart of yours. You broke off your engagement, I think. You must have gone through a good deal."

"Are you feeling real sympathy for me? I doubt it." She turned her back on him and began once more to poke at the fire, which responded in little angry leaps.

Irritated beyond endurance he said—"Put down that poker."

She gave no heed but continued, with renewed energy it seemed, to poke the fire.

He shouted—"Put down that poker, Dilly!"

He sprang up, went to her and took the implement of torture from her, and led her to the sofa. He no sooner had done this than he regretted it, for she at once put both arms about his neck and found a place for her head on his shoulder. She said—"My engagement was rather a tame affair."

Mechanically he patted her shoulder. He said—"Really?"

"Compared to this."

There was a silence in which he remembered a brief affair he had had with a girl from British Guiana during a visit to the horse show in New York the year before. She had the same fuzzy hair as Dilly. He knit his brow, trying to remember her name.

Dilly asked—"Do you want me to tell you what is in my heart?"

"Naturally."

"Why naturally?"

"Well, I'm naturally sympathetic."

She tightened her hold on him. "My past and my future are so intermingled," she said. "At this moment I am trying to wrench myself free of both. To be only conscious of the present."

Merlin, displaced from the comfort of the sofa, now tried to scramble onto Renny's lap. At the same instant a loud thumping sounded from the grandmother's room.

Renny exclaimed—"There's Gran calling!"

"Damn your grandmother," said Dilly. "I have never been in such a house. There's no possibility of privacy—even at midnight."

Renny was already on his way to old Adeline's room. In it the light burned low. Colors were not distinguishable but were overlaid by a rich plum-colored dimness, as though the past of the one who lay there were made palpable, as though the passions and desires, givings and takings, of a century had cast a mysterious bloom upon the room.

Renny had closed the door behind him. He could just make out his grandmother's pale shape, raised in the bed.

"What is it?" he asked. "Anything wrong, Gran?"

"Bonaparte," she said, calling the parrot by his full name, "where is he?"

"In the drawing room, Gran. I'll bring him to you."

"How did I come to forget him?"

"Well, perhaps you were a little upset."

"Was it the brandy?"

"I dare say."

"Was I perhaps a little tight?"

"Maybe."

She chuckled and lay back on the pillows. The chuckle turned to deep laughter that came right up from her chest. "I can't help laughing," she said.

"Perhaps you're still a little tight."

Abruptly her tone changed to one of great seriousness. She said—"I was troubled about something. It's slipped out of my mind."

"Let it stay out, Gran. You have nothing to worry about. I'll fetch Boney."

He met Dilly carrying the drowsy parrot on his perch.

"I heard her ask for him," she said.

His eyebrows shot up. "What hearing!"

"All my senses are abnormally acute tonight."

"Can you see your way in the bedroom?"

She flashed him a look. "What did I say? I could see in the dark tonight."

The old voice came from the bed. "Free the bird."

Renny undid the chain that held him by the leg and set him on the leather bed that was painted in gorgeous fruit and flowers. He shook himself in sleepy pleasure and, peering down at the nightcapped head on the pillow, murmured:

"Peariee . . . Peariiee lal."

"Hear what he calls me? His dearest ruby. Bless his heart. Did you hear him?"

"Yes," they both said, gazing down on her. She spoke to the parrot then in soft Eastern words but he had tucked his head under his wing and looked remote as a carven bird on a tomb.

She peered up and asked—"Who is with you, Renny?"

"Dilly."

"Dilly who?"

"Dilly Warkworth."

"Ah. Kiss me, both of you, and go. I'm sleepy now."

Again in the hall they heard the grandfather's clock

strike the midnight hour. He said—"You'd better go to bed, Dilly."

She raised her face for inspection. "Do I look tired?"

"No. But I promised young Eden to see him. I'll bet he's tired."

He went in where the fire was, to see if it were safe for the night. When he came out he said—"What you need is to have someone put you across his knee and give you a good whacking."

On her look of outrage he put out the light.

Lady Buckley's voice came from above, in a contralto whisper. "Dilly, are you still down there?"

"My God—Yes!" answered Dilly, the first two words in a raging undertone, the last clearly, sweetly.

A tall pale figure leant over the banister. "In the *dark*, Dilly?" she demanded.

Renny leapt up the stairs to his aunt's side and to her surprise kissed her. "We've been attending to the fire and to Gran. Dilly's very tired. She's on her way up."

Augusta turned, with impressive deliberation, to her own bedroom, but she said—"I hope you are not too tired, Dilly, to give me a few moments."

Passing Renny, Dilly Warkworth remarked to him:

"I do so love these endless conferences. Do you think they will go on all night? Your grandmother and you. You and me. Lady Buckley and me. You and Eden. And there's your little brother calling you. He wants one too. Bless his heart!"

Wakefield's voice was coming from Renny's room where, because of his weak heart, he slept. Now he called out—"Renny . . . Renny . . . Renny," in a small pathetic voice. "I'm not feeling very well."

Renny bent over the bed and laid his hand on the small body.

"There's nothing wrong with you," he soothed. "Go to sleep, there's a good fellow."

"Isn't my heart beating fast?"

"A bit fast. I'll sit here till you're quiet."

"My legs feel funny."

"I'll rub them."

The rhythmic rubbing of the thin thighs, the monotonous humming of "A hundred pipers and a'," had their effect. The light coming in from the passage no longer glimmered in Wakefield's eyes. They were closed. They flew open for a moment though when he said:

"I wish that girl Dilly'd go home."

"Why, Wake?"

"Well, for one thing, her mouth is too red. For another, her eyes keep looking at *you*. For another, she thinks she's clever. For another, she can't ride for sour apples. For another . . ." He tried to think of another objection but, drowned in comfort, sank asleep.

Every third step in the stairs that led to the top floor creaked, so that Eden was made aware of Renny's approach by a series of these punctuations. Each one ran threateningly through his nerves, and by the time Renny reached the top Eden was on his feet, facing him. Renny did not often come up to this room and now he threw a glance of distaste at its disorder. The bed showed that Eden had lain on it but the pillow was on the floor. Books were strewn over it. The short curtains at the windows had been tied in knots to let in all the light possible, and the wintry moon was framed in the western window. A rising gale was shaking the shutters which, after nearly a hundred years of struggle against those walls, still clung there. If there were few books in the library, the shelves in Eden's room were overflowing. Some lay on the floor. The open cupboard door revealed disorder within. Partly open drawers of the chest discovered garments half in, half out. The desk was littered. A pair of shoes lay in the middle of the floor and, near them, for some unguessed reason, an ash tray full of cigarette ends. Renny, whose belongings were kept in military order, said:

"I don't see how you live in this."

"I tidy up now and again. It just gets this way."

The light from the student's lamp cast a greenish pallor on Eden's face. He said—"Won't you sit down?" and began to clear the books from the armchair. For answer Renny perched on the edge of the desk.

"Have a cigarette?" Eden asked, with the air of a host.

"No, thanks." His intense gaze rested on Eden thoughtfully for a space, in silence, then he said—"What are you going to do about this Indigo Lake business?"

"What can I do? Well—I'm terribly sorry but I'm just as helpless as any of the others."

"Did you invest *all* of your commission, Eden?"

"No. Not quite all."

"You put part of it in the bank?"

"Yes."

"Let's see your deposit book."

Eden hesitated. Hot color surged up from his neck.

"Show me the book," Renny repeated.

Eden flung open a drawer of the desk, searched for a moment, handed the little red book to his elder, then jamming his hands into his pockets, turned to stare out of the window. Now the pale light of the moon was on his face. The moon was soon to be hidden by a snow-laden cloud. The first snowflakes whistled past the pane.

Renny studied the brief column of deposits. There were no withdrawals.

"You've been thrifty," he remarked.

"Something new for me, eh?" There was bitterness in his voice, as he added—"I had an object in saving." He felt what was about to come and now it came.

Renny said—"You must realize that we can't allow Dilly Warkworth to lose such a sum because of one of us and while she's visiting at Jalna."

Eden wheeled to face him. He said:

"She went into it with her eyes open."

"And you didn't seek her out and lead her to believe that here was the chance of a lifetime?"

"I believed so myself."

"Why did you keep these transactions secret?"

"Nobody wanted to tell the others."

"What others? Me?"

"I tried to tell you that day coming from town, but you wouldn't listen."

"Were you trying to confide in me or were you out to catch another sucker for Kronk?"

Eden paled. "Do you realize what you're accusing me of?"

"I say that your object all through this was to build up

your own little nest egg. Why—even your poor old grandmother was game for you." His voice rose. "By God, you ought to be ashamed of yourself!"

Eden blazed back—"You don't know what it is not to have a bean of your own."

"I know what it is to have responsibilities I have trouble in meeting."

"I'll soon be off your hands, I hope."

Renny now spoke quietly. "I don't want you—or any of you boys—off my hands. But I will not stand for a guest in the house losing money through you."

"I suppose you want me to fork over a thousand dollars for Dilly!"

"Exactly that."

Eden said, in a shaking voice—"Very well. I will, but I think it's damned hard."

"On the contrary, you're getting off easily. The uncles have been very decent. So has Meg—everyone. And that brings me to Piers."

"Good God," cried Eden. "You're not going to tell me to pay him back?"

"I certainly am. Piers worked hard—with hands and back—to earn the money he gave you—"

"He didn't *give* it to me!"

"He *entrusted* it to you to invest for him."

"You make it sound as though I were a swindler like Kronk. By jingo, I begin to wish I'd skipped out with the funds too."

"There's only one thing for you to do where these two are concerned. If you didn't repay Piers he'd hold it against you for years. I know Piers. And who could blame him? I don't want hard feeling in the house. When you've settled with those two you'll still have a hundred and sixty-three dollars left. Not so bad, eh?" He returned the deposit book to Eden. "Come, sit down and write those two cheques. Let me see you do it. You'll sleep all the better."

Eden broke out—"I can't do it tonight."

"But you will first thing in the morning?"

"Yes—though I still don't see—"

"You will when you think about it quietly. You'll be glad you did it."

Eden looked tired and deflated. He said—"It isn't giving up the money that I mind. I wasn't going to save it."

"Well—whatever ideas you had for spending it, you can forget for the present and put your nose to the grindstone or you'll be failing in your exams. Good-night."

He was gone.

Gone too the dreams of Europe. The walls of the lecture room pressed about Eden. He felt suffocated by the smell of dusty corridors. He heard the voice of the lecturer droning on, punctuated by the winter coughing of the students. He was caught, subdued, trapped! He flung open the window and the icy air flooded in, as though the lake had escaped its shores. A few snowflakes drifted in, shone in the lamplight, then melted at the first contact—like his hopes, he thought.

The sharpness of the air had its effect. He realized that what he was feeling was not despair but disappointment. His hopes were only postponed. For the present he must continue with the work he hated. Yet he felt no will for conflict with his own inclination. What he wanted he wanted so badly!

He stretched his arms and threw back his head. He saw how his elongated shadow on the wall made the form of a figure on a cross . . . He remained motionless in that position, staring at the shadow, till a shudder of cold shook him. He went to the window, closed it with a bang, then sat down in front of the desk and buried his face in his arms.

In the room directly beneath Eden's, Lady Buckley and Dilly Warkworth were engaged in a discussion as to the date of their sailing. Augusta was saying:

"But, my dear child, we have already outstayed the time when we had expected to return."

"Yes. Now we are in the time of the worst storms. You are not a very good sailor. Neither am I. I suggest that we wait till January."

Lady Buckley began to take down her long hair. She

laid the many hairpins in a meticulous mound. She said—
"There are other things than storms, Dilly."

Dilly knelt, in rather a spectacular fashion, at the older
woman's feet. "It's true," she said, "that my feelings
are . . ." She hesitated.

"Involved, Dilly?"

"Yes. Involved."

"I fear it is hopeless."

"Has he said anything—about me—against me—to
you?"

"He has spoken with circumspection."

"Lady Buckley—I love this family—I love this place—
It kills me to think of leaving. Why do you say it is hopeless?"

Lady Buckley began to comb her hair with a large ivory
comb. She looked compassionately down at Dilly. "I
have known him—" there was a silent agreement between
them not to mention him by name—"all his life. He is
hotheaded. Impulsive. If he had been going to fall in love
with you he would have done it before now. It would be
obvious to all." Dilly rose and stood up straight, though
not even then was she as tall as Lady Buckley.

"This is different," she said. "It's been a slow developing. You see, we both were so taken up by the horse
show. We thought of nothing else—or believed so. But
—all the while . . ."

Augusta could not refrain from asking—"You thought
of nothing else?"

"Well, occasionally I gave a thought to him but he—
well, I wouldn't have him otherwise."

"I doubt," said Augusta, "that you will get him any-
wise."

20.

Paying the Piper

EDEN SMILED AS HE HANDED the cheque to Dilly.

"But what is it?" she asked, drawing back.

"The bread you cast on the waters of Indigo Lake."

She peered at the cheque without taking it from him, then put her hands behind her back like a child.

"No, no, I won't take it."

"Nonsense. You must."

"But there is no reason in it. My eyes were open. Nobody forced me."

"Everybody says I led you into it."

"Eden, I don't blame you. I blame nobody. Why should you be the scapegoat?"

"I don't know. But I am."

"I refuse to take the money."

His heart leapt in relief, but then he saw the weakening in her face, her hand moved tentatively toward the cheque. As she took it she declared—"I'll tear it up." But she didn't tear it up. She folded it neatly and tucked it inside her belt. Then slipping her arm through his she said:

"I've been dreading to meet my man of business. He's terribly strict with me about money. It's ridiculous but I'm afraid of him."

"You've no need to be afraid now."

As soon as he could he escaped from her. He escaped from the house. He could hear the voice of the family lawyer, Mr. Patton, coming from his grandmother's room. He had been sent for to discover how deeply she was involved in the fateful stocks. An article in the morning

paper had confirmed the swindle. A warrant had been is-
sued for Kronk's arrest. It was found that the furniture
in both office and apartment had been bought on the in-
stallment plan and was still unpaid for. Mrs. Kronk had
gone to visit a sister in New York for the time being. A
glimpse of Mr. Patton's face through a crack of the library
door, as he entered the house, had shown him wearing
an expression appropriate to a funeral. The resonant melancholy of his voice further enhanced the illusion. He
might have been reading the funeral service.

Eden hoped and prayed that Mr. Patton would not ask
for an interview with him. He would make himself scarce,
that was certain. As he stood there, the lawyer's voice
ceased and Boney cried, with heartless gusto:

"Gold, you old devil! Buckets of gold!"

Eden fled.

Outdoors he found himself in a snowstorm. Snowflakes,
large and intricately shaped, were moving erratically in
the icy air, blown by a variable wind. Some of them, as
though finding no place indulgent toward their rest, moved
upward again and disappeared.

He saw footprints of dog but no dog. Footprints of
squirrel but no squirrel. There was no living thing. He
turned up his collar and ran toward the apple house, from
where came sounds of hammering. He guessed that Piers
might be there. The door stood ajar and he could see
Piers "heading in" a barrel of Northern Spies. He was
wearing a light gray cardigan. His muscular figure, his fair
complexion, stood in relief against the darkness within.
Each time he brought down the hammer on the barrel, it
was as though to relieve his rage within.

Eden stood in the doorway regarding with appreciation
the picture Piers made, foretasting the act he was to per-
form. Then, in a pause from the banging, he said, in his
pleasant voice:

"Oh, hullo, Brother Piers!"

Piers gave him his look of an angry young rustic and
again picked up the hammer.

Eden descended the three stone steps into the apple
house. What sweetness of scent was there! What rosy,

russet and golden-green shapes, lying cheek to cheek!
Eden forgot his errand and stood there enchanted.

"Well," Piers demanded, "what do you want?"

"I'll give you three guesses."

"How the hell should I know?" His look now became
wary, as though he suspected Eden of further designs on
him.

Eden took the cheque from his pocket and laid it down
on top of the barrel. "There you are," he said.

Piers looked. He read the words "Imperial Bank of
Canada. Pay to the order of Piers Whiteoak." He saw
the signature. His mouth fell open. He could scarcely
believe his good fortune.

He stammered—"S-surely you're not . . ."

"Surely I am. And I advise you to cash the blasted
thing as soon as possible or I may change my mind."

"You really mean I'm to have my money back?"

"I do."

Piers took the cheque, folded it carefully, unbuttoned
his cardigan, placed the cheque in the pocket of his pullover, buttoned himself up again, without speaking. Then
he turned to Eden. "Thanks," he muttered, and Eden
saw that there were tears in his eyes. Not just a few tears
but so many that in another moment they would be running down his cheeks.

Eden did not wait for that. He hastened away through
the falling snow. Suddenly he wanted to run along the
path that soon would be obliterated, and on through the
birch wood to the pine wood. He felt a lightness in him.
Poems he wanted to write came raging into his head. And
not only into his head but through his whole being. He
felt himself as an instrument, tuned up, ready for playing.

21.

Skating

PIERS, WHEN EDEN HAD LEFT HIM, remained, still as a statue, staring out through the open door after that swiftly moving figure. A few snowflakes drifted in and instantly dissolved. A red squirrel scrambled down the roof, peered in at the door, then fled in panic. Then came the sound of hoofbeats.

Piers was conscious of the tears on his cheeks. He wiped them with the back of his hand, threw down the hammer, and bounded up the steps. He saw the mare Cora, with Renny mounted, cantering toward the stables. He shouted his brother's name. Renny drew rein and waited for him, scanning his rosy face and wet blue eyes with an amused scrutiny.

"I bet you'll never guess what's happened," Piers said, breathless.

"What?"

"Eden has given me back my money."

"Good for him."

"You could have knocked me down with a feather."

"And only last night you wanted to knock him down!"

"Upon my word, Renny, I could hardly believe my eyes. Look." He produced the cheque. "He said I'd better cash it right off, to be sure of the money. Can I take the car and go to the bank?"

"What about the apples?"

"I'll finish them when I come back and take them to the station."

"Very well."

Cora was pawing up clots of snow, rolling her luminous eyes in impatience.

Piers, still in a daze, asked—"Do you think Eden's paying anyone else back?"

"Dilly."

Piers looked shocked. *"Dilly!* Why the dickens should *she* be paid back? She's knowing enough. She has plenty of money."

"She's a visitor."

"Phew. I didn't know Eden had it in him to pony up like this. I respect him for it."

"Good." Renny patted Cora's neck. She felt the welcome pressure of his knees in the way that meant "Go." Her whole muscular yet delicately adjusted being was freed, and she cantered along the path in feminine gaiety, arching her neck, dancing a little sidewise at the shadow of a pigeon on the snow, her long fine tail streaming.

The branch bank upon which the cheque was drawn was in the village of Stead less than ten miles away. Piers ran to the shed beside the stable where the car was kept, fearful that Eden by hook or crook might have withdrawn the money before his arrival. At Jalna the status of the motorcar was an inferior one. By most of the family, any sort of treatment was considered good enough for it. Piers was the only one who was anxious about its well-being, who would wash it or try to keep its engine in order. For the others, if the car would go, well enough; if it would not go, execrations were its lot.

This morning, after considerable grunting and groaning it decided to go. As it jolted along the quiet country road Piers sang for joy—" 'Pack up your troubles in your old kit bag and smile, smile, smile!' "

The hand of progress had not yet laid its devastating touch on this road that ran by the lake. The oaks and pines, in their primeval grandeur, beneath which moccasined Indians had passed to meet the first traders, stood in ignorance of the advancing axe, the coming bungalow, the filth of factory.

All Pier's dreams of affluence were now concentrated on getting his money back. Just to have it safe within the leather wallet which was the one thing he possessed that had been his father's. There were two women ahead of him, at the teller's wicket in the bank and he waited his turn in an onrush of anxiety. He slid Eden's cheque through the wicket. The teller, with a nonchalant eye, looked it over, just as though cheques of equal importance were his daily fare.

The teller turned over the cheque, examined the endorsement by Piers, then, with a smile handed over the money and asked how things were going at Jalna. He had been at the horse show and seen Piers riding his favorite polo pony. Piers, with an air equaling that of the teller in nonchalance, said he had reason to hope that the game of polo would regain its popularity—the finest game in the world!

Out in the street once more he was in no hurry to go home. He would like to celebrate his good fortune in some way but what was there to do?

A milkman's horse, not yet rough shod for the icy roads, had fallen. Piers helped to put it once more on its legs. He peered in through the frosty window of the bakery. The things inside looked good and he was suddenly hungry. He saw shiny Chelsea buns at fifteen cents the dozen. They were huge and with rich syrupy centres. He strolled into the shop and bought a dozen. He wondered what the woman behind the counter would do if he casually laid that massive roll of bank notes on the counter. Probably faint. Anyhow she'd think he was showing off and he didn't like that. Almost surreptitiously he extracted a bill from the envelope given him by the teller and pushed it across the counter to her. She drew back, as though she had been stung.

"Why, that's a twenty-dollar one," she said.

He went fiery red. Much embarrassed he retrieved it and turning his back to her, searched for something smaller.

"What you bought came to fifteen cents," she said—as though he didn't know!

"Haven't you any silver?" she inquired, with a freezing note in her voice, as though he had insulted her.

"No silver," he muttered, and found he had nothing smaller than a ten-dollar bill. He produced it and the woman looked at him as though she thought he'd been robbing the bank.

"I'm sorry," she said, still freezing, "but I haven't change for that."

Another customer entered and came up to the counter.

Piers muttered—"I guess I'll not take them then." He turned to leave the bakery and saw that the new customer was Pheasant Vaughan.

Their eyes met. They smiled in surprise and pleasure.

Pheasant then turned primly toward the woman.

"Have you Scotch shortbread?" she asked. "Like you make for Christmas?"

"It will be made in a few days, if you'll come in then." The woman smiled at Pheasant and now ignored Piers. "Is there anything else?" she asked.

"No, thanks . . . Well, yes. I'll have a dozen of the ladyfingers." She took out her little purse, perfectly composed.

Piers had an idea. "Could you lend me fifteen cents?" he asked in a low voice. "I've nothing less than a ten-dollar bill." He tried to make this sound normal.

She looked her astonishment, almost disbelief, but she took fifteen cents from her purse and laid it on the counter near him.

He pushed the silver across to the woman and picked up the bag of Chelsea buns. He and Pheasant turned away together, as though they had come in together.

"What did you buy?" she asked, with childish curiosity.

He opened the top of the bag to show her. "Oo," she said, "I love them."

He said—"I guess they don't make ice cream this time of year. I'd like some."

He asked the woman, who answered with a note of reproof that it was not the season for ice cream, but that she could make them a cup of coffee. Motorists sometimes came in for coffee in this cold weather. There were four little tables standing at the back of the shop.

"All right," Piers said loftily to the woman. "Make us some, please."

It wasn't till he had Pheasant seated at a table that he

leant over her and whispered—"I'll go to the bank and get some small bills. Back in a jiffy." Off he strode.

Pheasant discovered a tiny looking glass on the wall and tiptoed to it to see how she looked. She put her hat straight and tweaked a bit of hair from under it at each ear. The woman was in the room behind, making the coffee. Soon Piers could be seen running past the window, then entering composedly by the door. Pheasant was waiting with dignity at the table.

He dropped into the chair opposite her. He said:

"I don't often meet you. What I mean is you don't go about much, do you?"

She answered sedately—"I've no need to go about a lot."

"How's that?" he asked, looking suddenly and deeply into the golden brown of her eyes.

"Well, I've everything I need at home."

"You mean you don't *want* to go out?"

"When I want to go, I go," she said severely.

"That's funny," he said, and they lapsed into a rather depressed silence.

The smell of coffee came to them. Then the woman appeared with a small tray, the coffee pot, cream jug, and two cups. "Anything to eat?" she asked.

Pheasant looked at the bags containing the Chelsea buns and the ladyfingers. She said—"We have plenty to eat, thank you."

Piers gave her a quelling look. With a jerk of the head toward the glass case he said—"Bring us some of those splits, with the whipped cream inside."

The woman now seemed to admire him. She gave him a look that suggested it and then brought a blue plate with six round white buns on it, whipped cream thickly filling their two halves.

"Shall I pour?" Pheasant asked.

He nodded and gave all his attention to her pretty manipulating of the cups.

"Would you like forks?" the woman asked.

"It would be better," said Piers.

They ate, and sipped their coffee in silence for a little. In spite of all his care over the whipped cream Piers got a little moustache of it. He turned his face mischievously to Pheasant. "Look," he said.

She looked, and the sight was enough to send her off into soundless laughter. Feeling doggish he joined in laughing at himself. The woman looked back from the front of the shop and smiled.

Pheasant could not eat more than two buns, so Piers devoured the other four.

"Funny," he said, "we don't often do this."

"We couldn't," she said, decisively.

"Why not, I'd like to know."

"We shouldn't be let."

"Well—for heaven's sake! I'd like to know who'd stop me."

"Maybe not you but I shouldn't."

"Are they very strict with you? I mean Maurice and Mrs. Clinch."

Looking rather remote she answered—"I do what I like. Generally, I mean."

"Then why do you say what you said?"

"Well. People might talk."

"Do you mean say we're engaged or something like that?"

Her only answer was an embarrassed little laugh.

He went on—"I suppose the day will come when we're both engaged."

"I suppose."

"To somebody else, of course."

"Of course. Somebody else."

Piers noticed an ash tray on the table and took a cigarette from a packet in his pocket and lighted it. He glanced at the woman to see if she objected but she only smiled. Another customer had entered.

Piers said—"Dilly Warkworth smokes. In public too."

"For goodness' sake. She didn't win a first at the show, did she?"

"She says herself that she was no good. You'd have done better, Pheasant."

In silence she watched his quiet inhaling of the cigarette. Absent-mindedly he blew a perfect smoke ring.

"Oo," she breathed. "I wish I could."

"I'll show you."

"Not here."

"Some other place?"

"Yes." Their eyes met, were held, in tremulous fascination on her part, in powerful conscious masculinity on his. Both felt they had advanced in intimacy.

He drew the heavy bank envelope from his pocket and held it for her to peep inside. She drew back astonished. "Wherever did you get it?"

He answered easily—"Been dabbling a bit in mining stock. Gold."

Pheasant was impressed even more than he had expected.

"Gold!" she exclaimed. "However did you know how to do it?"

"It's easy enough," he said, "if you know the ropes." He returned the envelope to his pocket.

Pheasant's expression was one of profound respect.

"Just imagine!" she said. "But sometimes people lose their money. Mrs. Clinch was reading in the newspaper about a man who—"

Piers interrupted with some severity—"The thing is to know when to sell out."

In the street outside the shop he asked—"How are you going to get home?"

"Mrs. Clinch and I came by train. She's at a friend's house. I'm to meet her there."

"I wish you'd drive back with me."

He was not sorry when she declined saying she had so much to do. This had been a pleasant half hour but it was enough. Yet when she said she was going to have her skates sharpened, he was at once interested again. "You skate?" he asked. "Where?"

"Oh, the creek has made the loveliest pond in one of our fields. I'm the only one who goes. It's as smooth as glass."

He saw himself skating with her. He said, almost brusquely—"Mind if I come too?"

"If you like," she returned with dignity. "It's free. I skate every afternoon."

The very next day Piers arrived at the pond soon after Pheasant had put on her skates. He did not at once join her but stood concealed among some snow-laden bushes, watching her glide round and round the pond with more enjoyment than skill. Her pleasure in the rhythmic movement was obvious, from the red tassel on her cap to the bright blades of her newly sharpened skates. She had color in her cheeks, which was new to Piers. He felt a quickening desire to skate with her.

She did not see him till he flew past her, then turned with a flourish to face her, skating backward. He threw a bold beguiling look, as though to lead her to unheard of dangers and delights. He held out his two bare hands and she put her red-mittened hands in them. She ceased to take strokes but just put her two feet together and was drawn on by him. They moved away from the pond and up the narrow creek, which was wonderfully smooth beneath the film of snow that covered it.

She said—"How beautifully you skate. I didn't know anyone could skate so well."

"It's nothing. You should see the rink at the university and what some of the fellows can do."

"But it wouldn't be such fun as this."

A happy beam came from the blueness of his eyes.

"You bet it wouldn't," he said.

A twig, frozen in the ice, tripped him. He all but fell. He clutched her to him. He said—"It's getting a bit rough here. We'd better go back to the pond." Whatever he suggested was right, she thought. Their swaying movements, hand in hand, round the pond, dwarfed any excitements she had hitherto known. Piers was saying to himself—"Why—she's beautiful! Funny I never noticed it before." He said aloud—"I like your red cap and mitts. They're nice and bright."

"They were bought out of my Christmas money."

"But it's not Christmas yet!" he exclaimed, almost in consternation.

"I know. But I'm always given money for Christmas. Some while ahead. I buy what I like with it."

"But when the day comes. What then?"

"It's pretty much like a Sunday. Quiet, you know. But turkey of course. Once I had a tree. All by myself. I shall never forget that. It was planted afterward and it's still growing."

A warm pity for her surged through all his being. He thought of the great Christmas tree at Jalna, with presents for everyone. He wished he might invite her to join them. When they sat down to rest on the bank he said—"Christmas is a great day with us. Mysterious, you know. Everybody going about trying to hide something. Presents for everybody from everybody."

"It must be wonderful."

"Yes," he agreed judicially. "Though it's rather expensive." He gave a sudden explosion of laughter. "Not that cost signifies anything to me."

The silence of the countryside was heavy about them. Snow weighted the sky. Piers said—"I'll bring a shovel and clear the ice tomorrow. Will you be here—some time?"

She nodded happily.

Looking at her skates he asked—"Do you remember the day we kissed—by the bridge?"

"In a kind of way."

"In a *kind* of way. That's funny. How d' you mean *kind* of way?"

"It seems like a dream."

His eyes moved up as far as her mittens. "Like to try it again?" he asked.

"I think it would be better not."

"Why—I'd like to know?"

"Mrs. Clinch says habits grow on you."

He gave a snort and demanded—"What if it did?"

Pheasant took off her mittens and rubbed her palms together.

"Hands cold?" he asked.

"No. Too warm."

He picked up a mitten and drew it over his fingers. "Look," he said. "How small for me. I have the largest hands in the family."

She gave them a look askance, but said—"They're nice though. Manly, I mean."

"Oh, I don't know," he muttered, trying to hide his pleasure.

Now he lolled back on the snowy bank as though it were a quilt and gazed quietly up at the sky. He said:

"Now to go back to kissing."

She gave him her askance look. "How can we go back to something we hadn't begun?"

"Well, I suppose not," he said rebuffed, then added—"Anyhow I'm not much of a one to kiss. Not like the rest of my family."

Full of curiosity she asked—"Are they? When?"

"Oh, any old time. They're great kissers."

She turned her eyes, dark and wistful to his. She said—"Your brother Renny is the only person I can remember being kissed by."

"Well—I like that! So I'm nobody."

"You're different. I used to sit on his knee sometimes when he'd come to see Maurice. When I was young and he'd give me a kiss . . . Let's skate again."

They were scarcely on the ice when two other skaters appeared—young Finch and his friend, George Fennell. Piers was annoyed by this but Pheasant greeted them gladly. Soon all four were skimming about together, in a fashion so carefree, untrained and crude, that it would have been shocking to the grim experts of today.

22.

The Regaining of Equilibrium

MR. PATTON'S VISIT WAS VERY depressing to Adeline Whiteoak. He proved to her, in cold figures, how mistaken she had been to entrust the investing of a fairly large sum of money to an inexperienced youth like Eden and a scoundrel such as Kronk. He read aloud to her newspaper articles telling of the man's machinations in Canada and the United States. He told her just how much the poorer she was because of her recklessness, and though the figures went in at one of her ears and out of the other, the hard fact remained. He reduced her to a state of submission to his judgment which was to endure for the rest of her life, so far as investments were concerned.

When Mr. Patton had gone she collected what cash she had on hand, which was a little more than eleven dollars, and hid it in the bottom of the box where she kept her caps. She then experienced a feeling of relief, fed Boney a special tidbit, put on her second-best cap, and sent for Eden.

"You scallywag," she said, as soon as he was inside the door.

He said, under his breath—"Good God, have I got to go through this again!"

"Speak louder, you rascal," she said.

"Gran," he replied clearly, "I am in the same boat as you."

"What did you do with the money I gave you?" she demanded.

"Mr. Kronk took it, Gran. And he took mine and

Meg's and Uncle Nick's and Uncle Ernest's. Everybody's but Renny's."

"Ha, he didn't take Renny's, eh? Why?"

"Renny wouldn't invest, Gran."

She chuckled. "He's close, he is. Like his Scotch grandfather Dr. Ramsey. What do you say you have lost?"

"Practically everything, Gran."

"Everything, eh? Well, well—we're in the same boat then. But you'll not be able to say your old grandmother is close. Hand me that box. The one where I keep my caps."

She leaned forward, breathing hard, fumbling beneath the crisp lace and rosetted ribbon bows of the caps. She produced a five-dollar bill and thrust it into Eden's hand. She looked up at him, her face bright with the smile of her young womanhood that had enchanted those who knew her.

"Money always handy," she said, "to a young man."

Eden bent down to hug her. He was forgiven. That was the thing. She too embraced him. She asked:

"What day is it?"

"Saturday. Going to church tomorrow, Gran, in your new fur coat and all?"

She groaned at remembrance of the coat. But when the morning came she was ready to go, long before the time. An impressive collection of petticoats, underdrawers, overdrawers, vests and spencers were put on before she could be got into her black cashmere dress with the heavily beaded bodice and the lace ruching at throat and wrists. There were stockings and overstockings, shoes and overshoes, gloves and a muff. There was her widow's bonnet, with its voluminous veil. By the time she struggled into the new fur coat she was red in the face and panting. At last she was seated by that window in the drawing room which was nearest to the spot where Hodge would draw up the pair of bays and the old sleigh. He arrived promptly at half past ten, and for a quarter of an hour she regarded him complacently through the window. Out of the corner of his eye he glimpsed her black silhouette, set his hat at a more Sundayish angle. Hodge was proud of the bays and the old phaeton they drew for the greater part of the year and the capacious red sleigh that emerged when there was snow on the ground. There were few such equipages about nowadays. Strangers turned to stare at the glossy pair, with their polished, nickel-mounted harness and flowing manes and tails. For threescore years and ten, horses had been impatiently pawing the ground as they awaited the coming of Adeline Whiteoak.

Seated by the window she could tell by the way the tails and manes of the horses were blown that there was a high wind. She made up her mind that if she felt the cold this would be her last outing till spring, new fur coat or no. However, she was at this moment so very warm that she was overcome and fell asleep. She dreamed that it was sixty years back and she was waiting for her husband to come to church with her. She dreamed that it was a hot summer's day. She was dreadfully warm and Philip was late. Unusual for him. She felt herself becoming annoyed, then really angry. Whatever could he be doing? If anyone were kept waiting it should not be she! Then she heard a step, felt a hand on her shoulder. The step was quick—a running step—the hand was small . . . Philip had sent one of the children with a message from him. She turned her head, raised her heavy eyelids, and looked into the face of her youngest grandson.

"Wake up, my grandmother," he said, with his most dignified air. "The church bells will soon be ringing."

"Ha, where am I?" She was dazed, her long crepe veil had fallen over her face.

"On your way to church, my grandmother. In your new fur coat."

"Fur coat! In summer!"

"It's winter, Granny. Almost Christmas."

Renny and Piers came into the room . . . Still a bit dazed she was lifted to her feet. On her either side they supported her descent over the icy front steps to the sleigh. With a heave they got her into it and she sank, a great bundle of fur, into the comfort of the seat. The great black bearskin rug was drawn up about her. She had not, since waking, felt able to utter more than a mumbled word or two but now the ice-cold air revived her. She smiled into Renny's face and said:

"I was ready too soon. Who's coming with me?"

He stood bareheaded, the snow falling on his red hair.

"Where's your hat?" she demanded. "I won't have my grandson going to church bareheaded."

"It's in the car, Gran."

"Who's coming in the sleigh with me?"

Her two sons appeared, wearing topcoats with large fur collars. They climbed in and seated themselves beside her. Hodge eased the reins, but before the horses dashed off Wakefield clambered to the seat beside him. The many silver bells, those that were strung right around the bellies of the horses, and the large deep-toned ones that hung above their shoulders, set up a mellow jingling. Over the polished bright red back of the sleigh a second bearskin rung adorned by tails was placed. This was to rest one's body against and also to make a fine show as it streamed out behind. Above it floated old Adeline's voluminous veil. The muscles rippled beneath the glittering flanks of the horses. The scarlet tassel on Wakefield's cap bobbed. Nicholas and Ernest waved a good-bye to those on the steps. Down the drive and out of sight they went, the horses' hooves sending clots of clean snow over the rug that wrapped the knees of Hodge and Wakefield.

The motorcar, in its blackness, was a melancholy sight after the sleigh. Its grunting as it started was an offense to the ear after the music of the bells. Behind the wheel was Renny. Meg quickly secured the seat beside him. Dilly, Eden, and Piers sat together in the back. Lady Buckley, who suffered a migraine, had remained in her room. Last of the family to appear was Finch. He ran out of the house, dressed for church, but with a distraught expression, one hand held to his cheek.

Meg said—"No room in the car, dear. You'll just run across the fields like a good boy."

"I don't wanna go," he mumbled. "My tooth aches."

His sister looked her compassion. "What a shame. But if you will look on the top shelf of my bedroom cupboard, you'll find a bottle with toothache drops. They'll soon make it better."

"It *aches*," he muttered. "I can't go."

Renny said—"I know all about these headaches and toothaches that appear just at churchtime."

"But this is *real*. It aches likes the dickens."

"You didn't speak of it yesterday."

"It only began ten minutes ago."

"Don't let me hear any more about it."

Piers said—"We shall be late."

Off they went, leaving Finch on the snowy steps, the cold wind causing the tooth to jump fairly out of his head. He staggered into the hall, kicking the door shut after him. He said loudly—"I won't go. I won't! I'm damned if I will."

"Wot's the trouble?" inquired Wragge.

"Nobody cares how I suffer!" shouted Finch.

"Toothache, is it?"

"Raging. I wish they had it."

"You can't tell me nothing about toothache. Every tooth in me 'ead 'ad a bout of it—one time or another. There's no peace till you 'ave them all out."

"Oh, gosh, I don't want to do that."

"It's the only cure. But for relief a big mouthful of whiskey, 'eld in the mouth, is pretty good."

"Oh, oh," moaned Finch. "It's jumping."

Wragge brought him, from the dining room, whiskey in a glass. "Try this," he said.

Finch took a large mouthful; tilted his head to allow the aching tooth the full benefit of it; swallowed it; took another, while Wragge watched him solicitously. He fixed his eyes, in which hope lightened the misery, on Wragge. After a little he solemnly nodded.

Wragge said—"Swallow. Then tike another mouthful. 'Old it. Swallow. I never knew it to fail. On the tooth or in the stomach whiskey 'as a beficial effect." As Finch followed his directions he added—"Of course, you'll never 'ave any real comfort till you 'as them all out. That's what I've found."

Finch violently shook his head at this suggestion—choked—swallowed—took more whiskey. A look of benign relief came into his eyes. As he swallowed the last mouthful he executed a few steps of a jig with great agility.

"Did the trick, eh?" grinned Wragge.

"You bet. Why, it's practically stopped. I believe if I took the least little drop more it would stop."

"Right you are," said Wragge and brought him more.

A glowing warmth ran through all Finch's being. A warm grateful relief. Yet he felt at the same time a rebellious anger toward his eldest brother. Tyrant. Unfeeling tyrant who had a mouthful of teeth that never gave any trouble, yet would goad a sufferer like himself to go to church.

"Feel pretty good now?" Wragge asked. "Able for the windy walk across the fields?"

"Not on your life," said Finch.

"Well, I can't say I blime you."

"I'll show him," Finch added, in a loud aggressive voice, "whether he can order me about as though I was a dog. I've no intention of going to church. I never did intend to. I don't think much of churchgoing anyhow. What good does it do you?"

"None that I've discovered." Wragge was still grinning. "That is for me. With your family it's different. Your grandfather built the church. His descendants 'as got to keep it going."

"Not me," snarled Finch. "I'll be damned if I go . . . bloody damned if I go!"

In a mysterious way Wragge seemed to be floating round and round him, and always with that mischievous grin on his face, his eyes laughing.

"I doan't blime you," Rags repeated.

"I've stood about enough," yelled Finch. "From this time forward I'm going to go my own way and I'm sorry for anyone who interferes with me."

Out of a face large as a pumpkin that floated somewhere near the ceiling Rags reiterated—"Doan't blime . . . doan't blime you."

Finch watched this pumpkin face as it floated, at first with curiosity, then with a certain distaste. He found he was holding a glass in his hand. He tossed it up and caught it. He found this amusing, tossed it higher and higher. The last time it almost hit the ceiling and would have fallen to the floor had not Rags caught it.

As he caught the glass he said, with an abrupt change from his friendly manner to an air of faultfinding—" 'Ere —that's enough from you. Better lie down for a bit till you get over it."

"I am over it. D' you mean the pain?"

"I mean the cure. You need to lie daown."

"I know what I need and I don't like to be told. I'm not going to stand any more telling—see?"

"No offense meant," said Rags, friendly again.

Finch put an arm about Rags's shoulders. "None taken. And I chertainly am grateful for the way you stopped that pain. By the way—where just wash that pain?"

"In your fice. Toothache."

"Ah, yesh. Terrible toothache. Believe I'll go to the library and lie down. Feel funny."

But he turned in the wrong direction and found himself in the drawing room. He was surprised to discover the piano there and stood dazedly regarding it for some minutes . . . Then a clearness descended on his brain like a mystic hand. His brain was so clear that he felt himself capable of anything—even capable of playing the piano. He always had wanted to play the piano and now he discovered that he could.

He had some difficulty in making his way to the piano. A footstool was directly in his path and the detour he made in order to pass it brought him directly in front of the fireplace. The piano was not to be seen. But he saw his own reflection in the mirror above the mantelpiece. His face appeared flushed to him and rather splendid. He took a long pleasurable look at it before he again set out in search of the piano.

When he found it he discovered that the stool was too high. He twirled it till it became too low. However, it was fun twirling it and he kept this up for some time. Finally sinking upon it he laid his hands on the keyboard. He drooped there for a space blinking at the keys, which were strangely blurred. He waited, watching himself, as an outsider might have watched him, with a cool impersonal interest.

Then he heard himself beginning to play. Softly at first, with an exquisite singing tone, as of the first rippling of the frozen streams in springtime. Then the music grew stronger, as other streams added the power of their waters. Gradually the volume increased till all the rivers set free were shouting in their exaltation. His body swayed, his hands were raised high and brought down with a crash, as the floodwaters, heaving with broken ice, crashed in ferocious surrender into the sea . . . He realized now that he was not alone but that a great crowd in a magnificent concert hall were applauding him. Lights reflected in a thousand prisms in the chandeliers dazzled him. He knew that he should rise and bow but he had not the strength in his legs. All his power was in hands and arms. With the loud pedal down he played with greater volume, more splendid ferocity than ever.

The door of the drawing room was thrown open. Lady Buckley, her hands pressed to her ears, staggered toward him. She called his name but he was so rapt in his music that he did not hear her. He did not hear the four dogs in the hall. This canine quartette were, in the torture of their sensitive ears, rendering the air with their howls.

Lady Buckley staggered forward, a bandage about her aching head adding to the classic cast of her features, her long dressing gown threatening to trip her at every step, and laid her hands heavily on Finch's shoulders.

"Stop!" she commanded, in a stentorian voice.

His hands fell from the keys.

Silence that was almost palpable flooded the room. For a moment it lasted; then the quartette in the hall raised their voices in one last howl—high, shrill, and soprano from the Yorkshire terrier, quavering mournful baritones with all the misery of radio singers from the spaniels, heart-rending bass from the bobtailed sheep dog.

"How *dare* you cause such a riot?" demanded Augusta.

Speechless Finch raised a dazed face to hers.

"Have you lost your *reason?*" she demanded.

He could not speak.

What he had thought was the blaze of chandeliers was the glare of sunlight from a cloudless sky. His aunt's face hung above him. He smelled the camphor with which she had wet the cloth about her head. Behind his own head he felt the fullness of her breast and burrowed against it.

"Aunty," he breathed, and his breath went through her with a terrible shock.

"Finch," she mourned, "you have been *drinking*."

"Just whiskey," he mumbled, "for my tooth."

"You're *drunk*," she said.

"Thash's what made me able to play," he giggled.

"I was never more shocked," she said, and looked it. Indeed, her shock was so great that for the moment she forgot her migraine. She took him firmly by the arm and drew him to his feet.

An odd picture they made as they moved, clasped in a dizzy embrace, through the hall and into the library. There she laid him on the old leather couch and went to the trouble of covering him with a woollen afghan which she herself had knitted many years ago. But she said before she left him:

"I shall be obliged to speak to your brother about this."

That did not worry him. Nothing worried him. He fell into a heavy sleep.

Meantime the two parties arrived at the church.

The merry jangle of the sleigh bells mingled with the sonorous ringing of the church bell. Close behind the sleigh came the motorcar, chugging, bumping over the ruts, honking its urgency to the sleigh. Grandmother was half lifted out and, with Renny and Piers on either side, slowly, slowly she mounted the steep steps that led to the church. The frosty air made her wheeze. Nicholas, Dilly, Ernest, Meg, Eden, and Wakefield followed. Always she felt that she was being hurried, though everyone was suiting his pace to hers. She wanted the other churchgoers to have plenty of time on this morning to admire the beauty of her new fur coat. She spied the Misses Lacey, daughters of a retired English admiral, whom she had known all their lives. They were now aged sixty-three and sixty-four but had retained their fresh complexions and happy zest for life in this quiet spot.

"Dear Mrs. Whiteoak," they cried simultaneously, what a beautiful new fur coat!"

At this moment it seemed a burden to her, but when

she heard it admired she preened herself and stepped out more strongly. "It's a good coat," she said. " 'Twill do me the rest of my life."

"But," said Miss Lydia, "your other fur coat is so handsome still."

"Aye, 'twill do for a knockabout."

Nicholas winked at Miss Lacey, who had once wanted very badly to marry him and even now had a warm spot in her heart for him.

It seemed that the little procession would never reach the door of the church, so slow was its progress behind the shuffling leadership of old Mrs. Whiteoak. It was a relief to their ears when the clanging of the bell ceased. In the vestibule she said to Todd, the bell ringer—"It's high time you stopped that clamor. Didn't you see me coming?"

"Yes, indeed, Mrs. Whiteoak, ma'am," he said respectfully, his hands still clinging to the big rope, "but I thought you'd like a little music on the way."

That tickled her fancy and she gave him a gracious grin, inclining her head, massive in its widow's weeds. Along the aisle she progressed, and those already in the pews turned their heads to see her. The oldest of them could not remember the time when she was not there or picture the time when she would be no more seen.

Now the cushions for the pews, which she had donated in the first glow of her successful investing, caught and held her attention. In those pews that still were empty, they were stretched inviting, soft yet firm, and in a lovely shade of red. Those seated on them had a relaxed, armchair sort of look. Even those of the congregation whom nature had comfortably padded looked gratified, while relief was strongly mingled with gratitude on the faces of the thin ones.

Adeline Whiteoak saw that it was now too late to take back the cushions. Willy-nilly the expense of them must be borne by the remnant of her fortune. Never very good at figures, she now varied between looking on herself as impoverished or completely forgetting her loss.

Wakefield was in such haste to test the new cushions that he almost ran up the aisle to be first to reach the family pews. There were two of these. Into the foremost one went Piers, Eden, Dilly, and Ernest. Into the pew behind, Grandmother and Meg, with Wakefield between them, and Nicholas next the aisle. With an audible grunt the old lady sank onto her new cushion. Its comfort was nothing to her, because a cushion was always brought by Meg to put under her and another for her back. Now all the family, with that luxury beneath them, bent their heads in prayer, or the semblance of it. Miss Pink was softly playing the organ, her new winter hat an object of interest to the congregation. As the Whiteoaks straightened their backs Wakefield was bouncing on his seat. He was exhilarated by the resilience of the cushion till Nicholas, observing his unseemly conduct, reached behind Meg and gave him a fillip on the head. The little boy subsided against his grandmother and stroked the silky fur of her new coat.

"Do you think," Meg whispered to Nicholas, "that she should have the coat off?"

"Too much effort," he whispered back. "We should never get it on her again."

"Who?" demanded the grandmother.

"Who what, Granny?"

"Who's getting off or getting on?"

"It's your coat, Gran. Do you want it off?"

"I bought it to be seen. I'll keep it on, thanks."

Even more than Miss Pink's hat, it was indeed noticed. What with the hat, the coat, the new cushions in the pews, few of the congregation had eyes for the Rector and the lay reader when they took their places. But above all there was Miss Warkworth. Ever since she had come to Jalna Miss Warkworth had been the object of the most intense interest to the neighborhood. She was often the object of disapproval also. The redness of her lips was almost scandalous and she had been seen more than once to intensify their color, in public. She wore her hair short in the new fashion and curled all over her pretty head. She had an air of cool audacity, very different from the sweet expression of Miss Whiteoak, whom everyone admired. It was said that she was out, tooth and claw, to capture Renny Whiteoak. It was also said that she would meet her match in him. Now she stood between Eden and Ernest joining her sweet English voice to the lusty voices of the Whiteoaks in the processional hymn.

Renny Whiteoak was the lay reader, as had been his father and grandfather before him. He had hastened to the vestry and donned his surplice under the urgent eye of Mr. Fennell. As soon as he was in his place he cast a glance at the family to see if Finch had arrived. Finch was missing but there was Dilly blooming like a rose beside Uncle Ernest.

Mr. Fennell was reading, in his Sunday voice:

"To the Lord our God belong mercies and forgivenesses, though we have rebelled against him; neither have we obeyed the voice of the Lord our God, to walk in his laws which he set before us . . ." The service proceeded.

Dilly was looking extraordinarily pretty, thought Renny. But try as she would she could not look devout while Eden, without effort, looked rather like a young saint, with that face like his lovely mother's. And there was young Wake, again steadily bouncing on the cushion, in spite of the fillip Uncle Nick had given him. And there was Gran, looking mountainous, getting red in the face from the bulk of the new coat. Strange that Meg would not have taken it from her. Strange that Meg would allow the child to go bouncing. Well—he'd get something to bounce for, if he didn't behave himself . . . Renny noticed that his surplice was a little crumpled. It would be freshly laundered for Christmas. He must see that plenty of greenery was cut for decorating the church and holly ordered. A sudden recollection came to him of a Christmas when he was a very small boy. It had been the first Christmas after the death of his own mother. He and Meg had been sitting down there in that pew, with their grandmother and their father—the old widow and the young widower, all in black. Renny remembered his own little gray suit and the black band of crepe on his left arm. He was proud of its blackness because it made him seem more grown up and like his father. Often he would bend his head to look at it. But all the while he was thinking of the beautiful little iron train, with the wind-up engine, that he had glimpsed standing beneath the Christmas tree in the library when he and Meg had peeped through the keyhole. How he had quivered with longing to hold that key in his hand and wind up the locomotive!

It was the time of the Second Lesson. Renny stood behind the brass eagle of the lectern and read:

"And there shall be signs in the sun, and in the moon, and in the stars . . ."

Meg thought—"Now those sunspots we've been hearing of—they're bound to mean something—drought and a poor season for strawberries or floods, and seeds washed out of the ground . . ."

Renny read on— ". . . and upon the earth distress of nations, with perplexity, the sea and the waves roaring; men's hearts failing them for fear, and for looking after those things which are coming on the earth . . ."

To pass the time Eden played a game with Dilly. He had a pencil but no paper, so they used a blank page in the back of a hymnbook. First he wrote— "The congregation sag and snooze—"

He then handed the book to Dilly, who, after a moment's consideration added—"There are red cushions on the pews—"

She returned the hymnbook to him and he instantly wrote— "The reader reads so badly—"

This time Dilly nibbled the end of the pencil in perplexity but could think of nothing but to repeat the first line. She wrote, however— "The congregation sags and snoozes—"

He nudged her. "Go on."

She then added— "There are red cushions in the pewses—"

With a scowl he wrote— "I'm dying to kiss you madly."

Piers's strong hand reached in front of Eden, trying to get possession of the book. Dilly was clutching it delightedly. There was an incipient struggle, not lost on the Rector, the lay reader, or those in the nearby pews.

But now the organ pealed forth. The congregation rose and sang:

"O be joyful in the Lord, all ye lands: serve the Lord with gladness and come before his presence with a song."

All had risen but Grandmother, who too had seen the little scuffle. Muttering— "Young whelps, misbehaving in church." She took her stick and gave Eden a sharp poke in the back with it. This was so unexpected that the excellent note he had just struck, turned to an astonished grunt. He glared over his shoulder at his grandmother. "Behave yourself," she adjured, in a voice not drowned by the *Jubilate Deo*.

He turned and hissed at her— "Why should I be singled out?"

"Because you're the one I can reach," she hissed back but this time her voice was lost in the singing.

She enjoyed the little skirmish and settled back into the comfort of her fur coat like an old she-bear gone into hibernation for the winter. But she kept herself awake till Mr. Fennell had mounted the pulpit. Then he would, she knew, thank her for the cushions. He did indeed. Before beginning his sermon he said:

"We are enjoying on this Sunday morning still another benefit conferred on us by a member of that family which has been so generous with its gifts in the past—right from the time when Captain Whiteoak gave the land and built on it this church. Now the lady who was his beloved wife, and who, I am happy to say, is with us this morning, has donated cushions for all the pews in the church. This is a really splendid gift and one that I am sure you all deeply appreciate. The cushions are handsome and will add greatly to the physical comfort of our members. I can only hope that in this bodily comfort none of us will forget that we are in God's house . . . And now, in the name of the Father, the Son, and the Holy Ghost . . ."

Dilly's cheeks were flaming. Eden folded his arms and looked straight up into Mr. Fennell's face. Piers hung his head. But the grandmother's eyes were heavy with tears at the mention of Captain Whiteoak. The tears hung in her eyes till she blinked, then they trickled down either side of her strongly modeled, handsome old nose which defied the onslaught of time. Meg clasped her hand and squeezed it. Her family turned their heads to smile

at her. All the congregation craned to have a glimpse of
her, to make their offering of gratitude. Wakefield made
no attempt to conceal his self-importance. If he had himself donated the cushions he could not have felt more
the Triton among minnows.

The wintry sunshine penciled the shadows of bare
twigs on the windows. Its thin light was not flattering
but picked out worn spots, wrinkles and gray hairs,
showed how Farmer Tomkins had cut himself shaving,
how young Fred Miller was getting a boil, how the
brasses needed cleaning, and where there was a bit of
plaster loose. But the splashes of color from the stained-
glass window in memory of Captain Whiteoak were clear
and serene. In truth there was a serenity and confidence
about the whole scene, as though the actors, in pews,
choir, and pulpit, were playing parts they well understood, uttering lines well suited to them, feeling emotions
for which their forefathers had prepared them. Mr.
Fennell's sermon was not long. It was without rhetoric and
rather dull but his voice was pleasant, he preached of
goodness rather than sin, and no aspect of fear or doubt
entered into it.

As all rose at the end Piers managed to get possession
of the hymnbook and to tear out the page where the
verse was written.

The voices of the Whiteoaks, soprano, tenor and bari-
tone, led in the singing of the last hymn, the little choir
being quite helpless against them.

> " Let all the world in every corner sing,
>   My God and King!
> The heavens are not too high,
> His praise may thither fly;
>   The earth is not too low
>   His praises there may grow.
> Let all the world in every corner sing,
>   My God and King!"
>
> " Let all the world in every corner sing,
>   My God and King!
> The church with psalms must shout

> No door can keep them out;
>   But above all the heart
>   Must bear the largest part
> Let all the world in every corner sing,
>   My God and King!"

And such confirmed royalists were the Whiteoaks that the hymn's reference to their King might well have been understood by a listener to refer to their allegiance to George V.

Like an ancient battleship moving massively among lesser craft the grandmother made her way toward the door. The cushions in the new empty pews lay like quiet ripples on either side of her.

"Dear Mrs. Whiteoak," exclaimed the younger Miss Lacey, "never have I *known* such cushions! They're a perfect *dream!*"

"Never have I been so comfortable in church," added her sister. "I positively *luxuriated.*"

Everybody wanted to speak to her, to give her a word of thanks. She was in great good humor. In the vestibule she encountered Noah Binns. He had a piece of news to give her. It was that he had been appointed assistant gravedigger.

"That's what I am, from now on," he said with a leer. "Assistant gravedigger. Would you remember my father, ma'am? Eli Binns? We don't expect him to last more than a few days more. I'll be diggin' fer him pretty soon. That'll be my first. Quite an enigma fer me."

"Ah, that's sad," she answered.

Noah looked pious. He said— "The Lord giveth and the Lord taketh away. Nothing could be fairer than that."

Wakefield seemed to have heard those last words before. He pondered over them as he moved decorously through the vestibule. His eyes and Noah's met. All the way home, with the jingling of the bells as an accompaniment he chanted—"Nothing could be fairer than that."

Lady Buckley met Renny in the hall. She was feeling much better but was looking quite sallow. They two were for the moment alone. He put his arms about her and asked:

"Better, Aunty?"

"Better of the migraine but—" she compressed her lips.

He looked her over anxiously. "Something else—somewhere?"

"It is Finch," she answered, with a deep sigh.

"Finch? Is his tooth worse?"

"I only wish it were his tooth."

"Whatever is wrong?"

She took him by the lapel of his coat and said into his ear—"Finch was—and probably still is—*drunk*."

Renny drew back, as though from a woman demented. She saw this and repeated with great firmness—"Drunk —to the point of frenzy."

"Is he? Where?" he shot out.

"In there."

Renny threw open the door and the boy sprawled under the afghan was discovered.

Renny gave Augusta an anxious look. "Are you all right, Aunty?" he asked.

She drew herself up, offended. "Am I or am I not capable," she demanded, "to judge whether a person is in a frenzy?"

"He looks quiet enough now," said Renny.

"He is now *dead* drunk."

Renny strode into the room and bent over Finch. "Hm," he said, and straightened himself and scratched his chin. He wondered whether or not to wake the boy.

Lady Buckley continued— "The first manifestation was an outrageous uproar on the piano. Loud pedal down. A pounding that must surely have broken some strings. The din was horrible. Ill as I was I tottered downstairs and there was Finch *raging* up and down the keyboard and all four dogs howling."

"Well, I'll be damned."

"I must say," she added, "in justice to him, that he suffered himself to be led to the couch without any further disturbance."

"I wish I'd been here," said Renny.

"Oh, he did need a *man!*"

Renny patted her shoulder. "Just leave us for a bit, Aunty."

She hesitated, saying—"don't be too . . ."

"No, no, I won't."

Her voice trailed away, as did her long dressing gown.

He took the afghan off Finch. He then administered half a dozen hard slaps and thumps over the boy's bony person and ended by raising him to a sitting position by the ear.

With difficulty Finch opened his glazed eyes. He blubbered— "Ow—my ear! Whash amatter? Whatafidone?"

"You know damned well."

Finch put his fist to his face. "It was my tooth. It ached." He gave a dazed smile. "It 'sh better now. I took whiskey for it." He appeared not to have noticed the whacking he had got. Renny, observing this, gave it to him all over again.

Augusta had gone into the drawing room, closing the door after her, for she felt she could bear no more. In from outdoors now appeared Grandmother, a son on either side.

"I'm ready to drop," she declared in her strong old voice, "with the weight of the coat. Take it off me as fast as you can."

Divested of it she stood leaning on her stick, her eyes caught by the sight of Finch on the couch and Renny standing over him. As the second chastisement was taking place, she shuffled with all the haste that was in her to their side.

"What's this," she demanded. "What's going on?"

"This young fool," Renny said, "has been drinking."

"Him!" she cried. "And scarcely off his mother's milk! Flog him well for it, Renny. Of what use is your hand? My father always took a stick to his boys."

"I won't do it again," Finch got out. "I promish."

The room was now full of others, asking questions, rebuking, laughing, according to their natures. Wakefield came last, chanting in his shrill treble:

"An enigma! That's what he is. An enigma!" With the image of Noah Binns looming in his mind, he chanted

—"He got tight and he got licked. Nothing could be fairer than that!"

Meg took him by the hand and led him from the room.

Nicholas came from the drawing room with news that three strings of the piano were broken.

"Finch must pay for them out of his pocket money," Renny decreed.

"I'll pay," said Nicholas. "But he's not again to touch the piano. Augusta says the uproar was appalling."

Ernest added—"And if there is one thing above another that Augusta craves, it is peace."

"Don't we all?" grinned his mother who enjoyed nothing better than conflict.

Wragge now appeared carrying a small tray on which there were glasses of sherry.

"We'll have that in the drawing room, Rags," Renny said, and then asked in a lower tone—"Have you seen anything of this young man this morning?"

Rags looked with surprise at the figure on the couch. "I 'ad a glimpse of 'im, sir, 'holding to 'is fice. I think it was a toothache 'e 'ad."

Renny grinned, looking that moment extraordinarily like his grandmother. He said—"Well, I generally keep the spirits under lock and key. I shall have to be more careful in future, if the kids are going to take to drink."

"Yes indeed, sir," Rags agreed imperturbably.

Nicholas was filling his pipe, with the comfort of a man who had been through a church service. He remarked:

"The boy isn't fit to come to table. He'd better go up to his bed."

"Yes," agreed Renny. "Go up to bed, Finch."

"Good Lord," laughed Eden, "he's fallen asleep again."

"I'll wake him up," said Piers.

Renny said—"He can stay where he is," and covered him up with the afghan. His hair, wild as a brush heap, and his flushed miserable face were all that was left visible of him.

Eden picked up a crumpled half package of cigarettes that had fallen from Finch's pocket. "There isn't a crime," he said, "that this little boy doesn't experiment with. I believe these are mine." He helped himself to a cigarette

and was about to drop the remainder into his pocket when
Piers snatched them from him. Then Piers, remembering
Indigo Lake, returned them with a smile.

The procession moved into the drawing room and
Dilly came dancing down the stairs. She had on one of
the new-fashioned dresses with the terribly short skirt.
Ernest regarded her prettily shaped legs with interest,
but he remarked—"I always consider sherry as indigesti-
ble stuff."

"Nothing better for you before Sunday dinner," said
Nicholas. "Come along, Dilly, have a glass of sherry."
And he put an arm about the young woman.

For a brief moment she believed it to be Renny's
arm, for he was close on her other side, and she made
her eyes large at him. His look of abstraction, however,
undeceived her and she turned to Nicholas and clasped
his shoulder.

"Ha," grunted the grandmother ensconced with her
sherry. "This is good. I do like to go to morning service
and come home to a glass of sherry." She took a sip and
beamed about her. "My fur coat was no great weight at
all . . . D' you think they like the red cushions?"

"They love them," said Nicholas.

Ernest added—"It seems to me that the Rector spoke
very nicely of you, Mamma." As his niece came into the
room, he asked—"Can you tell me, Meggie, what we
are having for dinner?"

"A roast of veal, Uncle Ernest, stuffed. French fried
potatoes. Fritters. Lemon pie, with meringue. Nuts and
raisins."

Ernest set down his glass with a groan. "From my point
of view," he said, "it couldn't be worse."

"Shall I order something different for you?"

"Yes, have an egg poached for him," said Nicholas,
with seeming good humor.

Ernest returned tartly—"No, no, I prefer to eat what
the others do. In fact a little veal will do me no harm.
I shall eschew the nuts and raisins."

His mother nodded approval. She said—"I always
eschew my food well. It helps digestion."

"I said *es*chew, Mamma."

"So did I." With audible gusto she munched a little biscuit which Meg now brought her. She then turned to Dilly and Eden. "What were you young rascals up to in church?" she demanded benignly.

Piers came and stood in front of her. He said—"They're both poets, Gran. Listen to this." He produced a leaf from the hymnbook and read:

> " The congregation sag and snooze,
> There are red cushions on the pews,
> The reader reads so badly.
> The congregation sags and snoozes
> There are red cushions on the pewses—
> I want to kiss you madly! "

"Did they make it up?" asked the grandmother.

"Oh, yes, dear Mrs. Whiteoak," moaned Dilly, "and we're so ashamed."

"Nothing to be ashamed of. Quite a good poem. Now go ahead and do it."

"Kiss, do you mean?" asked Dilly, as though horrified.

"Certainly. Go ahead."

With a little scream Dilly held out her flowerlike cheek to Eden, who gave it a peck.

"That's not what I call kissing madly," said Grandmother. "Now that eldest grandson of mine. He could show you. Ha, ha—what about it, Renny?"

Dilly answered for him—"Oh, his mind is more on chastisement."

"Chastity," repeated the grandmother. "Ah, it's a great thing. A very great thing, as my father used to say—if you don't overdo it."

Augusta here rose, in great dignity. She said—"This is a strange Sunday. A most unedifying Sunday."

Meg nodded sadly—"Yes indeed, Aunt Augusta. Carousing at home. Writing ribald rhymes in church. And the strange thing is that the lesson Renny read was full of warnings—the sunspots and the like."

Renny said, from where he stood in the doorway:

"And there shall be signs in the sun, and in the moon, and in the stars . . . There was nothing about sunspots."

"But surely you agree," cried Meg, "that they all are *warnings*. These spots appear in the heavens—then disaster follows on the earth."

Wakefield here put in—"Nothing could be fairer than that."

"I like that rhyme," said the grandmother, "the one about the cushions I gave. I shall paste it in my scrapbook. Fetch me the book, Ernest."

"Bless your heart, old dear," said her son Nicholas. "No one has seen that scrapbook for thirty years."

"Have I pasted naught in it for all those years?"

"Nothing that I know of."

"Dear me," she sighed, "how time flies. What was the last thing I pasted in the book?"

Renny answered—"It was a newspaper cutting about the first time I rode at the horse show. I was seven."

Dilly hissed at him—"What a frightful egotist you are."

Piers presented his grandmother with the leaf from the hymnbook on which the jingle was written. However, as she was holding it between finger and thumb Boney flew down from his perch, secured it, and tore it to ribbons. At the same moment Wragge loudly sounded the gong for Sunday dinner, which effectively put all else out of the old lady's head.

Finch dimly heard the gong, was faintly conscious of the talk and clink of cutlery in the dining room. He was more and more conscious of the feeling of nausea which was creeping over him. The odor of the roast veal came through the cracks of the folding doors, the odor of rich gravy . . . The first wave of nausea passed but later on when the second wave attacked him he sprang from the couch and ran down the hall to the little room where the dogs slept and where there were taps and a basin. Groaning he bent over the basin.

When dinner was over Meg found him still in this room sitting on a stool near the window. She came in and laid her hand on his neck. She asked:

"Are you feeling better?"

He nodded, unable to speak.

"And you'll not do a wicked thing like that again, will you?"

Vigorously he shook his head.

She went on—"Everybody was *so* upset. For my part I could scarcely eat my dinner."

He shuddered. "Would you mind not talking about eating, Meg?"

She stroked his head, then drew back from him.

"Your *hair,*" she brought out, in disgust. "Whatever have you got on it?"

"I dunno. Why?"

"It's sticky. It must be washed. I shall wash it now."

He drew back in horror. "Oh, no, Meggie! No! You can't! I won't! Not my hair—please!" His voice broke in a squeak of misery.

Meanwhile Meg had removed her blouse and put on a large enveloping apron which she kept in this room. She had taken from the cupboard a cake of Windsor soap and a clean crash towel. Finch viewed these implements of torture with crapulent misery. Always he had hated hair washing but never so bitterly as now.

Meg now turned on the hot water in the basin. She demanded—"How often do you wash your hair?"

He was so miserable that she had to repeat the question before he took it in. Then he muttered:

"My hair gets washed when I have a bath."

"That's no way to do. No wonder it is in such a condition." She was intolerably brisk, dabbling her hand in the basin to test the temperature of the water.

He rose from his stool and made a zigzag movement toward the door. He said—"I'm not well enough. I *can't,* I tell you!"

"There is nothing you need do," Meg said, almost soothingly, "except to bend over the basin."

"No," he yelled. "I can't bend over the basin! I'll be sick again."

"Nonsense. It will make you feel better to have your head washed." Now her tone was commanding. She collared him, divested him of his jacket, pressed her hand on the back of his neck.

He bent over the basin. She made a lather on his head. She rubbed it in. He let himself go then, uttering noisy protests.

"Ouch! You're hurting me! Ow—my ear!"

"Which ear?"

"That one. I think someone hit me on it."

"Nonsense. Nobody hurt your ear. Bend lower."

There was no doubt about it. The hot water, the massage, the cold-water rinse that followed, made him feel better. By the time he had the second rinsing he was almost himself again. But he would not let Meg knew this. A listener up the hall might have thought he was on the rack.

Such a listener was Aunt Augusta. Her mother and brothers had retired for their after-dinner rest. She was enjoying the quiet of the drawing room when this turmoil disturbed her. She now swept to the scene.

"Stop!" she commanded loudly. "I will not allow this poor boy to be beaten again."

Meg was now enveloping Finch's head in the towel. "Don't worry, Aunt Augusta," she laughed. "Finch has just had his hair washed. People are coming to tea and I simply could not let him be seen looking the way he did. And he has *such* pretty hair when it is properly washed. Look." Proudly she lifted the towel from his head.

The two women now surveyed him with pleasure. His cheeks were now pink and his fine straight hair released from the towel was taking on golden-brown tints. He smiled sheepishly at them not knowing whether or no to be pleased with himself.

Meg put him by the heat of the glowing stove in the hall with a towel around his shoulders. With the dogs for company he meditated on the strangeness of life.

When teatime came he was there in the drawing room in his best suit, handing about cups of tea, carefully offering cake to the company. To one of these Meg might have been heard to remark:

"He is at the awkward age, you know, but he has an affectionate disposition and in some ways he is quite clever."

The conversation then moved to a more interesting subject, for teenagers had not yet been invented, nor were the peculiarities of very young people considered to be of importance.

23.

The Winter Moves On

CHRISTMAS CAME AND WENT in a mood that varied little from other Christmases at Jalna. Several members of the family felt that they had less than usual to spend on presents, which was natural, as their money losses had been considerable. Eden early announced that he would give nothing and expected nothing. However, at almost the last moment he had some verses accepted by one of the best American magazines and was so happy about it that he went to town and bought a necktie for each of his uncles and brothers, and lace-edged handkerchiefs for his aunt, his sister, and Dilly. For his grandmother he bought a bottle of smelling salts which she sniffed with such zest that she first sneezed, then coughed and all but choked, and had to be revived with brandy. This was the one untimely incident in an otherwise auspicious day.

Nicholas had made up his mind that his presents that year were to be better than usual. He would show that a bit of unlucky speculation did not affect his giving. As for Dilly, she was recklessly generous and said it was the best Christmas she ever had enjoyed. But to Piers it brought pleasure of a new sort. This was the heady pleasure of thinking of someone besides himself—to the complete exclusion of himself.

Thanks to Eden, a miracle had happened in the return of his lost investment. He was no longer hoping to double or treble his money. It seemed a magnificent thing just to have it once again in his possession. He made up his mind to buy Pheasant the most exciting Christmas present she ever had had. He spent a good deal of his time in pondering over what this was to be. Something to wear, that was certain. But what? He brought the conversation around to broaches (in these days they managed to meet quite often) but Pheasant let it be known that she already had a broach and she considered one broach quite enough for any girl. Of course, he might buy her a ring but there was a finality about a ring from which he shied away. A ring should be given only to seal an engagement. He brought the conversation round to earrings but Pheasant affirmed that earrings hurt and that she had no desire for them. What she did like was rings and never had possessed one. These conversations were carried on quite impersonally on her side, with no expectation of a present. Piers experienced the keenest enjoyment in them, in watching the expressions of her changeful little face, the drawing down in puzzlement of her brows, the judicial compressing of her sensitive lips.

One point which had to be considered was whether Maurice Vaughan, her father, would allow her to accept a present of jewelry. Piers felt that it would be best, on the whole, for the present to be kept secret for the time being, and worn only when they were together.

The next thing he thought of was a bracelet, but when he asked her whether she liked bracelets she showed no interest in them whatever. They were sitting on the snowy bank beside the frozen pond and the one thing which seemed to interest Pheasant at the moment was a broken bootlace. She had tied it in a knot and the knot pressed on her instep.

"It hurts awfully," she said. "I think I'll go home."

He examined the knot. "You've made a bad job of tying it," he said. "I can tie one that won't hurt. Take off the boot and I'll fix it for you."

Pheasant well knew that Mrs. Clinch would not approve of her removing her boot in front of Piers Whiteoak. Mrs. Clinch had devastating things to say about the goings-on of young women since the war. She had read that there were girls in London who now carried their own latchkeys and let themselves in at all hours. She fastened on this as one of the greatest evils, which was rather strange, as at Vaughanlands the front door was never locked. Neither Mrs. Clinch nor Pheasant had the slightest desire to go out or in at all hours. As for the danger from burglars, it was not even considered.

The thought of a girl's having a latchkey all her own was somehow fascinating to Pheasant. She pictured herself as coming home at midnight from some scene of revelry, inserting the latchkey in the large old lock, of which the actual key lay in a drawer of the hatrack, and entering the house on tiptoe, creeping past the room where Maurice slept and flinging off her velvet cloak in her own room, flinging it off with a weary gesture, sated with late hours and pleasure. Strangely enough the thought came to her now as she took off her boot and gave it to Piers. She asked:

"What do you think of latchkeys? For young women, I mean."

He turned his wide blue gaze on her. "Latchkeys? What for?"

"Why, to get in and out with." And she added, in a hushed tone—"Late at night."

"Where?" he asked, beginning to pluck at the knot with his fingernails.

"In London."

"Oh, *there*. You should hear the things Dilly tells. She often goes."

"What sort of things?"

"Oh, rather wild things."

"Does she tell in front of your grandmother and your aunt and your sister?"

"No. She doesn't."

"Do you approve?"

"Never thought about it." Now he had untied and re-tied the knot. "Put out your foot," he ordered, in a suddenly peremptory tone. Now he was kneeling in the snow. He held the boot invitingly before her.

"I can put it on." She was suddenly shy.

"All right." He dropped the boot, jumped up and stood on his skates, staring at a little red squirrel that was reaching in a stump for a nut it had hidden there. "You ought to be hibernating," he said, and made a snowball and threw at it.

Now Pheasant was sorry and somehow ashamed. She wished she had let him put the boot on her. She wrestled with the bootlace but could not lace it up.

"Ready?" he asked briskly.

"I can't manage it."

"That's what you get for being so proper."

"Oh, Piers. You are mean."

He wheeled, knelt down in front of her. Her small foot planted on the snow looked somehow pathetic. Skillfully he laced up the boot.

"Bend your foot and see if the knot hurts," he said.

It no longer hurt. It was quite comfortable.

As she looked down at him kneeling there, a feeling of tenderness toward him almost overcame her. She felt sorry for them both. She said—"What a pity we are not birds, so we could fly."

"Yes," he agreed, unexpectedly, for she had thought he would laugh at her. "It would be fun if we could fly together."

She plucked at a leaf of brown bracken that stuck up through the snow. It was when she bent her head that he noticed how round and slender and captivating was her neck.

"Do you like necklaces?" he asked, almost breathless in the excitement of this new idea.

"Do you intend to go into the jewelry business?" she asked. "Your mind seems sort of set on it."

"I've never known a girl like you," he answered in an annoyed tone. "No matter what I suggest you don't like it."

"I suppose," she said, feeling hurt, "you've had lots of girl friends."

He got to his feet and brushed the snow from his knees. "A considerable few," he answered.

"What were their names?"

He looked blank. "How could I remember?"

"Then I suppose you'll forget my name—later on."

"Oh, you'll be taking a new name, one of these days."

"What, for instance?"

"Whiteoak, perhaps."

At this they both laughed rather nervously, then a silence fell. To break it Pheasant said—"If there's one thing above another that I do like it's a necklace. I mean a real one. Not just a string of beads."

"I suppose," he probed, "that you have a very good one."

"I have beads but no necklace."

Now he knew what her Christmas present was to be. A necklace. A really good one, with pretty semiprecious stones in it.

They were gay and laughed for sheer pleasure in the skimming round and round the little pond, with the western sun reddening their faces.

Piers was a little sobered by the price he had to pay for the necklet he chose. Yet what a moment it was when Pheasant opened the blue velvet box and discovered it lying there in its nest of white satin . . . the fine gold chain, the flowerlike pendant of turquoise and tiny pearls.

"Not for me! Not for me—surely!" she cried.

He had brought it at a lucky moment. They were alone in the living room at Vaughanlands. Piers had chosen a time when he knew Maurice to be in town with Renny.

"Yes, for you." He tried not to look important.

"But it's beautiful!"

"It is rather nice." Nonchalantly he took his chin in his hand and stared out of the window.

"*Nice!*" she cried. "Oh, Piers—why did you ever do it?"

Now he looked straight at her. "I like you, don't I?"

"Well, perhaps . . . I suppose you do . . . but then—" she faltered.

"Then what?" he asked, as though trying to corner her.

"Oh, I don't know. I don't know anything except that I love it."

"*It,*" repeated Piers.

"Why not?"

"Why not me?"

"Of course I do—at this moment."

"Only at this moment!"

"All the time—naturally."

They laughed nervously, as though at some witty but rather dangerous repartee.

She was wearing a high-necked blue serge dress and she now took the necklet from its box and said, controlling her voice—"Thank you, again and again."

"Don't mention it," he said stiffly. Then he added—"What about trying it on?"

"With this dress? Never."

"But I'd like to see it on you."

She bit her lip in embarrassment. "As a matter of fact, I haven't anything fit to wear with it, excepting my brown satin best dress."

"This thing," Piers said, as though contemptuously, "should be worn on the skin."

"With a low-necked dress, you mean."

"Of course."

"I'd better put it away till summer," she said. "I'll get a new summer dress especially for it . . . What about Maurice? What will he say?"

"Good Lord, Maurice mustn't see it. He'd think it odd. He'd likely tell Renny and . . ." Piers could not go on. He could not tell her of the row he'd get into at home if— Now he said, his breath coming quick—"I wish you'd wear it every day, under your dress. Then nobody will see it till—" He hesitated and looked about him, as though for same way of escape. But he could not escape from himself and the urge that drove him.

"Till when?" she asked, large-eyed.

"Till we come out into the open." His voice was husky. The palms of his hands moist. A paralyzing silence enveloped them. It was a relief to hear Mrs. Clinch coming.

Piers was a favorite with her and she smiled when she saw him.

"You're quite a stranger," she said.

"I'm a working man, Mrs. Clinch," he laughed.

"It's news to me," she said, "when I hear of any of the folks at Jalna working."

"Now I call that insulting." He gave his jolly smile. "We do a lot of hard work."

"Hard work! None of you knows what real work is."

"My grandfather was a pioneer, like Pheasant's grandfather."

"Gentry, all of them," said the housekeeper, "with plenty of money to hire other folks to work for them. Not but what I like your sort better than some of the upstarts I see nowadays. Money is all they have."

"We certainly haven't much."

"Would you like a cooky?" she inquired. "I've some in the oven."

"Thanks. I'll go to the kitchen for them."

"No. I'll bring 'em in here." Piers's boyish vitality put new life into her. Angular though she was she almost bustled from the room.

Like two culprits Piers and Pheasant smiled secretly at each other.

"Got it safe?" he whispered.

She patted the front of her dress. "In here."

"Shall you wear it?"

"All the time. Underneath."

"I think it's rather nice, don't you?"

"Perfectly lovely."

He frowned judicially. "It isn't a cheap thing, you know."

"It must have cost the earth!"

He smiled, gratified. "Well, not quite."

She said, almost tragically—"You shouldn't have done it, Piers."

"Why?" he demanded, as though defying all of his family, with Maurice and Mrs. Clinch into the bargain.

"Oh, because."

"Because why?" He came close to her and looked deep into the golden-brown depths of her eyes.

"You know," she whispered.

"I only know," he said, "that you're the sweetest . . ."

Mrs. Clinch's step was approaching. They drew apart, and when she appeared with a plate of cookies they were examining with rapt interest a steel engraving of Lady Butler's "The Roll Call."

During these winter months Dilly's pursuit of Renny was as earnest as Piers's pursuit of Pheasant. Yet it was more difficult, because while he was more accessible to attack, he was at the same time even more shy, and decidedly fiercer. They were like two hunters, out after two different sorts of prey. They differed also in their motives, for Piers did not yet know whether he intended a direct kill or whether the pursuit itself was enough, but Dilly was quite sure of what she wanted. She wanted to see the red-haired master of Jalna lying mortally wounded at her feet.

He was fleet in avoiding her, for he perceived the huntress's glitter in her eye. Safe in his bedroom he counted the days till her departure on the shiny calendar that hung above his washing stand. Ruefully he examined his reflection in the looking glass as that of a man about whom the toils were closing. The women of his family were on Dilly's side. His grandmother was constantly reminding him that the girl had brass, and God knew he needed it. His aunt remarked what a handsome pair they made, and told him of the fine property in Leicestershire to which she was heir. His sister told him how she had learned to love Dilly and how she was the only girl she ever met whom she could welcome as a sister at Jalna. Even Wakefield developed a clinging attitude toward Dilly (nobody but he and she knew how many chocolates she fed him) and showed such a partiality for her that Meg became a little jealous. One thing was certain, the child had small appetite for his meals and suffered two bilious bouts inside a fortnight.

His uncles had a decided affection for the girl but they said nothing to push Renny into this marriage.

Ernest said, stroking his long finely boned face with his long white hand—"I have remained single and shall remain single to the end of my life. There is a spirit in me which refuses to bend the neck to the yoke of matrimony. But you, my dear boy—would, I imagine, find great pleasure in the companionship of a congenial woman. The question is—is Dilly congenial?"

Renny asked—"How did this question come up? I didn't bring it up."

"Really, I don't know," answered Ernest. "It's the long winter, I suppose."

Renny stared at him. "I wish the family would get something else on their minds."

"It's difficult for them—you see I don't include myself—" returned Ernest, "when there is such a desirable young woman in the house—and you."

"Leave me out of it."

"Yes indeed, I quite agree."

"If she is so desirable, why didn't that other fellow toe the scratch?"

"From what Augusta tells me, Dilly did well to escape."

"I wish I could."

Ernest laughed heartlessly. "You are well able to look after yourself, dear boy."

Nicholas now joined them, and Ernest said to him— "We have just been speaking of Dilly."

Nicholas, filling his pipe, growled—"Steer clear of matrimony. I tried it. Never would again."

Ernest objected—"But Renny must marry. He must carry on the name."

Nicholas said—"Piers is bound to. He's the type. Let him do it."

"Just the same," said Renny, "this girl is a menace. I wish she'd go."

"I shall miss her bright presence in the house." And Ernest drew a comfortable sigh.

"From now on," said Renny, "I intend to live more and more in the stable."

He kept his word and there were days when he was scarcely seen in the house. He had two rather peculiar horsy friends who visited him often but were not made welcome by Meg. They would sit in his little office in the stable, discussing the characteristics, the pedigrees of various horses by the hour. They would drink whiskey and water, smoke till the air was blue, even sometimes have a game of cards, all in the peaceful knowledge that, in the stable beyond, there were no complications of human intercourse, but only the direct and godlike simplicity of beautiful and powerful beasts.

"I love the harness horse," Mr. Chase would say. "And

I saw a beauty last week. She was for sale and you ought to buy her, Mr. Whiteoak."

"I don't go in for breeding harness horses, as you well know. It's a waste of time."

"That there Cora of yours is a lovely mare," Mr. Crowdy would add. "What a shoulder! What a firm, level back! What legs!"

"Yes," Renny would agree. "Money can't buy her."

And on and on they would talk till the early dusk began to fall, when the two friends would depart in their old Ford and Renny would stand in the door of the stable, staring longingly at the lights coming out in the house. "Upon my word," he thought, "it hardly seems like home any more."

He went back into his office and looked at the calendar and counted the days till she would go. "By God, she'll get me yet," he thought, as he felt himself weakening.

The very next day she appeared at the stables wearing her riding clothes. It was the first of March and a great thaw had set in. Huge snowdrifts which had withstood the ever increasing power of the sun now succumbed, sank, drew into themselves, and disappeared. Little rivulets chased each other all about the farm land. Sparrows fervently took baths in icy puddles. The earth presented its dark face to the sun's inspection. Dilly came right to the office and knocked peremptorily on the door.

He knew who it was before opening it and he looked about him, as though for a place to hide. Then she knocked again, playing a little tune on the door with her knuckles.

He opened it and greeted her with an unamiable grin. "Well," he said, "so it's you, Dilly."

"I didn't know a winter could be so long," she said. "Couldn't we go for a ride?

"We could indeed, if you like riding in icy slush. The horses certainly don't."

She came into the office. "I heard Piers say at lunch that the roads are quite good now and I heard you say last night that the horses need exercising." Her eyes rested on the calendar. "What a pretty calendar! Why have you made a circle with a red pencil round the twenty-first of March?"

He looked at that date as though he had not seen it before, then answered—"It is the equinox. Surely you know that."

"I want to know what it *means*." She stood straight, looking into his eyes.

"Why, the sun crosses the equator, doesn't it?"

"*I* cross the *Atlantic!*" she cried. "Do you mean to say that you're making a red-letter day of it?"

"Is that the date when you leave?" he asked innocently.

"It is. You know that very well. Really—you have the most perfectly abnormal sadistic nature I have ever known."

"Go on," he said, "this is just the way to make me love you."

"I don't want you to love me! I want you to go on hating me."

"Come out to the stable," he said, "and get on the scales and let me weigh you. I believe you've gained considerably since coming to Jalna."

"I'd rather," she cried, "be too plump, than thin as a bone as you are."

He answered tranquilly—"Curves in a woman can be very alluring."

"You suggest weighing me to sneer at me."

"No. To put you in a good humor. Children always like to be weighed."

"You think I behave childishly," she wailed.

He moved his arm so that he could see his wrist watch. "We have time for a ride," he said. "Supposing we go. I'll ride Cora and you shall ride Prince Eitel. He's a fairly new acquisition. He's well behaved, though a bit lively. Do you mind?"

"There's nothing on earth I should like so well," she cried, melting as the snowdrifts had melted. "Now we're friends again, aren't we? How heavenly!" And she held out her plump white hand, which he at once clasped in a determined air of masculine reconciliation.

As they passed the various stalls and loose boxes their occupants, by some subtle means of communication, let it be known to the farthest corner that there was riding in the air. The winter had been so long. To be sure, a canter on well-packed snow was a pleasant thing but the wind could be bitter cold and the deep ruts of winter roads were not liked by horse or rider. But now there was warmth in the sunshine that turned the clean straw to spears of gold. Through the open upper half of a door came a new smell. Elegantly sculptured necks were arched in anticipation. Lustrous eyes glowed and deep-throated whickers demanded—"Am I to be chosen?"

Cora and Prince Eitel were saddled and led out. Renny looked Dilly over with an appraising eyes as she was mounted. He thought he never had seen her so attractive. She stroked the Prince's neck and called him "darling." She seemed to feel that he was going to do something for her.

As they trotted past the house there was Meg on the porch, wearing only a cotton dress and hugging herself with her plump arms.

"Have a nice ride," she called.

"It's divine to be on horseback," Dilly called back.

"He's a beauty—the horse you're on!"

"He's like a rocking chair."

Meg shouted—"You two look lovely together!"

Pretending not to have heard Dilly asked—"What did she say?"

"She said we looked funny together."

"I don't believe it."

"That's what she said."

"I *heard*. And she said *lovely*."

"Rather silly remark. But I suppose she meant the horses."

"You never would agree that I could look lovely."

"You're not my type, as I've told you." He cast a critical glance at her. "Your right knee is out."

She clamped it to the Prince's side and they disappeared from Meg's gaze into the green tunnel of the drive where the lowest branches of the spruce and hemlock swept the ground and the topmost now welcomed the first crow.

"Listen!" exclaimed Renny, when it uttered its bold caw. "Spring is coming!"

"It must be divine here in springtime," she said, raising her eyes to the promise of black wings now spread against a pale blue sky.

"It is," he agreed. "It comes suddenly and everyone is glad. Though for myself I enjoy all seasons. Just as I enjoy all moods in a woman."

"You can be very sweet," she said. "But when you're disagreeable the effect on me is devastating. Oh, there's some terrible lack in me! You feel it, I know. Can you tell me what it is?" She rode close beside him now, through the big gate and onto the road.

"Yes," he answered tersely. "Horse sense."

"You devil," she said, pushing so close to him that Cora capered in annoyance, slipped, and went dangerously close to the ditch.

The road was a little muddy, with melting snow at the sides and a subdued gurgling in the ditches. On either side the farm lands still looked wintry. There was that air of flat desertion, as though, all slept, not in peace, not in serenity, but in the season that was no season, in a longing without object.

"Which way are we going?" she asked, in a small meek voice.

Always showing off, he thought, and answered—"To the lake-shore road. It will be better there." His eyes were following with admiration the easy grace of Prince Eitel's gait. He had been a good buy.

The pair exchanged amiable words as they ambled along the miles to the lake-shore road, which the sun had almost dried and where they passed two wagons and met a single motorcar.

Prince Eitel, Renny thought, carried himself as a prince should. He moved with charm and distinction. Not that he was better than Cora. No horse could surpass her, but he was wonderfully good, and Dilly had never appeared to greater advantage. Renny was conscious of his thoughts warming dangerously toward her, and she, when she spoke, said the right thing. Her eyes, when she turned to look into his—but no—better not meet that look of challenge and promise—for if he gave in to her, though she might pretend that she did not care a rip for marriage—he saw that in the pout of her lips now—she would marry him in the end—as sure as she sat astride the Prince.

He knew that road yard by yard, not mile by mile as a motorist would know it. He knew the rise beyond a clump of cedars, where a huge old stump lay at which Cora invariably ducked her head and shied. He knew the very bend in the road where the icy wind struck you. He knew that place where the lake was washing away the shore, nearer and nearer the road. The ditch into which a runaway horse had once thrown him and broken his leg.

They turned into a side road and passed through a gate into a field where Renny saw a farmer at work. He had arranged to buy a load of gravel from the man and the pit was at the far end of the field. Near it was a small stream. Cora lightly jumped the stream but Prince Eitel, in a playful mood, refused. He danced and gamboled at its edge, while Dilly happily showed off her horsemanship for the benefit of the two men. Then he made up his mind that he would jump, but Dilly had allowed him to dance farther down the stream and the place where he went over was near the edge of the pit. He jumped with great power, making for an instant a brilliant picture against the sky, then landed with his forefeet in slushy gravel, looking straight down into the pit. Shouts of warning had been too late to prevent the near disaster.

Terror shook the Prince to his vitals. Rigid as a horse in bronze he kept his balance, like a rider in bronze Dilly gripped him with her thighs. He uttered a snort of terror, glaring down into the pit. He then gave a trumpet-like scream, reared to his hind legs, turned short on them, and proceeded to express the violence of the fear he had experienced by a display of plunging, kicking, and shying. There was nothing the two men could do but watch and pray that Dilly would not be thrown.

She was not thrown, and when Prince Eitel had recovered himself she rode over to where Renny was and exclaimed quite jauntily, though her cheeks were white—"What fun!"

Never had he admired her so much. But now admiration was fired by desire. He really wanted her, he thought, and when they returned to Jalna he would ask her to marry him. Yes, he would marry her and everybody would be pleased. It had taken him some time to be sure of his feelings but now he was sure. Dilly was magnificent.

And all the way home she did nothing to destroy the aura with which this incident had surrounded her. She was rather quiet, rather gentle, bending to speak soothing words to the Prince and pat him.

In the stable yard at Jalna there was a pleasant bustle. The old carriage had been brought out and was being washed and polished for the grandmother's first spring outing. Wright was clipping the long hair from the legs of a team of farm horses. A hen was cackling loudly as a stableboy drove her from where she had no business to be. A rooster was crowing. Piers had been exercising his favorite among the horses, an aged polo pony which followed him about like a dog and was now eating a carrot from his hand. Ben, the sheep dog, was supervising all this with an air of great sagacity.

Piers came to help Dilly dismount and she poured out the story of her narrow escape. It was surprising how this terrifying incident sounded no more than feminine exaggeration the way Dilly now related it. And she had been so cool, so collected.

"You'd never believe, Piers," she cried, "how completely shattered Renny and I were. At first we simply rocked with hysterical laughter. Then we clung to each other, in tears. Didn't we, Renny?"

"Of course. And we were still mounted when we did all this," said Renny, his eyes now teasing rather than loverlike. "Take Dilly to the house, Piers, and give her a drink. She's been through a good deal."

"Aren't you coming?" asked Dilly.

"Not yet. Scotchmere tells me there are two men waiting for me in my office." He followed the old groom into the stable.

The two men were Messrs. Crowdy and Chase, the former bubbling over with plans for winning the King's Plate with a fine young horse he had lately purchased.

Chase, in his quiet way, was as absorbed as Crowdy, yet both had seen Dilly from the little window in his office. When their first greetings to Renny were over, Mr. Crowdy, spreading a thick palm, inscribed on it, with a stubby forefinger, a cryptic sign whose meaning was known only to himself, and said:

"A fine figure of a young lady. Very fine. A winner. In any class."

And Chase added—"There's no woman so satisfactory a companion as a good horse, Mr. Whiteoak. There's something about a good horse that makes a man happy and peaceful." By the time Renny joined the family for the evening meal the idea of making a proposal of marriage had quite left his mind. He felt free and untroubled.

Eden, throughout the long winter, wrote more poetry than ever before. He made a pretence of working at his books. He did indeed attend lectures and take notes, but in the seclusion of his own room he did little but read and write poetry. On the journeyings to and from the town he sat slumped in his seat in the train with young Finch opposite, his eyes not seeing the wintry landscape, his imagination fiery from within. In its generous glow he scarcely was aware of what day of the week it was, except for the pleasure of the week end when he was free.

"He gets lazier and lazier," Renny observed to Nicholas. "I don't know what to do with him. He's going to fail in his exams again, as sure as fate."

"He will be all right," said Nicholas. "There's good stuff in Eden. He may surprise us yet."

"I don't doubt that he'll surprise us. But I do doubt that the surprise will be pleasant."

"His poetry," said Ernest, "is good. I stick to that. Has he told you he has had another poem accepted by *Harper's?*"

"Yes."

"Did he read it to you?"

"Yes. But he can't live on poetry. When I talk of work he looks tragic."

Eden was always a problem. Finch was often a problem. Doubtless Wake would be a problem. Of the four youngest Whiteoaks Piers was the only one to be depended on, a boy easily understood, thought his elders, little dreaming what was going on inside his head.

A professor with whom Eden had become friendly advised him to send a collection of his poems to a firm of New York publishers, Messrs. Cory and Parsons. The thought of doing this had not before occurred to him. He felt diffident about it, but Ernest, when he was told of the suggestion, agreed with enthusiasm. He urged the boy to bring all the verse he had written to his room and they would go over them together, selecting, choosing titles for the poems, polishing—if Eden would be willing to let Ernest offer a suggestion now and again. Eden was willing and a happy time they had together. New lyrics poured from Eden in an ardent stream. So eager, so careless was the flow that scarcely had the idea of a new poem been generated in his imagination before it had taken form and was transferred to paper. In this period of flowering, the anxieties, the tension of the days of Indigo Lake were forgotten. Ernest knew he was doing wrong in encouraging Eden to waste so much of his time but he could not help himself. Always he had hoped to have something of his own published and had not given up hope, though he had not yet brought himself to the point of submitting a finished manuscript to a publisher.

24.

Indoor Sport

ALL THROUGH THE WINTER the house with its five chimneys seemed to be sunk in meditation. From the chimneys smoke rose, like its meditations made palpable. On one side or other of the roof the snow would melt, as the warmth of the sun increased, and the pigeons would come and sit on the sunny slope of it, passing the word in low tones that a time was coming for love and rivalry and the wonder of eggs in the nest. Sometimes a mass of snow would slide off the roof with a loud rumble like distant thunder. The grandmother would speak of the old days when passenger pigeons would fly overhead in a cloud that darkened the sun, and bluebirds in a small blue cloud, a time when the wild birds had scarcely learned to be afraid.

"Ah, those were the days," she said to Dilly. "The birds were scarce afraid. The people had not grown soft. They'd leave their grand homes and come out here to the Colony and rough it. There was no fear in the land. We had a glorious time of it—my husband and I. We built this house, you know."

"What fun!"

"Indeed, 'twas fun." And she added, in a tone of melancholy unusual to her—" 'Twere better I had been a man!"

"Why, dear Mrs. Whiteoak?"

"Because then I should have been dead long ago."

"But why?"

"Ah, they don't last as we do. They're not made for lasting."

"I think men are magnificent," cried Dilly. "See how they can fight in a war!"

"Ah, but they get killed or come home and die. We outlast them." Now she gave a grin of satisfaction. "Take my two sons. They'll never live as long as me. Nicholas has the gout, Ernest has indigestion. When I was their age I had neither pain nor ache. I'll live to be a hundred."

"I am sure you will."

"Aye. But the winter is long. Very long. What was that you said about fun?"

"I said you must have had fun in the old days."

"We had indeed . . . Heigho, I'd like a good laugh."

"Let's dress up," cried Dilly.

"Dress up?"

"Yes. All the others are out in their rooms. Let's dress up for tea. One day when I was in the attic with Meg, I saw all sorts of clothes. I could bring some here to your room. What a surprise we'd give everybody when they came to tea! Do say I may."

It was not quite clear to old Mrs. Whiteoak just what Dilly meant to do. The girl talked so fast. But she liked Dilly's animation. She longed to do something different, with a strange resurgence of youthful enterprise in her veins. She struck her knee with her clenched hand and said:

"Fetch the clothes! We'll dress up."

Dilly darted from the room and up the stairs. She flew up them, light as a bird, trying to rid herself of the feeling that this house gave her. It gave her the feeling that it was watching her, watching all the people under its roof. Thinking there were four women and five men, all unattached, each living for her or himself. This was, of course excepting the Wragges, who were both for and sometimes against each other. Three virile young men and one lively young woman unattached. The house did not approve of this sort of situation and somehow communicated this disapproval to Dilly or so it seemed to her, for she had an ardent imagination.

Upstairs the bedroom doors stood slightly ajar. She had a glimpse of Nicholas stretched on a chaise longue, with Nip curled up on his middle. Bubbling snores came from under his drooping gray moustache. Sometimes he appeared to be dissatisfied with these noises and would substitute for them scornful hissing noises, like a locomotive getting up steam. The copy of *Nicholas Nickleby* which he had been reading hung from his handsome hand. Ernest did not snore but lay, with a sweet, peaceful expression, on his bed, the coverlet drawn neatly over him and his cat, Sasha, asleep on the pillow next his. Augusta sat at the writing bureau in her room writing letters in her fine Italian hand. From Meg's room came the sound of her voice, reading aloud to Wakefield. The others were out.

Up in the attic Dilly threw open the door of a long dark cupboard that smelt of moth camphor. So dark it was that for a moment she despaired of finding anything. When she had been there with Meg they had had an oil lamp to light them. But now, light or dark, Dilly must do something to deck herself to astonish Renny. She went to the very end of the cupboard and groped for some things Meg had discovered to her.

In the meantime the grandmother had dropped asleep again. But Dilly was not one to steal away without disturbing her. She said, in her high clear voice:

"Mrs. Whiteoak, do you or don't you want to?"

The old lady woke and without hesitation answered—"I do want to," though she had completely forgotten what was in question.

"Good," said Dilly and flung down the armful of clothes. She was all excitement.

The garments were a rose-colored crinoline with rose and white panniers, a pale blue satin bodice trimmed with lace and little bunches of flowers, and a man's hunting costume of breeches and pink coat. The former Adeline Whiteoak had brought with her in a sailing vessel from the old land, the latter had been worn by Nicholas when he rode to hounds in England.

"These things are so picturesque, dear Mrs. Whiteoak," cried Dilly. "They will be just what is needed to brighten us all up at teatime."

The grandmother leant forward in her chair to peer at the faded, camphor-smelling bundle.

"What are they?" she demanded.

"A crinoline of yours and hunting togs. Meg told me they belong to her Uncle Nicholas."

"Bless my soul! And what are we going to do with them?"

"Dress up! Won't it be fun? I've always wanted to know what I should look like in a crinoline and this is a beauty." She began to undress.

"But me," demanded the old lady. "What about me?"

"You are to wear the hunting clothes. You said just now you wished you'd been a man—"

"Never wished any such thing—except when I was going to have a baby."

"But you said something that gave me the idea. I thought it would be such fun." Dilly was now wearing the crinoline and struggling to fasten the bodice. "But what a *tiny* waist you had, dear Mrs. Whiteoak. This is practically killing me." She was panting, her face was flushed.

Adeline Whiteoak watched her with an odd smile bending her lips. Pictures from the past crowded into her mind. She heard the sound of a violin and the clatter of a hansom cab on the London street.

"My waist was small," she said.

Dilly exclaimed—"And I can imagine how gracefully this crinoline swayed about you!"

"Aye. I moved well."

Dilly could scarcely bear to take her eyes off her reflection. She swayed and twirled before the pier glass. However, the little glass clock on the mantelpiece striking four brought her to the task on hand, to get old Mrs. Whiteoak into the hunting clothes. Almost she wished she had not thought of anything so absurd, but her high spirits had infected Adeline, who now said:

"Bring me the breeches."

Scarcely able to bend for the tightness of the bodice Dilly extracted the breeches from the heap on the floor. Adeline threw back the skirt of her dressing gown and extended her legs, clad in long woollen stockings and flannel drawers. Dilly drew on the nether garments and, because she herself was strong as a boy, was able to divest her of her dressing gown and clothe her in waistcoat and pink coat. Adeline herself was now moved to an amazing alacrity of both body and mind. She stood leaning on her stick, critically surveying her reflection in the pier glass. She said:

"I need boots, a cap and a stock. Open your little drawer and you will find large linen handkerchiefs in it. They were my Philip's. One of them will make me a stock."

Neat-fingered, Dilly folded the linen into the semblance of a stock and secured it with a broach. She said:

"I'll bring shoes and cap in a jiffy." She flew up the stairs to Renny's clothes cupboard and there found his shining riding boots and black velvet cap. His belongings had a fascination for her. On the way down she hugged the boots to her bosom and kissed the cap.

Scarcely was she back in the grandmother's room when the rest of the family began to assemble in the drawing room for tea. Wakefield came sliding down the banister followed by Meg upbraiding him. The approach of Nicholas was heralded by the shrill barking of Nip, whose favorite hour of the twenty-four this was. Augusta and Ernest descended together, amiably conversing. Piers came, innocent and pink-cheeked, from a stolen interview with Pheasant. Finch came, brooding on a girl he had seen in the street the day before. He did not know who she was. He did not want to know, but he could not get her out of his mind. Eden came, a letter from Messrs. Cory and Parsons, the New York publishers, burning in his breast pocket. Renny was the last to come. His eyes swept the family circle, the blazing fire, the laden tea table, the unusual sight of his grandmother's empty chair. He demanded:

"Where's Gran?"

Ernest answered—"She and Dilly are closeted in her room. They've some sort of secret. They'll be here."

"That girl," said Nicholas, "is not capable of assisting Mamma. I must go."

"I'll go," said Renny.

He turned out into the hall and there encountered one of the strangest sights he ever had seen. He stood dumfounded as the pair approached him. His face was well-molded by nature to express astonishment, from the arched eyebrows, the carven nose, to the spirited mouth. His features now expressed that emotion to its utmost. He was speechless. Here was an elegant young lady of the eighteen-fifties who resembled Dilly Warkworth, accompanied by a very elderly gentleman in hunting costume who bore a bizarre likeness to a portrait he had seen in Ireland of his great-great-grandfather, the old Marquess of Killiekeggan.

In truth, Adeline Whiteoak, nearing the century mark in age, was swept at this moment by an amazing rejuvenation. It had been a struggle to get herself into the male attire. The boots had been hardest of all. But it had been the change from the lace-trimmed cap to the velvet cap which had worked the greatest transformation. More even than the breeches. With her hair tucked out of sight, with the shadow of the cap's peak on her face, she no longer looked the feeble old woman, but a handsome eldery rake of the Regency period.

Scarcely leaning on Dilly, she passed Renny and entered the drawing room with a jaunty air. The effect of this entrance was galvanic. The company, seated like an audience, now rose like an audience, drawn to their feet by that superb but fantastic entrance. Ernest was the first to recognize his mother.

"Mamma!" he exclaimed.

Then Augusta put all the force of her amazed disapproval into the same word.

Their mother with an ancient, rakish elegance, half tottered, half swaggered, toward her chair. The parrot, Boney, as though the better to see her, hung head down on his perch.

"So it is really my grandmother?" cried Wake.

"It is," said Meg, "and I call it wicked."

The young men, Eden and Piers, were charmed. They addressed her as "Your Lordship," placed her chair for her, and brought her tea. Dilly danced round the room, swaying her crinoline, her burning eyes on Renny. Everybody began to talk at once—Nicholas to recall the time when he had last worn that hunting pink—Ernest to bring out an old daguerreotype of his great-grandfather and point out the likeliness between it and the figure in the wing chair. Boney could not recognize his mistress and shouted his bewilderment and outrage. Wragge, bringing in a second supply of tea—for everyone was unusually thirsty—all but dropped the pot.

When Finch beheld his grandmother, he stared open-mouthed. "Like a duck in a thunderstorm," said Piers.

"Why—why—" gasped Finch. "What's it all about? What's happened to Gran?"

"It's an enigma," said Wakefield.

Finch stood looking down on the bizarre figure in the hunting clothes, then gave a hysterical giggle. He stared down at his grandmother, giggling, and as she looked up into his face she too began to giggle. The awkward boy and the old lady in her strange attire made a picture irresistibly droll. Everyone began to explode in laughter. Adeline, with a shaking hand, set down her cup and saucer and gave herself up to laughter. Boney screamed with laughter.

"Mamma's face is crimson," Ernest remarked, pulling himself together. "This is very bad for her."

"It must stop," said Augusta, suddenly grave and rather ashamed of herself.

"Mamma," Nicholas said loudly, "control yourself."

"I can't," she gasped, her face now purple.

They gathered about her solicitous—all but Finch, who held his aching side and appeared to be on the verge of hysteria.

"Behave yourself, sir," ordered Nicholas.

"I can't," wailed Finch.

"Renny, come and straighten up this young 'un. He's killing my mother."

"I'll do it," said Piers and taking Finch under the arms, ran him out of the drawing room into the study and gently, carefully closed the door behind them.

Augusta gave Dilly a look of deep reproach. She said —"I find nothing amusing in turning my mother into a figure of fun."

"You were laughing," said Dilly boldly.

Nicholas said—"We all were laughing and it's time we stopped." He bent over his mother and lifted the velvet cap from her head. The disordered hair released, she ap-

peared once more as a very old woman. She still shook
with what was now almost silent laughter. Meg came with
smelling salts. Ernest drew with difficulty the heavy boots
from her feet. Augusta came hastening with her dressing
gown. The change was completed and now no more than
a roguish smile lit her face.

"Ha," she said, "I haven't enjoyed myself so—not in
years! But now I want my tea and very hungry I am.
Blackberry jam, please. And a muffin. Bless my heart,
that was fun. Where's Dilly?"

The young woman, midway between feeling pleased
with herself and being in disgrace, flew to the grandmother
and embraced her. "What fun!" she cried.

"Indeed 'twas fun. There's nothing like a bit of dressing up, to pass the time." And she made this remark as
complacently as though she had all the time in the world
to spare.

Dilly swayed near Renny, her crinoline, though faded,
still exhaling the perfume of a romantic past. She sought
to transmit a shock of her desire into his body but he
produced nothing for her but an ironic smile.

As soon as Eden was able to get Renny apart from the
others, he took the publishers' letter from his pocket. "I
had this to-day," he said, trying to speak nonchalantly. "I
thought you might like to see it."

He expected no sympathetic understanding and got
none.

Renny, after knitting his brows over the letter, remarked
—"It's brief enough. I can't think they are much interested."

Eden said, heatedly—"You must understand, Renny,
that publishers in a city like New York are busy people.
They haven't time to write a long screed to a new author.
The point is that they are *considering* the poems. They
may publish them."

"Hmph. I see that they think there are scarcely enough
poems for a book."

"That's nothing! I have others in my room." Before
he could stop himself he added—"I'm writing new ones
every day!"

"I'll bet you are! When you ought to be studying."

"I don't neglect my work."

"Come now!"

"I go to lectures."

His brother's eyebrows shot up. "You go to lectures—and fill your notebooks with verse! It won't do, Eden. Either you must put your back into your studies or give them up and help Piers with the horses and farm."

Eden said despairingly—"Can't you understand what it means to me to have such encouragement?"

"I do understand that it would be damn bad for you."

"Oh, Lord God," cried Eden and flung himself across the passage to Ernest's room, where he and his uncle exulted together. By the time they had read the letter from Messrs. Cory and Parsons half a dozen times they were convinced that the publishers would not only produce the poems but that the book would make Eden's name. He sat up half the night writing a new poem.

As for Dilly, from that day she gave up her attempt to become the mistress of Jalna. Lady Buckley and she shortly sailed for England, Augusta to return to her home in Devonshire and Dilly to the arms of her family. From there she wrote, before a month had passed, of her engagement to a cousin on her father's side. In this letter (to Renny) she declared—"I am happier than ever before in this strange life of mine—devoted to my fiancé but—I still think you are wildly attractive!"

25.

Nothing Could Be Fairer

WHEN THE PLEASURE OF MEETING on the pond to skate was gone with the winter's cold, Piers and Pheasant still contrived their secret meetings. He had become the very lodestar of her life, by whose light all that she thought or did was illumined. Yet strangely the idea of marrying him had never entered her head. Marriage to her was something remote and romantic which one read of in books but did not contemplate for oneself. It was a subject indeed which she consciously put out of her mind because her parents had not been married, because Maurice Vaughan and Meg Whiteoak had not married, and because it was somehow her fault that they had not. It was enough for her that spring and summer lay ahead and that, in the warmth of the evenings, their meetings could be longer.

On this early evening they had arranged to meet on the little rustic bridge that spanned the stream down in the ravine. The stream, in ardent relish of its freedom, moved swiftly between its moist banks, where, as yet, there was no growth but only drowsy promise. The air was charged with the sound of running water.

Pheasant said—"What a delicious sound! I could listen to it all night. Yet I hate the sound of water running out of a tap, don't you?"

"I've never thought about it. But I guess the water out of a tap would be a good deal cleaner. Think of the frogs and eels and water rats down there."

"Oh, I like to think of them." Her face was almost passionately alight. "They've had such a long winter.

They're awake now—hopping and slithering and scuttling about—getting ready to—" She did not finish the sentence but leant over the railing, picturing those activities down below.

He finished for her. "Getting ready to mate."

She raised her face to smile into his. "Oh, Piers, how exciting for them!"

"Yes," he agreed, "and for me too."

"You do like creatures, don't you?" she exclaimed, pleased with him.

"Oh, pretty well . . . But I like you better."

"Naturally." Again she leant over the rail.

He looked at the back of her neck where a short brown lock had found a nesting place.

"Why naturally?"

"Because it seems only natural to like your best friend better than things that live in the water."

"What I mean is, you make so little of it."

Now she stood up straight and faced him astonished. "I make little of it!" she cried. "Why Piers, your caring for me is the greatest thing in my life." Color swept into her cheeks. "It's the *only* thing in my life!"

At these words an extraordinary change came over the scene. The chatter of the stream ceased and a strange breathless silence enveloped them. The very color of the trees changed, for the red sunset pushed the evening aside and burnished them to a new life, so that every needle on the pines seemed sharpened and polished. Suddenly the trunks of the trees became as pillars in a cathedral. The two on the bridge became painted figures on a screen. The only sound came from within and that was the beating of their hearts. She was the first to speak. She whispered:

"I shouldn't have said that."

"Why?" he wanted to know.

"Because it wasn't proper."

"*Proper!* Oh, Pheasant—don't bring Mrs. Clinch into this."

Now he moved swiftly and took her in his arms. He said, into the soft hair that hid her ear—"I'm going to marry you, if you'll have me. Will you?"

"Yes, Piers."

Now the stream was in motion again, hastening as though to make up for lost time to tell their secret to the lake. They heard voices and the barking of dogs. They climbed the steep path to the little wood where they were safe.

From this time they never missed a day for meeting. They were an engaged couple and Piers waited only for the propitious moment to declare the fact to the family. But it was hard to find that moment—hard to make up his mind to face the obstacles that he knew lay in his way. With the coming of spring the newly aroused force of his passion made him sometimes contemptuous of the others and he wanted to leap from his bed, arouse the household, and announce his engagement. But when morning came he wanted only to enjoy his love in peace.

One morning Renny took him into his little office in the stables and remarked:

"I hear that you're meeting Pheasant Vaughan every day."

This was so unexpected that Piers could only mutter— "We meet pretty often."

"Why?" Renny shot the question at him and at the same time his mobile brows came down in a frown.

Piers would have liked to answer—"Because I love her and am going to marry her," but all he said was— "Well, there's not much to do."

Renny said—"I suppose the time has come when you need a girl to go about with. But, Piers," his eyes held his brother's, "you can't go about with Pheasant. You know why."

"It wasn't her fault, was it?" Piers asked loudly.

"No, but you'll find out that in life the innocent often have to suffer."

"She won't suffer through me!" His ready color flamed.

"What! Are you telling me you have made her fond of you?"

The words all but tumbled out of Piers—"Yes, she and I love each other. We're going to be married." But he did not speak. Only his angry blue eyes made response.

"Is there anything between you two?" demanded Renny.

Like a sulky boy Piers muttered his lie. "Nothing." And hated himself for lying.

Renny spoke almost soothingly now. "You understand that there can't be, Piers—because of Meg?"

"I expect I do—though it seems pretty hard."

"How long have you known?"

"For years. Eden told me when I was only a kid."

"Well, it was a great pity things went wrong because the marriage would have been ideal for Meggie—and Maurice too."

"My God," cried Piers. "Why couldn't she forgive him?"

"Meg's not the girl to forgive that sort of thing. Then the Vaughans'—Maurice's parents—taking in the child made it worse. The child was the constant disgrace."

Hot love for Pheasant ran through Piers's body, but he could not speak. Not yet. He could not face Renny in open rebellion. He would wait a little, save money (for Renny was paying him good wages), then, when the time was ripe, explode the bombshell. Nothing Meg might say or do could hinder him.

Later he came to believe that he had not been afraid to tell Renny of the engagement but had deliberately planned its concealment till an appointed time. Now, in Renny's office, he said:

"I'm in no hurry to marry."

"That's right," said Renny. "Never fall for the first girl who attracts you. In fact you should wait your turn to marry."

"Good Lord," Piers's eyes opened wide, "I might never marry!"

"What a catastrophe," laughed Renny. Then he added seriously—"No, your type must not be lost from Jalna. You are the authentic Whiteoak. It's up to you to breed, but see that you choose the right mate."

He felt that he knew how to handle Piers. He could see that the boy was pleased. He put his arm about Piers's shoulders and added—"I'm not forbidding you to see Pheasant. Only you must not put ideas into her head. She's a dear little thing and I don't want to see her hurt. And understand—a marriage between you is impossible."

Piers thought—"There he goes—the autocrat—the Rajah of Jalna! Why do we knuckle under to him? He's spoilt. He's like Gran. Lord, I pity his wife when he brings himself to marry."

Yet the touch of that arm on his body, the magnetism that emanated from the eldest Whiteoak to every member of the tribe, inevitably drew him. Piers hung his head, his lips had a boyish pout, but then he raised eyes to Renny's and muttered assent. He even smiled in response to Renny's pat of approval.

After this he and Pheasant were more cautious in meeting, and this was made easier by an early spring. There were many quiet spots where young lovers could meet.

Wakefield Whiteoak ran on and on, faster and faster. He was late for the one o'clock dinner but he had had a good morning. His lessons at the Rectory with Mr. Fennell had gone well, from his point of view, for he had escaped with no wearisome addition to his learning, which he considered already sufficient for any boy; and he had had agreeable nourishment, in the form of lemon soda and sponge cakes, from the little shop of Mrs. Brawn.

Glorious, glorious life! When he reached the field where the stream was, the breeze had become a wind that ruffled up his hair and whistled through his teeth as he ran. It was as good a playfellow as he wanted, racing him, blowing the clouds about for his pleasure, shaking out the blossoms of the wild cherry tree like spray.

As he ran, he flung his arms forward alternately like a swimmer; he darted off at sudden tangents, shying like a skittish horse, his face now fierce with rolling eyes, now blank as a gamboling lamb's.

It was an erratic progress, and as he crept through his accustomed hole in the hedge onto the lawn, he began to be afraid that he might be very late.

He entered the house quietly and heard the clink of dishes and the sound of voices in the dining room. Dinner was in progress. No one paid any attention to Wakefield as he slipped quietly into his place, for a subject of great interest to all was being discussed.

A collection of Eden's poems was to be published in the

fall and that by Messrs. Cory and Parsons of New York. Dissension that was almost pleasurable, in that it was blown to exhilarating heat by a breath from the outer world, raged about the table. Meg was proud of the boy, yet fearful lest this success might take him away from home. Ernest too was proud of Eden, recalling the literary ambitions he himself had cherished. Nicholas, pleased but judicial. Renny sceptical of Eden's ability to earn a living by his pen, mourning the hard cash spent on Eden's study for the law. Piers laughing at versifying, flaunting his own bucolic occupation. Grandmother bewildered, demanding explanation. Eden, jubilant, angry, boastful, and sulky, in turn.

Now, standing alone on the drive, the warm sun on his back, the wind ruffling his hair, Eden recalled with a smile the scene that had followed. When he was with his family, how often they irritated and angered him. Yet, away from them, his appreciation of them was almost romantic. He would not have had them otherwise, from stormy-tempered old Gran down to little Wakefield. The time would come, he knew, when he would leave the family, the old house, behind him. He knew that his spirit could not be contained by Jalna. Yet he wondered, a little wryly, whether the outside world would inspire him to truer poetry than had sprung from him under this roof . . . Yes, surely it would! His imagination pressed forward, trying to foresee what lay ahead of him . . . This coming summer he would go on a canoeing trip into the North. That, for a long while, he had wanted to do. In the fall he would go down to New York. Mystery beckoned there, the strangeness of an unknown country.

He raised his arms above his head and stretched them, as though to break bonds. By that movement he roused the flock of pigeons sunning themselves on the roof. They swept upward, with a whirring of wings, circled overhead, with feet tucked neatly beneath downy breasts and a show of blue and gray and buff to delight the eye, then sped, in playful panic, toward the woods.

Eden saw that the Virginia creeper which covered the front of the house and festooned itself over the porch, was in tiny bud. The buds were rosy in the sunshine. Soon they would spread themselves in green leaf and, by the time they reddened in the fall, what might he not have done? His blood sang with the urge to live.

Heavy footsteps clumped along the gravel drive. Then appeared Noah Binns, a spade over his shoulder. Eden could not stop himself. He said gayly:

"Hullo, Noah. What do you suppose? I'm having a book published. A book of poetry!"

Noah's slate-colored eyes did not light. He stopped, stared at Eden, and grunted—"Huh."

"Ever read poetry?" asked Eden.

Noah shook his head. "No time fer such fiddle-faddle. I'm on my way to dig a grave."

"A grave," repeated Eden, the light going out of his face.

Noah thrust his spade into the gravel. "Aye, a grave. Two graves this week I've dug. It's an unhealthy year."

"Strange," said Eden, his eyes resting on the scene before him. "Everything looks full of promise."

"Promise!" cackled Noah. "Promises made to be broken. Budding and blight. Bugs and passing on."

"Sad. Very sad," Eden said absently.

" 'Tain't sad. Not at all." Noah spoke with unction. "The Lord giveth and the Lord taketh away. Nothing could be fairer than that."

MAZO DE LA ROCHE

Her achievement makes me think of Trollope and Galsworthy: I am too close to her work to attempt a comparison in quality, but I do know that neither of them ever created more living people.

In America where her books have sold more than a million six hundred thousand copies, readers feel personally responsible for each member of the Whiteoak family. They write to our author imploring her not to let the Master of Jalna sell any more of the property; not to let Finch marry the wrong woman. They show their pleasure in the resemblance of young Adeline to her great-grandmother.

In Europe where her novels have been translated into 15 languages, Jalna beckons as a wonderful Canadian sanctuary for those whose homes have been destroyed in the war. From the Balts in a DP camp, from Hollanders who found happiness in her books when there was no relief from the Nazi occupation, from Norway and Switzerland, and from France I have seen literally scores of letters thanking Mazo for the hope and the humanity which she held out to them. I think the Whiteoaks are bigger than any Dominion. The quick-tempered, loyal Renny and Piers, the subtle and sensitive Eden, the vulnerable Finch, young Wakefield and the Uncles are bound together in an intense family loyalty and zest for life—in them are the qualities which bind together any big family anywhere.

—EDWARD WEEKS

Romantic Fiction

If you like novels of passion and daring adventure that take you to the very heart of human drama, these are the books for you.

☐	AFTER—Anderson	Q2279	1.50
☐	THE DANCE OF LOVE—Dodson	23110-0	1.75
☐	A GIFT OF ONYX—Kettle	23206-9	1.50
☐	TARA'S HEALING—Giles	23012-0	1.50
☐	THE DEFIANT DESIRE—Klem	13741-4	1.75
☐	LOVE'S TRIUMPHANT HEART—Ashton	13771-6	1.75
☐	MAJORCA—Dodson	13740-6	1.75

Buy them at your local bookstores or use this handy coupon for ordering:

Anya Seton

Tempestuous Novels of Passion and Violence

☐	AVALON	23308-1	1.95
☐	DEVIL WATER	23633-1	2.25
☐	FOXFIRE	X2916	1.75
☐	GREEN DARKNESS	C2728	1.95
☐	KATHERINE	23497-5	2.25
☐	MY THEODOSIA	23034-1	1.95
☐	THE TURQUOISE	23088-0	1.95

Dorothy Eden

Ms. Eden's novels have enthralled millions of readers for many years. Here is your chance to order any or all of her bestselling titles direct by mail.

☐	AN AFTERNOON WALK	23072-4	1.75
☐	DARKWATER	23153-4	1.75
☐	THE HOUSE ON HAY HILL	X2839	1.75
☐	LADY OF MALLOW	23167-4	1.75
☐	THE MARRIAGE CHEST	23032-5	1.50
☐	MELBURY SQUARE	22973-4	1.75
☐	THE MILLIONAIRE'S DAUGHTER	23186-0	1.95
☐	NEVER CALL IT LOVING	23143-7	1.95
☐	RAVENSCROFT	22998-X	1.50
☐	THE SHADOW WIFE	23699-4	1.75
☐	SIEGE IN THE SUN	Q2736	1.50
☐	SLEEP IN THE WOODS	23706-0	1.95
☐	SPEAK TO ME OF LOVE	22735-9	1.75
☐	THE TIME OF THE DRAGON	23059-7	1.95
☐	THE VINES OF YARRABEE	23184-4	1.95
☐	WAITING FOR WILLA	23187-9	1.50
☐	WINTERWOOD	23185-2	1.75

Buy them at your local bookstores or use this handy coupon for ordering:

FAWCETT BOOKS GROUP, P.O. Box C730, 524 Myrtle Avenue, Pratt Station Brooklyn, N.Y. 11205

Please send me the books I have checked above. Orders for less than 5 books must include 60¢ for the first book and 25¢ for each additional book to cover mailing and handling. Postage is FREE for orders of 5 books or more. Check or money order only. Please include sales tax.

Name_____   Books $_____

Address_____   Postage _____

City_____ State/Zip_____   Sales Tax _____

Total $_____

Please allow 4 to 5 weeks for delivery

Victoria Holt

Over 20,000,000 copies of Victoria Holt's novels are in print. If you have missed any of her spellbinding bestsellers, here is an opportunity to order any or all direct by mail.

☐	BRIDE OF PENDORRIC	23280-8	1.95
☐	THE CURSE OF THE KINGS	23284-0	1.95
☐	THE HOUSE OF A THOUSAND LANTERNS	23685-4	1.95
☐	THE KING OF THE CASTLE	23587-4	1.95
☐	KIRKLAND REVELS	X2917	1.75
☐	THE LEGEND OF THE SEVENTH VIRGIN	23281-6	1.95
☐	LORD OF THE FAR ISLAND	22874-6	1.95
☐	MENFREYA IN THE MORNING	23076-7	1.75
☐	MISTRESS OF MELLYN	23124-0	1.75
☐	ON THE NIGHT OF THE SEVENTH MOON	23568-0	1.95
☐	THE QUEENS' CONFESSION	23213-1	1.95
☐	THE SECRET WOMAN	23283-2	1.95
☐	THE SHADOW OF THE LYNX	23278-6	1.95
☐	THE SHIVERING SANDS	23282-4	1.95

Buy them at your local bookstores or use this handy coupon for ordering:

BESTSELLERS

☐	BEGGAR ON HORSEBACK–Thorpe	23091-0	1.50
☐	THE TURQUOISE–Seton	23088-0	1.95
☐	STRANGER AT WILDINGS–Brent	23085-6	1.95
	(Pub. in England as Kirkby's Changeling)		
☐	MAKING ENDS MEET–Howar	23084-8	1.95
☐	THE LYNMARA LEGACY–Gaskin	23060-0	1.95
☐	THE TIME OF THE DRAGON–Eden	23059-7	1.95
☐	THE GOLDEN RENDEZVOUS–MacLean	23055-4	1.75
☐	TESTAMENT–Morrell	23033-3	1.95
☐	CAN YOU WAIT TIL FRIDAY?–	23022-8	1.75
	Olson, M.D.		
☐	HARRY'S GAME–Seymour	23019-8	1.95
☐	TRADING UP–Lea	23014-7	1.95
☐	CAPTAINS AND THE KINGS–Caldwell	23069-4	2.25
☐	"I AIN'T WELL–BUT I SURE AM	23007-4	1.75
	BETTER"–Lair		
☐	THE GOLDEN PANTHER–Thorpe	23006-6	1.50
☐	IN THE BEGINNING–Potok	22980-7	1.95
☐	DRUM–Onstott	22920-3	1.95
☐	LORD OF THE FAR ISLAND–Holt	22874-6	1.95
☐	DEVIL WATER–Seton	23633-1	2.25
☐	CSARDAS–Pearson	22885-1	1.95
☐	CIRCUS–MacLean	22875-4	1.95
☐	WINNING THROUGH INTIMIDATION–	23589-0	2.25
	Ringer		
☐	THE POWER OF POSITIVE	23499-1	1.95
	THINKING–Peale		
☐	VOYAGE OF THE DAMNED–	22449-X	1.75
	Thomas & Witts		
☐	THINK AND GROW RICH–Hill	23504-1	1.95
☐	EDEN–Ellis	23543-2	1.95

Buy them at your local bookstores or use this handy coupon for ordering:

Please allow 4 to 5 weeks for delivery